6581

THE STORY-MAKERS

Second Edition

A Selection of Modern Short Stories
Edited and with an introduction by
RUDY WIEBE

Copyright © 1987 Gage Educational Publishing Company
A Division of Canada Publishing Corporation

All rights reserved. No part of this publication may be reproduced in any form without permission in writing from the publisher. Reproducing passages from this publication by mimeographing or by photographic, electrostatic, or mechanical means without the written permission of the publisher is an infringement of copyright law.

Care has been taken to trace ownership of copyright material contained in this text. The publishers will gladly take any information that will enable them to rectify any reference or credit in subsequent editions.

Canadian Cataloguing in Publication Data

Main entry under title:

The Story-makers

First ed. published: Toronto : Macmillan of Canada, 1970.
ISBN 0-7715-5606-3

1. Short stories, American. 2. Short stories, Canadian (English).* 3. Short stories. 4. American fiction—20th century. 5. Canadian fiction (English)—20th century.* 6. Fiction— 20th century. I. Wiebe, Rudy, 1934- .

PN6014.S76 1987   813'.01'08   C86-094818-8

Editor: Kathy Austin
Designer: Craig Allen
Cover Illustration: Mary Allen
ISBN: 0-7715-**5606-3**
1 2 3 4 5 6 7 AP 93 92 91 90 89 88 87
Printed and Bound in Canada

CONTENTS

Acknowledgments

For permission to reprint copyright material grateful acknowledgment is made to the following:

"The Molesters" from *Expensive People* by Joyce Carol Oates. Copyright © 1968 by Joyce Carol Oates. Reprinted by permission of the publisher, Vanguard Press, Inc.

"A Very Old Man with Enormous Wings" from *Collected Stories* by Gabriel García Márquez, translated from the Spanish by Gregory Rabassa. Copyright © 1972 by Gabriel García Márquez. Reprinted by permission of Harper & Row, Publishers, Inc.

"The Conversion of the Jews" from *Goodbye Columbus* by Philip Roth. Copyright © 1959 by Philip Roth. Reprinted by permission of Houghton Mifflin Company.

"The Wind Blows" from *Short Stories* by Katherine Mansfield. Courtesy of The Society of Authors as the literary representative of the Estate of Katherine Mansfield.

"A North American Education" from *A North American Education* by Clark Blaise. Copyright © 1971 by Clark Blaise. Reprinted by permission of Doubleday & Company, Inc.

"Thanks for the Ride" from *Dance of the Happy Shades* by Alice Munro. By permission of McGraw-Hill Ryerson Ltd.

"Falling in Love" by Sandra Birdsell from *Ladies of the House*. Copyright © 1984 by Sandra Birdsell. Reprinted by permission of Turnstone Press.

"The Horse Dealer's Daughter" from *The Complete Short Stories of D. H. Lawrence. Vol. II* by D. H. Lawrence. Copyright © 1934 by Frieda Lawrence, renewed © 1962 by Angelo Ravagli and C. Montague Weekley, Executors of the Estate of Frieda Lawrence Ravagli. Reprinted by permission of Viking Penguin, Inc.

"The Sin of Jesus" by Isaac Babel from *Lyubka the Cossack and Other Stories* translated by Andrew R. MacAndrew. Copyright © 1963 by Andrew R. MacAndrew. Reprinted by permission of New American Library.

"Your Lover Just Called" from *Too Far to Go: The Maples*

Stories by John Updike. Copyright © 1979 by John Updike. Reprinted by permission of Alfred A. Knopf, Inc.

"The Chorus Girl" from *Select Tales* by Anton Chekhov, translated by Constance Garnett. By permission of Chatto & Windus Publishers.

"A Field of Wheat" by Sinclair Ross from *The Lamp at Noon and Other Stories*. Used by permission of The Canadian Publishers, McClelland and Stewart Limited, Toronto.

"Seeing is Believing" by Rudy Wiebe from *Kunapipi*, Vol. 6, #2, 1984. Copyright © 1984 by Rudy Wiebe. Aarhus, Denmark.

"That Evening Sun" from *The Collected Stories of William Faulkner* by William Faulkner. Copyright © 1931 and renewed © 1959 by William Faulkner. Reprinted by permission of Random House, Inc.

"Counterparts" from *Dubliners* by James Joyce. Copyright © 1916 by B. W. Huebsch. Definitive text copyright © 1967 by the Estate of James Joyce. Reprinted by permission of Viking Penguin, Inc.

"The Plague Children" by Jack Hodgins from *The Barclay Family Theatre*. Copyright © 1981 by Jack Hodgins. Reproduced by permission of the author and Macmillan of Canada (A Division of Canada Publishing Corporation).

"Waiting for the Rodeo" by Aritha van Herk. First published in *Canadian Fiction Magazine 1984*. Copyright © Aritha van Herk. By permission of the author.

"Be Fruitful and Multiply" by Madeleine Ferron from *Coeur de sucre*, Montreal 1966 Hurtubise HMH. Translated by Sheila Watson (1974). Reprinted by permission of Editions Hurtubise HMH, Montreal.

"If One Green Bottle...." by Audrey G. Thomas. Originally appeared in *Ten Green Bottles*, Bobbs-Merrill New York, 1967. Copyright © Audrey G. Thomas. Reprinted by permission of the author.

"You Could Look It Up" by James Thurber from *My World—And Welcome to It*, published by Harcourt Brace Jovanovich, Inc. Copyright © 1942 James Thurber; © 1970 Helen W. Thurber and Rosemary A. Thurber. Used by permission.

"After the Storm" by Ernest Hemingway from *Winner*

Take Nothing. Copyright © 1933 Charles Scribner's Sons; copyright renewed © 1961 Mary Hemingway. Reprinted with the permission of Charles Scribner's Sons.

"The Guest" from *Exile and the Kingdom* by Albert Camus, translated by Justin O'Brien. Copyright © 1957, 1958 by Alfred A. Knopf, Inc. Reprinted by permission of the publisher.

"The Post Card" from *Eighteen Stories* by Heinrich Böll, translated by Leila Vennewitz. Copyright © 1966 by Heinrich Böll. Reprinted by permission of Joan Daves, Literary Agent.

"The Children's Campaign" by Pär Lagerkvist from "Onda Sagor" (Evil Tales). Copyright © 1986 by the Estate of Pär Lagerkvist. Reprinted by permission of the publisher, Albert Bonniers Förlag.

"The Secret Room" by Alain Robbe-Grillet, translated by Barbara Wright. From *Snapshots* and *Towards a New Novel*. Reprinted by permission of John Calder (Publishers) Ltd.

"The Second Death" by Graham Greene from *Collected Stories*. Published by William Heinemann Ltd. and The Bodley Head Ltd. Reprinted by permission of Laurence Pollinger Limited, U.K.

"When It Happens" from *Dancing Girls* by Margaret Atwood. Copyright © 1977 by Margaret Atwood. Used by permission of The Canadian Publishers, McClelland and Stewart Limited, Toronto.

"A Country Doctor" from *The Penal Colony* by Franz Kafka, translated by Willa and Edwin Muir. Copyright © 1948, 1976 by Schocken Books Inc. Reprinted by permission of Schocken Books Inc.

"Gimpel the Fool" by Isaac Bashevis Singer from *A Treasury of Yiddish Stories*, edited by Irving Howe and Eliezer Greenberg. Copyright © 1953, 1954 by The Viking Press, Inc. Copyright renewed © 1982 by Irving Howe and Mrs. Eva Greenberg. Reprinted by permission of Viking Penguin, Inc.

"Revelation" from *Everything that Rises Must Converge* by Flannery O'Connor. Copyright © 1964, 1965 by Flannery O'Connor. Reprinted by permission of Farrar, Straus and Giroux, Inc.

PREFACE

The continuing interest in a concise anthology of short fiction that makes its selection from both classic and contemporary world writing justifies a new edition of *The Story-Makers*. Part of its seventeen-year popularity seems to be the juxtaposition of the short story in English, as represented by British, Canadian, and United States stories, with fiction translated from other world languages. Further, when the original edition of this book appeared in 1970, it was the first to give any wider place to Canadian stories in a world context; the growth and fictional sophistication of Canadian short stories since 1967 has justified this editorial stance and numerous anthologies now follow it.

This edition of *The Story-Makers* contains thirty stories. Twenty authors remain the same as in the 1970 edition, though three (Kafka, Updike, and Wiebe) are represented by different stories. Ten new authors are added: two twentieth-century giants (Joyce and Lawrence), seven dominant Canadian writers (Atwood, Birdsell, Blaise, Ferron, Hodgins, van Herk, and Thomas), and Gabriel García Márquez. The latter, Columbian, writer seems to find the inspiration for his wonderfully modern stories in the ancient tradition of folklore and legend.

No startlingly new development in writing the short story has appeared since 1970, but the self-conscious, self-reflexive making of fictions has certainly been accentuated. Therefore, if I were writing a full-length introduction to this book today I would underscore what was already discernible in the 1970 edition: the modern short story has developed not only from *dreaming... recounting... explaining... instruction...* and *making an imitation*; it has also developed into what it is from *the very desire itself to make story*. That is, making a short story now is justification enough for its existence; it needs neither to dream, recount, explain, instruct or imitate anything, though in the process of becoming itself it may do all five. The process, the making itself often seems the writer's primal objective, and the question of *where* that making takes place—in the act of writing or in the act of reading the writing—then becomes the further point at issue. In the present selection, stories like "The Secret Room" and "Seeing is Believing" reveal this tendency most clearly. The first shapes itself out of the stasis of time and place in a painting, moving not only over the captured (painted) moment like a camera in space/place but apparently also forward and backward in a time before the painted instant occurred; the second returns again and again to a continuing conversation between unidentified conversants, its parts separated by bits of fairy tale, hunting narrative and travelogue (which turns into magic nightmare), while language play, literary theory, sexual innuendo intersect into what may be a whole or perhaps a scattering of discreet story parts. In such cases the structure itself, not the content, becomes the larger story.

Except for some minor editorial changes, the 1970 introduction is included here as originally written. Several of the story examples cited do not appear in this edition, but rather than restructure the entire piece, I have let them remain; the interested reader can easily find them in other sources.

Finally, the way the word "story" was used in the original introduction has found some objection; it seems that certain readers find the phrase "to make story" wrong, even insulting! Perhaps they parallel it with "to make water," which I also find a perfectly acceptable English construction and no more problematic than "to make breakfast" or "to make love," though the actions they describe could perhaps be considered prettier. The fact is that in the phrase "to make story," the word "story" is used generically, and as such it is consistent with the title. So, to use the traditional proofreader term, I say *stet*.

Rudy Wiebe
Edmonton, 1987

INTRODUCTION

The impulse to make story needs no defence. Where it arises, who knows. It simply is, like the impulse to sing, to dance, to play games. It would seem, however, that story-making is the uniquely human of these impulses for, though many animals sing, play games, perform intricate and beautiful dances, it still remains to be discovered whether any make stories. Therefore, a little human conjecture may not be out of place.

For us, to make story is to entertain: we entertain ourselves as we entertain our listeners. In other words, the emotional impulse to make story drives toward the principle of pleasure. At best, good story does what it does while pleasurably seducing both teller and listener out of their world into its own and, again at best, this seduction may both illuminate the world in which teller and listener actually are and often be the more pleasurable as the seduction becomes less immediate: story worth pondering is story doubly enjoyed. Which, if you grant, still does not explain why we should find story a pleasure.

Further, it is easy to imagine that the impulse to make story and submit to it is rooted in our necessity to label. Wherever we live we invent symbols (a picture, a sound, an act) for things, apparently in order to relate in an essentially human way to the things themselves. This relation we seem to find both necessary and enjoyable. In Genesis, for example, Adam discovers a fundamental quality in animals *while in the process of naming them*: not one of the animals is a fit mate for him.[1] Helen Keller's brilliant mind is finally unjailed from its deaf-and-dumb body when she grasps the connection between the pressure of Teacher's fingers and the water spilling over her hand.[2] Or, the small child staring across the prairie from a dome-car, asking, "Daddy, what's that?" "Can't you see?" the father growls. "Yes," the child replies, "but what *is* it?" And only when the conductor reveals that it *is* the Sweet Grass Hills can there be brief peace and quiet.

The very act of shaping a symbol (a distinctive sound, a distinctive touch) for a thing, then, somehow releases us, provides us with a strange insight and mastery; and enjoyment. Perhaps, in a similar way, to overlay an actual happening with words (i.e., symbol) is to provide such insight and enjoyment that we drive for the overlay whether a happening has really taken place or not. That is, we not only recount, we also invent, story.

I can also imagine that the impulse to make story is connected with our awareness of time. Time ends all acts, the more pleasurable often the more quickly. But time can be partly overcome by story. So, after a year's journey far from her friends, the Eskimo Higilaq sings to them in the festival snowhouse:

> *Wishing to begin to walk,*
> *Wishing to begin to walk,*
> *To Kuluksuk I proceeded to walk.*[3]

> *When my stomach was empty in me,*
> *To Kuluksuk I proceeded to walk.*

1. Genesis, chapter 2, verses 19 and 20.
2. Helen Keller, *The Story of My Life*, 1903, p. 23.

In eighteen verses she expands on what happened during her walking; from the encounter with a flooded river to making stone pots, from having no bows to shoot the bull caribou to their inability to "procure a companion" to the one seal that falls their victim, and to the final event of an upset sled:

> *I no longer having possessions on the sled,*
> *Since I did not become angry, I laughed aloud at it!*
> *And to Kuluksuk I proceeded to walk.*

We encounter her journey almost a century later. Story *is*, much longer than the fact.

Obviously I have shored up my two conjectures about story with stories. That may be circular reasoning or, in the best tradition of the revered scientific method, merely examining the thing for evidence concerning itself. In any case, I imagine that story has existed as long as humanity and language (perhaps longer than language: story can be mimed) and I further imagine that the early forms of it developed from

> *. . . dreaming how we wish things were;*
> *. . . recounting what happened;*
> *. . . explaining why things are as they are;*
> *. . . instructing ourselves and our children;*
> *. . . making an imitation.*

These areas certainly overlap and they are stated in no necessary order except that the last has, in modern times among civilized peoples, developed into the most complex; it has largely taken over the field of written story.

3. *Report of the Canadian Arctic Expedition, 1913-18*, Volume XIV, Ottawa, 1925, record IV. C. 80.

STORY DREAMING HOW WE WISH THINGS WERE

If human beings were before we had words, I imagine we already dreamt, wishing the world different. Things happen; lightning strikes, you step on a thorn; mostly what you can do about it is dream. Perhaps a wild psychedelic whirl of a dream for a thousand and one nights, perhaps a short, homely little dream like the following:

The Nixie

A little brother and sister were playing by a well, and as they were playing, both plopped in. Down in the well was a nixie who said, "Now I've got you! Now you're to work good and hard for me," and led them away with her. She gave the girl hard, tangled flax to spin, and she had to carry water in a cask with no bottom. The boy was supposed to chop down a tree with a dull ax, and all they got to eat were dumplings as hard as rocks. Finally the children got so impatient that they waited till one Sunday when the nixie was at church and ran away.

When church was out, the nixie saw that the birds had flown and set after them with long strides. However, the children spied her from afar, and the girl threw a brush behind her; this produced a huge mountain of brushes, with thousands and thousands of briars, which the nixie had to climb over with a great deal of trouble, though she finally got across. When the children saw that, the boy threw a comb behind him; this produced a huge mountain of combs, with thousands and thousands of teeth. The nixie, however, knew how to hold onto them and finally got over them. Then the girl threw a mirror behind her, which produced a mountain of mirrors and was so very, very slippery that she couldn't get over it. Then she thought, "I'll hurry home and fetch my ax and cut the mountain of mirrors in two," but by the time she'd got back and had chopped up the glass, the children had long since fled far away, and the nixie had to trudge back to her well.[4]

Things happen here too: you fall in wells, and you get enslaved for no reason except accident. And nixies even go to church! But you also have all the resources, strange as they are, to handle the implacable forces that pursue you, and eventually we all get what we deserve. That's dream.

Whatever graspable motives emerge from fairy and folk tale are direct and changeless: witches are forever hateful, lovers love in everlasting faithfulness and happiness. Of such dream quality little remains in contemporary story. Invariably that little is revealed by children: Ozzie in "The Conversion of the Jews" can, while he's sitting on the roof high above everyone he knows, dream that he can really change people. Or by persons we oh-so-mature adults would call child-like: Gimpel ("Gimpel the Fool") with his renunciation of everything in this world, Mrs. Turpin ("Revelation") with her illustrated-Bible vision. When the primitive encounters the modern world (Oolulik in my own story of that title), the dream is broken. We, like Myra in Tennessee Williams's "The Field of Blue Children," have "sense enough to see that it is impossible." Sadly, too much sense to dream well.

4 *The Grimms' German Folk Tales*, translated by Magoun and Krappe, Carbondale, 1960, p. 289.

STORY RECOUNTING WHAT HAPPENED

The earliest development of this form is no doubt autobiography (it happened to me) followed closely by biography (it happened to them) and, after perhaps generations, by history (it happened to our tribe, that group of nations, etc.). It moves from one extreme—say, the fisherman telling once more about the fish that got away—through an incredible spectrum to the other extreme—say, Winston Churchill's *History of the English Speaking Peoples*. Besides, it can include every conceivable combination of information from generally accepted fact through informed surmise to the sheerest tall tale. Two fishermen and two historians often disagree widely as to what happened, omitting altogether the even more difficult problem of 'why'.

Such circumstances need hardly surprise us. We all are to an extent limited in what we can take in (only God, presumably, can see all, including pure fact.) This is a verity every good story-maker knows, the quality of story depends rather less on what happens than on how the story is made, and if you can begin your story with "I was there; this really happened" you already have long hold on your audience. Then, if you can with skill shape facts and events to show the human meanings behind them (events taken by themselves in the order in which they happen very rarely show deeper human meaning), you have truly memorable story. How much you mix actual fact and fancy is not so important as that the story whole move us to understand 'what happened' in a profounder human way.

Modern people with our stress on objectively verifiable evidence, with our determination to 'demythologize' down to the scrapped bones of possible fact, find it hard to understand that more primitive peoples lay little or no stress on the supposed difference between fact and fiction. Earthy, real Odysseus lives easily in the perfectly told Greek story with fantastic one-eyed Polyphemus; Jonah and his Jewish hatred of the Assyrians lives with ease in the perfectly told story of the fantastic fish and even more fantastic conversion of the Ninevites to a Jewish prophet. The legendary lives of the saints, the Icelandic sagas, the local legends of special places and strange events— all are basic forms of the story explaining what happened. And they gain much of their strength from stressing that actuality of event, or at least its haunting possibility.

While drawing the limits of possibility a good deal tighter than the ancients, the story of 'what happened' is very strong in modern writing. The examples range from Akutagawa's "In a Grove," which gives a multi-witness account of the 'what' (and gradually the 'why') of a single event, to Singer's "Gimpel the Fool," a single-witness account of an entire lifetime. Few readers would take the 'I's of these stories literally: Ryūnosuke Akutagawa cannot be seven witnesses even if he died a suicide in Japan in 1927, and Isaac B. Singer is alive and writing with great success in New York; obviously no (holy?) fool. But Updike's "Wife-Wooing" is a little more tangled, and many naïve (not primitive) readers would perhaps find the story more 'real' if they knew that John Updike's wife actually played an old piano in their Sunday school and that, after seven years of marriage, they did have three children. Thurber's narrator insists again and again on the veracity of his story by appealing to the newspaper (literate humanity's daily record of history), though a few things don't fit: he never mentions the name of his team, he cannot remember certain key names, and the date, considering the exploits, is most strangely vague. All of which characterizes the tall tale of the master story-maker at work entertaining readers with 'what happened'. Ha.

STORY EXPLAINING WHY THINGS ARE AS THEY ARE

Today we have the scientist with unnumbered devices and records and sense-extensions to explain the why and what of ourselves and the phenomena around us; ancient people had only myth. And though in modern times we can, by scientific law and experiment, explain and understand a good deal in between, regarding beginnings and ends we have mostly myths still.

The Blackfoot Myth of Beginnings

Old Man was travelling about, south of here, making the people. He came from the south, travelling north, making animals and birds as he passed along. He made the mountains, prairies, timber and brush first. So he went along, travelling northward, making things as he went, putting rivers here and there, and falls on them, putting red paint here and there in the ground— fixing up the world as we see it to-day. He made the Milk River [i.e. the Teton River in Montana] and crossed it, and, being tired, went up on a little hill and lay down to rest. As he lay on his back stretched out on the ground, with arms extended, he marked himself out with stones— the shape of his body, head, legs, arms, and everything. There you can see those rocks to-day. After he had rested, he went on northward, and stumbled over a knoll and fell down on his knees. Then he said, "You are a bad thing to be stumbling against"; so he raised up two large buttes there, and named them the Knees, and they are called so to this day. He went on further north, and with some of the rocks he carried with him he built the Sweet Grass Hills.

Old Man covered the plains with grass for the animals to feed on. He marked off a piece of ground, and in it he made to grow all kinds of roots and berries—camas, wild carrots, wild turnips, sweet-root, bitter-root, sarvis berries, bull berries, cherries, plums, and rosebuds. He put trees in the ground. He put all kinds of animals on the ground. . . .

One day Old Man determined that he would make a woman and a child; so he formed them both—the woman and the child, her son—of clay. After he had moulded the clay in human shape, he said to the clay, "You must be people," and then he covered it up and left it, and went away. The next morning he went to the place and took the covering off, and saw that the clay shapes had changed a little. The second morning there was still more change, and the third still more. The fourth morning he went to the place, took the covering off, looked at the images, and told them to rise and walk; and they did so. They walked down to the river with their Maker, and then he told them that his name was *Nà pi*, Old Man.

As they were standing by the river, the woman said to him, "How is it? Will we always live, will there be no end to it?" He said: "I have never thought of that. We will have to decide it. I will take this buffalo chip and throw it in the river. If it floats, when people die, in four days they will become alive again; they will die for only four days. But if it sinks, there will be an end to them." He threw the chip into the river, and it floated. The woman turned and picked up a stone, and said: "No, I will throw this stone in the river; if it floats we will always live, if it sinks people must die, that they may always be sorry for each other" [i.e., that their surviving friends may always remember them]. The woman threw the stone into the water, and it sank. "There," said Old Man, "you have chosen. There will be an end to them."

It was not many nights after, that the woman's child died, and she cried a great deal for it. She said to Old Man: "Let us change this. The law that you first made, let that be a law." He said: "Not so. What is made law must be law. We will undo nothing that we have done. The child is dead, but it cannot be changed. People will have to die."

That is how we came to be people. It is he who made us. . . .

Old Man teaches them how to kill buffalo and make fire.

Also Old Man said to the people: "Now, if you are overcome, you may go and sleep, and get power. Something will come to you in your dream, that will help you. Whatever these animals tell you to do, you must obey them, as they appear to you in your sleep. Be guided by them. If anybody wants help, if you are alone and travelling, and cry aloud for help, your prayer will be answered. It may be by the eagles, perhaps by the buffalo, or by the bears. Whatever animal answers your prayer, you must listen to him."

That was how the first people got through the world, by the power of their dreams. . . .

After he had taught those people these things, he started off again, travelling north, until he came to where Bow and Elbow rivers meet [i.e., the present site of Calgary, Alberta]. There he made some more people, and taught them the same things. From here he again went on northward. When he had come nearly to the Red Deer's River, he reached the hill where the Old Man sleeps. There he lay down and rested himself. The form of his body is to be seen there yet. . . .

This is as far as the Blackfeet followed Old Man. The Crees know what he did further north.[5]

A story of beginnings that reveals a basic way of seeing the world. In it divinity is man with super-human knowledge and powers; he travels, gets tired, is forgetful, and amuses himself; life is mostly journey, animals and plants are perfect as they are, under Old Man's teaching man dominates animals; man gains strength from dreams, and death comes through woman; people are created several times, at several places. There is something sacred in the number 'four'.

Today we officially leave our speculations regarding origins to the scientist, and they, of necessity, are forever changing; however, vestiges remain in some contemporary stories. Dave Godfrey's "The Hard-Headed Collector" with its incredible journey across a continent is essentially a myth of why things are as they are. Arina in "The Sin of Jesus" and the two terrified friends in "The Second Death" encounter

5. George B. Grinnell, *Blackfoot Lodge Tales*, New York, 1921, p. 137 ff.

(explain?) the basic 'why' of existence in direct and somehow beyond-human terms. On the whole, however, people in today's story do not look so far back or forward; what is under one's nose seems concern enough.

STORY INSTRUCTING OURSELVES AND OUR CHILDREN

Certain kinds of instruction (how to find food to fill your belly, for example) are easily conveyed by demonstration. Other matters humans deem important (like moral qualities) are harder to demonstrate than talk about, perhaps because they are concerned with ideals purer in the mind than in the actuality. To convey such instruction, the story (where anything is possible) is a perfect vehicle.

A wolf stole a lamb from the flock, and was carrying it off to devour it at his leisure when he met a lion, who took his prey away from him and walked off with it. He dared not resist, but when the lion had gone some distance he said, "It is most unjust of you to take what's mine away from me like that." The lion laughed and called out in reply, "It was justly yours, no doubt! The gift of a friend, perhaps, eh?"

A typical Aesop fable, sharp, unelaborated, concrete; fundamentally different from the fairy tale quoted earlier. This obviously means to drive us toward some moral understanding, though the animal characters serve somewhat to disguise the easy meaning; and that may be exactly their use. By analogy the moral teaching certainly relates to humanity, but the precise comment on justice is not stated. The mind must infer it.

The parable is another ancient teaching story; its characters are usually human and, unlike the fable, it depends less on irony and much more on the complex human situation it evokes to make its meaning clear.

The Man and his Two Sons

Once there was a man who had two sons. The younger one said to his father, "Father, give me the share of the property that will come to me." So he divided up his property between the two of them. Before very long, the younger son collected all his belongings and went off to a foreign land, where he squandered his wealth in the wildest extravagance. And when he had run through all his money, a terrible famine arose in that country, and he began to feel the pinch. Then he went and hired himself out to one of the citizens of that country who sent him out into the fields to feed the pigs. He got to the point of longing to stuff himself with the food the pigs were eating, and not a soul gave him anything.

Then he came to his senses and cried aloud, "Why, dozens of my father's hired men have got more food than they can eat and here am I dying of hunger! I will get up and go back to my father, and I will say to him, 'Father, I have done wrong in the sight of Heaven and in your eyes. I don't deserve to be called you son any more. Please take me on as one of your hired men.'" So he got up and went to his father. But while he was still some distance off, his father saw him and his heart went out to him, and he ran and fell on his neck and kissed him. But his son said,

'Father, I have done wrong in the sight of Heaven and in your eyes. I don't deserve to be called your son any more. . . ." "Hurry!" called out his father to the servants, "fetch the best clothes and put them on him! Put a ring on his finger and shoes on his feet, and get that calf we've fattened and kill it, and we will have a feast and a celebration. For this is my son—I thought he was dead, and he's alive again. I thought I had lost him, and he's found!" And they began to get the festivities going.

But the elder brother was out in the fields, and as he came near the house, he heard music and dancing. So he called one of the servants across to him and enquired what was the meaning of it all. "Your brother has arrived, and your father has killed the calf we fattened because he has got him home again safe and sound," was the reply. But he was furious and refused to go inside the house. So his father came outside and called him. Then he burst out, "Look, how many years have I slaved for you and never disobeyed a single order of yours, and yet you have never given me so much as a young goat, so that I could give my friends a dinner? But when that son of yours arrives, who has spent all your money on prostitutes, for *him* you kill the calf we've fattened!" But the father replied, "My son, you have been with me all the time and everything I have is yours. But we *had* to celebrate and show our joy. For this is your brother; I thought he was dead—and he's alive. I thought he was lost—and he is found."[6]

6. Luke, chapter 15; from *The Gospels translated into Modern English*, by J. B. Phillips, London, 1952.

The conclusion here is rather more cryptic than that of the fable, partly because the story is much more complex, partly because it drives toward at least two equally possible responses by the elder son. Therein lies the crux of the teaching: every listener knows how the elder should respond, but the given evidence offers little hope and, without directly saying a word on the subject, the story-maker Jesus has taught not necessarily a moral (as a fable does) but something perhaps even more essential about the nature of human beings.

Neither fables nor parables are allegories, though the allegory probably developed from the other two. In allegory characters, places, situations stand in a one-to-one relationship with a system of ideas outside the precise story. The returning son does stand for the 'repentant sinner' and the father for 'God's love'; that is allegorical, but certainly the party the father throws does not stand for a divinely organized binge, nor does the elder son stand for those who have never sinned; according to Jesus there are none such.

It is difficult to separate the strands of fable, parable, and allegory in most modern stories. There are strong elements of all three in "The Children's Campaign," for example, though parable predominates. Kafka's "The Hunter Gracchus" is more difficult still; it can be argued that the hunter himself is Christ, the boatman the Church, and the harbour any community, but fitting every detail of the story into a one-to-one relationship with an abstract scheme will lead inevitably to silliness. And in realistic stories, like "That Evening Sun" for example, though we can say that Nancy stands for 'negro womanhood', or even 'oppressed womanhood in general', and in that role her story teaches us something, we are nevertheless more concerned with her as a *particular* woman than with what she abstractly represents.

STORY MAKING AN IMITATION

Ancient Chinese and Egyptian drawings show story-tellers at work. The myths of Wotan, Jesus' parables, the Icelandic sagas, the Arabian Nights tales, the hero legends of the Middle Ages, Boccaccio's *Decameron*, and Chaucer's *Canterbury Tales* are only a few of humanity's great story collections. Yet it can be argued that story in the literary form of the short story has existed only for a little over a century.

As George P. Elliott has said so well, "In literature, as in painting, realism is the art of manifesting an idea by means of arranging the appearances of actual things into a recognizable likeness."[7] In this sense, realistic fiction did not emerge until eighteenth-century England, and in its short story form not until the nineteenth century. Then it came into being at about the same time in Russia (Gogol), the United States (Irving, Hawthorne, Poe), France (Mérimée, Balzac), and Germany (Hoffmann). The first major critical statement is made by Poe in 1842 while reviewing Hawthorne's *Twice-told Tales*:

A skilful literary artist has constructed a tale. If wise, he has not fashioned his thoughts to accommodate his incidents; but having con-ceived, with deliberate care, a certain unique or single effect or be wrought out, he then invents such incidents—he then combines such events as may best aid him in establishing this precon-ceived effect. If his very initial sentence tend not to the outbringing of this effect, then he has failed in his first step. In the whole composition there should be no word written, of which the ten-

7. Elliott, G. P., "A Defence of Fiction" in *Types of Prose Fiction*, New York, 1964, p. 20.

dency, direct or indirect, is not to the one pre-
established design. And by such means, with
such skill and care, a picture is at length painted
which leaves in the mind of him who contem-
plates it with a kindred art, a sense of the fullest
satisfaction.[8]

The word 'tale' has, since an article by Brander
Matthews in 1884, been changed to short story but
the description holds: primacy on the literary artist,
the single effect, the conciseness, the attempt to draw
a picture which makes us recognize, perhaps with
a jolt very much like a jolt of fear, "Ah-h, life is like
that." This making of a picture is no slavish copying
of the actual life scene; far from it. As stated earlier,
life is usually so scattered that meaningful patterns
rarely occur. The maker selects and orders the event
pattern in such a way that the impression of recognizable life is felt, an *impression* (not real life itself)
that may be more powerful and incisive than if we
had actually lived through the event, because the
maker is lending his or her eyes out and we see more
deeply with these than we do with our own.

The way modern story gets at the deeper facts of
life can be reviewed briefly by discussing the basic
elements of the short story. We will do so from the
point of view of the story-maker, not that of the critic.

I. *Theme.* Seen by the critic, theme is "the abstract
concept which is made concrete through its repre-
sentation in person, action, and image."[9] Seen by the
maker, theme is the yeast that holds, permeates,
shapes story into its uniqueness, the excitement that

8. *Graham's Magazine*, May 1842.
9. *A Handbook to Literature*, ed. Thrall, et al., New York, 1960,
    p. 486.

begins your work and that keeps your audience bound with you, the iron that, as Frank O'Connor has it, "plummets to the bottom of the mind."[10] A theme is never original with a story; if it were, it would be unrecognizable to anyone; rather, it is a human truth larger than any individual. Anyone can think up a dozen in five minutes and some of them may be suitable for stories. Blood is thicker than water, in crucial situations everyone likes to have a second chance; these are possible story themes and they are certainly not universally true, which is also a characteristic of theme in general. Sometimes blood is *not* thicker than water!

Since Frank O'Connor goes on record in many places stressing theme in story, a thematic study of his "Guests of the Nation" is illuminating. Other stories might be "The Second Death" and "Waiting for the Rodeo" and (a cruncher) "The Secret Room." A story may have several themes; deciding which, if any, is the most important goes a long way in determining what the story means. If anything.

II. *Point of View.* In an obvious sense the authority which leads us into a story is the maker. However, realistic fiction has discovered that a prime method for giving us a convincing impression of life is for the maker not to appear to speak; in other words, the story seems to reach the audience through no maker at all, but rather it simply seems to happen. The maker's problem becomes one of deciding upon a means of perception: "What 'eye' or what 'mind' placed in a certain position, or so established as to make it possible for it to be shifted from one position to another, is best suited to the task of revealing the

10.Frank O'Connor, *The Lonely Voice*, Cleveland, 1965, p. 216.

totality of the subject?"[11] An incisive study of this matter is done by Wayne C. Booth, *The Rhetoric of Fiction* (Chicago, 1961); as introduction here, a drastically schematized view must do, keeping in mind that no law requires a story to stick to one point of view and that the same point of view used in different stories will give quite different impressions.

1. *First Person Narrator.* "It happened while I was there"—and either I was *uninvolved* or *involved*. First person *uninvolved* is often used to narrate slightly incredible events. Sensible persons report what they saw; their own characters play no part except that they must appear trustworthy and so add credence to the oddities that occur. Dr. Watson in *The Adventures of Sherlock Holmes* is a good example; in this selection "You Could Look It Up" serves well. The *first person involved* is a much more complex situation, as a study of "The Molesters" or "That Evening Sun" or "After the Storm" will indicate. Can you believe what these narrators tell you? After all, some are only children, and under great stress. Obviously, too, adults like the narrator of "After the Storm" see what happens to themselves in a very different light than we possibly can. In other words, the more the narrator is involved, the less reliable the story may be on a straightforward level; the greater depth (and audience pleasure) of the story may be the one of which the narrator, because of immaturity or character, can have no comprehension. On the other hand, children sometimes see more truly than biassed adults.

A further complication is shown in "The Second Death" and "Oolulik." For most of the story the narrators remain uninvolved; he is active, but vital

11. Gordon and Tate, eds. *The House of Fiction*, New York, 1960, p. 437.

questions do not affect him. Then, suddenly, he is involved to the depths of his moral being. What is the complete story then?

2. *Camera-eye Narrator.* The camera whirs. It makes no comments, it simply stares, listens, and records. Either externally—it records actions, the words spoken; or internally—mounted inside the brain of the main character, it records the pictures, the sentences, the word clusters that transpire there. In its most severe form the *camera-eye external* point of view is like reading a play script. Hemingway's famous short story "The Killers" is a good fiction example, as is Robbe-Grillet's "The Secret Room.' What I call *camera-eye internal* is usually designated "stream of consciousness," a fictional development of the past fifty years which resembles the movie technique of montage: clusters of words, ideas, images flash before the reader in seeming chaos to present, as it were, the associative flux in a character's mind without transitions or explanatory tags like 'he thought' and so on. A most severe use of this technique is Molly Bloom's soliloquy at the end of *Ulysses*. A somewhat softened version is found in many stories in this selection, most clearly perhaps in "The Wind Blows" where many exclamations, sentences, even whole paragraphs are recorded exactly as Matilda would be thinking them; they are in her idiosyncratic rhythms and these tell us as much about her conscious and subconscious life as her actions and what she says aloud.

This point of view must not be labelled 'omniscient'; it is not that, but limits itself more or less strictly to an objective recording of either externals or internals. And yet—is not the very way we are guided into and through "The Secret Room" a comment? And what of "The Sin of Jesus?" Sometimes it is external, sometimes internal. Where, really, is the camera hung that records these stories?

3. *Third Person Narrator.* Again there are two useful distinctions: the third person omniscient and the third person central intelligence.

Third person omniscient is exactly that: the viewpoint moves over the landscape, closes in or backs off from any scene or character, goes fully into any character's mind. In other words, this narrator knows everything, can be anywhere, inside or outside any character at any depth. It is a technique well suited to the novel; in the short story it requires immense skill so as not to confuse, overextend, or inform too much. Clearly, no one has unlimited length to tell all, even if one wished to, and some stories concentrate mostly on one character with brief flashes into others, as in "The Conversion of the Jews." "The House on the Esplanade" (Anne Hébert) moves through the sensations of the three main characters in careful order, but it begins with the 'I' of a narrator speaking to the 'you' of the reader. Hébert is combining a very ancient 'I-you' oral story technique with a modern one of rendering inner states; the progress of this story's point of view deserves careful study. The same is true of George Elliott's "The Commonplace," whose opening viewpoint is the 'we' of an entire community, which then smoothly moves into and shifts between the two teenagers. It is worth noting that Elliott skirts getting deeply inside either of the Sunbirds. Why?

Third person central intelligence is a cumbersome phrase but it is an accurate description: the action of a story is evaluated by one superior mind at the centre of that action. Henry James theorized this point of view and his disciple, Percy Lubbock, elaborated by stating that the real actors in a story become the "thoughts, emotions, and sensations of the hero"; that this method "represents the mind of the narrator [i.e., the 'he' of the story] is in itself a kind of action."[12] The way in which this method almost immeasurably widens the narrowness and bias that must go with the first person narrator can best be seen by comparing "Thanks for the Ride" or "The Post Card" with 'The Guest" or "Revelation." They are all beautiful stories in their own way and could not be told other than they are, but the point of view in the last two opens areas and dimensions to which the first two are inevitably closed.

III. *Action and Character.* The classic approach to art is that there is no discernible difference between action and character. Henry James stated: "What is character but the determination of incident? What is incident but the illustration of character?"[13] What a character does, that character is, and story is then either good or bad as that action shows character either well or badly. The 'action story' and 'character story' distinctions mean nothing; so-called action stories are bad if they are not true to their subject— if they, for example, fail to show the true depths of characters—but they are good if they show shallowness if it is actually there. It is possible, I suppose, for a baseball manager to actually be two-dimensional in the extreme; in that case "You Could Look It Up" would be a 'good' story in the classical sense. It may be that it is impossible to write any other kind of

12. Percy Lubbock, *The Craft of Fiction*, New York, 1921, 1957, p. 148.
13. Henry James, "The Art of Fiction" in *The Future of the Novel*, edited by Leon Edel, 1956, p. 15.

story about ballplayers except a simplistic surface one because all ballplayers are really such persons; whether it is in the nature of their occupation, or whatever, professional athletes simply have no profound human depth. But most of us would feel there is something drastically wrong with that, and certainly a fat farm woman in a rural doctor's office would seem no more hopeful than ballplayers—yet look at "Revelation."

The answer is so obvious that it is almost banal: some actions (and some professional activities!) can better show profound human depths than others. If the maker chooses to remain on the level of farcical action, then the maker's characters remain there too. Modern writers have shucked all taboos and explored any and every human activity, digging for what depth any action may reveal. They have found the sexual area rich; none have been able to do much with the more rudimentary actions of elimination, however, though enough have tried. In a classic sense James remains correct. Not even in the most elementary story is there much point in looking at action divorced from character, or vice versa. They are of the same essence; they are either made well or made badly.

IV. *Setting and Character.* Henry James's dictum was made in 1884, and it would be surprising indeed if, after Sigmund Freud and global wars, there did not now exist a significant difference of opinion about human character. The development of the 'stream of consciousness' technique undermines the statement by stressing process rather than state: character is what it is ever becoming, but it is impossible to capture, once and for all, what a character is at a given moment. Character is neither consistent nor static; people are neither responsible nor irresponsible.

They simply are, whatever they are, and that may and does change with the stimuli that trigger them, either internally or externally. James Joyce begins to move in this direction in *Ulysses*; in the theatre of the absurd and the French anti-novel such theory seems to have reached a kind of ultimate in character anonymity and even indescribability. Everything is beyond the individual's control—is there any significance to imagining that an individual is really responsible for anything? "The meaning of the world around us can no longer be considered as other than fragmentary, temporary, and even contradictory, and is always in dispute. How can a work of art set out to illustrate any sort of meaning which is known in advance?" asks Alain Robbe-Grillet.[14] Life is a succession of moments, and the only thing that can be done is study its surface minutely.

Hence "The Secret Room" and "Black Angels" (Bruce Jay Friedman). Do they seem to get closer to an impression of life in our decade than "The Chorus Girl" or "Rocking-Chair" (Morley Callaghan)? Where do "After the Fair" (Dylan Thomas) and "The Molesters" belong in this spectrum? The theory of the anti-novelists and absurdists may be (very inadequately) pulled together by: "Surface is all." The state of things that surround modern humanity at any given moment to a large extent determines what kind of characters we are at that moment. We are ever changing and becoming, and, no more than a child, can we ourselves do much to determine that state or those things. So goes this theory.

Perhaps it does explain a little why 'reasonable' people continue to murder themselves so ruthlessly

14. *Program and Notes* for the International Writers' Conference, Edinburgh, 1962, p. 43.

in this century. Read the war stories here included.

V. *Time.* The possible relationships between story-time (the time required to completely read or listen to a story) and time-in-the-story are infinite and therefore forever exciting to the story-maker. In conversation, story-time and time-in-the-story presumably coincide: that gives you scene. When twenty years is traversed in a sentence or paragraph, you have panorama. The mixture of scene and panorama is a major determinant of story pace. There are no rules about these matters in story-making (there once were in drama, for example) and "Gimpel the Fool" and "The Secret Room" provide extremes in time relationship between which most of the other stories fall.

A further aspect of time is chronology. The modern story-maker knows that the imagination is informed neither by clock nor by calendar; that Marcel Proust's statement of "the inseparableness of us from the past" also has a corollary in the inseparableness of us from what we see as our future. Therefore fiction is never limited by historical chronology; the past and the future and the present hold only possibilities, as "The Second Death" and "The Wind Blows" demonstrate.

Nothing will be said here about irony, symbolism, style, and other such things which the story has in common with other art forms. If you allow for a kind of hiatus roughly in the middle to accommodate such human staples as play, loneliness, and war, the stories in this collection have been arranged in the order of the ages of human beings. And the last two lead beyond earth and death to a glimpse of heaven itself.

The Iglulik Eskimos of the Canadian Arctic coast believe that everyone is a poet; shaping poems requires no special gift which any one human does not have. Though we may doubt this concerning poetry, certainly in one significant way every human being is a story-maker; many persons, like many Eskimo singers, actually do tell beautiful stories without the conscious attempt at making anything beautiful. But most of us are not primitives and can never be, no matter how much we might wish it. Literary stories do require special gifts to make well, and they are well made when they give us pleasure. The stories in this selection vary drastically in substance and range, but all have given me very deep pleasure in ways too numerous to explicate. In the last analysis that seems to me sufficient reason for their appearance here.

Joyce Carol Oates

THE
MOLESTERS

I AM SIX YEARS OLD. There, at the end of the porch,
is the old lilac tree. Everything is blurred with light,
because there was a fog the night before and it is
lifting slowly. I am sitting on the porch step playing
with something—a doll. It has no clothes and is
scuffed. It is neither a boy nor a girl; its hair was
pulled off; its body is smooth and its eyes staring
as if they saw something that frightened them. In
the lilac tree some blackbirds are arguing. Not too
far away is the cherry orchard; the birds fly over from
the cherry trees and in a minute will fly back again.
My father has put tin foil up in the trees to scare
the birds away, but it doesn't work. If I lean forward
I can see the brilliant tin foil gleaming high up in
the trees—it moves with the rocking of the limbs,
in the wind. My father has gone to work and does
not come home until supper. The odor of supper and
the harsh sound of my father's car turning into the
cinder drive go together; everything goes together.

I climb up into the lilac tree. The first branch is
hard to hold. The birds fly away. The doll is back
there, by the steps. My grandmother gave me that
doll, and the funny thing about it is this: I never

remember it or think about it until I see it lying
somewhere, then I pick it up and hug it. There is
a little chair in the lilac tree made by three branches
that come together. I like to sit here and hide. Once
I fell down and cried and Mommy ran out onto the
porch, but that was a long time ago when I was little.
I am much bigger now. My legs dangle beneath me,
scuffed like the doll's skin. My knees are marred with
old scratches that are about to flake off and one milky
white scar that will never go away.

My mother comes outside. The chickens run toward
her even though they know it isn't time to be fed;
they come anyway. My mother puts something up
on the clothesline. The clothesline is always up,
running from tree to tree.

"What are you doing?" Mommy says. I thought
she couldn't see me but she can.

"Can I go down to the crick?" I ask her.

There, in the grass, her feet are almost hidden. The
grass is jagged and seems like waves of water. "Tommy
isn't home," she says, without looking around. She
finishes hanging the towels up—she has clothespins
in her pocket and they make her stomach look funny.
"Why do you always want to play there?" she says.
"Can't you play up here?"

"Tommy can go down anytime—"

"Tommy's bigger, Tommy doesn't fall down." She
looks past me. There is something soft about her face—
nothing bad stays in it. When I was little I kept going
back into the kitchen to make sure she was there
and she was always there. The big kids teased me
and said she was gone, but she was always there.
She would pick me up with a laugh.

I take the path through the field to the creek. There
is more than one path: a path from our house and
the Sullivans' house, and a path for fishermen who

come from the road. Our path runs along flat but curves around, and there are prickly bushes that scratch you. By the creek the path dips downhill and goes to the bank. The fishermen's path comes down from the road, alongside the bridge. Fishermen leave their cars up on the road and come down the path, slipping and sliding because it is so steep. When fishermen come we have to leave. Mommy says we have to leave. One of the big boys threw stones in the creek once, to scare the fish away, and the fisherman ran up to the Sullivans' house and was mad. He was from the city.

The creek has a smell I like. I always forget it until I come back to it; there it is. There are big flat white rocks by the shore, covered with dried-up moss that is green in the water but white outside. This is what smells. It smells dry and strange; there is something dead about it. There are dead things by the creek. Little fish and yellow birds and toads; once a garter snake. The fishermen throw little fish down on the stones and let them rot. When the fishermen are from around here we can stay and watch—they're like my father, they talk like him. When they're from the city they talk different.

Everybody has their rocks. Tommy's rock is the biggest one and nobody can sit on it but him. I have a rock too. I sit on it and my feet get in the water by mistake. That's bad. My mother will holler. I try not to let them slip in but my rock is too little, I can't sit on it right. I let my feet go back in the water. I like the way the water feels.

I have a dam made out of stones, between two rocks. When I look around I see the fisherman behind me.

He has a strange dark face; I saw someone like him in a movie once. He has a fishing pole and a paper bag and some things in his pockets. His hat looks dusty. "Do you live up there?" he says. He has a nice voice.

That makes me think of my mother. I don't know how to talk to grownups. They talk too loud to you, and something is always wrong. I don't say anything to him. There are two crabs behind the dam, little ones. Their bodies are soft to touch but they'd bite you if they could; their pincers are too little. Tommy and the boys use them for fishing, instead of worms.

"Do you live close by here?"

The fisherman is squatting on the bank now. His hat is off and next to him. He has dark hair. I tell him yes. My face is prickly, because of him looking at it. There is something funny about him.

"How old are you?" he says.

They always ask that. I don't answer but let a stone fall in the water to show I'm not afraid of him.

"Are you fishing?"

"No."

"What are you doing?"

He is squatting on the bank and calling over to me. A grownup would just walk out and see what I had, or he would walk away; he wouldn't care. This man is squatting and watching me. The bank is bare from people always standing on it. We play here all the time. When I was little I could look down from higher up and see the boys down here, playing. Mommy wouldn't let me come down then. Now I can come down by myself, alone. I am getting big. The bank tilts down toward the creek, and there are a whole lot of stones and rocks where the creek is dried up, then the water begins but is shallow, like where I am, but then farther out it is deep and only the big rocks stick up. The boys can wade out there but not me. There are holes somewhere too; it is dangerous to walk out there. Then, across the creek, is a big tangle of bushes and trees. Somebody owns that land. On this side nobody owns it, but that side has a fence. Farther down where the bushes are gone, cows come down to the creek sometimes. The boys throw stones at them. When I throw a stone it goes up in the air and comes down right away.

"What have you got there?"

"A dam."

He smiles and puts his hand to his ear. "A what?"

I don't answer him, but pretend to be fixing something.

"Can I come look?" he says.

I tell him yes. Up there, nobody cares about what I do, except if I break or spill something; then they holler. This man is different. He is like my father but not like him because he talks to me. My father says things to me but doesn't talk to me, he doesn't look at me for long because there are too many other things going on. He is always driving back and forth in the car. This man looks right at me. His eyes are dark, like Daddy's. He left his hat back on the bank. His hair is funny. He must have been out in the sun because his skin is dark. He is darker than Tommy with his suntan.

"A little dam," he says. "Well, that's real nice."

The crabs are inside yet. He doesn't see them.

"I got two crabs," I say.

The man bends down right away to look. I can smell something by him, something sweet. It makes me think of the store down the road. "Hey, look at that—I see them crabs. They'd like to bite a nice little girl like you."

I pick up one of the crabs to show him I'm not afraid. I am never afraid of crabs but only of fish that they catch and tear off the hook and let lay around

to die. They flop around on the grass, bleeding, and
their eyes look right at you. I'm afraid of them but
not of crabs.

"Hey, don't let him bite you!" The man laughs.

"He can't bite."

The crab gets away and falls back into the water.
It swims backward in quick little jerks and gets under
a rock. It is the rock the man has his foot on. He
has big black shoes like my father's, but caked with
mud and cracked. He stands with one foot on a rock
and the other in a little bit of water. He can do that
if he wants to, nobody can holler at him.

"Do you like to play down here?"

"Yes."

"Do you go to school?"

"I'm going next year."

The sun comes out and is bright. When I look up
at him my eyes have to squint. He is bending over
me. "I went to school too," he says. He smiles at me.
"Hey, you got yourself dirty," he says.

I look down and there is mud on me, on my knees
and legs and arms. It makes me giggle.

"Will your mommy be mad?" he says. Now, slowly,
he squats down. He is leaning over me the way some
of them in town do, my mother's people. You can
smell smoke or something in their breaths and it isn't
nice, it makes me not like them. This man smells of
something like candy.

"Little girls shouldn't get dirty," he says. "Don't
you want to be nice and clean and pretty?"

I splash in the water again because I know it's all
right. He won't holler.

"Little boys like to be dirty but little girls like to
be clean," he says. He talks slow, like he was doing
something dangerous—walking from rock to rock, or
trying to keep his balance on a fence.

"You've got some stuff in your hair," he says. He touches my hair. I stop what I'm doing and am quiet, like when Mommy takes burrs out. He rubs the top of my head and my neck. "Your hair is real nice," he says.

"It's got snarls underneath. She has to cut them out."

"It's real pretty hair," he says. "Hey, you know in the city little girls have two daddies. One goes to work and the other stays home to play. Do you know that?"

Something makes me giggle. His hand is on my shoulder. He has dark, staring eyes with tight lines around them. He looks like he is staring into a lamp.

"Would you like another daddy?" he says.

"I got a daddy."

He touches my arm. He looks at me as if he was really seeing me. He is not thinking about anybody else; in a minute he won't stand up and yell out to somebody else, like my mother does. He is really with me. He puts his finger to his mouth to get it wet and then he rubs at the dirt on my arm. "I wouldn't never spank no little girl of mine either," he says. He shifts forward. His legs must ache, bent so tight like that. "You think they'd spank you at home for being dirty?"

"I can wash it off." I put my arm in the water. When you knock over a stone in the water a little puff of mud comes and hides the crabs that jump out—that saves them. When you can see again they're all hid.

"Maybe you better get washed up down here. I sure wouldn't want you to get spanked again," the man says. His voice is soft, like music. His hands are warm and heavy but I don't mind them. He is holding my arm; with his thumb he is rubbing it. I look but can't see any dirt where he is rubbing it.

"Hey, don't touch your hair. You'll get mud in it," he says. He pulls my hand away. "You can wash right here in the crick. They won't never know you were dirty then. Okay? We can keep it a secret."

"Tommy has some secrets."

"It can be a secret, and we'll be friends. Okay? Don't you tell anybody about it."

"Okay."

"I'll get you all nice and clean and then we'll be friends. And you won't tell them about it. I can come back here to visit sometimes." He looks back at the bank for something. "I got some real nice licorice in there. You like that, huh?"

I tell him yes.

"When you get cleaned up you can have some then. I bet you like it."

He smiles when I say yes. Now I know what the smell is about him—licorice. It reminds me of the store down the road where the licorice sticks are standing up in a plastic thing and when you touch them they're soft. They stick to your teeth.

"Little girls don't know how to wash themselves," he says. He pats water on my arm and washes it. I sit there and don't move. There is nothing that hurts, like there is sometimes with a washcloth and hot water. He washes me slow and careful. His face is serious; he isn't in a hurry. He looks like somebody that is listening to the radio but you can't hear what he hears.

He washes my legs. "You're a real pretty little girl," he says. "They shouldn't spank you. Shouldn't nobody spank you. I'd kill them if I saw it." He looks like he might cry. Something draws his face all in, and his eyes seem to be going in, looking somewhere inside him.

"But I'll get you clean, nice and clean," he says. "Then you can have some licorice."

"Is it from the store?"

He moves his hand on my back, slow, like you pet a cat. The cat makes his back go stiff and I do the same thing. I understand what it is like to be a cat.

"Do you want to walk in the water a little?"

"I can't do that."

"Just here. By these rocks."

"They don't let me do it."

I look at him, waiting for permission. My shoes are already soaked. But if I play out in the sun afterward then they will get dry.

"Sure. They ain't nowhere around here. *I* say you can do it," he whispers. He leans back and watches me. Because he is so close I am safe and it's all right to wade in the water. Nobody else ever sat and watched me so close. Nobody else ever wanted me to walk in the water and would sit there to catch me if I tripped.

"Is it nice? Does the water feel nice?"

The water comes up to my knees in the deepest place. I can't go out any farther than this. I was swimming somewhere, but not here; we go to a lake. There they have sand and people lying on blankets, but here there isn't anything except stones. The stones are sharp sometimes.

After a while the man stands up. His face is squinting in the sun. He walks alongside me, watching me; his feet will get wet. Something makes me yawn. I feel tired. I look down and see that I am making clouds of mud underwater.

"You better come out now," he says.

When I step out on the stones my shoes make a squishy noise. It makes me laugh to see the water running out. Inside my shoes my toes are cold.

He takes my hand and walks with me back to the bank. His hand is very warm. "You had a real nice time out there, didn't you?" he says. "Little girls like to play in the water and get clean."

He wets his finger and rubs something on my face. I close my eyes until it's clean.

The licorice stick isn't as good as the ones at the store. I want to take it back home but the man says no, I have to eat it down here. I keep yawning and want to go to bed. When I play in the water I get tired, the sun makes my eyes tired.

The man washes my hands with creek water, his own hands wet and rubbing with mine like he was washing his own.

"This is our own secret and don't never tell anybody," he says.

He wipes our hands on his shirt. He is squatting down all the time to be just as tall as I am. He has a black comb he combs my hair with, but there are snarls underneath and he has to stop. He pulls the hairs out of the comb.

"Now you have another daddy, and don't never tell them," he says.

When I turn around to look at him from higher up on the path, he is bending to get his fishing pole. I forgot about looking at the pole and want to run back to see it, if it's a glass pole like some of them, but now he looks like somebody I don't know. With his back to me he is like some fisherman from the city that I don't know and am afraid of.

II

I AM SIX YEARS OLD. At this time we are still living in the country; in a few years we will move to the city, in with my grandmother. But now my father is still well enough to work. My brother and his friends have gone on a bike trip. They have mustard sandwiches wrapped in wax paper and emptied pop bottles with water in them. I went out to the road and watched them ride away. Nobody cared about me; the boys call me baby if they are nice and push me away and tease me if they're bad. I hate my brother because he pushes me with his hand, like people do in the movies when they want to knock somebody out of the way. "Move it, kid," he says and pushes me. If I run to Mommy it won't do any good. He is four years older than me and so I can never catch up to him.

The day is hot. It's August, in the morning. The high grass in the orchard is dried up; the birds are always fighting in the trees; the leaves churn to show their sleek black wings. Tommy has a BB gun and shoots the birds sometimes, but when they hear the noise they fly away; birds are smart. The cat ate one of the dead birds and then threw up the feathers and stuff, right on the kitchen floor.

I am playing with my doll. Inside, Mommy is still canning cherries. On Sundays Daddy sits out front under the tree and tries to sell baskets of cherries to people that drive by. You can't go out by him and talk because he is always mad. The kitchen is ugly and hot. There are steamed jars everywhere, and bowls of cherries. Once I liked cherries, but the last time they made me sick. I saw a little worm in a cherry, by the pit. Twenty-five years from now I will drive by cherry orchards and the nausea will rise up in me; a tiny white worm. My mind will always be pushed back to this farm, and there is nothing I can do about it. I will never be able to get away.

Today is a weekday. Later on I will learn the number of it, from hearing so much about it. But now I know

nothing except there are two or three days until
Sunday, when Daddy stays home and sits out in front
and waits for cars to stop.

My mother comes outside to see where I am. She
wears an old dress with cherry stains on it. The stains
make me look at them, they remind me of something.
Of blood. She has her hair pushed back. Her hair
is streaked up in front, by the sun, but brown
everywhere else. There is a picture of her when she
had long hair; she isn't my mother but somebody
else. Around the house she is barefoot. Her legs look
strong; she could probably run fast if she wanted to
but she never wants to. Everything is slow around
her. The chickens are nervous, picking in the dirt and
watching her for food. They jerk their heads from side
to side. If she raises her hand they will flutter their
wings, waiting to be fed.

My mother comes over to me where I am sitting
on the branches. She brushes my hair out of my eyes.
"Can't you wait for Tommy to come back, to go down
there?" she says.

"I want to play with my dam," I tell her. I lean
back so she can't touch my hair. When she works
in the kitchen her pale hands are stained from cherries.
I don't like them to touch me then. When she gives
me my bath they're like that too. I don't always like
her. I can like her if I want to, but I don't have to.
I like Daddy better, on purpose, even though Mommy
is nicer to me. She never knows what I am thinking.

"I can take you down in a while, myself," she says.
"Okay?"

I stare down at nothing. My face gets hard.

"What the hell is so good about playing in that
dirty water?" she says.

This makes my heart beat hard, with hating her.

Her eyebrows are thin and always look surprised.

I see her pluck at them sometimes. That must hurt. She stands with her hands thrust in her pockets, and her shoulders slump. I always know before she does what she is going to say.

"All right, then, go on down. But don't get wet."

I run around back of our orchard and through the next-door neighbor's field. Nothing is planted there. Then a path begins that goes down the big hill to the creek. In August the creek is shallow and there is filth in little patches in it, from sewers up creek. Fishermen fish anywhere along the creek, but there are some spots they like more than others. We always play by the rocks. There are also pieces of iron lying around, from when the new bridge was built. I can't remember any other bridge, but there was one.

I have my own little rock, that Tommy lets me have. It is shaped like a funny loaf of bread and has little dents in it. It looks like birds chipped at it, but they couldn't do that. When I come down and run through the bushes, some yellow birds fly up in surprise. Then everything is quiet. I walk in the water right away, to get my shoes wet. I hate my mother. Yesterday she was sitting on Daddy's lap; she was barefoot and her feet were dirty. They told me to come by them but I wouldn't. I ran outside by myself. Down at the creek I am happier by myself, but something makes me shiver. It is too quiet. If I was to fall in the water and drown nobody would know about it or care.

A man drowned in this creek, a few miles away. It was out back of a tavern. I heard my father talk about it.

When I look around there is a man standing on the bank. His car is parked up on the road but I didn't see it before. The man waves at me and grins. I can see his teeth way out here.

"Real nice day to play in the water," he says.

I narrow my eyes and watch him. Something touches the back of my neck, trying to tell me something. I start to shiver but stop. He reminds me of the man that drowned. Maybe his body wasn't taken out of the creek but lost. This man is too tall. His arms hang down. He has a fishing pole in one hand that is long and gawky like he is. There is something about the way he is standing—with his legs apart, as if he thought somebody might run and knock him down—that makes my eyes get narrow.

"You live around here?" he says.

He takes off his hat and tosses it down as if he was tired of it. Now I know what he is: a colored man. I know what a colored man is like. But this one isn't black like the one my grandmother pointed out when we were driving. This one has a light brown skin. When Tommy gets real brown he's almost that dark.

"How old are you?" he says.

I should run past him and up the hill and go home. I know this. Mommy told me so. But something makes me stay where I am. To make Mommy sorry, I will stay here, right where I am. I think of her watching me, standing up on top of the hill and watching and feeling sorry for me.

"I'm six," I tell the man. With my head lowered I can still see him through my lashes. My eyes are half closed.

Everything is prickly and strange. Like when you are going to be sick but don't know it yet and are just waiting for something to happen. Something is going to happen. Or like when there is a spider on the ceiling, in just the second before you turn your head to see it. You know it's there but don't know why. There is something between us like a wet soft cobweb that keeps us watching each other, the colored man and me. I can tell he is afraid too.

"What are you doing?" he says. He squats down on the bank. He puts the fishing pole and the bag behind him. He looks like a dog waiting for his dish; he knows he can't come until it's ready. I could throw a stone at him, and he could reach out and catch it with a laugh.

"Can I come look?" he says.

He gets up slowly. His legs are long and he walks like he isn't used to walking. He comes right out to where I am and looks at what I have: a little dam made with stones between my rock and another rock. The water is running slowly through it. Nothing can stop that water. There is scum on it, greasy spots, and I touch them with my finger even though I hate them.

"I got two crabs in here," I tell the man.

I can hear him breathing when he bends down to look. A smell of licorice by him—and this makes me know I should run away. Men smell like smoke or something. They smell like beer, or the outside, or sweat. He is different from them.

"A crab would like to bite a nice little girl like you," he says. Right in the middle of talking he makes a swallowing sound. I keep playing in the water just like I was alone. I seem to see my mother coming out on the porch, frowning and making that sharp line like a cut between her eyebrows. She looks down and sees my doll on the stps, by itself. If she would come down to get me I would be all right. But she won't. She will just go back in the house and forget about me.

Now the colored man squats beside me. He is still taller than I am. I am sitting with my feet in the water, and it makes me think of how the water might stop me, pulling at my feet, if I wanted to run. The water is quiet. If an airplane would fly past we could look up at it, but nothing happens. After a while the man starts to talk to me.

He says I have mud on me. Yes, this is right. It is like in a dream; maybe he put the mud on me somehow when I wasn't watching. I'm afraid to look at him, but his voice is soft and nice. He talks about little boys and little girls. I know he is not a daddy from the way he talks.

"Your hair is real nice," he says.

As soon as he touches me I am not afraid. He takes something out of my hair and shows me—a dried-up leaf. We both laugh.

He is bending toward me. His eyes are funny. The eyelid is sleepy and would push down to close the eyes, except the eyeball bulges too much. It can't see enough. We are so close together that I can see tiny little threads of blood in his eyes. He smells nice. Dark skin like that is funny to me, I never saw it so close. I would like to touch it but I don't dare. The man's mouth keeps moving. Sometimes it is a smile, then it gets bigger, then it changes back to nothing. It is as if he doesn't know what it's doing. His teeth are yellowish. The top ones are big, and when he smiles I can see his gums—a bright pink color, like a dog's. When he breathes his nostrils get small and then larger. I can almost see the warm air coming out of him, mixed with the smell of licorice and the dark smell of his skin.

He touches my shoulders and arms. He is saying something. He talks about my father and says he knows him, and he would like to be my father too. But he is not like any of the fathers because he talks in a whisper and nobody does that. He would not hit me or get mad. His eyelids come down over his big eyes and he must see me like you see something in a fog. His neck has a cord in it or something that moves; my grandmother has that too. It is the only ugly thing about him.

Now he is washing me. His breath is fast and warm against my skin. "They'll spank you if you're not clean. You got to be clean. All clean," he says. When he pulls my shirt off over my head the collar gets stuck by my nose and hurts me, but I know it is too late to run away. The water keeps coming and making a noise. "Now this. Hold on here," he says, with his voice muffled as if it was pushed in a pillow, and he pulls my shorts down and takes them off.

I can't stop shivering now. He stares at me. His hand is big and dark by my arm. I say I want to go home, and my voice is a surprise, because it is ready to cry. "Now you just be nice," he says. He moves his hand on my back so that I am pressed up by him. I wait for something to hurt me but nothing hurts me. He would never hurt me like they would. His breath is fast and he could be drowning, and then he pushed me back a little. "Why don't you walk in the water a little?"

His forehead is wrinkled, and in the wrinkles there are drops of sweat that won't run down. I wouldn't want to touch his hair. He stares at me while I wade in the water. Everywhere he touched me I feel strange, and where he looks at me I feel strange. I know how he is watching. I can feel how he likes me. He would never hurt me. Something that makes me want to laugh comes up into my throat and almost scares me.

The sun is hot and makes me tired.

He takes my clothes and dresses me on the bank. He is very quiet. He drops my shirt and picks it up again, right away. Then with his long forefinger he rubs my arm down to the wrist, as if he doesn't understand what it is. His hands are real funny inside—a pink color, not like the rest of him. His fingernails are light too but ridged with dirt.

"Don't leave yet," he says. "Please. Sit and eat this with me."

When we eat the licorice he seems to forget about it, even when it's in his mouth. He forgets to chew it. I can see something coming into his eyes that makes him forget about me; he is listening to something.

We have a secret together that I won't ever tell.

When I come home Mommy is still in the kitchen. But everything looks different. It is the same but different. The air is wet. The way Mommy looks at me when I come in is different. She is smoking a cigarette.

"For Christ's sake, look at your shoes!"

She might be going to hit me, and I jerk back. But she just bends down and starts to unlace my shoe. "Just lucky for you these are the old ones," she says. The top of her head is damp. I can see her white scalp in places right through her hair. "Come on, put your foot up," she says, tugging at my shoe.

When the shoes are off she straightens up, and her face shows that she feels something hurt her.

"What the hell is that?" she says.

My heart starts to pound. "What?"

"On your teeth."

She stares at me. I can see the little lines on her face that will get to be like Grandma's.

"I said what is that? What have you been eating?"

I try to pull away from her. "Nothing."

"What have you been eating? Licorice? Who gave it to you?"

Her face gets hard. She leans down to me and sniffs, like a cat. I think of how I hate her because she can know every secret.

"Who gave it to you?"

"Nobody."

"I said who gave it to you!"

She slaps me. Her hand moves so fast both of us are afraid of it. She makes me cry.

"Who gave it to you? Who was it? Was it somebody down at the creek?"

"A man . . . a man had it—"

"What man?"

"A man down there."

"A fisherman?"

"Yes."

Her head is moving a little, rocking back and forth as if her heart began to pound too hard. "Why did he gave it to you? Were you alone?"

"He liked me."

"Why did he give it to you?"

Her eyes are like the cat's eyes. They are too big for her face. What I see in them is terrible.

"Did he . . . did he do anything to you?" she says. Her voice is getting higher. "What did he do? What did he do?"

"Nothing."

She pulls me in from the door, like she doesn't know what she is doing. "God," she says. She doesn't know I can hear it. "My God. My God."

I try to push against her legs. I would like to run back out the door and away from her and back down to the creek.

"What did he do?" she says.

I am crying now. "Nothing. I like him. I like him better than you!"

She pulls me to the kitchen chair and knocks me against it, as if she was trying to make me sit on it but forgot how. The chair hurts my back. "Tell me what he did!" she screams.

She knocks me against the chair again. She is trying
to hurt me, to kill me. Her face is terrible. It is
somebody else's. She is like somebody from the city
come to get me. It seems to me that the colored man
is hiding behind me, afraid of her eyes and her
screaming, that awful voice I never heard before. She
is trying to get both of us.

"What did he do? Oh, my God, my God!" Her words
all run together. She is touching me everywhere, my
arms, my legs. Her fingers want to pinch me but she
won't let them. "He took your clothes off, didn't he?"
she says. "He took them off. He took them off—this
is on backwards, this is . . ."

She begins to scream. Her arms swing around and
one of the jars is knocked off the table and breaks
on the floor. I try to get away from her. I kick her
leg. She is going to kill me, her face is red and
everything is different, her voice is going higher and
higher and nothing can stop it. I know from the way
her eyes stare at me that something terrible happened
and that everything is changed.

III

I AM SIX YEARS OLD. Down at the creek, I am trying
to sit on a rock but my feet keep sliding off. Am I
too big for the rock now? How big am I? Am I six
years old or some other age? My toes curl inside my
shoes but I can't take hold of the rock.

The colored man leans toward me and touches my
hair. "I'm going to be your new daddy," he says.

The colored man leans toward me and touches my
shoulders. His hand is warm and heavy.

The colored man leans toward me and puts his
big hand around the back of my neck. He touches
me with his mouth, and then I can feel his teeth and

his tongue all soft and wet on my shoulder. "I love you," he says. The words come back inside my head over and over, so that I am saying that to him: "I love you."

Then I am in the water and it touches me everywhere. I start to scream. My mouth tries to make noises but I can't hear them until somebody saves me.

"Honey, wake up. Wake up!"

My mother is by the bed. She pulls me awake.

"What's wrong, honey?" she says. "What did you dream about?"

In the light from the lamp her face is lined and not pretty.

I can hear myself crying. My throat is sore. When I see her face it makes me cry harder. What if they all come in behind her, all those people again, to look at me? The doctor had something cold that touched me. I hated them all. I wanted them to die.

But only my father comes in. He stumbles against the bureau. "Another one of them dreams, huh?" he says in a voice like the doctor's. He is walking fast but then he slows down. The first night he was in here before my mother, to help me.

My mother presses me against her. Her hands rub my back and remind me of something ... the creek again, and the dead dry smell and the rush of terror like ice that came up in me, from way down in my stomach. Now it comes again and I can't stop crying.

"Hey, little girl, come on now," my father says. He bends over me with his two hands on his thighs, frowning. He stares at me and then at my mother. He is wondering who we are.

"We better drive her back to the doctor tomorrow," he says.

"Leave her alone, she's all right," my mother says.

"What the hell do you know about it?"

"She wasn't hurt, it's all in her head. It's in her head," my mother says sharply. She leans back and looks at me as if she is trying to look inside my head. "I can take care of her."

"Look, I can't take this much longer. It's been a year now—"

"It has not been a year!" my mother says.

My crying runs down. It always stops. Then they go out and I hear them walk in the kitchen. Alone in bed, I lie with my legs stiff and my arms stiff; something bad will happen if I move. I have to stay just the way I am when they snap off my light, or something will happen to me. I have to stay like this until morning.

They are out in the kitchen. At first they talk too low for me to hear, then louder. If they argue it will get louder. One night they talked about the nigger and I could hear them. Tommy could hear them too; I know he was awake. The nigger was caught and a state trooper that Daddy knows real well kicked him in the face—he was kicked in the face. I can't remember that face now. Yes, I can remember it. I can remember some face. He did something terrible, and what was terrible came onto me, like black tar you can't wash off, and they are sitting out there talking about it. They are trying to remember what that nigger did to me. They weren't there and so they can't remember it. They will sit there until morning and then I will smell coffee. They are talking about what to do, what to do with me, and they keep trying to remember what that nigger did to me.

My mother's voice lifts sleepily. "Oh, you bastard!" she says. Something made of glass touches something else of glass.

The rooster out back has been crowing for hours.

"Look," says my father, and then his voice drops

and I can't hear it. I lie still with my legs and arms stiff like they were made of ice or stone, trying to hear him. I can never hear him.

"... time is it?" says my mother.

The room is starting to get light and so I know everything is safe again.

Gabriel García Márquez

A VERY OLD MAN WITH ENORMOUS WINGS

A Tale For Children
Translated by Gregory Rabassa

ON THE THIRD DAY of rain they had killed so many crabs inside the house that Pelayo had to cross his drenched courtyard and throw them into the sea, because the newborn child had a temperature all night and they thought it was due to the stench. The world had been sad since Tuesday. Sea and sky were a single ash-gray thing and the sands of the beach, which on March nights glimmered like powdered light, had become a stew of mud and rotten shellfish. The light was so weak at noon that when Pelayo was coming back to the house after throwing away the crabs, it was hard for him to see what it was that was moving and groaning in the rear of the courtyard. He had to go very close to see that it was an old man, a very old man, lying face down in the mud, who, in spite of his tremendous efforts, couldn't get up, impeded by his enormous wings.

Frightened by that nightmare, Pelayo ran to get Elisenda, his wife, who was putting compresses on the sick child, and he took her to the rear of the courtyard. They both looked at the fallen body with mute stupor. He was dressed like a ragpicker. There were only a few faded hairs left on his bald skull and very few teeth in his mouth, and his pitiful condition of a drenched great-grandfather had taken away any sense of grandeur he might have had. His huge buzzard wings, dirty and half-plucked, were forever entangled in the mud. They looked at him so long and so closely that Pelayo and Elisenda very soon overcame their surprise and in the end found him familiar. Then they dared speak to him, and he answered in an incomprehensible dialect with a strong sailor's voice. That was how they skipped over the inconvenience of the wings and quite intelligently concluded that he was a lonely castaway from some foreign ship wrecked by the storm. And yet, they called in a neighbor woman who knew everything about life and death to see him, and all she needed was one look to show them their mistake.

"He's an angel," she told them. "He must have been coming for the child, but the poor fellow is so old that the rain knocked him down."

On the following day everyone knew that a flesh-and-blood angel was held captive in Pelayo's house. Against the judgment of the wise neighbor woman, for whom angels in those times were the fugitive survivors of a celestial conspiracy, they did not have the heart to club him to death. Pelayo watched over him all afternoon from the kitchen, armed with his bailiff's club, and before going to bed he dragged him out of the mud and locked him up with the hens in the wire chicken coop. In the middle of the night, when the rain stopped, Pelayo and Elisenda were still killing crabs. A short time afterward the child woke up without a fever and with a desire to eat. Then they felt magnanimous and decided to put the angel on a raft with fresh water and provisions for three days and leave him to his fate on the high seas. But when they went out into the courtyard with the first light of dawn, they found the whole neighborhood in front of the chicken coop having fun with the angel, without the slightest reverence, tossing him things to eat through the openings in the wire as if he weren't a supernatural creature but a circus animal.

Father Gonzaga arrived before seven o'clock, alarmed at the strange news. By that time onlookers less frivolous than those at dawn had already arrived and they were making all kinds of conjectures concerning the captive's future. The simplest among them thought that he should be named mayor of the world. Others of sterner mind felt that he should be promoted to the rank of five-star general in order to win all wars. Some visionaries hoped that he could be put to stud in order to implant on earth a race of winged wise men who could take charge of the universe. But Father Gonzaga, before becoming a priest, had been a robust woodcutter. Standing by the wire, he reviewed his catechism in an instant and asked them to open the door so that he could take a close look at that pitiful man who looked more like a huge decrepit hen among the fascinated chickens. He was lying in a corner drying his open wings in the sunlight among the fruit peels and breakfast leftovers that the early risers had thrown him. Alien to the impertinences of the world, he only lifted his antiquarian eyes and murmured something in his dialect when Father Gonzaga went into the chicken coop and said good morning to him in Latin. The parish priest had his first suspicion of an imposter when he saw that he did not understand the language of God or know how to greet His ministers. Then he noticed that seen close up he was much too human: he had an unbearable smell of the outdoors, the back side of his wings was strewn with parasites and his main feathers had been mistreated by terrestrial winds, and nothing about him measured up to the proud dignity of angels. Then he came out of the chicken coop and in a brief sermon warned the curious against the risks of being ingenuous. He reminded them that the devil had the bad habit of making use of carnival tricks in order to confuse the unwary. He argued that if wings were not the essential element in determining the difference between a hawk and an airplane, they were even less so in the recognition of angels. Nevertheless, he promised to write a letter to his bishop so that the latter would write to his primate so that the latter would write to the Supreme Pontiff in order to get the final verdict from the highest courts.

His prudence fell on sterile hearts. The news of the captive angel spread with such rapidity that after a few hours the courtyard had the bustle of a marketplace and they had to call in troops with fixed bayonets to disperse the mob that was about to knock the house down. Elisenda, her spine all twisted from sweeping up so much marketplace trash, then got the idea of fencing in the yard and charging five cents admission to see the angel.

The curious came from far away. A traveling carnival arrived with a flying acrobat who buzzed over the crowd several times, but no one paid any attention to him because his wings were not those of an angel but, rather, those of a sidereal bat. The most unfortunate invalids on earth came in search of health: a poor woman who since childhood had been counting her heartbeats and had run out of numbers; a Portuguese man who couldn't sleep because the noise of the stars disturbed him; a sleepwalker who got up at night to undo the things he had done while awake; and many others with less serious ailments.

In the midst of that shipwreck disorder that made the earth tremble, Pelayo and Elisenda were happy with fatigue, for in less than a week they had crammed their rooms with money and the line of pilgrims waiting their turn to enter still reached beyond the horizon.

The angel was the only one who took no part in his own act. He spent his time trying to get comfortable in his borrowed nest, befuddled by the hellish heat of the oil lamps and sacramental candles that had been placed along the wire. At first they tried to make him eat some mothballs, which, according to the wisdom of the wise neighbor woman, were the food prescribed for angels. But he turned them down, just as he turned down the papal lunches that the penitents brought him, and they never found out whether it was because he was an angel or because he was an old man that in the end he ate nothing but eggplant mush. His only supernatural virtue seemed to be patience. Especially during the first days, when the hens pecked at him, searching for the stellar parasites that proliferated in his wings, and the cripples pulled out feathers to touch their defective parts with, and even the most merciful threw stones at him, trying to get him to rise so they could see him standing. The only time they succeeded in arousing him was when they burned his side with an iron for branding steers, for he had been motionless for so many hours that they thought he was dead. He awoke with a start, ranting in his hermetic language and with tears in his eyes, and he flapped his wings a couple of times, which brought on a whirlwind of chicken dung and lunar dust and a gale of panic that did not seem to be of this world. Although many thought that his reaction had been one not of rage but of pain, from then on they were careful not to annoy him, because the majority understood that his passivity was not that of a hero taking his ease but that of a cataclysm in repose.

Father Gonzaga held back the crowd's frivolity with formulas of maidservant inspiration while awaiting the arrival of a final judgment on the nature of the captive. But the mail from Rome showed no sense of urgency. They spent their time finding out if the prisoner had a navel, if his dialect had any connection with Aramaic, how many times he could fit on the head of a pin, or whether he wasn't just a Norwegian with wings. Those meager letters might have come and gone until the end of time if a providential event had not put an end to the priest's tribulations.

It so happened that during those days, among so many other carnival attractions, there arrived in town the traveling show of the woman who had been changed into a spider for having disobeyed her parents. The admission to see her was not only less than the admission to see the angel, but people were permitted to ask her all manner of questions about her absurd state and to examine her up and down so that no one would ever doubt the truth of her horror. She was a frightful tarantula the size of a ram and with the head of a sad maiden. What was most heart-rending, however, was not her outlandish shape but the sincere affliction with which she recounted the details of her misfortune. While still practically a child she had sneaked out of her parents' house to go to a dance, and while she was coming back through the woods after having danced all night without permission, a fearful thunderclap rent the sky in two and through the crack came the lightning bolt of brimstone that changed her into a spider. Her only nourishment came from the meatballs that charitable souls chose to toss into her mouth. A spectacle like that, full of so much human truth and with such a fearful lesson, was bound to defeat without even trying that of a haughty angel who scarcely deigned to look at mortals. Besides, the few miracles attributed to the angel showed a certain mental disorder, like the blind man who didn't recover his sight but grew three new teeth, or the paralytic who didn't get to walk but almost won the lottery, and the leper whose sores sprouted sunflowers. Those consolation miracles, which were more like mocking fun, had already ruined the angel's reputation when the woman who had been changed into a spider finally crushed him completely. That was how Father Gonzaga was cured forever of his insomnia and Pelayo's courtyard went back to being as empty as during the time it had rained for three days and crabs walked through the bedrooms.

The owners of the house had no reason to lament. With the money they saved they built a two-story mansion with balconies and gardens and high netting so that crabs wouldn't get in during the winter, and with iron bars on the windows so that angels wouldn't get in. Pelayo also set up a rabbit warren close to town and gave up his job as bailiff for good, and Elisenda bought some satin pumps with high heels and many dresses of iridescent silk, the kind worn on Sunday by the most desirable women in those times. The chicken coop was the only thing that didn't receive any attention. If they washed it down with creolin and burned tears of myrrh inside it every so often, it was not in homage to the angel but to drive away the dungheap stench that still hung everywhere like a ghost and was turning the new house into an old one. At first, when the child learned to walk, they were careful that he not get too close to the chicken coop. But then they began to lose their fears and got

used to the smell, and before the child got his second
teeth he'd gone inside the chicken coop to play, where
the wires were falling apart. The angel was no less
standoffish with him than with other mortals, but
he tolerated the most ingenious infamies with the
patience of a dog who had no illusions. They both
came down with chicken pox at the same time. The
doctor who took care of the child couldn't resist the
temptation to listen to the angel's heart, and he found
so much whistling in the heart and so many sounds
in his kidneys that it seemed impossible for him to
be alive. What surprised him most, however, was the
logic of his wings. They seemed so natural on that
completely human organism that he couldn't understand why other men didn't have them too.

When the child began school it had been some time
since the sun and rain had caused the collapse of
the chicken coop. The angel went dragging himself
about here and there like a stray dying man. They
would drive him out of the bedroom with a broom
and a moment later find him in the kitchen. He seemed
to be in so many places at the same time that they
grew to think that he'd been duplicated, that he was
reproducing himself all through the house, and the
exasperated and unhinged Elisenda shouted that it
was awful living in that hell full of angels. He could
scarcely eat and his antiquarian eyes had also become
so foggy that he went about bumping into posts. All
he had left were the bare cannulae of his last feathers.
Pelayo threw a blanket over him and extended him
the charity of letting him sleep in the shed, and only
then did they notice that he had a temperature at
night, and was delirious with the tongue twisters of
an old Norwegian. That was one of the few times
they became alarmed, for they thought he was going
to die and not even the wise neighbor woman had

been able to tell them what to do with dead angels.

And yet he not only survived his worst winter, but seemed improved with the first sunny days. He remained motionless for several days in the farthest corner of the courtyard, where no one would see him, and at the beginning of December some large, stiff feathers began to grow on his wings, the feathers of a scarecrow, which looked more like another misfortune of decrepitude. But he must have known the reason for those changes, for he was quite careful that no one should notice them, that no one should hear the sea chanteys that he sometimes sang under the stars. One morning Elisenda was cutting some bunches of onions for lunch when a wind that seemed to come from the high seas blew into the kitchen. Then she went to the window and caught the angel in his first attempts at flight. They were so clumsy that his fingernails opened a furrow in the vegetable patch and he was on the point of knocking the shed down with the ungainly flapping that slipped on the light and couldn't get a grip on the air. But he did manage to gain altitude. Elisenda let out a sigh of relief, for herself and for him, when she saw him pass over the last houses, holding himself up in some way with the risky flapping of a senile vulture. She kept watching him even when she was through cutting the onions and she kept on watching until it was no longer possible for her to see him, because then he was no longer an annoyance in her life but an imaginary dot on the horizon of the sea.

Philip Roth

THE CONVERSION OF THE JEWS

"YOU'RE A REAL ONE for opening your mouth in the first place," Itzie said. "What do you open your mouth all the time for?"

"I didn't bring it up, Itz, I didn't," Ozzie said.

"What do you care about Jesus Christ for anyway?"

"I didn't bring up Jesus Christ. He did. I didn't even know what he was talking about. Jesus is historical, he kept saying. Jesus is historical." Ozzie mimicked the monumental voice of Rabbi Binder.

"Jesus was a person that lived like you and me," Ozzie continued. "That's what Binder said—"

"Yeah? ... So what! What do I give two cents whether he lived or not. And what do you gotta open your mouth!" Itzie Lieberman favored closed-mouthedness, especially when it came to Ozzie Freedman's questions. Mrs. Freedman had to see Rabbi Binder twice before about Ozzie's questions and this Wednesday at four-thirty would be the third time. Itzie preferred to keep *his* mother in the kitchen; he settled for behind-the-back subtleties such as gestures, faces, snarls and other less delicate barn-yard noises.

"He was a real person, Jesus, but he wasn't like

God, and we don't believe he is God." Slowly, Ozzie was explaining Rabbi Binder's position to Itzie, who had been absent from Hebrew School the previous afternoon.

"The Catholics," Itzie said helpfully, "they believe in Jesus Christ, that he's God." Itzie Lieberman used "the Catholics" in its broadest sense—to include the Protestants.

Ozzie received Itzie's remark with a tiny head bob, as though it were a footnote, and went on. "His mother was Mary, and his father probably was Joseph," Ozzie said. "But the New Testament says his real father was God."

"His *real* father?"

"Yeah," Ozzie said, "that's the big thing, his father's supposed to be God."

"Bull."

"That's what Rabbi Binder says, that it's impossible—"

"Sure it's impossible. That stuff's all bull. To have a baby you gotta get laid," Itzie theologized. "Mary hadda get laid."

"That's what Binder says: 'The only way a woman can have a baby is to have intercourse with a man.' "

"He said *that*, Ozz?" For a moment it appeared that Itzie had put the theological question aside. "He said that, intercourse?" A little curled smile shaped itself in the lower half of Itzie's face like a pink mustache. "What you guys do, Ozz, you laugh or something?"

"I raised my hand."

"Yeah? Whatja say?"

"That's when I asked the question."

Itzie's face lit up. "Whatja ask about—intercourse?"

"No, I asked the question about God, how if He could create the heaven and earth in six days, and make all the animals and the fish and the light in six days—the light especially, that's what always gets me, that He could make the light. Making fish and animals, that's pretty good—"

"That's damn good." Itzie's appreciation was honest but unimaginative: it was as though God had just pitched a one-hitter.

"But making light . . . I mean when you think about it, it's really something," Ozzie said. "Anyway, I asked Binder if He could make all that in six days, and He could *pick* the six days he wanted right out of nowhere, why couldn't He let a woman have a baby without having intercourse."

"You said intercourse, Ozz, to Binder?"

"Yeah."

"Right in class?"

"Yeah."

Itzie smacked the side of his head.

"I mean, no kidding around," Ozzie said, "that'd really be nothing. After all that other stuff, that'd practically be nothing."

Itzie considered a moment. "What'd Binder say?"

"He started all over again explaining how Jesus was historical and how he lived like you and me but he wasn't God. So I said I *understood* that. What I wanted to know was different."

What Ozzie wanted to know was always different. The first time he had wanted to know how Rabbi Binder could call the Jews "The Chosen People" if the Declaration of Independence claimed all men to be created equal. Rabbi Binder tried to distinguish for him between political equality and spiritual legitimacy, but what Ozzie wanted to know, he insisted, vehemently, was different. That was the first time his mother had to come.

Then there was the plane crash. Fifty-eight people had been killed in a plane crash at La Guardia. In studying a casualty list in the newspaper his mother had discovered among the list of those dead eight Jewish names (his grandmother had nine but she counted Miller as a Jewish name); because of the eight she said the plane crash was "a tragedy." During free-discussion time on Wednesday Ozzie had brought to Rabbi Binder's attention this matter of "some of his relations" always picking out the Jewish names. Rabbi Binder had begun to explain cultural unity and some other things when Ozzie stood up at his seat and said that what he wanted to know was different. Rabbi Binder insisted that he sit down and it was then that Ozzie shouted that he wished all fifty-eight were Jews. That was the second time his mother came.

"And he kept explaining about Jesus being histor-ical, and so I kept asking him. No kidding, Itz, he was trying to make me look stupid."

"So what he finally do?"

"Finally he starts screaming that I was deliberately simple-minded and a wise guy, and that my mother had to come, and this was the last time. And that I'd never get bar-mitzvahed if he could help it. Then, Itz, then he starts talking in that voice like a statue, real slow and deep, and he says that I better think over what I said about the Lord. He told me to go to his office and think it over." Ozzie leaned his body towards Itzie. "Itz, I thought it over for a solid hour, and now I'm convinced God could do it."

Ozzie had planned to confess his latest transgression to his mother as soon as she came home from work. But it was a Friday night in November and already dark, and when Mrs. Freedman came through the door she tossed off her coat, kissed Ozzie quickly on the face, and went to the kitchen table to light the three yellow candles, two for the Sabbath and one for Ozzie's father.

When his mother lit the candles she would move her two arms slowly towards her, dragging them through the air, as though persuading people whose minds were half made up. And her eyes would get glassy with tears. Even when his father was alive Ozzie remembered that her eyes had gotten glassy, so it didn't have anything to do with his dying. It had something to do with lighting the candles.

As she touched the flaming match to the unlit wick of a Sabbath candle, the phone rang, and Ozzie, standing only a foot from it, plucked it off the receiver and held it muffled to his chest. When his mother lit candles Ozzie felt there should be no noise; even breathing, if you could manage it, should be softened. Ozzie pressed the phone to his breast and watched his mother dragging whatever she was dragging, and he felt his own eyes get glassy. His mother was a round, tired, gray-haired penguin of a woman whose gray skin had begun to feel the tug of gravity and the weight of her own history. Even when she was dressed up she didn't look like a chosen person. But when she lit candles she looked like something better; like a woman who knew momentarily that God could do anything.

After a few mysterious minutes she was finished. Ozzie hung up the phone and walked to the kitchen table where she was beginning to lay the two places for the four-course Sabbath meal. He told her that she would have to see Rabbi Binder next Wednesday at four-thirty, and then he told her why. For the first time in their life together she hit Ozzie across the face with her hand.

All through the chopped liver and chicken soup

part of the dinner Ozzie cried; he didn't have any appetite for the rest.

On Wednesday, in the largest of the three basement classrooms of the synagogue, Rabbi Marvin Binder, a tall, handsome, broad-shouldered man of thirty with thick strong-fibered black hair, removed his watch from his pocket and saw that it was four o'clock. At the rear of the room Yakov Blotnik, the seventy-one-year-old custodian, slowly polished the large window, mumbling to himself, unaware that it was four o'clock or six o'clock, Monday or Wednesday. To most of the students Yakov Blotnik's mumbling, along with his brown curly beard, scythe nose, and two heel-trailing black cats, made of him an object of wonder, a foreigner, a relic, towards whom they were alternately fearful and disrespectful. To Ozzie the mumbling had always seemed a monotonous, curious prayer; what made it curious was that old Blotnik had been mumbling so steadily for so many years, Ozzie suspected he had memorized the prayers and forgotten all about God.

"It is now free-discussion time," Rabbi Binder said. "Feel free to talk about any Jewish matter at all— religion, family, politics, sports—"

There was silence. It was a gusty, clouded November afternoon and it did not seem as though there ever was or could be a thing called baseball. So nobody this week said a word about that hero from the past, Hank Greenberg—which limited free discussion considerably.

And the soul-battering Ozzie Freedman had just received from Rabbi Binder had imposed its limitation. When it was Ozzie's turn to read aloud from the Hebrew book the rabbi had asked him petulantly why he didn't read more rapidly. He was showing no progress. Ozzie said he could read faster but that if he did he was sure not to understand what he was reading. Nevertheless, at the rabbi's repeated suggestion Ozzie tried, and showed a great talent, but in the midst of a long passage he stopped short and said he didn't understand a word he was reading, and started in again at a drag-footed pace. Then came the soul-battering.

Consequently when free-discussion time rolled around none of the students felt too free. The rabbi's invitation was answered only by the mumbling of feeble old Blotnik.

"Isn't there anything at all you would like to discuss?" Rabbi Binder asked again, looking at his watch. "No questions or comments?"

There was a small grumble from the third row. The rabbi requested that Ozzie rise and give the rest of the class the advantage of his thought.

Ozzie rose. "I forget it now," he said, and sat down in his place.

Rabbi Binder advanced a seat towards Ozzie and poised himself on the edge of the desk. It was Itzie's desk and the rabbi's frame only a dagger's-length away from his face snapped him to sitting attention.

"Stand up again, Oscar," Rabbi Binder said calmly, "and try to assemble your thoughts."

Ozzie stood up. All his classmates turned in their seats and watched as he gave an unconvincing scratch to his forehead.

"I can't assemble any," he announced, and plunked himself down.

"Stand up!" Rabbi Binder advanced from Itzie's desk to the one directly in front of Ozzie; when the rabbinical back was turned Itzie gave it five-fingers off the tip of his nose, causing a small titter in the room. Rabbi Binder was too absorbed in squelching

Ozzie's nonsense once and for all to bother with titters. "Stand up, Oscar. What's your question about?"

Ozzie pulled a word out of the air. It was the handiest word. "Religion."

"Oh, now you remember?"

"Yes."

"What is it?"

Trapped, Ozzie blurted the first thing that came to him. "Why can't He make anything He wants to make!"

As Rabbi Binder prepared an answer, a final answer, Itzie, ten feet behind him, raised one finger on his left hand, gestured it meaningfully towards the rabbi's back, and brought the house down.

Binder twisted quickly to see what had happened and in the midst of the commotion Ozzie shouted in the rabbi's back what he couldn't have shouted to his face. It was a loud, toneless sound that had the timbre of something stored inside for about six days.

"You don't know! You don't know anything about God!"

The rabbi spun back towards Ozzie. "What?"

"You don't know—you don't—"

"Apologize, Oscar, apologize!" It was a threat.

"You don't—"

Rabbi Binder's hand flicked out at Ozzie's cheek. Perhaps it had only been meant to clamp the boy's mouth shut, but Ozzie ducked and the palm caught him squarely on the nose.

The blood came in a short, red spurt on to Ozzie's shirt front.

The next moment was all confusion. Ozzie screamed, "You bastard, you bastard!" and broke for the classroom door. Rabbi Binder lurched a step backwards, as though his own blood had started

flowing violently in the opposite direction, then gave
a clumsy lurch forward and bolted out the door after
Ozzie. The class followed after the rabbi's huge blue-
suited back, and before old Blotnik could turn from
his window, the room was empty and everyone was
headed full speed up the three flights leading to the
roof.

If one should compare the light of day to the life of
man: sunrise to birth; sunset—the dropping down
over the edge—to death; then as Ozzie Freedman
wiggled through the trapdoor of the synagogue roof,
his feet kicking backwards bronco-style at Rabbi
Binder's outstretched arms—at that moment the day
was fifty years old. As a rule, fifty or fifty-five reflects
accurately the age of late afternoons in November,
for it is in that month, during those hours, that one's
awareness of light seems no longer a matter of seeing,
but of hearing: light begins clicking away. In fact, as
Ozzie locked shut the trapdoor in the rabbi's face,
the sharp click of the bolt into the lock might momentarily have been mistaken for the sound of the heavier
gray that had just throbbed through the sky.

With all his weight Ozzie kneeled on the locked
door; any instant he was certain that Rabbi Binder's
shoulder would fling it open, splintering the wood
into shrapnel and catapulting his body into the sky.
But the door did not move and below him he heard
only the rumble of feet, first loud then dim, like
thunder rolling away.

A question shot through his brain. "Can this be
me?" For a thirteen-year-old who had just labeled his
religious leader a bastard, twice, it was not an
improper question. Louder and louder the question
came to him—"Is it me? Is it me?"—until he discovered himself no longer kneeling, but racing crazily

towards the edge of the roof, his eyes crying, his throat screaming, and his arms flying everywhichway as though not his own.

"Is it me? Is it Me ME ME ME! It has to be me— but is it!"

It is the question a thief must ask himself the night he jimmies open his first window, and it is said to be the question with which bridegrooms quiz themselves before the altar.

In the few wild seconds it took Ozzie's body to propel him to the edge of the roof, his self-examination began to grow fuzzy. Gazing down at the street, he became confused as to the problem beneath the question: was it, is-it-me-who-called-Binder-a-bastard? or, is-it-me-prancing-around-on-the-roof? However, the scene below settled all, for there is an instant in any action when whether it is you or somebody else is academic. The thief crams the money in his pockets and scoots out the window. The bridegroom signs the hotel register for two. And the boy on the roof finds a streetful of people gaping at him, necks stretched backwards, faces up, as though he were the ceiling of the Hayden Planetarium. Suddenly you know it's you.

"Oscar! Oscar Freedman!" a voice rose from the center of the crowd, a voice that, could it have been seen, would have looked like the writing on scroll. "Oscar Freedman, get down from there. Immediately!" Rabbi Binder was pointing one arm stiffly up at him; and at the end of that arm, one finger aimed menacingly. It was the attitude of a dictator, but one—the eyes confessed all—whose personal valet had spit neatly in his face.

Ozzie didn't answer. Only for a blink's length did he look towards Rabbi Binder. Instead his eyes began to fit together the world beneath him, to sort out people from places, friends from enemies, participants from spectators. In little jagged starlike clusters his friends stood around Rabbi Binder, who was still pointing. The topmost point on a star compounded not of angels but of five adolescent boys was Itzie. What a world it was, with those stars below, Rabbi Binder below ... Ozzie, who a moment earlier hadn't been able to control his own body, started to feel the meaning of the word control: he felt Peace and he felt Power.

"Oscar Freedman, I'll give you three to come down."

Few dictators give their subjects three to do anything; but, as always, Rabbi Binder only looked dictatorial.

"Are you ready, Oscar?"

Ozzie nodded his head yes, although he had no intention in the world—the lower one or the celestial one he'd just entered—of coming down even if Rabbi Binder should give him a million.

"All right then," said Rabbi Binder. He ran a hand through his black Samson hair as though it were a gesture prescribed for uttering the first digit. Then, with his other hand cutting a circle out of the small piece of sky around him, he spoke. "One!"

There was no thunder. On the contrary, at that moment, as though "one" was the cue for which he had been waiting, the world's least thunderous person appeared on the synagogue steps. He did not so much come out the synagogue door as lean out, onto the darkening air. He clutched at the doorknob with one hand and looked up at the roof.

"Oy!"

Yakov Blotnik's old mind hobbled slowly, as if on crutches, and though he couldn't decide precisely what the boy was doing on the roof, he knew it wasn't good—that is, it wasn't-good-for-the-Jews. For Yakov

Blotnik life had fractionated itself simply: things were either good-for-the-Jews or no-good-for-the-Jews.

He smacked his free hand to his in-sucked cheek, gently. "Oy, Gut!" And then quickly as he was able, he jacked down his head and surveyed the street. There was Rabbi Binder (like a man at an auction with only three dollars in his pocket, he had just delivered a shaky "Two"); there were the students, and that was all. So far it-wasn't-so-bad-for-the-Jews. But the boy had to come down immediately, before anybody saw. The problem: how to get the boy off the roof?

Anybody who has ever had a cat on the roof knows how to get him down. You call the fire department. Or first you call the operator and you ask her for the fire department. And the next thing there is great jamming of brakes and clanging of bells and shouting of instructions. And then the cat is off the roof. You do the same thing to get a boy off the roof.

That is, you do the same thing if you are Yakov Blotnik and you once had a cat on the roof.

When the engines, all four of them, arrived, Rabbi Binder had four times given Ozzie the count of three. The big hook-and-ladder swung around the corner and one of the firemen leaped from it, plunging headlong towards the yellow fire hydrant in front of the synagogue. With a huge wrench he began to unscrew the top nozzle. Rabbi Binder raced over to him and pulled at his shoulder.

"There's no fire ..."

The fireman mumbled back over his shoulder and, heatedly, continued working at the nozzle.

"But there's no fire, there's no fire ..." Binder shouted. When the fireman mumbled again, the rabbi grasped his face with both his hands and pointed it up at the roof.

To Ozzie it looked as though Rabbi Binder was trying to tug the fireman's head out of his body, like a cork from a bottle. He had to giggle at the picture they made: it was a family portrait—rabbi in black skullcap, fireman in red fire hat, and the little yellow hydrant squatting beside like a kid brother, bareheaded. From the edge of the roof Ozzie waved at the portrait, a one-handed, flapping, mocking wave; in doing it his right foot slipped from under him. Rabbi Binder covered his eyes with his hands.

Firemen work fast. Before Ozzie had even regained his balance, a big, round, yellowed net was being held on the synagogue lawn. The firemen who held it looked up at Ozzie with stern, feelingless faces.

One of the firemen turned his head towards Rabbi Binder. "What, is the kid nuts or something?"

Rabbi Binder unpeeled his hands from his eyes, slowly, painfully, as if they were taped. Then he checked: nothing on the sidewalk, no dents in the net.

"Is he gonna jump, or what?" the firemen shouted.

In a voice not at all like a statue, Rabbi Binder finally answered. "Yes, Yes, I think so ... He's been threatening to ..."

Threatening to? Why, the reason he was on the roof, Ozzie remembered, was to get away; he hadn't even thought about jumping. He had just run to get away, and the truth was that he hadn't really headed for the roof as much as he'd been chased there.

"What's his name, the kid?"

"Freedman," Rabbi Binder answered. "Oscar Freedman."

The fireman looked up at Ozzie. "What is it with you, Oscar? You gonna jump, or what?"

Ozzie did not answer. Frankly, the question had just arisen.

"Look, Oscar, if you're gonna jump, jump—and if you're not gonna jump, don't jump. But don't waste our time, willya?"

Ozzie looked at the fireman and then at Rabbi Binder. He wanted to see Rabbi Binder cover his eyes one more time.

"I'm going to jump."

And then he scampered around the edge of the roof to the corner, where there was no net below, and he flapped his arms at his sides, swishing the air and smacking his palms to his trousers on the downbeat. He began screaming like some kind of engine, "Wheeeee ... wheeeeee," and leaning way out over the edge with the upper half of his body. The firemen whipped around to cover the ground with the net. Rabbi Binder mumbled a few words to Somebody and covered his eyes. Everything happened quickly, jerkily, as in a silent movie. The crowd, which had arrived with the fire engines, gave out a long, Fourth-of-July fireworks oooh-aahhh. In the excitement no one had paid the crowd much heed, except, of course, Yakov Blotnik, who swung from the doorknob counting heads. "Fier und tsvansik ... finf und tsvantsik ... Oy, Gut!" It wasn't like this with the cat.

Rabbi Binder peeked through his fingers, checked the sidewalk and net. Empty. But there was Ozzie racing to the other corner. The firemen raced with him but were unable to keep up. Whenever Ozzie wanted to he might jump and splatter himself upon the sidewalk, and by the time the firemen scooted to the spot all they could do with their net would be to cover the mess.

"Wheeeee ... wheeeee ..."

"Hey, Oscar," the winded fireman yelled, "What the hell is this, a game or something?"

"Wheeeee ... wheeeee ..."

"Hey, Oscar—"

But he was off now to the other corner, flapping his wings fiercely. Rabbi Binder couldn't take it any longer—the fire engines from nowhere, the screaming suicidal boy, the net. He fell to his knees, exhausted, and with his hands curled together in front of his chest like a little dome, he pleaded, "Oscar, stop it, Oscar. Don't jump, Oscar. Please come down ... Please don't jump."

And further back in the crowd a single voice, a single young voice, shouted a lone word to the boy on the roof.

"Jump!"

It was Itzie. Ozzie momentarily stopped flapping.

"Go ahead, Ozzie—jump!" Itzie broke off his point of the star and courageously, with the inspiration not of a wise-guy but of a disciple, stood alone. "Jump, Ozz, jump!"

Still on his knees, his hands still curled, Rabbi Binder twisted his body back. He looked at Itzie, then, agonizingly, back to Ozzie.

"Oscar, DON'T JUMP! PLEASE, DON'T JUMP ... please please ..."

"Jump!" This time it wasn't Itzie but another point of the star. By the time Mrs. Freedman arrived to keep her four-thirty appointment with Rabbi Binder, the whole little upside down heaven was shouting and pleading for Ozzie to jump, and Rabbi Binder no longer was pleading with him not to jump, but was crying into the dome of his hands.

Understandably Mrs. Freedman couldn't figure out

what her son was doing on the roof. So she asked.

"Ozzie, my Ozzie, what are you doing? My Ozzie, what is it?"

Ozzie stopped wheeeeeing and slowed his arms down to a cruising flap, the kind birds use in soft winds, but he did not answer. He stood against the low, clouded, darkening sky—light clicked down swiftly now, as on a small gear—flapping softly and gazing down at the small bundle of a woman who was his mother.

"What are you doing, Ozzie?" She turned towards the kneeling Rabbi Binder and rushed so close that only a paper-thickness of dusk lay between her stomach and his shoulders.

"What is my baby doing?"

Rabbi Binder gaped up at her but he too was mute. All that moved was the dome of his hands; it shook back and forth like a weak pulse.

"Rabbi, get him down! He'll kill himself. Get him down, my only baby ..."

"I can't," Rabbi Binder said. "I can't ..." and he turned his handsome head towards the crowd of boys behind him. "It's them. Listen to them."

And for the first time Mrs. Freedman saw the crowd of boys, and she heard what they were yelling.

"He's doing it for them. He won't listen to me. It's them." Rabbi Binder spoke like one in a trance.

"For them?"

"Yes."

"Why for them?"

"They want him to ..."

Mrs. Freedman raised her two arms upward as though she were conducting the sky. "For them he's doing it!" And then in a gesture older than pyramids, older than prophets and floods, her arms came slapping down to her sides. "A martyr I have. Look!" She tilted her head to the roof. Ozzie was still flapping softly. "My martyr."

"Oscar, come down, *please*," Rabbi Binder groaned.

In a startlingly even voice Mrs. Freedman called to the boy on the roof. "Ozzie, come down, Ozzie. Don't be a martyr, my baby."

As though it were a litany, Rabbi Binder repeated her words. "Don't be a martyr, my baby. Don't be a martyr."

"Gawhead, Ozz—*be* a Martin!" It was Itzie. "Be a Martin, be a Martin," and all the voices joined in singing for Martindom, whatever *it* was. "Be a Martin, be a Martin ..."

Somehow when you're on a roof the darker it gets the less you can hear. All Ozzie knew was that two groups wanted two new things: his friends were spirited and musical about what they wanted; his mother and the rabbi were even-toned, chanting, about what they didn't want. The rabbi's voice was without tears now and so was his mother's.

The big net stared up at Ozzie like a sightless eye. The big, clouded sky pushed down. From beneath it looked like a gray corrugated board. Suddenly, looking up into that unsympathetic sky, Ozzie realized all the strangeness of what these people, his friends, were asking: they wanted him to jump, to kill himself; they were singing about it now—it made them that happy. And there was an even greater strangeness: Rabbi Binder was on his knees, trembling. If there was a question to be asked now it was not "Is it me?" but rather "Is it us? ... Is it us?"

Being on the roof, it turned out, was a serious thing. If he jumped would the singing become dancing? Would it? What would jumping stop? Yearningly,

Ozzie wished he could rip open the sky, plunge his hands through, and pull out the sun; and on the sun, like a coin, would be stamped JUMP OR DON'T JUMP.

Ozzie's knees rocked and sagged a little under him as though they were setting him for a dive. His arms tightened, stiffened, froze, from shoulders to fingernails. He felt as if each part of his body were going to vote as to whether he should kill himself or not— and each part as though it were independent of *him*.

The light took an unexpected click down and the new darkness, like a gag, hushed the friends singing for this and the mother and rabbi chanting for that.

Ozzie stopped counting votes, and in a curiously high voice, like one who wasn't prepared for speech, he spoke.

"Mamma?"

"Yes, Oscar."

"Mamma, get down on your knees, like Rabbi Binder."

"Oscar—"

"Get down on your knees," he said, "or I'll jump."

Ozzie heard a whimper, then a quick rustling, and when he looked down where his mother had stood he saw the top of a head and beneath that a circle of dress. She was kneeling beside Rabbi Binder.

He spoke again. "Everybody kneel." There was the sound of everybody kneeling.

Ozzie looked around. With one hand he pointed towards the synagogue entrance. "Make *him* kneel."

There was a noise, not of kneeling, but of body-and-cloth stretching. Ozzie could hear Rabbi Binder saying in a gruff whisper, "... or he'll *kill* himself," and when next he looked there was Yakov Blotnik off the doorknob and for the first time in his life upon his knees in the Gentile posture of prayer.

As for the firemen—it was not as difficult as one

might imagine to hold a net taut while you are kneeling.

Ozzie looked around again; and then he called to Rabbi Binder.

"Rabbi?"

"Yes, Oscar."

"Rabbi Binder, do you believe in God?"

"Yes."

"Do you believe God can do Anything?" Ozzie leaned his head out in the darkness. "Anything?"

"Oscar, I think—"

"Tell me you believe God can do Anything."

There was a second's hesitation. Then: "God can do Anything."

"Tell me you believe God can make a child without intercourse."

"He can."

"Tell me!"

"God," Rabbi Binder admitted, "can make a child without intercourse."

"Mamma, you tell me."

"God can make a child without intercourse," his mother said.

"Make *him* tell me." There was no doubt who *him* was.

In a few moments Ozzie heard an old comical voice say something to the increasing darkness about God.

Next, Ozzie made everybody say it. And then he made them all say they believed in Jesus Christ— first one at a time, then all together.

When the catechizing was through it was the beginning of evening. From the street it sounded as if the boy on the roof might have sighed.

"Ozzie?" A woman's voice dared to speak. "You'll come down now?"

There was no answer, but the woman waited, and

when a voice finally did speak it was thin and crying,
and exhausted as that of an old man who has just
finished pulling the bells.

"Mamma, don't you see—you shouldn't hit me.
He shouldn't hit me. You shouldn't hit me about
God, Mamma. You should never hit anybody about
God—"

"Ozzie, please come down now."

"Promise me, promise me you'll never hit anybody
about God."

He had asked only his mother, but for some reason
everyone kneeling in the street promised he would
never hit anybody about God.

Once again there was silence.

"I can come down now, Mamma," the boy on the
roof finally said. He turned his head both ways as
though checking the traffic lights. "Now I can come
down ..."

And he did, right into the center of the yellow net
that glowed in the evening's edge like an overgrown
halo.

Katherine Mansfield

THE WIND BLOWS

SUDDENLY—DREADFULLY—she wakes up. What has happened? Something dreadful has happened. No—nothing has happened. It is only the wind shaking the house, rattling the windows, banging a piece of iron on the roof and making her bed tremble. Leaves flutter past the window, up and away; down in the avenue a whole newspaper wags in the air like a lost kite and falls, spiked on a pine tree. It is cold. Summer is over—it is autumn—everything is ugly. The carts rattle by, swinging from side to side; two Chinamen lollop along under their wooden yokes with the straining vegetable baskets—their pigtails and blue blouses fly out in the wind. A white dog on three legs yelps past the gate. It is all over! What is? Oh, everything! And she begins to plait her hair with shaking fingers, not daring to look in the glass. Mother is talking to grandmother in the hall.

"A perfect idiot! Imagine leaving anything out on the line in weather like this.... Now my best little Teneriffe-work tea-cloth is simply in ribbons. *What* is that extraordinary smell? It's the porridge burning. Oh, heavens—this wind!"

She has a music lesson at ten o'clock. At the thought the minor movement of the Beethoven begins to play in her head, the trills long and terrible like little rolling drums.... Marie Swainson runs into the garden next door to pick the "chrysanths" before they are ruined. Her skirt flies up above her waist; she tries to beat it down, to tuck it between her legs while she stoops, but it is no use—up it flies. All the trees and bushes beat about her. She picks as quickly as she can, but she is quite distracted. She doesn't mind what she does—she pulls the plants up by the roots and bends and twists them, stamping her foot and swearing.

"For heaven's sake keep the front door shut! Go round to the back," shouts someone. And then she hears Bogey:

"Mother, you're wanted on the telephone. Telephone, Mother. It's the butcher."

How hideous life is—revolting, simply revolting.... And now her hat-elastic's snapped. Of course it would. She'll wear her old tam and slip out the back way. But Mother has seen.

"Matilda. Matilda. Come back im-me-diately! What on earth have you got on your head? It looks like a tea cosy. And why have you got that mane of hair on your forehead."

"I can't come back, Mother. I'll be late for my lesson."

"Come back immediately!"

She won't. She won't. She hates Mother. "Go to hell," she shouts, running down the road.

In waves, in clouds, in big round whirls the dust comes stinging, and with it little bits of straw and chaff and manure. There is a loud roaring sound from the trees in the gardens, and standing at the bottom of the road outside Mr. Bullen's gate she can hear the sea sob: "Ah! ... Ah! ... Ah-h!" But Mr. Bullen's drawing-room is as quiet as a cave. The windows are closed, the blinds half pulled, and she is not late. The-girl-before-her has just started playing MacDowell's

"To an Iceberg." Mr. Bullen looks over at her and half smiles.

"Sit down," he says. "Sit over there in the sofa corner, little lady."

How funny he is. He doesn't exactly laugh at you ... but there is just something ... Oh, how peaceful it is here. She likes this room. It smells of art serge and stale smoke and chrysanthemums ... there is a big vase of them on the mantelpiece behind the pale photograph of Rubinstein ... *à mon ami Robert Bullen*.... Over the black glittering piano hangs "Solitude"— a dark tragic woman draped in white, sitting on a rock, her knees crossed, her chin on her hands.

"No, no!" says Mr. Bullen, and he leans over the other girl, puts his arms over her shoulders and plays the passage for her. The stupid—she's blushing! How ridiculous!

Now the-girl-before-her has gone; the front door slams. Mr. Bullen comes back and walks up and down, very softly, waiting for her. What an extraordinary thing. Her fingers tremble so that she can't undo the knot in the music satchel. It's the wind.... And her heart beats so hard she feels it must lift her blouse up and down. Mr. Bullen does not say a word. The shabby red piano seat is long enough for two people to sit side by side. Mr. Bullen sits down by her.

"Shall I begin with scales," she asks, squeezing her hands together. "I had some arpeggios, too."

But he does not answer. She doesn't believe he even hears ... and then suddenly his fresh hand with the ring on it reaches over and opens Beethoven.

"Let's have a little of the old master," he says.

But why does he speak so kindly—so awfully kindly—and as though they had known each other for years and years and knew everything about each other.

He turns the page slowly. She watches his hand—
it is a very nice hand and always looks as though
it had just been washed.

"Here we are," says Mr. Bullen.

Oh, that kind voice—Oh, that minor movement.
Here come the little drums....

"Shall I take the repeat?"

"Yes, dear child."

His voice is far, far too kind. The crotchets and
quavers are dancing up and down the stave like little
black boys on a fence. Why is he so ... She will not
cry—she has nothing to cry about....

"What is it, dear child?"

Mr. Bullen takes her hands. His shoulder is there—
just by her head. She leans on it ever so little, her
cheek against the springy tweed.

"Life is so dreadful," she murmurs, but she does
not feel it's dreadful at all. He says something about
"waiting" and "marking time" and "that rare thing,
a woman," but she does not hear. It is so comfortable
... for ever ...

Suddenly the door opens and in pops Marie Swainson hours before her time.

"Take the allegretto a little faster," says Mr. Bullen,
and gets up and begins to walk up and down again.

"Sit in the sofa corner, little lady," he says to Marie.

The wind, the wind. It's frightening to be here in her
room by herself. The bed, the mirror, the white jug
and basin gleam like the sky outside. It's the bed that
is frightening. There it lies, sound asleep.... Does
Mother imagine for one moment that she is going
to darn all those stockings knotted up on the quilt
like a coil of snakes? She's not. No, Mother. I do not
see why I should.... The wind—the wind! There's a
funny smell of soot blowing down the chimney. Hasn't

anyone written poems to the wind? ... "I bring fresh flowers to the leaves and showers." ... What nonsense.

"Is that you, Bogey?"

"Come for a walk round the esplanade, Matilda. I can't stand this any longer."

"Right-o. I'll put on my ulster. Isn't it an awful day!" Bogey's ulster is just like hers. Hooking the collar she looks at herself in the glass. Her face is white, they have the same excited eyes and hot lips. Ah, they know those two in the glass. Good-bye, dears; we shall be back soon.

"This is better, isn't it?"

"Hook on," says Bogey.

They cannot walk fast enough. Their heads bent, their legs just touching, they stride like one eager person through the town, down the asphalt zigzag where the fennel grows wild and on to the esplanade. It is dusky—just getting dusky. The wind is so strong that they have to fight their way through it, rocking like two old drunkards. All the poor little pahutukawas on the esplanade are bent to the ground.

"Come on! Come on! Let's get near."

Over by the breakwater the sea is very high. They pull off their hats and her hair blows across her mouth, tasting of salt. The sea is so high that the waves do not break at all; they thump against the rough stone wall and suck up the weedy, dripping steps. A fine spray skims from the water right across the esplanade. They are covered with drops; the inside of her mouth tastes wet and cold.

Bogey's voice is breaking. When he speaks he rushes up and down the scale. It's funny—it makes you laugh—and yet it just suits the day. The wind carries their voices—away fly the sentences like little narrow ribbons.

"Quicker! Quicker!"

It is getting very dark. In the harbour the coal hulks show two lights—one high on a mast, and one from the stern.

"Look, Bogey. Look over there."

A big black steamer with a long loop of smoke streaming, with the portholes lighted, with lights everywhere, is putting out to sea. The wind does not stop her; she cuts through the waves, making for the open gate between the pointed rocks that lead to ... It's the light that makes her look so awfully beautiful and mysterious.... *They* are on board leaning over the rail arm in arm.

"... Who are they?"

"... Brother and sister."

"Look, Bogey, there's the town. Doesn't it look small? There's the post office clock chiming for the last time. There's the esplanade where we walked that windy day. Do you remember? I cried at my music lesson that day—how many years ago! Good-bye, little island, good-bye...."

Now the dark stretches a wing over the tumbling water. They can't see those two any more. Good-bye, good-bye. Don't forget.... But the ship is gone, now.

The wind—the wind.

Clark Blaise

A NORTH AMERICAN
EDUCATION

ELEVEN YEARS AFTER the death of Napoleon, in
the presidency of Andrew Jackson, my grandfather,
Boniface Thibidault, was born. For most of his life
he was a *journalier*, a day labourer, with a few years
off for wars and buccaneering. Then at the age of
fifty, a father and widower, he left Paris and came
alone to the New World and settled in Sorel, a few
miles down river from Montreal. He worked in the
shipyards for a year or two then married his young
housekeeper, an eighteen-year-old named Lise Beau-
dette. Lise, my grandmother, had that resigned look
of a Quebec girl marked early for a nursing order
if marriage couldn't catch her, by accident, first. In
twenty years she bore fifteen children, eight of them
boys, five of whom survived. The final child, a son,
was named Jean-Louis and given at birth to the
Church. As was the custom with the last boy, he was
sent to the monastery as soon as he could walk, and
remained with the Brothers for a dozen years, taking
his meals and instructions as an apprentice.

It would have been fitting if Boniface Thibidault,
then nearly eighty, had earned a fortune in Sorel—
but he didn't. Or if a son had survived to pass on

his stories—but none were listening. Or if Boniface himself had written something—but he was illiterate. Boniface was cut out for something different. One spring morning in 1912, the man who had seen two child brides through menopause stood in the mud outside his cottage and defied Sorel's first horseless carriage to churn its way through the April muck to his door, and if by the Grace of God it did, to try going on while he, an old man, pushed it back downhill. Money was evenly divided on the man and the driver, whom Boniface also defamed for good measure. The driver was later acquitted of manslaughter in Sorel's first fatality and it was never ascertained if Boniface died of the bumping, the strain, or perhaps the shock of meeting his match. Jean-Louis wasn't there. He left the church a year later by walking out and never looking back. He was my father.

The death of Boniface was in keeping with the life, yet I think of my grandfather as someone special, a character from a well-packed novel who enters once and is never fully forgotten. I think of Flaubert's *Sentimental Education* and the porters who littered the decks of the *Ville-de-Montereau* on the morning of September 15, 1840, when young Frédéric Moreau was about to sail. My grandfather was already eight in 1840, a good age for cabin boys. But while Frédéric was about to meet Arnoux and his grand passion, Boniface was content to pocket a tip and beat it, out of the novel and back into his demimonde.

I have seen one picture of my grandfather, taken on a ferry between Quebec and Levis in 1895. He looks strangely like Sigmund Freud: bearded, straw-hatted, buttoned against the river breezes. It must have been a cold day—the vapour from the nearby horses steams in the background. As a young man he must have been, briefly, extraordinary. I think of

him as a face in a Gold Rush shot, the one face that
seems both incidental and immortal guarding a claim
or watering a horse, the face that seems lifted from
the crowd, from history, the face that could be
dynastic.

And my father, Jean-Louis Thibidault, who became
Gene and T.B. Doe—he too stands out in pictures.
A handsome man, a contemporary man (and yet not
even a man of this century. His original half-brothers
back in France would now be 120 years old; he would
be, by now, just seventy); a salesman and business-
man. I still have many pictures, those my mother gave
me. The earliest is of a strong handsome man with
very short legs. He is lounging on an old canvas chaise
under a maple tree, long before aluminum furniture,
long before I was born. A scene north of Montreal,
just after they were married. It is an impressive
picture, but for the legs, which barely reach the grass.
Later he would grow into his shortness, would learn
the vanities of the short and never again stretch out
casually, like the tall. In another picture I am standing
with him on a Florida beach. I am five, he is forty-
two. I am already the man I was destined to be; he
is still the youth he always was. My mother must
have taken the shot—I can tell, for I occupy the
centre—and it is one of those embarrassing shots
parents often take. I am in my wet transparent under-
pants and I've just been swimming at Daytona Beach.
It is 1946, our first morning in Florida. It isn't a
vacation; we've arrived to start again, in the sun. The
war is over, the border is open, the old black Packard
is parked behind us. I had wanted to swim but had
no trunks; my father took me down in my underwear.
But in the picture my face is worried, my cupped
hands are reaching down to cover myself, but I was
late or the picture early—it seems instead that I am

pointing to it, a fleshy little spot on my transparent pants. On the back of the picture my father had written:

Thibidault et fils,
Daytona, avr/46

We'd left Montreal four days before, with snow still grey in the tenements' shadow, the trees black and budless over the dingy winter street. Our destination was a town named Hartley where my father had a friend from Montreal who'd started a lawn furniture factory. My father was to become a travelling salesman for Laverdure's Lawn Laddies, and I was to begin my life as a salesman's son. As reader of back issues, as a collector of cancelled stamps (the inkier the better), as student and teacher of languages.

Thibidault et fils; Thibidault and son. After a week in Hartley I developed worms. My feet bled from itching and scratching. The worms were visible; I could prick them with pins. My mother took me to a clinic where the doctor sprayed my foot with a liquid freeze. Going on, the ice was pleasant, for Florida feet are always hot. Out on the bench I scraped my initials in the frost of my foot. It seemed right to me (before the pain of the thaw began); I was from Up North, the freezing was a friendly gesture for a Florida doctor. My mother held my foot between her hands and told me stories of her childhood, ice-skating for miles on the Battleford River in Saskatchewan, then riding home under fur rugs in a horse-drawn sleigh. Though she was the same age as my father, she was the eldest of six—somewhere between them was a missing generation. The next morning the itching was worse and half a dozen new worms radiated from the ball of my foot. My mother then consulted her old *Canadian*

Doctor's Home Companion—my grandfather Blanken-ship had been a doctor, active for years in curling circles, Anglican missions, and crackpot Toryism—and learned that footworms, etc., were unknown in Canada but sometimes afflicted Canadian travellers in Tropical Regions. Common to all hot climes, the book went on, due to poor sanitation and the unspeakable habits of the non-white peoples, even in the Gulf Coast and Indian Territories of our southern neigh-bour. No known cure, but lack of attention can be fatal.

My mother called in a neighbour, our first contact with the slovenly woman who lived downstairs. She came up with a bottle of carbolic acid and another of alcohol, and poured the acid over the worms and told me to yell when it got too hot. Then with alcohol she wiped it off. The next morning my foot had peeled and the worms were gone. And I thought, inspecting my peeled, brown foot, that in some small way I had become less northern, less hateful to the kids around me though I still sounded strange and they shouted after me, "Yankee, Yankee!"

My father was already browned and already spoke with a passable southern accent. When he wasn't on the road with Lawn Laddies he walked around bare-foot or in shower clogs. But he never got worms, and he was embarrassed that I had.

Thibidault and son: he was a fisherman and I always fished at his side. Fished for what? I wonder now—he was too short and vain a man to really be a fisherman. He dressed too well, couldn't swim, de-spised the taste of fish, shunned the cold, the heat, the bugs, the rain. And yet we fished every Sunday, wherever we lived. Canada, Florida, the Middle West, heedless as deer of crossing borders. The tackle box

(oily childhood smell) creaked at our feet. The fir-
lined shores and pink granite beaches of Ontario
gleamed behind us. Every cast became a fresh hope,
a trout or *doré* or even a muskie. But we never caught
a muskie or a trout, just the snake-like fork-boned
pike that we let go by cutting the line when the plug
was swallowed deep. And in Florida, with my father
in his Harry Truman shirts and sharkskin pants, the
warm bait-well sloshing with half-dead shiners, we
waited for bass and channel cat in Okeechobee,
Kissimmee and a dozen other bug-beclouded lakes.
Gar fish, those tropical pike, drifted by the boat. Gators
churned in a narrow channel and dragonflies lit on
my cane pole tip. And as I grew older and we came
back North (but not all the way), I remember our
Sundays in Cincinnati, standing shoulder-to-shoulder
with a few hundred others around a clay-banked tub
lit with arc-lamps. Scummy pay-lakes with a hot dog
stand behind, a vision of hell for a Canadian or a
Floridian, but we paid and we fished and we never
caught a thing. Ten hours every Sunday from Memorial Day to Labour Day, an unquestioning ritual that
would see me dress in my fishing khakis, race out
early and buy the Sunday paper before we left (so
I could check the baseball averages—what a normal
kid I might have been!), then pack the tacklebox and
portable radio (for the Cincinnati doubleheader) in
the trunk. Then I would get my father up. He'd have
his coffee and a few cigarettes then shout, "Mildred,
Frankie and I are going fishing!" She would be upstairs
reading or sewing. We were still living in a duplex;
a few months later my parents were to start their
furniture store and we would never fish again. We
walked out, my father and I, nodding to the neighbours (a few kids, younger than I, asked if they could
go, a few young fathers would squint and ask, "Not

again, Gene?"); and silently we drove, and later, silently, we fished.

Then came a Sunday just before Labour Day when I was thirteen and we didn't go fishing. I was dressed for it and the car was packed as usual, but my father drove to the County Fair instead. Not the Hamilton County Fair in Cincinnati—we drove across the river into Boone County, Kentucky, where things were once again southern and shoddy.

I had known from the books and articles my mother was leaving in the bathroom that I was supposed to be learning about sex. I'd read the books and figured out the anatomy for myself; I wondered only how to ask a girl for it and what to do once I got there. Sex was something like dancing, I supposed, too intricate and spontaneous for a boy like me. And so we toured the Fair Grounds that morning, saying nothing, reviewing the prize sows and heifers, watching a stock-car race and a miniature rodeo. I could tell from my father's breathing, his coughing, his attempt to put his arm around my shoulder, that this was the day he was going to talk to me about sex, the facts of life, and the thought embarrassed him as much as it did me. I wanted to tell him to never mind; I didn't need it, it was something that selfish people did to one another.

He led me to a remote tent far off the fairway. There was a long male line outside, men with a few boys my age, joking loudly and smelling bad. My father looked away, silent. So this is the place, I thought, where I'm going to see it, going to learn something good and dirty, something they couldn't put on those Britannica Films and show in school. The sign over the entrance said only: *Princess Hi-Yalla. Shows Continuously.*

There was a smell, over the heat, over the hundred

men straining for a place, over the fumes of pigsties and stockyards. It was the smell of furtiveness, rural slaughter and unquenchable famine. The smell of boy's rooms in the high school. The smell of sex on the hoof. The "Princess" on the runway wore not a stitch, and she was already lathered like a racehorse from her continuous dance. There was no avoiding the bright pink lower lips that she'd painted; no avoiding the shrinking, smiling, puckering, wrinkled labia. "Kiss, baby?" she called out, and the men went wild. The lips smacked us softly. The Princess was more a dowager, and more black than brown or yellow. She bent forward to watch herself, like a ventriloquist with a dummy. I couldn't turn away as my father had; it seemed less offensive to watch her wide flat breasts instead, and to think of her as another native from the *National Geographic*. She asked a guard for a slice of gum, then held it over the first row. "Who gwina wet it up fo' baby?" And a farmer licked both sides while his friends made appreciative noises, then handed it back. The Princess inserted it slowly, as though it hurt, spreading her legs like the bow-legged rodeo clown I'd seen a few minutes earlier. Her lower mouth chewed, her abdomen heaved, and she doubled forward to watch the progress. "Blow a bubble!" the farmer called, his friends screamed with laughter. But a row of boys in overalls, my age, stared at the woman and didn't smile. Nothing would amaze them—they were waiting for a bubble. Then she cupped her hand underneath and the gum came slithering out. "Who wants this?" she called, holding it high, and men were whistling and throwing other things on the stage: key rings, handkerchiefs, cigarettes. She threw the gum toward us—I remember ducking as it came my way, but someone caught it. "Now then," she said, and her voice was as loud as a gospel singer's, "baby's fixin' to have herself a cig'rette." She walked to the edge of the stage (I could see her moist footprints in the dust), her toes curled over the side. "Which of you men out there is givin' baby a cig'rette?" Another farmer standing behind his fat adolescent son threw up two cigarettes. The boy, I remember, was in overalls and had the cretinous look of fat boys in overalls: big, sweating, red-cheeked, with eyes like calves' in a roping event. By the time I looked back on stage, the Princess had inserted the cigarette and had thrust baby out over the runway and was asking for matches. She held the match herself. And the cigarette glowed, smoke came out, an ash formed.

I heard moaning, long low moans, and I felt the eyes of a dozen farmers leap to the boy in overalls. He was jumping and whimpering and the men were laughing as he tried to dig into his sealed-up pants. Forgetting the buttons at his shoulders, he was holding his crotch as though it burned. He was running in place, moaning, then screaming, "Daddy!" and I forgot about the Princess. Men cleared a circle around him and began clapping and chanting, "Whip it out!" and the boy was crying, "Daddy, I cain't hold it back no more!"

My father grabbed me then by the elbow, and said, "Well, have you seen enough?" The farm boy had collapsed on the dirt floor, and was twitching on his back as though a live wire were passed through his body. A navy-blue stain that I thought was blood was spreading between his legs. I thought he'd managed to pull his penis off. My father led me out and he was mad at me for something—it was *me* who had brought him there, and his duties as my father— and just as we stepped from the tent I yelled, "Wait— it's happening to me too." I wanted to cry with embarrassment for I hadn't felt any urgency before entering the tent. It seemed like a sudden, irresistible need to urinate, something I couldn't hold back. But worse than water; something was ripping at my crotch. My light-coloured fishing khakis would turn brown in water, and the dark stain was already forming.

"Jesus Christ—are you *sick?* That was an old woman—how could *she* ... how could *you* ..." He jerked me forward by the elbow. "Jesus God," he muttered, pulling me along down the fairway, then letting me go and walking so fast I had to run, both hands trying to cup the mess I had made. Thousands of people passed me, smiling, laughing. "I don't know about you," my father said. *"I think there's something wrong with you,"* and it was the worst thing my father could say about me. We were in the car. I was crying in the back seat. "Don't tell me someone didn't see you—didn't you think of that? Or what if a customer saw *me*—but you didn't think of that either, did you? Here I take you to something I thought you'd like, something any *normal* boy would like, and—"

I'd been afraid to talk. The wetness was drying, a stain remained. "You know Murray Lieberman?" my father asked a few minutes later.

"The salesman?"

"He has a kid your age and so we were talking—"

"Never mind." I said.

"Well, what in the name of God is wrong with two fathers getting together, eh? It was supposed to *show* you what it's like, about women, I mean. It's better than any drawing, isn't it? You want books all the time? You want to *read* about it, or do you want to see it? At least now you *know*, so go ahead and read. Tell your mother we were fishing today, O.K.? And *that*—that was a Coke you spilled, all right?"

And no other talk, man-to-man, or father-to-son, had ever taken place.

I think back to Boniface Thibidault—how would he, how *did* he, show his sons what to do and where to do it? He was a Frenchman, not a North American; he learned it in Paris, not in a monastery as my father had. And I am, partially at least, a Frenchman too. My father should have taken me to a *cocotte*, to his own mistress perhaps, for the initiation, *la déniasement*. And I, in my own love-making, would have forever honoured him. But this is North America and my father, despite everything, was in his silence a Quebec Catholic of the nineteenth century. Sex, despite my dreams of something better, something nobler, still smells of the circus tent, of something raw and murderous. Other kinds of sex, the adjusted, contented, fulfilling sex of school and manual, seems insubstantial, willfully ignorant of the depths.

At thirteen I was oldest of eighty kids on the block, a thankless distinction, and my parents at fifty had a good twenty years on the next oldest, who, it happened, shared our duplex.

There lived on that street, and I was beginning to notice in that summer before the sideshow at the county fair, several girl brides and one or two maturely youthful wives. The brides, under twenty and with their first or second youngsters, were a sloppy crew who patrolled the street in cut-away shorts and bra-less elasticized halters that had to be pulled up every few steps. They set their hair so tightly in pin curlers that the effect, at a distance, was of the mange. Barefoot they pushed their baby strollers, thighs sloshing as they walked, or sat on porch furniture reading movie magazines and holding tinted plastic baby bottles between their knees. Though they sat in the sun all day they never tanned. They were spreading week by week while their husbands, hard athletic gas-pumpers, played touch football on the street every Sunday.

But there were others; in particular the wife next door, our two floors being mirror images of the other, everything back-to-back but otherwise identical. What was their name? She was a fair woman, about thirty, with hair only lightly bleached and the kind of figure that one first judges slightly too plump until something voluptuous in her, or you, makes you look again and you see that she is merely extraordinary; a full woman who had once been a lanky girl. She had three children, two of them girls who favoured the husband, but I can't quite place his name or face. Her name was Annette.

She was French. That had been a point of discussion once. Born in Maine, she would often chat with my father in what French she remembered while her husband played football or read inside. By that time I had forgotten most of my French. And now I remember the husband. His name was Lance— Lance!—and he was dark, square-shouldered, with a severe crewcut that sliced across an ample bald spot. He travelled a lot; I recall him sitting in a lawn chair on summer evenings, reading the paper and drinking a beer till the mosquitoes drove him in.

And that left Annette alone, and Annette had no friends on the block. She gave the impression, justified, of far outdistancing the neighbourhood girls. Perhaps she frightened them, being older and by comparison, a goddess. She would sit on a lawn chair in the front yard, on those male-less afternoons of toddling children and cranky mothers and was so stunning in a modest sundress that I would stay inside and peek at her through a hole I had cut in the curtains. Delivery trucks, forced to creep through the litter of kids and abandoned toys, lingered longer than they had to, just to look. At thirteen I could stare for hours, unconscious of peeping, unaware, really, of what I wanted or expected to see. It was almost like fishing, with patience and anticipation keeping me rooted.

My parents were at the new property, cleaning it up for a grand opening. I was given three or four dollars a day for food and I'd spend fifty or sixty cents of it on meaty and starchy grease down at the shopping centre. I was getting fat. Every few days I carried a bulging pocketful of wadded bills down to the bank and cashed them for a ten or twenty. And the bills would accumulate in my wallet. I was too young to open an account without my parents' finding out; the question was how to spend it. After a couple of weeks I'd go downtown and spend astounding sums, for a child, on stamps.

While I was in the shopping centre I began stealing magazines from the drugstore. The scandal mags, the Hollywood parties, the early *Playboy* and its imitators—I stole because I was too good to be seen buying them. I placed them between the pages of the *Sporting News*, which I also read cover-to-cover, then dropped a wadded five-dollar bill in the newspaper honour box, raced home, and feasted. Never one for risks, I burned the residue or threw them out in a neighbour's garbage can, my conscience clear for a month's more stealing and secret reading. There was never a time in my life when sex had been so palpable; when the very sight of any girl vaguely developed or any woman up to forty and still in trim could make my breath come short, make my crotch tingle under my baggy pants. In the supermarket, when young mothers dipped low to pick a carton of Cokes from the bottom shelf, I dipped with them. When the counter girl at the drugstore plunged her dipper in the ice cream tub, I hung over the counter to catch a glimpse of her lacy bra; when the neighbour women hung out their clothes, I would take the stairs two at a time to watch from above. When those young wives hooked their thumbs under the knitted elastic halters and gave an upward tug, I let out a little whimper. How close it was to madness; how many other fat thirteen- and fourteen-year-olds with a drop more violence, provocation, self-pity or whatever, would plunge a knife sixty times into those bellies, just to run their fingers inside the shorts and peel the halter back, allowing the breasts to ooze aside? And especially living next to Annette whose figure made flimsy styles seem indecent and modest dresses maddening. Her body possessed the clothes too greedily, sucked the material to her flesh. She was the woman, I now realize, that Dostoyevski and Kazantzakis and even Faulkner knew; a Grushenka or the young village widow, a dormant body that kindled violence.

The duplexes were mirror images with only the staircases and bathrooms adjoining. In the summer with Annette at home, her children out playing or taking a nap, her husband away, or just at work, she took many baths. From wherever I sat in our duplex watching television or reading my magazines, I could hear the drop of the drain plug in her bathroom, the splash of water rushing in, the quick expansion of the hot water pipes.

I could imagine the rest, exquisitely. First testing the water with her finger, then drying the finger on her shorts and then letting them drop. Testing the water again before unhooking the bra in a careless sweep and with another swipe, peeling off her panties. The thought of Annette naked, a foot away, made the walls seem paper-thin, made the tiles grow warm. Ear against the tiles I could hear the waves she made as she settled back, the squeaking of her heels on the bottom of the tub as she straightened her legs, the wringing of a face cloth, plunk of soap as it dropped. The scene was as vivid, with my eyes closed and my hot ear on the warm tile, as murders on old radio shows. I thought of the childhood comic character who could shrink himself with magic sand; how for me that had always translated itself into watching the Hollywood starlets from their bathroom heating registers. But Annette was better or at least as good, and so available. If only there were a way, a shaft for midgets. It wasn't right to house strangers so intimately without providing a way to spy. I looked down to the tile floor—a crack? Something a bobby pin could be twisted in, just a modest, modest opening? And I saw the pipes under the sink, two slim swannecks, one for hot, one for cold, that cut jaggedly through the tile wall—they had to connect! Then on my hands and knees I scraped away the plaster that held the chromium collar around the pipe. As I had hoped, the hole was a good quarter-inch wider than the pipes and all that blocked a straight-on view of the other bathroom were the collars on Annette's pipes. It would be nothing to punch my way through, slide the rings down, and lie on the tile floor in the comfort of my own bathroom and watch it all; Annette bathing! Ring level was below the tub, but given the distance the angle might correct itself. But detection would be unbearable; if caught I'd commit suicide. She was already out of the bath (but there'll be other days, I thought). She took ten-minute baths (how much more could a man bear?), the water was draining and now she was running the lavatory faucet which seemed just over my head. How long before she took another bath? It would seem, now that I had a plan, as long as the wait between issues of my favourite magazines.

I rested on the floor under the sink until Annette left her bathroom. Then I walked down to the shopping centre and had a Coke to steady myself. I bought a nailfile. When I got back Annette was sitting in her yard, wearing a striped housedress and looking, as usual, fresh from a bath. I said hello and she smiled very kindly. Then I turned my door handle and cried, "Oh, no!"

"What is it, Frankie?" she asked, getting up from her chair.

"I left my key inside."

"Shall I call your father?"

"No," I said, "I think I can get in through the window. But could I use your bathroom first?"

"Of course."

I checked upstairs for kids. Then I locked myself inside and with the new file, scraped away the plaster and pulled one collar down. Careful as always, aware that I would make a good murderer or a good detective, I cleaned up the plaster crumbs. I'd forgotten to leave our own bathroom light on, but it seemed that I could see all the way through. Time would tell. *Take a bath*, I willed her, as I flushed the toilet. It reminded me of fishing as a child, trying to influence the fish to bite. It's very hot, sticky, just right for a nice cool bath . . . My own flesh was stippled, I shivered as I stepped outside and saw her again. She'd soon be *mine*—something to do for the rest of the summer! My throat was so tense I couldn't even thank her. I climbed inside through the living-room window that I had left open.

I took the stairs two at a time, stretched myself out under the sink to admire the job. I'd forgotten to leave *her* light on, but I thought I could see the white of her tub in the darkened bathroom, and even an empty tub was enough to sustain me.

How obvious was the pipe and collar? It suddenly seemed blatant, that she would enter the bathroom, undress, sit in the tub, turn to the wall, and scream. Do a peeper's eyes shine too brightly? In school I'd often been able to stare a kid into turning around— it was now an unwanted gift.

You're getting warm again, Annette. Very, very hot. You want another bath. You're getting up from the chair, coming inside, up the stairs ... I kept on for hours till it was dark. I heard the kids taking baths and saw nothing. The white of the bathtub was another skin of plaster, no telling how thick. I'd been cheated.

Another day. There had to be another link—I had faith that the builders of duplexes were men who provided, out of guilt, certain amenities. Fans were in the ceiling. Windows opened on the opposite sides, the heating ducts were useless without a metal drill. Only the medicine cabinets were left. They had to be back-to-back. I opened ours, found the four corner screws, undid them, took out the medicines quietly (even my old Florida carbolic acid), then eased the chest from its plaster nest. It worked. I was facing the metal backing of Annette's medicine chest. The fit was tight and I could never take a chance of tampering with hers—what if I gave it a nudge when Lance was shaving and the whole thing came crashing down, revealing me leaning over my sink in the hole where our medicine chest had been?

The used-razor slot. A little slot in the middle. I popped the paper coating with the nailfile. I darkened our own bathroom. If Annette opened her chest, I'd see her. But would she open it with her clothes off?

Was she tall enough to make it count? How many hours would I have to stand there, stretched over the sink, waiting, and could I, every day, put the chest back up and take it down without some loud disaster? What if my father came home to shave, unexpectedly?

I waited all afternoon and all evening and when eight o'clock came I ended the vigil and put the chest back up. With a desire so urgent, there *had* to be a way of penetrating an inch and a half of tile and plaster. When she was in her bath I felt I could have devoured the walls between us. Anything *heard* so clearly had to yield to vision—that was another natural law—just as anything dreamt had to become real, eventually.

I became a baby-sitter; the oldest kid on the block, quiet and responsible. I watched television in nearly every duplex on the street, ignored the whimpers, filled bottles, and my pockets bulged with more unneeded cash. I poked around the young parents' bedrooms and medicine cabinets, only half-repelled by the clutter and unfamiliar odours, the stickiness, the greyness of young married life in a Midwest suburb. I found boxes of prophylactics in top drawers and learned to put one on and to walk around with it on until the lubrication stuck to my underwear. Sex books and nudist magazines showing pubic hair were stuffed in nightstands, and in one or two homes I found piles of home-made snaps of the young wife when she'd been slim and high school young, sitting naked in the sun, in a woods somewhere. She'd been posed in dozens of ways, legs wide apart, fingers on her pubic hair, tongue curled between her teeth. Others of her, and of a neighbour woman, on the same living-room sofa that I was sitting on: fatter now, her breasts resting on a roll of fat around her middle, her thighs shadowed where the skin had grown soft. *This is the girl I see every day*, pushing that carriage, looking like a fat girl at a high school hang-out. Those bigger girls in my school, in bright blue sweaters, earrings, black curly hair, bad skin, black corduroy jackets, smoking. They became like this; they *are* like this.

These were the weeks in August, when my mother was leaving the articles around. Soon my father would take me to the county fair. There were no answers to the questions I asked, holding those snapshots, looking again (by daylight) at the wife (in ragged shorts and elastic halter) who had consented to the pictures. They were like murder victims, the photos were like police shots in the scandal magazines, the women looked like mistresses of bandits. There was no place in the world for the life I wanted, for the pure woman I would someday, somehow, marry.

I baby-sat for Annette and Lance, then for Annette alone, and I worked again on the lavatory scheme, the used-razor slot, and discovered the slight deficiencies in the architecture that had thrown my calculations off. I could see from their bathroom into ours much better than I could ever see into theirs. Annette kept a neat house and life with her, even I could appreciate, must have been a joy of lust and efficiency, in surroundings as clean and attractive as a *Playboy* studio.

One evening she came over when my parents were working, to ask me to baby-sit for a couple of hours. Lance wasn't in. Her children were never a problem and though it was a week night and school had begun, I agreed. She left me a slice of Lance's birthday cake, and begged me to go to sleep in case she was late.

An hour later, after some reading, I used her bathroom, innocently. If only I lived here, with

Annette over there! I opened her medicine chest to learn some more about her: a few interesting pills "for pain," Tampax Super (naturally, I thought), gauze and adhesive, something for piles (for him, I hoped). And then I heard a noise from our bathroom; I heard our light snap on. My parents must have come home early.

I knew from a cough that it wasn't my mother. The Thibidault medicine chest was opened. I peered through the razor slot and saw young fingers among our bottles, blond hair and a tanned forehead: Annette. She picked out a jar, then closed the door. I fell to the floor and put my eye against the pipes. Bare golden legs. Then our light went out.

I looked into our bathroom for the next few seconds then ran to Annette's front bedroom where the youngest girl slept, and pressed over her crib to look out the window. She was just stepping out and walking slowly to the station wagon of Thibidault Furniture, which had been parked. She got in the far side and the car immediately, silently, backed away, with just its parking lights on ...

And that was all. For some reason, perhaps the shame of my complicity, I never asked my father why he had come home or why Annette had been in our bathroom. I didn't have to—I'd gotten a glimpse of Annette, which was all I could handle anyway. I didn't understand the rest. *Thibidault et fils*, fishing again.

Jean-Louis Thibidault, twice-divorced, is dead; buried in Venice, Florida. Bridge of Sighs Cemetery. I even asked his widow if I could have him removed to Sorel, Quebec. She didn't mind, but the *prêtre-vicaire* of my father's old parish turned me down. When my father was born, Venice, Florida, was five miles offshore and fifty feet underwater. The thought of him buried there tortures my soul.

There was another Sunday in Florida. A hurricane was a hundred miles offshore and due to strike Fort Lauderdale within the next six hours. We drove from our house down Las Olas to the beach (Fort Lauderdale was still an inland city then), and parked half a mile away, safe from the paint-blasting sand. We could hear the breakers under the shriek of the wind, shaking the wooden bridge we walked on. Then we watched them crash, brown with weeds and suspended sand. And we could see them miles offshore, rolling in forty feet high and flashing their foam like icebergs. A few men in swimming suits and woollen sweaters were standing in the crater pools, pulling out the deep-sea fish that had been stunned by the trip and waves. Other fish littered the beach, their bellies blasted by the change in pressure. My mother's face was raw and her glasses webbed with salt. She went back to the car on her own. My father and I sat on the bench for another hour and I could see behind his crusty sunglasses. His eyes were moist and dancing, his hair stiff and matted. We sat on the bench until we were soaked and the municipal guards rounded us up. Then they barricaded the boulevards and we went back to the car, the best day of fishing we'd ever had, and we walked hand in hand for the last time, talking excitedly, dodging coconuts, power lines, and shattered glass, feeling brave and united in the face of the storm. My father and me. What a day it was, what a once-in-a-lifetime day it was.

THANKS FOR THE RIDE

MY COUSIN GEORGE AND I were sitting in a restaurant called Pop's Cafe, in a little town close to the Lake. It was getting dark in there, and they had not turned the lights on, but you could still read the signs plastered against the mirror between the fly-speckled and slightly yellowed cutouts of strawberry sundaes and tomato sandwiches.

"Don't ask for information," George read. "If we knew anything we wouldn't be here" and "If you've got nothing to do, you picked a hell of a good place to do it in." George always read everything out loud —posters, billboards, Burma-Shave signs, "Mission Creek. Population 1700. Gateway to the Bruce. We love our children."

I was wondering whose sense of humour provided us with the signs. I thought it would be the man behind the cash register. Pop? Chewing on a match, looking out at the street, not watching for anything except for somebody to trip over a crack in the sidewalk or have a blowout or make a fool of himself in some way that Pop, rooted behind the cash register, huge and cynical and incurious, was never likely to do. Maybe not even that; maybe just by walking up and down, driving up and down, going places, the rest of the world proved its absurdity. You see that judgment on the faces of people looking out of windows, sitting on front steps in some little towns; so deeply, deeply uncaring they are, as if they had sources of disillusionment which they would keep, with some satisfaction, in the dark.

There was only the one waitress, a pudgy girl who leaned over the counter and scraped at the polish on her fingernails. When she had flaked most of the polish off her thumbnail she put the thumb against her teeth and rubbed the nail back and forth absorbedly. We asked her what her name was and she didn't answer. Two or three minutes later the thumb came out of her mouth and she said, inspecting it: "That's for me to know and you to find out."

"All right," George said. "Okay if I call you Mickey?"

"I don't care."

"Because you remind me of Mickey Rooney," George said. "Hey, where's everybody go in this town? Where's everybody go?" Mickey had turned her back and begun to drain out the coffee. It looked as if she didn't mean to talk any more, so George got a little jumpy, as he did when he was threatened with having to be quiet or be by himself. "Hey, aren't there any girls in this town?" he said almost plaintively. "Aren't there any girls or dances or anything? We're strangers in town," he said. "Don't you want to help us out?"

"Dance hall down on the beach closed up Labour Day," Mickey said coldly.

"There any other dance halls?"

"There's a dance tonight out at Wilson's *school*," Mickey said.

"That old-time? No, no, I don't go for that old-time. *All-a-man left* and that, used to have that down

in the basement of the church. Yeah, *ever'body swing*—
I don't go for that. Inna basement of the *church*,"
George said, obscurely angered. "You don't remember
that," he said to me. "Too young."

I was just out of high-school at this time, and George
had been working for three years in the Men's Shoes
in a downtown department store, so there was that
difference. But we had never bothered with each other
back in the city. We were together now because we
had met unexpectedly in a strange place and because
I had a little money, while George was broke. Also
I had my father's car, and George was in one of his
periods between cars, which made him always a little
touchy and dissatisfied. But he would have to rear-
range these facts a bit, they made him uneasy. I could
feel him manufacturing a sufficiency of good feeling,
old-pal feeling, and dressing me up as Old Dick, good
kid, real character—which did not matter one way
or the other, though I did not think, looking at his
tender blond piggish handsomeness, the nudity of
his pink mouth, and the surprised, angry creases that
frequent puzzlement was beginning to put into his
forehead, that I would be able to work up an Old
George.

I had driven up to the Lake to bring my mother
home from a beach resort for women, a place where
they had fruit juice and cottage cheese for reducing,
and early-morning swims in the Lake, and some
religion, apparently, for there was a little chapel
attached. My aunt, George's mother, was staying there
at the same time, and George arrived about an hour
or so after I did, not to take his mother home, but
to get some money out of her. He did not get along
well with his father, and he did not make much money
working in the shoe department, so he was very often
broke. His mother said he could have a loan if he

would stay over and go to church with her the next day. George said he would. Then George and I got away and drove half a mile along the lake to this little town neither of us had seen before, which George said would be full of bootleggers and girls.

It was a town of unpaved, wide, sandy streets and bare yards. Only the hardy things like red and yellow nasturtiums, or a lilac bush with brown curled leaves, grew out of that cracked earth. The houses were set wide apart, with their own pumps and sheds and privies out behind; most of them were built of wood and painted green or grey or yellow. The trees that grew there were big willows or poplars, their fine leaves greyed with the dust. There were no trees along the main street, but spaces of tall grass and dandelions and blowing thistles—open country between the store buildings. The town hall was surprisingly large, with a great bell in a tower, the red brick rather glaring in the midst of the town's walls of faded, pale-painted wood. The sign beside the door said that it was a memorial to the soldiers who had died in the First World War. We had a drink out of the fountain in front.

We drove up and down the main street for a while, with George saying: "What a dump! Jesus, what a dump!" and "Hey, look at that! Aw, not so good either." The people on the street went home to supper, the shadows of the store buildings lay solid across the street, and we went into Pop's.

"Hey," George said, "is there any other restaurant in this town? Did you see any other restaurant?"

"No," I said.

"Any other town I ever been," George said, "pigs hangin' out the windows, practically hangin' off the trees. Not here. Jesus! I guess it's late in the season," he said.

"You want to go to a show?"

The door opened. A girl came in, walked up and sat on a stool, with most of her skirt bunched up underneath her. She had a long somnolent face, no bust, frizzy hair; she was pale, almost ugly, but she had that inexplicable aura of sexuality. George brightened, though not a great deal. "Never mind," he said. "This'll do. This'll do in a pinch, eh? In a pinch."

He went to the end of the counter and sat down beside her and started to talk. In about five minutes they came back to me, the girl drinking a bottle of orange pop.

"This is Adelaide," George said. "Adelaide, Adeline—Sweet Adeline. I'm going to call her Sweet A, Sweet A."

Adelaide sucked at her straw, paying not much attention.

"She hasn't got a date," George said. "You haven't got a date have you, honey?"

Adelaide shook her head very slightly.

"Doesn't hear half what you say to her," George said. "Adelaide, Sweet A, have you got any friends? Have you got any nice, young little girl friend to go out with Dickie? You and me and her and Dickie?"

"Depends," said Adelaide. "Where do you want to go?"

"Anywhere you say. Go for a drive. Drive up to Owen Sound, maybe."

"You got a car?"

"Yeah, yeah, we got a car. C'mon, you must have some nice little friend for Dickie." He put his arm around this girl, spreading his fingers over her blouse. "C'mon out and I'll show you the car."

Adelaide said: "I know one girl might come. The guy she goes around with, he's engaged, and his girl came up and she's staying at his place up the beach, his mother and dad's place, and—"

"Well that is certainly int-er-esting," George said. "What's her name? Come on, let's go round and get her. You want to sit around drinking pop all night?"

"I'm finished," Adelaide said. "She might not come. I don't know."

"Why not? Her mother not let her out nights?"

"Oh, she can do what she likes," said Adelaide. "Only there's times she don't want to. I don't know."

We went out and got into the car, George and Adelaide in the back. On the main street about a block from the cafe we passed a thin, fair-haired girl in slacks and Adelaide cried: "Hey stop! That's her! That's Lois!"

I pulled in and George stuck his head out of the window, whistling. Adelaide yelled, and the girl came unhesitatingly, unhurriedly to the car. She smiled, rather coldly and politely, when Adelaide explained to her. All the time George kept saying: "Hurry up, come on, get in! We can talk in the car." The girl smiled, did not really look at any of us, and in a few moments, to my surprise, she opened the door and slid into the car.

"I don't have anything to do," she said. "My boy friend's away."

"That so?" said George, and I saw Adelaide, in the rear-vision mirror, make a cross warning face. Lois did not seem to have heard him.

"We better drive around to my house," she said. "I was just going down to get some Cokes, that's why I only have my slacks on. We better drive around to my house and I'll put on something else."

"Where are we going to go," she said, "so I know what to put on?"

I said: "Where do you want to go?"

"Okay, okay," George said. "First things first. We gotta get a bottle, then we'll decide. You know where to get one?" Adelaide and Lois both said yes, and then Lois said to me: "You can come in the house and wait while I change, if you want to." I glanced in the rear mirror and thought that there was probably some agreement she had with Adelaide.

Lois's house had an old couch on the porch and some rugs hanging down over the railing. She walked ahead of me across the yard. She had her long pale hair tied at the back of her neck; her skin was dustily freckled, but not tanned; even her eyes were light-coloured. She was cold and narrow and pale. There was derision, and also great gravity, about her mouth. I thought she was about my age or a little older.

She opened the front door and said in a clear, stilted voice: "I would like you to meet my family."

The little front room had linoleum on the floor and flowered paper curtains at the windows. There was a glossy chesterfield with a Niagara Falls and a To Mother cushion on it, and there was a little black stove with a screen around it for summer, and a big vase of paper apple blossoms. A tall, frail woman came into the room drying her hands on a dishtowel, which she flung into a chair. Her mouth was full of blue-white china teeth, the long cords trembled in her neck. I said how-do-you-do to her, embarrassed by Lois's announcement, so suddenly and purposefully conventional. I wondered if she had any misconceptions about this date, engineered by George for such specific purposes. I did not think so. Her face had no innocence in it that I could see; it was knowledgeable, calm, and hostile. She might have done it, then, to mock me, to make me into this caricature of The Date, the boy who grins and shuffles in the front hall and waits to be presented to the nice girl's family. But that was a little far-fetched. Why should she want to embarrass me when she had agreed to go out with me without even looking into my face? Why should she care enough?

Lois's mother and I sat down on the chesterfield. She began to make conversation, giving this the Date interpretation. I noticed the smell in the house, the smell of stale small rooms, bedclothes, frying, washing, and medicated ointments. And dirt, though it did not look dirty. Lois's mother said: "That's a nice car you got out front. Is that your car?"

"My father's."

"Isn't that lovely! Your father has such a nice car. I always think it's lovely for people to have things. I've got no time for these people that's just eaten up with malice 'n envy. I say it's lovely. I bet your mother, every time she wants anything, she just goes down to the store and buys it—new coat, bedspread, pots and pans. What does your father do? Is he a lawyer or doctor or something like that?"

"He's a chartered accountant."

"Oh. That's in an office, is it?"

"Yes."

"My brother, Lois's uncle, he's in the office of the CPR in London. He's quite high up there, I understand."

She began to tell me about how Lois's father had been killed in an accident at the mill. I noticed an old woman, the grandmother probably, standing in the doorway of the room. She was not thin like the others, but as soft and shapeless as a collapsed pudding, pale brown spots melting together on her face and arms, bristles of hairs in the moisture around her mouth. Some of the smell in the house seemed to come from her. It was a smell of hidden decay, such as there is when some obscure little animal has died under the verandah. The smell, the slovenly, confiding voice—something about this life I had not known, something about these people. I thought: my mother, George's mother, they are innocent. Even George, George is innocent. But these others are born sly and sad and knowing.

I did not hear much about Lois's father except that his head was cut off.

"Clean off, imagine, and rolled on the floor! Couldn't open the coffin. It was June, the hot weather. And everybody in town just stripped their gardens, stripped them for the funeral. Stripped their spirea bushes and peenies and climbin' clemantis. I guess it was the worst accident ever took place in this town.

"Lois had a nice boy friend this summer," she said. "Used to take her out and sometimes stay here overnight when his folks weren't up at the cottage and he didn't feel like passin' his time there all alone. He'd bring the kids candy and even me he'd bring presents. That china elephant up there, you can plant flowers in it, he brought me that. He fixed the radio for me and I never had to take it into the shop. Do your folks have a summer cottage up here?"

I said no, and Lois came in, wearing a dress of yellow-green stuff—stiff and shiny like Christmas wrappings—high-heeled shoes, rhinestones, and a lot of dark powder over her freckles. Her mother was excited.

"You like that dress?" she said. "She went all the way to London and bought that dress, didn't get it anywhere round here!"

We had to pass by the old woman as we went out. She looked at us with sudden recognition, a steadying of her pale, jellied eyes. Her mouth trembled open, she stuck her face out at me.

"You can do what you like with my gran'daughter,"

she said in her old, strong voice, the rough voice of a country woman. "But you be careful. And you know what I mean!"

Lois's mother pushed the old woman behind her, smiling tightly, eyebrows lifted, skin straining over her temples. "Never mind," she mouthed at me, grimacing distractedly. "Never mind. Second childhood." The smile stayed on her face; the skin pulled back from it. She seemed to be listening all the time to a perpetual din and racket in her head. She grabbed my hand as I followed Lois out. "Lois is a nice girl," she whispered. "You have a nice time, don't let her mope!" There was a quick, grotesque, and, I suppose, originally flirtatious, flickering of brows and lids. "'Night!"

Lois walked stiffly ahead of me, rustling her papery skirt. I said: "Did you want to go to a dance or something?"

"No," she said. "I don't care."

"Well you got all dressed up—"

"I always get dressed up on Saturday night," Lois said, her voice floating back to me, low and scornful. Then she began to laugh, and I had a glimpse of her mother in her, that jaggedness and hysteria. "Oh, my God!" she whispered. I knew she meant what had happened in the house, and I laughed too, not knowing what else to do. So we went back to the car laughing as if we were friends, but we were not.

We drove out of town to a farmhouse where a woman sold us a whisky bottle full of muddy-looking homemade liquor, something George and I had never had before. Adelaide had said that this woman would probably let us use her front room, but it turned out that she would not, and that was because of Lois. When the woman peered up at me from under the

man's cap she had on her head and said to Lois,
"Change's as good as a rest, eh?" Lois did not answer,
kept a cold face. Then later the woman said that if
we were so stuck-up tonight her front room wouldn't
be good enough for us and we better go back to the
bush. All the way back down the lane Adelaide kept
saying: "Some people can't take a joke, can they? Yeah,
stuck-up is right—" until I passed her the bottle to
keep her quiet. I saw George did not mind, thinking
this had taken her mind off driving to Owen Sound.

We parked at the end of the lane and sat in the
car drinking. George and Adelaide drank more than
we did. They did not talk, just reached for the bottle
and passed it back. This stuff was different from
anything I had tasted before; it was heavy and
sickening in my stomach. There was no other effect,
and I began to have the depressing feeling that I was
not going to get drunk. Each time Lois handed the
bottle back to me she said "Thank you" in a mannerly
and subtly contemptuous way. I put my arm around
her, not much wanting to. I was wondering what was
the matter. This girl lay against my arm, scornful,
acquiescent, angry, inarticulate and out-of-reach. I
wanted to talk to her then more than to touch her,
and that was out of the question; talk was not so
little a thing to her as touching. Meanwhile I was
aware that I should be beyond this, beyond the first
stage and well into the second (for I had a knowledge,
though it was not very comprehensive, of the orderly
progression of stages, the ritual of back- and front-
seat seduction). Almost I wished I was with Adelaide.

"Do you want to go for a walk?" I said.

"That's the first bright idea you've had all night,"
George told me from the back seat. "Don't hurry,"
he said as we got out. He and Adelaide were muffled
and laughing together. "Don't hurry back!"

Lois and I walked along a wagon track close to the bush. The fields were moonlit, chilly and blowing. Now I felt vengeful, and I said softly, "I had quite a talk with your mother."

"I can imagine," said Lois.

"She told me about that guy you went out with last summer."

"This summer."

"It's last summer now. He was engaged or something, wasn't he?"

"Yes."

I was not going to let her go. "Did he like you better?" I said. "Was that it? Did he like you better?"

"No, I wouldn't say he liked me," Lois said. I thought, by some thickening of the sarcasm in her voice, that she was beginning to be drunk. "He liked Momma and the kids okay but he didn't like me. *Like me*," she said, "What's that?"

"Well, he went out with you—"

"He just went around with me for the summer. That's what those guys from up the beach always do. They come down here to the dances and get a girl to go around with. For the summer. They always do."

"How I know he didn't *like* me," she said, "he said I was always bitching. You have to act grateful to those guys, you know, or they say you're bitching."

I was a little startled at having loosed all this. I said: "Did you like him?"

"Oh, sure! I should, shouldn't I? I should just get down on my knees and thank him. That's what my mother does. He brings her a cheap old spotted elephant—"

"Was this guy the first?" I said.

"The first steady. Is that what you mean?"

It wasn't. "How old are you?"

She considered. "I'm almost seventeen. I can pass

for eighteen or nineteen. I can pass in a beer parlour. I did once."

"What grade are you in at school?"

She looked at me, rather amazed. "Did you think I still went to school? I quit that two years ago. I've got a job at the glove-works in town."

"That must have been against the law. When you quit."

"Oh, you can get a permit if your father's dead or something."

"What do you do at the glove-works?" I said.

"Oh, I run a machine. It's like a sewing machine. I'll be getting on piecework soon. You make more money."

"Do you like it?"

"Oh, I wouldn't say I loved it. It's a job—you ask a lot of questions," she said.

"Do you mind?"

"I don't have to answer you," she said, her voice flat and small again. "Only if I like." She picked up her skirt and spread it out in her hands. "I've got burrs on my skirt," she said. She bent over, pulling them one by one. "I've got burrs on my dress," she said. "It's my good dress. Will they leave a mark? If I pull them all—slowly—I won't pull any threads."

"You shouldn't have worn that dress," I said. "What'd you wear that dress for?"

She shook the skirt, tossing a burr loose. "I don't know," she said. She held it out, the stiff, shining stuff, with faintly drunken satisfaction. 'I wanted to show you guys!" she said, with a sudden small explosion of viciousness. The drunken, nose-thumbing, toe-twirling satisfaction could not now be mistaken as she stood there foolishly, tauntingly, with her skirt spread out. "I've got an imitation cashmere sweater at home. It cost me twelve dollars," she said.

"I've got a fur coat I'm paying on, paying on for next winter. I've got a fur coat—"

"That's nice," I said. "I think it's lovely for people to have things."

She dropped the skirt and struck the flat of her hand on my face. This was a relief to me, to both of us. We felt a fight had been building in us all along. We faced each other as warily as we could, considering we were both a little drunk, she tensing to slap me again and I to grab her or slap her back. We would have it out, what we had against each other. But the moment of this keenness passed. We let out our breath; we had not moved in time. And the next moment, not bothering to shake off our enmity, nor thinking how the one thing could give way to the other, we kissed. It was the first time, for me, that a kiss was accomplished without premeditation, or hesitancy, or over-haste, or the usual vague ensuing disappointment. And laughing shakily against me, she began to talk again, going back to the earlier part of our conversation as if nothing had come between.

"Isn't it funny?" she said. "You know, all winter all the girls do is talk about last summer, talk and talk about those guys, and I bet you those guys have forgotten even what their names were—"

But I did not want to talk any more, having discovered another force in her that lay side by side with her hostility, that was, in fact, just as enveloping and impersonal. After a while I whispered: "Isn't there some place we can go?"

And she answered: "There's a barn in the next field."

She knew the countryside; she had been there before.

We drove back into town after midnight. George and Adelaide were asleep in the back seat. I did not think

Lois was alseep, though she kept her eyes closed and did not say anything. I had read somewhere about *Omne animal*, and I was going to tell her, but then I thought she would not know Latin words and would think I was being—oh, pretentious and superior. Afterwards I wished that I had told her. She would have known what it meant.

Afterwards the lassitude of the body, and the cold; the separation. To brush away the bits of hay and tidy ourselves with heavy unconnected movements, to come out of the barn and find the moon gone down, but the flat stubble fields still there, and the poplar trees, and the stars. To find our same selves, chilled and shaken, who had gone that headlong journey and were here still. To go back to the car and find the others sprawled asleep. That is what it is: *triste. Triste est.*

That headlong journey. Was it like that because it was the first time, because I was a little, strangely drunk? No. It was because of Lois. There are some people who can go only a little way with the act of love, and some others who can go very far, who can make a greater surrender, like the mystics. And Lois, this mystic of love, sat now on the far side of the car-seat, looking cold and rumpled, and utterly closed up in herself. All the things I wanted to say to her went clattering emptily through my head. *Come and see you again—Remember—Love*—I could not say any of these things. They would not seem even half-true across the space that had come between us. I thought: I will say something to her before the next tree, the next telephone pole. But I did not. I only drove faster, too fast, making the town come nearer.

The street lights bloomed out of the dark trees ahead; there were stirrings in the back seat.

"What time is it?" George said.

"Twenty past twelve."

"We musta finished that bottle. I don't feel so good. Oh, Christ, I don't feel so good. How do you feel?"

"Fine."

"Fine, eh? Feel like you finished your education tonight, eh? That how you feel? Is yours asleep? Mine is."

"I am not," said Adelaide drowsily. "Where's my belt? George—oh. Now where's my other shoe? It's early for Saturday night, isn't it? We could go and get something to eat."

"I don't feel like food," George said. "I gotta get some sleep. Gotta get up early tomorrow and go to church with my mother."

"Yeah, I know," said Adelaide, disbelieving, though not too ill-humoured. "You could've anyways bought me a hamburger!"

I had driven around to Lois's house. Lois did not open her eyes until the car stopped.

She sat still a moment, and then pressed her hands down over the skirt of her dress, flattening it out. She did not look at me. I moved to kiss her, but she seemed to draw slightly away, and I felt that there had after all been something fraudulent and theatrical about this final gesture. She was not like that.

George said to Adelaide: "Where do you live? You live near here?"

"Yeah. Half a block down."

"Okay. How be you get out here too? We gotta get home sometime tonight."

He kissed her and both the girls got out.

I started the car. We began to pull away, George settling down on the back seat to sleep. And then we heard the female voice calling after us, the loud, crude, female voice, abusive and forlorn:

"Thanks for the ride!"

It was not Adelaide calling; it was Lois.

Sandra Birdsell

FALLING IN LOVE

I GET OFF THE BUS and I stand beside the highway at Jordon Siding, wondering what to do now. I've come to a dead end. Stopped by the reality of a churned-up landscape. For shitsake, as Larry, the past-love-of-my-life, would say. Today, in late June, while the fields around me are growing towards harvest, I am empty. I'm split in two. One part of me can think, what are you going to do? And the other is off somewhere, wandering through empty rooms, bumping into dusty furniture, hoping that this may be a dream. And that Larry is still here.

"I'm sorry you didn't know, ah," the bus driver searches for the correct word. Am I Miss or Ma'am? He pushes his cap back onto his chunky, sandy head and glances down and then away from my breasts which nudge out against Larry's denim shirt. No, I'm not wearing a bra. His glance is at once shifty and closed as though he, too, is guilty of betraying me. And immediately, I'm glad that at least I have not made the mistake of being pregnant. Grateful that I never gave in to those odd flashes of desire to make love without a contraceptive, to play a kind of roulette game with sex.

"Didn't they tell you when you bought the ticket that the road was under construction?" the bus driver asks. His eyes take in the shoebox I carry beneath my arm, tied closed with butcher string, air holes punched in it so Satan can breathe. A going-away present from Larry, a black rabbit. He has taken off, Larry has, has flown the coop and left me with the rabbit and one measly shirt to remind me of him. Larry, I'm remembering you in the briny smell of armpits.

I remember this morning, the acne-faced girl in the coffee shop at the bus depot in Manitou saying something about having to go to Winnipeg and then back south to get to Agassiz. But my mind wasn't paying attention. I was aware instead of her squinty mean eyes enjoying the lapsed state of my affair. Larry Cooper is wild, I'd been warned, and he's lazier than a pet coon. And I told myself that they were just jealous. There are no callipers wide enough to measure the scoured sides of my stupidity. This year, I have learned something about the eternal combustion engine, about love.

Before me, where I should be making my connection with another Grey Goose bus that will carry me thirty miles east across farming country to Agassiz and back into the bosom of my family, the road is a muddy upheaval of rocks, slippery clay and top-soil. Under destruction. The whole world is under destruction. Larry used the word 'dead-end'. And so he has turned the other way, headed down the highway to Montreal to work in his brother-in-law's car rental business.

If you love someone, let him go, Larry's mother said. And if he comes back, he's yours. Whatever you do, don't take this thing personal, okay? Larry's like that. Every spring, he takes off. Spring fever, it's in his blood, she said. And then she evicted me.

"You'd better get back on the bus and make your connection in Winnipeg," the driver says and it's clear from his tone that he's decided I'm a Miss which gives him certain authority. I'm aware of faces in the windows looking out at me, slight amusement at my predicament. I see in the window my greasy black hair tied up into a pony tail, Larry's shirt, my jeans held at the waist with safety pins because I have lost ten pounds. My luggage is an Eaton's shopping bag.

When I woke up and discovered Larry missing, I didn't worry at first because he often went out riding before dawn. He liked to be alone in the early morning. Larry liked to watch the sun rise. He's out ripping off truck parts, you mean, his mother said, raising an artfully plucked eyebrow and flicking cigarette ashes into her coffee cup. But she didn't know Larry the way I thought I did. He would come back to me, crawl beneath the sheets, hairy limbs still cool from the early morning air, breath minty and sweet, and he would wind himself around me and describe the colour of the sun on a barn roof, or the distinct clatter of a tractor starting up. On such a morning, he brought Satan to me because he said its shiny black coat, its constant nibbling reminded him of me. On such a morning, he came home and invented a gadget that cooked weiners electrically. He stuck wires into each end of the weiner, plugged it into the wall and instant, cooked weiner. Another morning, he was inspired to try to build a more effective water pump.

I lay in bed waiting for Larry, looking up at the new ceiling tiles overhead. His mother let us live rent-free in those three rooms above the butcher shop if we fixed the caved-in ceiling. I liked the suite the way it was when we first moved in, sawdust and shavings ankle-deep on the floor, ceiling slats dangling free, the lone lightbulb suspended by a single twined wire. It was early Canadian Catastrophe. It reminded me that when I met Larry, I was sitting in the hotel cafe in Agassiz, between jobs, waiting for the world to end. For a year, I'd had the feeling that a bomb was going to drop and that would be the end of us all. For this reason, I left school. I was filling in time, waiting, and then Larry walked in and I thought that if the bomb fell that day, I'd rather be dead with him than anyone else.

But Larry wouldn't live with a caved-in ceiling and when he'd fixed that, he enamelled the kitchen counters black. And the paint never quite dried and if we let a dish stand on it overnight, it became permanently stuck there. And then I went crazy and hand-stitched curtains for the windows in the front room. Larry nailed Christmas tree lights onto the wall above the couch and we made love in their multicoloured glow. We made love every single day for six months.

I waited for Larry to return and listened at the same time to the rats thumping about in the butcher shop below, dragging bones from the bone box. (I never minded the rats, I figured they worked hard for what they got.) Above me, near the ceiling, a shaft of light came through the small window, spotlighting Larry's note taped to the closet door. I knew before reading it that Larry had left me. I have this built-in premonition for bad news. As I reached for the note, I could smell Larry, like alkali, dry, metallic, in the palms of my hands. And scattered in the sheets were his c-shaped blond pubic hairs. I read the note and it was as though a thick, black, woollen hood had fallen suddenly into place over my head.

Two days later, Larry's mother dropped by. She told me to get out of bed. She wanted her sheets back. She had me clean out the fridge. I have brought along the left-overs of our relationship in the shopping bag. Lettuce for Satan, a dimpled, wilted grapefruit and one beer. And resentment, which is a thick sludge clogging my chest. If Larry, by some miracle, showed up now, I would jump on his skinny back, grab hold of his blond hair and wrestle him to the ground. I would stomp on his adam's apple.

"Forget it," I say to the bus driver. "I'm not going all the way to Winnipeg. Just forget it."

He laughs. "I don't see what choice you have." He puts his sunglasses back on and I can see myself in them. And it seems to me that he, along with everyone else, conspires against me. That I have never had a choice.

"You looked at my ticket when I got on. Why didn't you say something?"

"I thought you knew."

I pick up the shopping bag and begin to walk away. "Well, I didn't. And I'm not spending three bloody hours on the bus. So, I guess I'll walk."

He blocks my way. "Whoa, Agassiz is thirty miles away. And it's going to be one hot day." He scans the cloudless sky.

Larry, you creep. This is all your fault. "What's it to you whether I walk or ride?"

The driver's thick neck flares red. He steps aside. "Right. It's no skin off my nose. If you want to walk thirty miles in the blazing sun, go ahead. It's a free country."

The bus roars down the highway, leaving me in a billow of hot sharp-smelling smoke. The sound of the engine grows fainter and then I'm alone, facing that churned-up muddy road where no vehicle could ever pass. Thirty bloody miles. God-damn you, Larry. I hear a meadowlark trilling and then a squealing rhythmic sound of metal on metal. It comes from a BA gas sign swinging back and forth above two rusting gas bowsers that stand in front of a dilapidated wood-frame building. Jordon Siding garage and store. Eureka. A telephone. I will call home and say, guess what? No, I'll say, it's your prodigal daughter, to get them thinking along charitable lines. I have seen the light. But all that is another issue, one I don't have the energy to think about. Plants fill the dusty store window and off to one side, a tiny yard, freshly laundered clothes flutter from a clothesline.

I enter the dim interior and feel surrounded. The atmosphere is dreary, relentlessly claustrophobic. It's a typical country store and yet it reminds me of old things, of fly-specked calendars, lambs and young girls in straw hats smiling with cherry-painted lips, innocent smiles. And me pulling a toboggan through the streets of Agassiz each New Year, collecting calendars, trekking through the fragile blue sphere of a winter night that seemed to embrace all ages so that as I bumped along ice and snow I thought, years ago, someone like me was doing this, may still be doing this. But at the same time, I felt the world dangling like a bauble about to shatter on the floor. I went to the garages, grocery stores, the bank. I needed many calendars because during the coming year each time a month ended, I wrote messages on the backs of the spent time and hid the messages in the garden, in flower pots, beneath stones, for people from another world to discover when I would be gone. A fly buzzes suddenly against the window, trapped between the foliage of the plants and the glass. Beyond, a counter, glass casing, but there's nothing inside it but shelf-lining, old newspapers.

"Hello, anyone here?" I call in the direction of the back rooms behind the varnished counter where I imagine potatoes boil in a pot, a child sleeps on a blanket on the floor while its mother ignores my voice, sits in an over-stuffed chair (the type Larry and I inherited with our suite, an olive green, scratchy velour couch and chair), reading a magazine. What is she reading? I wonder. I look about me. No telephone in sight.

Outside once again, I face that bleak landscape and begin walking in the direction of Agassiz. I face the sun and walk off to the side of the road, following the deep imprint left behind by one of the monstrous yellow machines that sits idle in the field beyond. Why aren't there any men on the machines? Why aren't they working today? I begin to feel uneasy. The sounds of the countryside rise up and Satan thumps violently against his box in answer. Around me stretch broad fields dotted with clumps of trees. In the distance a neat row of elms, planted as a windbreak, shade a small farmhouse and outbuildings. Overhead, the flat cloudless sky, no perspective, I cannot gauge distance. It's as though this is a calendar picture of a landscape and I have somehow entered it. Except for yellow grasshoppers sprinting up before my feet and the tireless hovering of flies above the ditches, there is no movement anywhere. I turn around. The garage is still the same distance. I can turn back and wait for a car and hitch a ride to Winnipeg. I could go back to Manitou. But it seems to me that I have been set in this direction, that it's inevitable. I walk for an hour. Satan continues to struggle. I stop to rest, lift the lid off the box a crack and push wilted lettuce through to him. I sit down, take Larry's note from my shirt pocket and unfold it on my knee.

Dear Lureen,
    I'm sorry if you got your hopes up. Like the song goes, you always hurt the one you love, the one you shouldn't hurt at all. That's life. But this town

is a dead-end. You know what I mean. I think I'll
take my sister up on her offer.

You are okay. Don't think I'm leaving because
of you. I know you will get over me. Anyway, if
it works out, I'll send you some money. I might
send you enough to come to Montreal. I'll see. It
just depends.

You can have Satan. I don't trust my mother to
look after him anyway. Once, she forgot to feed
my goldfish and they all turned belly-up. Notice,
I am leaving you my denim shirt because you liked
it so much.

Tell the old lady not to get in a sweat.

Luv U,
Larry.

Whatever you do, Larry's mother said when he
introduced us, don't get married. A cigarette dangled
from one corner of her mouth and she squinted at
me hard through the blue smoke. She was blonde
like Larry and I thought that at one time she must
have been beautiful, you could see flashes of it
sometimes when she wasn't being sarcastic. I'm only
telling you for your own good, she said later when
Larry was out of the room. He's like his father. Lazier
than a pet coon.

Larry was not lazy. He could pull the head off a
motor, ream out the cylinders, do a ring and valve
job in two days flat. I'd tell him I wanted to go to
the dance at Rock Lake and he'd rebuild the trans-
mission that afternoon so we could go. He opened
the housing, called me down the stairs to come and
see the giant cogs, how the gears were supposed to
mesh. And I couldn't help think that the combustion
engine is a joke, or at least a hoax perpetuated on
man to keep him busy tinkering so he can't think

about what's really happening. Wheels moving
wheels, moving pulleys, moving more metal and so
much motion for so little effect, arms, lifters, valves,
wheezing breathers, springs, filters, cylinders, shoes,
things pressing against other things, grinding, particles of chewed-up metal sifting into other important
parts. God, it was overwhelming. Faulty timing, a
coughing, farting engine, a rotten swaying front-end,
screeching wheelbearings, all these problems Larry
and I faced and overcame in six months.

Okay Larry, I said, wanting to say, this is silly.
There has got to be a much simpler way than the
eternal combustion engine.

Internal, internal combustion engine, he said, and
anyway, you are paid not to think, but to do. So,
okay, I played the game. I soaked bolts and other
metal shapes in my dishpan, brushed them down with
Varsol, removed grease with a paring knife, had them
looking like new. I learned how to install brushes in
a generator. I took it apart in my lap. I thought the
copper wires were beautiful. And then, that what I
was doing was important. That maybe I'd like to have
a part in the running of the internal combustion
machine. And the next time Larry complained about
having to wash his feet with his socks on, maybe
I'd let him ride bareback for awhile. Maybe the two
of us could open a garage?

Larry flicked the end of my nose with a greasy
finger and said no way would he put in four years
getting his papers just to satisfy some government-
hired jerk who had never taken apart anything more
complicated than a Zippo lighter.

And always, we made it to the dance on time. That
night, we'd be cruising down the highway, eating up
the miles to Rock Lake, radio turned up full volume,
Larry driving with two fingers and reaching with his

other hand for me, naked beneath my sundress. And the gears would be meshing and the motor singing, the timing tuned just right and the radio playing all our favourite hits. And Larry would squeeze my breast and say, hey, honey bunch. Remind me to slow down long before we get to the corner, okay? I got no brakes.

Ancient history. Ancient bloody history. I rest my head against my knees and I don't want to cry, Larry's not worth it, but I do. And then I take the lid off the shoebox and I pet Satan for a few moments and then I carry him to the side of the road and drop him into the tall grass. He scurries away without a backward glance.

Do you think it's true, Larry said, turning away from me to examine his naked physique in the mirror, that a large ass means a short sex life? That's what my mother told me.

And I spent the next two hours convincing him that she was wrong and that he had the neatest, hardest, turned-in buttocks I had ever seen. Bullshit. I wish for Larry an extremely short sex life. May he never have sex again. I pick up the shopping bag, swing it back and forth a couple of times and let loose. It flies across the ditch and whacks against the telephone pole. Screw yourself Larry. Stick your scrawny dink in your ear.

Free now, I walk faster, arms swinging, following the fish-bone tire pattern pressed into the yellow clay. I will go to Winnipeg, look for work. Or I will go to bed and stay there. Or I could go back to school. And then I hear a sound, the sound of a motor geared down low—Larry? My heart leaps. I wouldn't put it past him. Larry can do anything. Even materialize out of thin air. I look up. There on the crest of the muddy graded mound is a pale blue car, the bullet-nosed shape of a '51 Studebaker. It slithers sideways first one way and then the other. It stops, starts, makes its way slowly towards me. I see a man behind the wheel, copper-red hair, a brushcut. Not Larry. The car comes to a stop and the man opens the door. I measure the distance to the farmhouse beyond. Could I outrun him? He unfolds from the seat. He's match-like, tall and thin. He stands up, shakes creases from his grey slacks, tiptoes across the ruts in shiny brown penny loafers and I begin to relax, he looks harmless. He stretches out a long pale hand to me, it looks fragile, like worn porcelain. I keep my hands behind my back. He doesn't seem to mind and folds his, one overtop the other across his stomach. He tilts back slightly on his heels and smiles down at me. "Well, well. Bless you. This is the day that the Lord hath made. Let's just take a moment to rejoice in it." He breathes deeply. "Thankyou Jesus."

God. A Pentecostal fanatic. One of the holy rollers.

"I saw you coming down from the corner and I said to myself, 'Now there's the reason God had for waking you up this morning.'" He lifts his hand suddenly, pokes a long finger into his red hair and scratches.

A grasshopper leaps up between us and lands on the roof of the car. I can see a resemblance between the insect and the man: long limbs, angles, ball-bearing shaped eyes.

"So, you're stranded then," he says.

"I didn't know about this." I indicate the upturned road.

"No matter," he says. He flutters his flimsy hand in my direction and catches himself on the chin in the process. I begin to like him. His smile is wide, lights up his steel grey eyes. "Everything works out for the good in the end. For those that trust in Him. Where are you hoping to get to?"

Life, I want to say. I am hoping to get through life, but I don't think I will. "Agassiz."

"Agassiz. Well, well. The heavenly Father has given me business just outside of Agassiz. I can get you close to it. Closer than this. Didn't I say everything would work out?"

He leads the way around to the passenger side, opens the door and suddenly I feel awkward. Larry would let me crawl through the window before he'd think to open a door for me. The car is like new inside. The seats are covered in clear plastic. A sheet of plastic lies on the floor. On the dash is what looks to be a deck of playing cards but the box says, "Thought for Today." Clipped to the sun visor is another card that reads, "I am a Flying Farmer."

He turns the car around in stages and soon we are bumping down the road, mud scraping against the bottom of the car. Despite the good condition of the car, there's a slight ticking and I want to tell him that he ought to watch the valves but I don't think it would be polite. I look over my shoulder and sure enough, tell-tale blue smoke billows from the exhaust. He's a clumsy driver, shifts gears too soon, strains the engine, rides the clutch. And then the tires grab hold of a groove of deep ruts and he speeds up, letting the car find its own path.

"So, what's your story?" he asks after awhile.

"Story?"

"Sure. The Lord sends me lots of people. I know when someone has a story."

And so I begin the way I always do, with the question that makes people frown or shrug or walk away. "Have you ever thought that at this very moment, someone may be pressing a button and that the world may come to an end? And we'll all be instant cooked weiners?"

He laughs. "Now why would I want to waste my time thinking about that? I couldn't live with those negative thoughts hanging over my head all the time. I know that He is able to keep me against that day. Whatever a man thinks, that's what he is. And I think about all the good things we've got." He thumps the wheel for emphasis, sticks his head out the window. "Look around you, this country is *beaudyfull*. Good crops this year. The fields are white unto the harvest. Thankyou Jesus." He begins to hum to himself as we slither down the road. Then he sucks something loose from his teeth. "Cooked weiners, my, my. That just won't happen. Know how I know? Because I wouldn't be here right now if that was true. The Lord would have returned already if it was the end of the world and I wouldn't be here. I'd be with Him."

I know the story. I have been brought up on this. Graves opening, the rapture of the saints. People reaching towards a shining light. Whenever I heard the story, I would imagine grabbing hold of a tree on the way up so I could stay behind. "How do you know that's true?"

He laughs once again. "And how do you know that it isn't? It takes more faith to believe that it isn't true than to believe that it is. Know why? Because of hope. Man is born with hope right in him and you've got to go against the grain not to believe. Now tell me, what's the story behind the story? What brings you here today, to this place, this time?"

And suddenly, my tongue takes off and I tell him everything, about being young and hiding pieces of paper from the calendar that say, Whoever finds this, my name was Lureen Lafreniere, I lived in Agassiz, Manitoba. This month, when I was running, I slipped and fell and cut my hand on a sharp piece of ice. Five stitches.

"For awhile, I stopped doing this, I thought it was a silly thing to do. But it came back to me, the feeling, so strong, that I couldn't sit still in school. I had to get up and move, just do something, because I felt that something terrible was going to happen that would prevent me from ... from...."

"From doing all the things you want to do even though you aren't even sure what it is you want to do."

"Yes."

"There's nothing new under the sun. I've heard that one before."

"Yes, but just when man says, nothing is new, everything is the same as yesterday, then comes the end. Therefore, watch and wait."

He smiles and his smile makes me smile. "You know your scripture. Bless you sister."

And then I tell him how I met Larry, about the past six months, about the feeling of impending doom leaving me. I talk to him as though I have known him for years and he doesn't ever interrupt, just says, "whoops" and "bless you" when we hit large clumps of mud. I talk non-stop, as though this man were sent for just this reason. And when I finish, he doesn't answer for a long time, just squints near-sightedly at the road and I think that I have made a mistake. I hold my breath and wait for his sermon. The Thou Shalt Nots.

"You love him," he says finally and puts a long, slender, cool hand overtop mine.

"Yeah." I realize this is true. That I am in love with Larry. While waiting for the world to end, I have fallen in love. I fell for Larry Cooper. I'm falling.

"Well, well. Love is great. Love is wonderful. The Lord knew what He was doing when He created Adam and Eve."

I wipe my eyes on Larry's denim shirt.

"That fella of yours will come back. You can be sure of that."

"He will?"

He squeezes my hand. "Believe it and it will happen. Tell yourself, Larry's coming back."

Shit. The power of positive thinking crap. "Larry's pretty stubborn, you don't know him like I do."

"Shh. I understand. You know Larry and you may be right. But that's only one side of it. Listen, this is my story. Long time ago, I was in a bad accident. A plane crash. I went down in the bush in northern Manitoba. I thought I was finished. I walked in circles for two days with a broken collarbone. When I came upon the plane the second time, I cried. Broke right down. And then a verse from the Bible came to me. It was, 'not by might, nor by power, but by my spirit.' It was the Lord telling me to trust Him. So I knelt in the bush and I prayed and I said, 'Okay God. I'm lost. I can't find the way myself. I've already tried. And I'm tired and I'm injured and so I have no choice. I'm going to trust you. Show me the way.' And I opened my eyes, got up, started walking and I hadn't walked more than five minutes and there in front of me was a road. A paved road. So you see, from my side of it, I was finished. There was nothing I could do. But from God's side, He had only just begun. And God knows Larry better than you do."

I want to say, I know how that happened. Often, when you try too hard, the answer escapes you. You have to give up and then the inner mind brings the answer to the surface. There wasn't anything supernatural about your experience. It happens all the time. I bite my tongue.

"That's very nice," I say.

He turns to me in astonishment. "Nice? I tell you

about my wonderful experience, how the Lord delivered me and you say, 'that's nice'? It was more than nice, sister. It was a frigging miracle."

Would an angel swear? I ponder the question later that evening as I lie in bed in the front bedroom of my house in Agassiz. He dropped me off three miles from town, near the elevators, and when I turned to tell him, as a favour, that he'd better get the valves checked, the car had vanished. And I was shocked. I sat down beside the road to think about it. I rubbed my stiff calf muscles, my feet burned as though I had walked a great distance. And I came to the conclusion that I had imagined meeting that man. The mind can do that. It was a way of coping with the situation I was in. But the question intrigues me. Would an angel swear? And was that swearing? I have always imagined swearing to mean to swear on something, to have to prove in some way the fact that you are telling the truth. The error of not being trustworthy.

The reception I received from my family was surprising. My mother was strangely tender, as though I had fallen ill with a fever. My younger brothers and sisters regarded me as someone who had come from a long way away, a distant relative, and they were guarded and shy. "Are you expecting?" my mother asked while the two of us changed the linen on the bed in the front bedroom. And I said no, but that I wished I was. She flicked the sheet and smoothed it straight. "No you don't," she said. "You just think you do, but you really don't."

As I lie in bed, the sounds around me are all familiar. The town siren blares out the ten o'clock curfew. The curtains on the window are the same ones I've had since I can remember. But I pull the sheet up around me and I feel like a guest, a visitor in the home I grew up in. How will I ever be able to sleep without Larry?

I remember our first date. Larry showing off, climbing up on a snowplow in the municipal yards, starting it and ripping through the chainlink fence before he could figure out how to stop it. And later, driving eighty miles to Manitou to crawl across the roof of the butcher shop, breaking a window to get into the suite. Still wearing our parkas, it was bitterly cold, I gave up my virginity while our breath hung in clouds of frost in the air above us and the beer we'd bought popped the caps and climbed up in frosty towers from the bottles. Afterward, teeth chattering, we chewed frozen malt and Larry warmed my hands in his armpits.

The memory climbs up the back of my throat, finds its way into my eyes, leaks down the sides of my face into the pillow. Okay God. I'll give you this one chance. This miracle involves another person, his own stubborn will. I clench my teeth. I feel as though I am levitating off the bed. This is it. Thanks for bringing Larry back to me.

I sigh. I'm calm. Tension seeps from me as I lie in the room where I have first thought of love and making it happen. And I hear the breeze in the trees outside the window. I have hidden many particles of time beneath their branches. I see the faint glow of the town. And if I got up, I would see the green watertower and the siren on it that orders the movement of my town. I would see the skating rink, my father coming down from the corner on his way home from the Hotel, to the news that Lureen's back home. And then I hear it, a jangle of keys that stiffens my spine, sends my heart jumping. Then a cough. I'm rigid, listening. A whistle. I leap down the bed, pull aside the curtains and below I see him, his narrow pale face turned up to the window, Larry in his white windbreaker, collar turned up, the glow of his cigarette.

"Larry?"

"For shitsake. What's keeping you?" he asks.

And I run barefoot down the stairs, through the rooms, out the front door and then Larry catches me by the wrist and pulls me to him, wraps me around his skinny shivering body.

"Blew a rod at Thunder Bay," he says. "I couldn't fix it."

Liar. "I'm sorry," I say. He kisses me. His mouth is chilly and warm at the same time. I wedge my tongue between his shivering lips.

He pulls away. "I caught a ride with a real weirdo. He offered me fifty bucks if I'd jerk him off. So I said to hell with it and I took the first bus going west."

"Hey honey bunch," I whisper into his neck, "let's go to the park. We can talk tomorrow."

"The park, what for?" But I can feel him growing hard against my stomach. "I haven't got anything on me. You know." His tongue answers mine and it's like the faint fluttering of a moth.

I link my arm through his and lead him in the direction I want to go. "Oh, by the way, I let the rabbit loose."

He stops walking, frowns. "What did you go and do that for?"

"Well, he was heavy, Larry. I suppose you never thought of that. And there I was, thirty miles from nowhere. I had to walk because the bloody road was under construction, so what was I supposed to do?"

"You've got all the brains," Larry says. "Why ask me?"

And we walk arm in arm down the road, Larry and me going to the park.

D. H. Lawrence

THE HORSE DEALER'S DAUGHTER

"WELL, MABEL, and what are you going to do with yourself?" asked Joe, with foolish flippancy. He felt quite safe himself. Without listening for an answer, he turned aside, worked a grain of tobacco to the tip of his tongue, and spat it out. He did not care about anything, since he felt safe himself.

The three brothers and the sister sat round the desolate breakfast table, attempting some sort of desultory consultation. The morning's post had given the final tap to the family fortunes, and all was over. The dreary dining room itself, with its heavy mahogany furniture, looked as if it were waiting to be done away with.

But the consultation amounted to nothing. There was a strange air of ineffectuality about the three men, as they sprawled at table, smoking and reflecting vaguely on their own condition. The girl was alone, a rather short, sullen-looking young woman of twenty-seven. She did not share the same life as her brothers. She would have been good-looking, save for the impassive fixity of her face, "bull dog," as her brothers called it.

There was a confused tramping of horses' feet

outside. The three men all sprawled round in their chairs to watch. Beyond the dark holly bushes that separated the strip of lawn from the highroad, they could see a cavalcade of shire horses swinging out of their own yard, being taken for exercise. This was the last time. These were the last horses that would go through their hands. The young men watched with critical, callous looks. They were all frightened at the collapse of their lives, and the sense of disaster in which they were involved left them no inner freedom.

Yet they were three fine, well-set fellows enough. Joe, the eldest, was a man of thirty-three, broad and handsome in a hot, flushed way. His face was red, he twisted his black mustache over a thick finger, his eyes were shallow and restless. He had a sensual way of uncovering his teeth when he laughed, and his bearing was stupid. Now he watched the horses with a glazed look of helplessness in his eyes, a certain stupor of downfall.

The great draft-horses swung past. They were tied head to tail, four of them, and they heaved along to where a lane branched off from the highroad, planting their great hoofs floutingly in the fine black mud, swinging their great rounded haunches sumptuously, and trotting a few sudden steps as they were led into the lane, round the corner. Every movement showed a massive, slumbrous strength, and a stupidity which held them in subjection. The groom at the head looked back, jerking the leading rope. And the cavalcade moved out of sight up the lane, the tail of the last horse, bobbed up tight and stiff, held out taut from the swinging great haunches as they rocked behind the hedges in a motion-like sleep.

Joe watched with glazed hopeless eyes. The horses were almost like his own body to him. He felt he was done for now. Luckily he was engaged to a woman as old as himself, and therefore her father, who was steward of a neighboring estate, would provide him with a job. He would marry and go into harness. His life was over, he would be a subject animal now.

He turned uneasily aside, the retreating steps of the horses echoing in his ears. Then, with foolish restlessness, he reached for the scraps of bacon-rind from the plates, and making a faint whistling sound, flung them to the terrier that lay against the fender. He watched the dog swallow them, and waited till the creature looked into his eyes. Then a faint grin came on his face, and in a high, foolish voice he said:

"You won't get much more bacon, shall you, you little b------?"

The dog faintly and dismally wagged its tail, then lowered its haunches, circled round, and lay down again.

There was another helpless silence at the table. Joe sprawled uneasily in his seat, not willing to go till the family conclave was dissolved. Fred Henry, the second brother, was erect, clean-limbed, alert. He had watched the passing of the horses with more sang-froid. If he was an animal, like Joe, he was an animal which controls, not one which is controlled. He was master of any horse, and he carried himself with a well-tempered air of mastery. But he was not master of the situations of life. He pushed his coarse brown mustache upwards, off his lip, and glanced irritably at his sister, who sat impassive and inscrutable.

"You'll go and stop with Lucy for a bit, shan't you?" he asked. The girl did not answer.

"I don't see what else you can do," persisted Fred Henry.

"Go as a skivvy," Joe interpolated laconically.

The girl did not move a muscle.

"If I was her, I should go in for training for a nurse," said Malcolm, the youngest of them all. He was the baby of the family, a young man of twenty-two, with a fresh, jaunty *museau*.

But Mabel did not take any notice of him. They had talked at her and round her for so many years, that she hardly heard them at all.

The marble clock on the mantelpiece softly chimed the half-hour, the dog rose uneasily from the hearth-rug and looked at the party at the breakfast table. But still they sat on in ineffectual conclave.

"Oh, all right," said Joe suddenly, apropos of nothing. "I'll get a move on."

He pushed back his chair, straddled his knees with a downward jerk, to get them free, in horsey fashion, and went to the fire. Still he did not go out of the room; he was curious to know what the others would do or say. He began to charge his pipe, looking down at the dog and saying, in a high, affected voice:

"Going wi' me? Going wi' me are ter? Tha'rt goin' further than tha counts on just now, dost hear?"

The dog faintly wagged its tail, the man stuck out his jaw and covered his pipe with his hands, and puffed intently, losing himself in the tobacco, looking down all the while at the dog with an absent brown eye. The dog looked up at him in mournful distrust. Joe stood with his knees stuck out, in real horsey fashion.

"Have you had a letter from Lucy?" Fred Henry asked of his sister.

"Last week," came the neutral reply.

"And what does she say?"

There was no answer.

"Does she *ask* you to go and stop there?" persisted Fred Henry.

"She says I can if I like."

"Well, then, you'd better. Tell her you'll come on Monday."

This was received in silence.

"That's what you'll do then, is it?" said Fred Henry, in some exasperation.

But she made no answer. There was a silence of futility and irritation in the room. Malcolm grinned fatuously.

"You'll have to make up your mind between now and next Wednesday," said Joe loudly, "or else find yourself lodgings on the curbstone."

The face of the young woman darkened, but she sat on immutable.

"Here's Jack Fergusson!" exclaimed Malcolm, who was looking aimlessly out of the window.

"Where?" exclaimed Joe, loudly.

"Just gone past."

"Coming in?"

Malcolm craned his neck to see the gate.

"Yes," he said.

There was a silence. Mabel sat on like one condemned, at the head of the table. Then a whistle was heard from the kitchen. The dog got up and barked sharply. Joe opened the door and shouted:

"Come on."

After a moment a young man entered. He was muffled up in overcoat and a purple woolen scarf, and his tweed cap, which he did not remove, was pulled down on his head. He was of medium height, his face was rather long and pale, his eyes looked tired.

"Hello, Jack! Well, Jack!" exclaimed Malcolm and Joe. Fred Henry merely said, "Jack."

"What's doing?" asked the newcomer, evidently addressing Fred Henry.

"Same. We've got to be out by Wednesday. Got a cold?"

"I have—got it bad, too."

"Why don't you stop in?"

"*Me* stop in? When I can't stand on my legs, perhaps I shall have a chance." The young man spoke huskily. He had a slight Scotch accent.

"It's a knockout, isn't it," said Joe, boisterously, "if a doctor goes round croaking with a cold. Looks bad for the patients, doesn't it?"

The young doctor looked at him slowly.

"Anything the matter with *you*, then?" he asked sarcastically.

"Not as I know of. Damn your eyes, I hope not. Why?"

"I thought you were very concerned about the patients, wondered if you might be one yourself."

"Damn it, no, I've never been patient to no flaming doctor, and hope I never shall be," returned Joe.

At this point Mabel rose from the table, and they all seemed to become aware of her existence. She began putting the dishes together. The young doctor looked at her, but did not address her. He had not greeted her. She went out of the room with the tray, her face impassive and unchanged.

"When are you off then, all of you?" asked the doctor.

"I'm catching the eleven-forty," replied Malcolm. "Are you goin' down wi' th' trap, Joe?"

"Yes, I've told you I'm going down wi' th' trap, haven't I?"

"We'd better be getting her in then. So long, Jack, if I don't see you before I go," said Malcolm, shaking hands.

He went out, followed by Joe, who seemed to have his tail between his legs.

"Well, this is the devil's own," exclaimed the doctor, when he was left alone with Fred Henry. "Going before Wednesday, are you?"

"That's the orders," replied the other.

"Where, to Northampton?"

"That's it."

"The devil!" exclaimed Fergusson, with quiet chagrin.

And there was silence between the two.

"All settled up, are you?" asked Fergusson.

"About."

There was another pause.

"Well, I shall miss yer, Freddy, boy," said the young doctor.

"And I shall miss thee, Jack," returned the other.

"Miss you like hell," mused the doctor.

Fred Henry turned aside. There was nothing to say. Mabel came in again, to finish clearing the table.

"What are *you* going to do, then, Miss Pervin?" asked Fergusson. "Going to your sister's, are you?"

Mabel looked at him with her steady, dangerous eyes, that always made him uncomfortable, unsettling his superficial ease.

"No," she said.

"Well, what in the name of fortune *are* you going to do? Say what you mean to do," cried Fred Henry, with futile intensity.

But she only averted her head, and continued her work. She folded the white tablecloth, and put on the chenille cloth.

"The sulkiest bitch that ever trod!" muttered her brother.

But she finished her task with perfectly impassive face, the young doctor watching her interestedly all the while. Then she went out.

Fred Henry stared after her, clenching his lips, his

blue eyes fixing in sharp antagonism, as he made a grimace of sour exasperation.

"You could bray her into bits, and that's all you'd get out of her," he said, in a small, narrowed tone.

The doctor smiled faintly.

"What's she *going* to do, then?" he asked.

"Strike me if *I* know!" returned the other.

There was a pause. Then the doctor stirred.

"I'll be seeing you tonight, shall I?" he said to his friend.

"Ay—where's it to be? Are we going over to Jessdale?"

"I don't know. I've got such a cold on me. I'll come round to the Moon and Stars, anyway."

"Let Lizzie and May miss their night for once, eh?"

"That's it—if I feel as I do now."

"All's one——"

The two young men went through the passage and down to the back door together. The house was large, but it was servantless now, and desolate. At the back was a small bricked house-yard, and beyond that a big square, graveled fine and red, and having stables on two sides. Sloping, dank, winter-dark fields stretched away on the open sides.

But the stables were empty. Joseph Pervin, the father of the family, had been a man of no education, who had become a fairly large horse dealer. The stables had been full of horses, there was a great turmoil and come-and-go of horses and of dealers and grooms. Then the kitchen was full of servants. But of late things had declined. The old man had married a second time, to retrieve his fortunes. Now he was dead and everything was gone to the dogs, there was nothing but debt and threatening.

For months, Mabel had been servantless in the big house, keeping the home together in penury for her ineffectual brothers. She had kept house for ten years. But previously it was with unstinted means. Then, however brutal and coarse everything was, the sense of money had kept her proud, confident. The men might be foul-mouthed, the women in the kitchen might have bad reputations, her brothers might have illegitimate children. But so long as there was money, the girl felt herself established, and brutally proud, reserved.

No company came to the house, save dealers and coarse men. Mabel had no associates of her own sex, after her sister went away. But she did not mind. She went regularly to church, she attended to her father. And she lived in the memory of her mother, who had died when she was fourteen, and whom she had loved. She had loved her father, too, in a different way, depending upon him, and feeling secure in him, until at the age of fifty-four he married again. And then she had set hard against him. Now he had died and left them all hopelessly in debt.

She had suffered badly during the period of poverty. Nothing, however, could shake the curious sullen, animal pride that dominated each member of the family. Now, for Mabel, the end had come. Still she would not cast about her. She would follow her own way just the same. She would always hold the keys of her own situation. Mindless and persistent, she endured from day to day. Why should she think? Why should she answer anybody? It was enough that this was the end, and there was no way out. She need not pass any more darkly along the main street of the small town, avoiding every eye. She need not demean herself any more, going into the shops and buying the cheapest food. This was at an end. She thought of nobody, not even of herself. Mindless and persistent, she seemed in a sort of ecstasy to be coming nearer to her fulfilment, her own glorification, approaching her dead mother, who was glorified.

In the afternoon she took a little bag, with shears and sponge and a small scrubbing brush, and went out. It was a gray, wintry day, with saddened, dark green fields and an atmosphere blackened by the smoke of foundries not far off. She went quickly, darkly along the causeway, heeding nobody, through the town to the churchyard.

There she always felt secure, as if no one could see her, although as a matter of fact she was exposed to the stare of every one who passed along under the churchyard wall. Nevertheless, once under the shadow of the great looming church, among the graves, she felt immune from the world, reserved within the thick churchyard wall as in another country.

Carefully she clipped the grass from the grave, and arranged the pinky white, small chrysanthemums in the tin cross. When this was done, she took an empty jar from a neighboring grave, brought water, and carefully, most scrupulously sponged the marble headstone and the coping-stone.

It gave her sincere satisfaction to do this. She felt in immediate contact with the world of her mother. She took minute pains, went through the park in a state bordering on pure happiness, as if in performing this task she came into a subtle, intimate connection with her mother. For the life she followed here in the world was far less real than the world of death she inherited from her mother.

The doctor's house was just by the church. Fergusson, being a mere hired assistant, was slave to the countryside. As he hurried now to attend to the outpatients in the surgery, glancing across the graveyard with his quick eye, he saw the girl at her task at the grave. She seemed so intent and remote, it was like looking into another world. Some mystical element was touched in him. He slowed down as he walked, watching her as if spellbound.

She lifted her eyes, feeling him looking. Their eyes met. And each looked again at once, each feeling, in some way, found out by the other. He lifted his cap and passed on down the road. There remained distinct in his consciousness, like a vision, the memory of her face, lifted from the tombstone in the churchyard, and looking at him with slow, large, portentous eyes. It *was* portentous, her face. It seemed to mesmerize him. There was a heavy power in her eyes which laid hold of his whole being, as if he had drunk some powerful drug. He had been feeling weak and done before. Now the life came back into him, he felt delivered from his own fretted, daily self.

He finished his duties at the surgery as quickly as might be, hastily filling up the bottles of the waiting people with cheap drugs. Then, in perpetual haste, he set off again to visit several cases in another part of his round, before teatime. At all times he preferred to walk if he could, but particularly when he was not well. He fancied the motion restored him.

The afternoon was falling. It was gray, deadened, and wintry, with a slow, moist, heavy coldness sinking in and deadening all the faculties. But why should he think or notice? He hastily climbed the hill and turned across the dark green fields, following the black cinder-track. In the distance, across a shallow dip in the country, the small town was clustered like smouldering ash, a tower, a spire, a heap of low, raw, extinct houses. And on the nearest fringe of the town, sloping into the dip, was Oldmeadow, the Pervins' house. He could see the stables and the outbuildings distinctly, as they lay towards him on the slope. Well, he would not go there many more times! Another resource would be lost to him, another place gone: the only company he cared for in the alien, ugly little town he was losing. Nothing but work, drudgery, constant hastening from dwelling to dwelling among the colliers and the ironworkers. It wore him out, but at the same time he had a craving for it. It was a stimulant to him to be in the homes of the working people, moving as it were through the innermost body of their life. His nerves were excited and gratified. He could come so near, into the very lives of the rough, inarticulate, powerfully emotional men and women. He grumbled, he said he hated the hellish hole. But as a matter of fact it excited him, the contact with the rough, strongly-feeling people was a stimulant applied direct to his nerves.

Below Oldmeadow, in the green, shallow, soddened hollow of fields, lay a square, deep pond. Roving across the landscape, the doctor's quick eye detected a figure in black passing through the gate of the field, down towards the pond. He looked again. It would be Mabel Pervin. His mind suddenly became alive and attentive.

Why was she going down there? He pulled up on the path on the slope above, and stood staring. He could just make sure of the small black figure moving in the hollow of the failing day. He seemed to see her in the midst of such obscurity, that he was like a clairvoyant, seeing rather with the mind's eye than with ordinary sight. Yet he could see her positively enough, whilst he kept his eye attentive. He felt, if he looked away from her, in the thick, ugly, falling dusk, he would lose her altogether.

He followed her minutely as she moved, direct and intent, like something transmitted rather than stirring in voluntary activity, straight down the field towards the pond. There she stood on the bank for a moment.

She never raised her head. Then she waded slowly into the water.

He stood motionless as the small black figure walked slowly and deliberately towards the center of the pond, very slowly, gradually moving deeper into the motionless water, and still moving forward as the water got up to her breast. Then he could see her no more in the dusk of the dead afternoon.

"There!" he exclaimed. "Would you believe it?"

And he hastened straight down, running over the wet, soddened fields, pushing through the hedges, down into the depression of callous wintry obscurity. It took him several minutes to come to the pond. He stood on the bank, breathing heavily. He could see nothing. His eyes seemed to penetrate the dead water. Yes, perhaps that was the dark shadow of her black clothing beneath the surface of the water.

He slowly ventured into the pond. The bottom was deep, soft clay, he sank in, and the water clasped dead cold round his legs. As he stirred he could smell the cold, rotten clay that fouled up into the water. It was objectionable in his lungs. Still, repelled and yet not heeding, he moved deeper into the pond. The cold water rose over his thighs, over his loins, upon his abdomen. The lower part of his body was all sunk in the hideous cold element. And the bottom was so deeply soft and uncertain, he was afraid of pitching with his mouth underneath. He could not swim, and was afraid.

He crouched a little, spreading his hands under the water and moving them round, trying to feel for her. The dead cold pond swayed upon his chest. He moved again, a little deeper, and again, with his hands underneath, he felt all around under the water. And he touched her clothing. But it evaded his fingers. He made a desperate effort to grasp it.

And so doing he lost his balance and went under, horribly, suffocating in the foul earthy water, struggling madly for a few moments. At last, after what seemed an eternity, he got his footing, rose again into the air and looked around. He gasped, and knew he was in the world. Then he looked at the water. She had risen near him. He grasped her clothing, and drawing her nearer, turned to take his way to land again.

He went very slowly, carefully, absorbed in the slow progress. He rose higher, climbing out of the pond. The water was now only about his legs; he was thankful, full of relief to be out of the clutches of the pond. He lifted her and staggered on to the bank, out of the horror of wet, gray clay.

He laid her down on the bank. She was quite unconscious and running with water. He made the water come from her mouth, he worked to restore her. He did not have to work very long before he could feel the breathing begin again in her; she was breathing naturally. He worked a little longer. He could feel her live beneath his hands; she was coming back. He wiped her face, wrapped her in his overcoat, looked round into the dim, dark gray world, then lifted her and staggered down the bank and across the fields.

It seemed an unthinkably long way, and his burden so heavy he felt he would never get to the house. But at last he was in the stable-yard, and then in the house-yard. He opened the door and went into the house. In the kitchen he laid her down on the hearthrug, and called. The house was empty. But the fire was burning in the grate.

Then again he kneeled to attend to her. She was breathing regularly, her eyes were wide open and as if conscious, but there seemed something missing in her look. She was conscious in herself, but unconscious of her surroundings.

He ran upstairs, took blankets from a bed, and put them before the fire to warm. Then he removed her saturated, earthy-smelling clothing, rubbed her dry with a towel, and wrapped her naked in the blankets. Then he went into the dining room, to look for spirits. There was a little whisky. He drank a gulp himself, and put some into her mouth.

The effect was instantaneous. She looked full into his face, as if she had been seeing him for some time, and yet had only just become conscious of him.

"Dr. Fergusson?" she said.

"What?" he answered.

He was divesting himself of his coat, intending to find some dry clothing upstairs. He could not bear the smell of the dead, clayey water, and he was mortally afraid for his own health.

"What did I do?" she asked.

"Walked into the pond," he replied. He had begun to shudder like one sick, and could hardly attend to her. Her eyes remained full on him, he seemed to be going dark in his mind, looking back at her helplessly. The shuddering became quieter in him, his life came back in him, dark and unknowing, but strong again.

"Was I out of my mind?" she asked, while her eyes were fixed on him all the time.

"Maybe, for the moment," he replied. He felt quiet, because his strength had come back. The strange fretful strain had left him.

"Am I out of my mind now?" she asked.

"Are you?" he reflected a moment. "No," he answered truthfully, "I don't see that you are." He turned his face aside. He was afraid now, because he felt dazed, and felt dimly that her power was stronger than his, in this issue. And she continued to look at him fixedly all the time. "Can you tell me where

I shall find some dry things to put on?" he asked.

"Did you dive into the pond for me?" she asked.

"No," he answered. "I walked in. But I went in overhead as well."

There was silence for a moment. He hesitated. He very much wanted to go upstairs to get into dry clothing. But there was another desire in him. And she seemed to hold him. His will seemed to have gone to sleep, and left him, standing there slack before her. But he felt warm inside himself. He did not shudder at all, though his clothes were sodden on him.

"Why did you?" she asked.

"Because I didn't want you to do such a foolish thing," he said.

"It wasn't foolish," she said, still gazing at him as she lay on the floor, with a sofa cushion under her head. "It was the right thing to do. I knew best, then."

"I'll go and shift these wet things," he said. But still he had not the power to move out of her presence, until she sent him. It was as if she had the life of his body in her hands, and he could not extricate himself. Or perhaps he did not want to.

Suddenly she sat up. Then she became aware of her own immediate condition. She felt the blankets about her, she knew her own limbs. For a moment it seemed as if her reason were going. She looked round, with wild eye, as if seeking something. He stood still with fear. She saw her clothing lying scattered.

"Who undressed me?" she asked, her eyes resting full and inevitable on his face.

"I did," he replied, "to bring you round."

For some moments she sat and gazed at him awfully, her lips parted.

"Do you love me, then?" she asked.

He only stood and stared at her, fascinated. His soul seemed to melt.

She shuffled forward on her knees, and put her arms round him, round his legs, as he stood there, pressing her breasts against his knees and thighs, clutching him with strange, convulsive certainty, pressing his thighs against her, drawing him to her face, her throat, as she looked up at him with flaring, humble eyes of transfiguration, triumphant in first possession.

"You love me," she murmured, in strange transport, yearning and triumphant and confident. "You love me. I know you love me, I know."

And she was passionately kissing his knees, through the wet clothing, passionately and indiscriminately kissing his knees, his legs, as if unaware of everything.

He looked down at the tangled wet hair, the wild, bare, animal shoulders. He was amazed, bewildered, and afraid. He had never thought of loving her. He had never wanted to love her. When he rescued her and restored her, he was a doctor, and she was a patient. He had had no single personal thought of her. Nay, this introduction of the personal element was very distasteful to him, a violation of his professional honor. It was horrible to have her there embracing his knees. It was horrible. He revolted from it, violently. And yet—and yet—he had not the power to break away.

She looked at him again, with the same supplication of powerful love, and that same transcendent, frightening light of triumph. In view of the delicate flame which seemed to come from her face like a light, he was powerless. And yet he had never intended to love her. He had never intended. And something stubborn in him could not give way.

"You love me," she repeated, in a murmur of deep, rhapsodic assurance. "You love me."

Her hands were drawing him, drawing him down to her. He was afraid, even a little horrified. For he had, really, no intention of loving her. Yet her hands were drawing him towards her. He put out his hand quickly to steady himself, and grasped her bare shoulder. A flame seemed to burn the hand that grasped her soft shoulder. He had no intention of loving her: his whole will was against his yielding. It was horrible. And yet wonderful was the touch of her shoulders, beautiful the shining of her face. Was she perhaps mad? He had a horror of yielding to her. Yet something in him ached also.

He had been staring away at the door, away from her. But his hand remained on her shoulder. She had gone suddenly very still. He looked down at her. Her eyes were now wide with fear, with doubt, the light was dying from her face, a shadow of terrible grayness was returning. He could not bear the touch of her eyes' question upon him, and the look of death behind the question.

With an inward groan he gave way, and let his heart yield towards her. A sudden gentle smile came on his face. And her eyes, which never left his face, slowly, slowly filled with tears. He watched the strange water rise in her eyes, like some slow fountain coming up. And his heart seemed to burn and melt away in his breast.

He could not bear to look at her any more. He dropped on his knees and caught her head with his arms and pressed her face against his throat. She was very still. His heart, which seemed to have broken, was burning with a kind of agony in his breast. And he felt her slow, hot tears wetting his throat. But he could not move.

He felt the hot tears wet his neck and the hollows of his neck, and he remained motionless, suspended through one of man's eternities. Only now it had become indispensable to him to have her face pressed close to him; he could never let her go again. He could never let her head go away from the close clutch of his arm. He wanted to remain like that for ever, with his heart hurting him in a pain that was also life to him. Without knowing, he was looking down on her damp, soft brown hair.

Then, as it were suddenly, he smelt the horrid stagnant smell of that water. And at the same moment she drew away from him and looked at him. Her eyes were wistful and unfathomable. He was afraid of them, and he fell to kissing her, not knowing what he was doing. He wanted her eyes not to have that terrible, wistful, unfathomable look.

When she turned her face to him again, a faint delicate flush was glowing, and there was again dawning that terrible shining of joy in her eyes, which really terrified him, and yet which he now wanted to see, because he feared the look of doubt still more.

"You love me?" she said, rather faltering.

"Yes." The word cost him a painful effort. Not because it wasn't true. But because it was too newly true, the *saying* seemed to tear open again his newly-torn heart. And he hardly wanted it to be true, even now.

She lifted her face to him, and he bent forward and kissed her on the mouth, gently, with the one kiss that is an eternal pledge. And as he kissed her his heart strained again in his breast. He never intended to love her. But now it was over. He had crossed over the gulf to her, and all that he had left behind had shriveled and become void.

After the kiss, her eyes again slowly filled with tears. She sat still, away from him, with her face drooped aside, and her hands folded in her lap. The tears fell very slowly. There was complete silence. He too sat there motionless and silent on the hearthrug. The strange pain of his heart that was broken seemed to consume him. That he should love her? That this was love! That he should be ripped open in this way! Him, a doctor! How they would all jeer if they knew! It was agony to him to think they might know.

In the curious naked pain of the thought he looked again to her. She was sitting there drooped into a muse. He saw a tear fall, and his heart flared hot. He saw for the first time that one of her shoulders was quite uncovered, one arm bare, he could see one of her small breasts; dimly, because it had become almost dark in the room.

"Why are you crying?" he asked, in an altered voice.

She looked up at him, and behind her tears the consciousness of her situation for the first time brought a dark look of shame to her eyes.

"I'm not crying, really," she said, watching him half frightened.

He reached his hand, and softly closed it on her bare arm.

"I love you! I love you!" he said in a soft, low vibrating voice, unlike himself.

She shrank, and dropped her head. The soft, penetrating grip of his hand on her arm distressed her. She looked up at him.

"I want to go," she said. "I want to go and get you some dry things."

"Why?" he said. "I'm all right."

"But I want to go," she said. "And I want you to change your things."

He released her arm, and she wrapped herself in the blanket, looking at him rather frightened. And still she did not rise.

"Kiss me," she said wistfully.

He kissed her, but briefly, half in anger.

Then, after a second, she rose nervously, all mixed up in the blanket. He watched her in her confusion, as she tried to extricate herself and wrap herself up so that she could walk. He watched her relentlessly, as she knew. And as she went, the blanket trailing, and as he saw a glimpse of her feet and her white leg, he tried to remember her as she was when he had wrapped her in the blanket. But then he didn't want to remember, because she had been nothing to him then, and his nature revolted from remembering her as she was when she was nothing to him.

A tumbling, muffled noise from within the dark house startled him. Then he heard her voice—"There are clothes." He rose and went to the foot of the stairs, and gathered up the garments she had thrown down. Then he came back to the fire, to rub himself down and dress. He grinned at his own appearance when he had finished.

The fire was sinking, so he put on coal. The house was now quite dark save for the light of a street-lamp that shone in faintly from beyond the holly trees. He lit the gas with matches he found on the mantelpiece. Then he emptied the pockets of his own clothes, and threw all his wet things in a heap into the scullery. After which he gathered up her sodden clothes, gently, and put them in a separate heap on the copper-top in the scullery.

It was six o'clock on the clock. His own watch had stopped. He ought to go back to the surgery. He waited, and still she did not come down. So he went to the foot of the stairs and called:

"I shall have to go."

Almost immediately he heard her coming down. She had on her best dress of black voile, and her hair was tidy, but still damp. She looked at him— and in spite of herself, smiled.

"I don't like you in those clothes," she said.

"Do I look a sight?" he answered.

They were shy of one another.

"I'll make you some tea," she said.

"No, I must go."

"Must you?" And she looked at him again with the wide, strained, doubtful eyes. And again, from the pain of his breast, he knew how he loved her. He went and bent to kiss her, gently, passionately, with his heart's painful kiss.

"And my hair smells so horrible," she murmured in distraction. "And I'm so awful, I'm so awful! Oh, no, I'm too awful." And she broke into bitter, heart-broken sobbing. "You can't want to love me, I'm horrible."

"Don't be silly, don't be silly," he said, trying to comfort her, kissing her, holding her in his arms. "I want you, I want to marry you, we're going to be married, quickly, quickly—tomorrow if I can."

But she only sobbed terribly, and cried:

"I feel awful. I feel awful. I feel I'm horrible to you."

"No, I want you, I want you," was all he answered, blindly, with that terrible intonation which frightened her almost more than her horror lest he should *not* want her.

Isaac Babel

THE SIN OF JESUS

Translated by Andrew R. MacAndrew

ARINA LIVED by the front staircase where the guests'
rooms were. Serioga, the janitor's assistant, lived under
the back stairs. Between them, there was shame. On
Palm Sunday, Arina presented Serioga with a pair
of twins. Water flows, stars shine, people make love.
Soon Arina was pregnant again. The sixth month was
rolling on—and how they do roll, those women's
months!—when Serioga was called into the Army.
There was the snag. So Arina said to him:

"There's no point in my waiting for you, Serioga.
We'll be parted for four years and in that time, I'd
say, I'll have at least three babies. Working in a hotel,
you know, is just like going around with your skirt
pulled up. The guest is always the boss, whatever
he is, even a Jew. So by the time you get out of the
Army, my insides will be pretty worn out and I won't
be much of a woman no more, so what's the good?"

"You have something there," Serioga said, nodding.

"Now there are some fellows who'd marry me if
I wanted. There's that contractor Trofimych, but he's
a brute. And there's Isai Abramych, the warden of
St. Nicholas' Church—he's old and weak, but what

good does your nasty male vigor do me? I'm sick of it as it is, and that's the truth, I'm telling you, just like I was confessing to a priest.... Three months from now, when the baby's born, I'll take it to a foundling home and get hitched to the old fellow."

When he heard that, Serioga removed his belt and bravely whacked Arina a few times on the belly.

"Hey," Arina says to him, "take it easy. It's your stuffing inside this belly, no one else's."

But there was plenty of beating and pushing and a flood of the man's tears and the woman's blood, but that's not the point. Well, finally the woman came to Jesus Christ and said to Him as follows:

"I," she said, "am Arina, the chambermaid from the Madrid and Louvre Hotel—you know, on Tverskaya Street. As you know, Lord Jesus, working in a hotel is just like going around with your skirt pulled up. Any guy who pays for his room must be treated like your lord and master, even if he's a Jew or something. Now, there walks on earth a servant of yours, Lord Jesus, one Serioga, the janitor's assistant, and last year, on Palm Sunday, I had twins by him...."

And she gave the Lord a complete picture of what had happened.

"But," the Lord asked, "what if Serioga refuses to go into the Army?"

"I guess the cops will come and drag him off."

"Cops?" the Lord said and sadly hung His head. "That's something that hadn't occurred to me.... Now, how about your trying to stay chaste for a while?"

"You mean for four years? Listening to you talk one would think it was easy for men to get rid of the beast in them. And even supposing they did, how would they reproduce themselves then? If you want to give me advice, you should talk sense!"

The Lord's cheeks turned red then, for the woman's words had touched Him on a sore spot. But He said nothing. No one can kiss his own ear, and God is aware of that too.

"Now here's what I'll do for you, God's servant, holy sinner, the Lord's handmaiden Arina," the Lord proclaimed in all His glory. "There's a little angel called Alfred hanging around my heaven and lately he's really got out of hand. He whines all the time. 'Why,' he says to me, 'did you have to promote me to Angel when I wasn't even twenty and was still full of sap!' So what would you say, Arina, if I lent you the angel Alfred for four years to serve as a husband? He'd help you pray, he'd protect you, and you could use him as your sweetheart too. As to becoming pregnant by him, you have nothing to fear: you'll never even get a duckling out of him, let alone a child, for while there's a lot of fun in him, there's not even a kopeck's worth of seriousness."

"Now, that's just what I need," the Lord's handmaiden Arina cried happily, "because that seriousness of theirs has made me almost kick the bucket three times in the past two years."

"So you'll have a blissful respite, God's child Arina, and may your prayers be as light as a song. So be it."

And they let it rest at that. Alfred was brought to her and he turned out to be a frail, delicate little guy with a pair of wings behind his bluish shoulders. And those wings seemed to flutter in a sort of rosy light, like a couple of doves playing in the sky at sunset. Arina grabbed him, pressed him in her arms, and sobbed with joy and feminine tenderness.

"Alfred, sweetie-pie, my consolation, my bridegroom . . ."

The Lord warned her though that, before they went to bed, she must remove his wings—they were attached like doors, on sort of hinges—and wrap them carefully in a clean sheet, because any brisk movement could easily snap a wing, which after all, is made only of infants' sighs.

The Lord blessed their union with a specially summoned choir of bishops who performed very loudly indeed. But there were no refreshments, nothing at all—that's strictly against their rules up there. When it was all over, Arina and Alfred, their arms around each other, descended on a silken ladder to earth.

They came to Petrovka Street—the most expensive shopping center, but nothing less would satisfy her now—and she bought for Alfred, who, by the way, was not only sockless but, besides, wore nothing at all and was in what we might call his natural state, patent-leather shoes, checked trousers, a hunting jacket, and a sky-blue velvet waistcoat.

"The rest, darling," she told him, "I'm sure we'll find at home."

Arina managed to get that day off at the hotel. Serioga arrived and started kicking up hell outside her door, but she didn't even go out to him.

"Mr. Nifantich," she told him from behind the closed door, "I happen to be washing my feet today, and therefore I beg you to leave without no more disturbance."

He said nothing and left. It was, of course, the angelic force that was beginning to manifest itself.

That evening, Arina produced a meal good enough for a big merchant, for she had plenty of ambition, that woman. A half bottle of vodka, a bottle of wine, a Danube herring with spuds, and a samovar for tea. No sooner had Alfred partaken of that earthly fruit than he fell dead asleep. So Arina immediately removed his wings from their hinges, packed them up, and carried him to her bed.

And now, on her tattered, sinful comforter, that heavenly wonder was stretched out, with a halo behind his head and light radiating from his body, its rosy beams alternating with the white moonbeams swaying around the room on their luminous legs. Arina cried and laughed and sang and prayed. Ah, Arina, what happiness you've struck on this battered earth! Blessed art thou among women!

They had emptied the half bottle and it showed. As soon as she was asleep, she rolled over, resting her belly, which had been swelling for six months now with Serioga's fruit, on Alfred. It wasn't enough for her to sleep with an angel, it wasn't enough that no one spat at the wall or snored or snorted; no, that wasn't enough for that frantic dame—she had to warm her sore and swollen belly too. And in her drunken state, she smothered God's angel, smothered him amidst her rejoicing, like one smothers a week-old infant—crushed him under her weight. And so that was the end of him and pale tears rolled from his angel's wings wrapped in a sheet.

Dawn came. Trees bowed their heads to the ground; in the distant northern forests, each pine turned into a priest and knelt down....

And again the woman stood before the Lord's throne. She stood there, strong and broad-shouldered, holding the young corpse in her thick, red arms.

"Behold, Lord—"

This time, Jesus' meek heart was unable to stand it and angrily He laid a curse on the woman.

"From this day on, Arina," the Lord said, "you're on your own. Let it be with you as it is on earth."

"But why, Lord?" Arina said in a very low voice.

"Was it me myself who made my body so heavy? Was it me who brewed that vodka? Was it me who made my stupid, lonely soul the way it is?"

"I've had just about as much of you as I can stand," cried the Lord Jesus. "You've smothered my angel. Ah, you slut—"

And a putrid wind carried Arina back to earth, straight to her room in the Madrid and Louvre Hotel on Tverskaya Street. And there, things were as bad as they could be, with Serioga drinking and running wild, for these were his last days before going into the army.

And the contractor Trofimych, just back from a trip to Kolomna, took one look at Arina, sturdy and red-cheeked, and cooed:

"Oh, your cute, fat little tummy," and so on.

Isai Abramych heard about that fat little tummy and he too came lisping tenderly to her.

"I, of course," he lisped, "cannot make you my lawful wedded wife after all that's happened. However," he added, "I don't see why we shouldn't go to bed together now, since ..."

If that old guy was to lie anywhere, it surely should have been under a few feet of cold earth rather than in bed with anyone, but no, he too must have a go at insulting her to her very soul. They were all after her like dogs who had broken their chains—the kitchen boys, the traveling salesmen, the foreigners, everyone—they all wanted to have some fun.

And that's the end of the story.

When she was due to deliver—for three months had rolled by—Arina stepped out into the courtyard, by the back staircase near the janitor's room, raised her huge belly toward the silky heavens, and made the following stupid statement:

"See, Lord, that's some belly for you! It'd sound

like a drum if you dropped peas on it. But I still can't see what it's all about and again, Lord, I never asked for it."

Lord Jesus washed Arina with His tears then, and He, the Saviour, knelt before her.

"Forgive me, Arina dear," He said, "forgive me, your sinful God, for having done this to you. . . ."

"No, there's no forgiveness for you, Lord Jesus," Arina said. "There just ain't."

John Updike

YOUR LOVER JUST
CALLED

THE TELEPHONE RANG, and Richard Maple, who
had stayed home from work this Friday because of
a cold, answered it: "Hello?" The person at the other
end of the line hung up. Richard went into the
bedroom, where Joan was making the bed, and said,
"Your lover just called."

"What did he say?"

"Nothing. He hung up. He was amazed to find me
home."

"Maybe it was *your* lover."

He knew, through the phlegm beclouding his head,
that there was something wrong with this, and found
it. "If it was *my* lover," he said, "why would she hang
up, since I answered?"

Joan shook the sheet so it made a clapping noise.
"Maybe she doesn't love you anymore."

"This is a ridiculous conversation."

"You started it."

"Well, what would you think, if you answered the
phone on a weekday and the person hung up? He
clearly expected you to be home alone."

"Well, if you'll go to the store for cigarettes I'll call
him back and explain what happened."

"You think I'll think you're kidding but I know that's really what *would* happen."

"Oh, come on, Dick. Who would it be? Freddie Vetter?"

"Or Harry Saxon. Or somebody I don't know at all. Some old college friend who's moved to New England. Or maybe the milkman. I can hear you and him talking while I'm shaving sometimes."

"We're surrounded by hungry children. He's fifty years old and has hair coming out of his ears."

"Like your father. You're not adverse to older men. There was that Chaucer section man when we first met. Anyway, you've been acting awfully happy lately. There's a little smile comes into your face when you're doing the housework. See, there it is!"

"I'm smiling," Joan said, "because you're so absurd. I have no lover. I have nowhere to put him. My days are consumed by devotion to the needs of my husband and his many children."

"Oh, so I'm the one who made you have all the children? While you were hankering after a career in fashion or in the exciting world of business. Aeronautics, perhaps. You could have been the first woman to design a nose cone. Or to crack the wheat futures cycle. Joan Maple, girl agronomist. Joan Maple, lady geopolitician. But for that fornicating brute she mistakenly married, this clear-eyed female citizen of our ever-needful republic—"

"Dick, have you taken your temperature? I haven't heard you rave like this for years."

"I haven't been betrayed like this for years. I hated that *click*. That nasty little I-know-your-wife-better-than-you-do *click*."

"It was some child. If we're going to have Mack for dinner tonight, you better convalesce now."

"It *is* Mack, isn't it? That son of a bitch. The divorce isn't even finalized and he's calling my wife on the phone. And then proposes to gorge himself at my groaning board."

"I'll be groaning myself. You're giving me a headache."

"Sure. First I foist off children on you in my mad desire for progeny, then I give you a menstrual headache."

"Get into bed and I'll bring you orange juice and toast cut into strips the way your mother used to make it."

"You're lovely."

As he was settling himself under the blankets, the phone rang again, and Joan answered it in the upstairs hall. "Yes...no...no...good," she said, and hung up.

"Who was it?" he called.

"Somebody wanting to sell us the *World Book Encyclopedia*," she called back.

"A very likely story," he said, with self-pleasing irony, leaning back onto the pillows confident that he was being unjust, that there was no lover.

Mack Dennis was a homely, agreeable, sheepish man their age, whose wife, Eleanor, was in Wyoming suing for divorce. He spoke of her with a cloying tenderness, as if of a favorite daughter away for the first time at camp, or as a departed angel nevertheless keeping in close electronic touch with the scorned earth. "She says they've had some wonderful thunderstorms. The children go horseback riding every morning, and they play Pounce at night and are in bed by ten. Everybody's health has never been better, Ellie's asthma has cleared up and she thinks now she must have been allergic to *me*."

"You should have cut all your hair off and dressed in cellophane," Richard told him.

Joan asked him, "And how's *your* health? Are you feeding yourself enough? Mack, you look thin."

"The nights I don't stay in Boston," Mack said, tapping himself all over for a pack of cigarettes, "I've taken to eating at the motel on Route 33. It's the best food in town now, and you can watch the kids in the swimming pool." He studied his empty upturned hands as if they had recently held a surprise. He missed his own kids, was perhaps the surprise.

"I'm out of cigarettes too," Joan said.

"I'll go get some," Richard said.

"And a thing of Bitter Lemon at the liquor store."

"I'll make a pitcher of Martinis," Mack said. "Doesn't it feel great, to have Martini weather again?"

It was that season which is late summer in the days and early autumn at night. Evening descended on the downtown, lifting the neon tubing into brilliance, as Richard ran his errand. His sore throat felt folded within him like a secret; there was something reckless and gay in his being up and out at all after spending the afternoon in bed. Home, he parked by his back fence and walked down through a lawn loud with fallen leaves, though the trees overhead were still massy. The lit windows of his house looked golden and idyllic; the children's rooms were above (the face of Judith, his bigger daughter, drifted preoccupied across a slice of her wallpaper, and her pink square hand reached to adjust a doll on a shelf) and the kitchen below. In the kitchen windows, whose tone was fluorescent, a silent tableau was being enacted. Mack was holding a Martini shaker and pouring it into a vessel, eclipsed by an element of window sash, that Joan was offering with a long white arm. Head tilted winningly, she was talking with the slightly pushed-forward mouth that Richard recognized as peculiar to her while looking into mirrors, conversing with her elders, or otherwise seeking to display herself to advantage. Whatever she was saying made Mack laugh, so that his pouring (the silver shaker head glinted, a drop of greenish liquid spilled) was unsteady. He set the shaker down and displayed his hands, the same hands from which a little while ago a surprise had seemed to escape, at his sides, shoulder-high. Joan moved toward him, still holding her glass, and the back of her head, done up taut and oval in a bun, with blond down trailing at the nape of her neck, eclipsed all of Mack's face but his eyes, which closed. They were kissing. Joan's head tilted one way and Mack's another to make their mouths meet tighter. The graceful line of her shoulders was carried outward by the line of the arm holding her glass safe in the air. The other arm was around his neck. Behind them an open cabinet door revealed a paralyzed row of erect paper boxes whose lettering Richard could not read but whose coloring advertised their contents— Cheerios, Wheat Honeys, Onion Thins. Joan backed off and ran her index finger down the length of Mack's necktie (a summer tartan) ending with a jab in the vicinity of his navel that might have expressed a rebuke or a regret. His face, pale and lumpy in the harsh vertical light, looked mildly humorous but intent, and moved forward, toward hers, an inch or two. The scene had the fascinating slow motion of action underwater, mixed with the insane silent suddenness of a television montage glimpsed from the street. Judith came to the window upstairs, not noticing her father standing in the massy shadow of the tree. Wearing a nightie of lemon gauze, she innocently scratched her armpit while studying a moth beating on her screen; and this too gave Richard a momentous sense, crowding his heart, of having been brought by the mute act of witnessing—like a child sitting alone at the movies—perilously close to the hidden machinations of things. In another kitchen window a neglected teakettle began to plume and to fog the panes with steam. Joan was talking again; her forward-thrust lips seemed to be throwing rapid little bridges across a narrowing gap. Mack paused, shrugged; his face puckered as if he were speaking French. Joan's head snapped back with laughter and triumphantly she threw her free arm wide and was in his embrace again. His hand, spread starlike on the small of her back, went lower to what, out of sight behind the edge of formica counter, would be her bottom.

Richard scuffled loudly down the cement steps and kicked the kitchen door open, giving them time to break apart before he entered. From the far end of the kitchen, smaller than children, they looked at him with blurred, blank expressions. Joan turned off the steaming kettle and Mack shambled forward to pay for the cigarettes. After the third round of Martinis, the constraints loosened and Richard said, taking pleasure in the plaintive huskiness of his voice, "Imagine my discomfort. Sick as I am, I go out into this bitter night to get my wife and my guest some cigarettes, so they can pollute the air and aggravate my already grievous bronchial condition, and coming down through the back yard, what do I see? The two of them doing the Kama Sutra in my own kitchen. It was like seeing a blue movie and knowing the people in it."

"Where do you see blue movies nowadays?" Joan asked.

"Tush, Dick," Mack said sheepishly, rubbing his thighs with a brisk ironing motion. "A mere fraternal kiss. A brotherly hug. A disinterested tribute to your wife's charm."

"Really, Dick," Joan said. "I think it's shockingly sneaky of you to be standing around spying into your own windows."

"Standing around! I was transfixed with horror. It was a real trauma. My first primal scene." A profound happiness was stretching him from within; the reach of his tongue and wit felt immense, and the other two seemed dolls, homuneuli, in his playful grasp.

"We were hardly doing anything," Joan said, lifting her head as if to rise above it all, the lovely line of her jaw defined by tension, her lips stung by a pout.

"Oh, I'm sure, by your standards, you had hardly begun. You'd hardly sampled the possible wealth of coital positions. Did you think I'd never return? Have you poisoned my drink and I'm too vigorous to die, like Rasputin?"

"Dick," Mack said, "Joan loves you. And if I love any man, it's you. Joan and I had this out years ago, and decided to be merely friends."

"Don't go Irish on me, Mack Dennis. 'If I love any mon, 'tis thee.' Don't give me a thought, laddie. Just think of poor Eleanor out there, sweating out your divorce, bouncing up and down on those horses day after day, playing Pounce till she's black and blue—"

"Let's eat," Joan said. "You've made me so nervous I've probably overdone the roast beef. Really, Dick, I don't think you can excuse yourself by trying to make it funny."

Next day, the Maples awoke soured and dazed by hangovers; Mack had stayed until two, to make sure there were no hard feelings. Joan usually played ladies' tennis Saturday mornings, while Richard amused the children; now, dressed in white shorts and sneakers, she delayed at home in order to quarrel. "It's desperate of you," she told Richard, "to try to make something of Mack and me. What are you trying to cover up?"

"My dear Mrs. Maple, I *saw*," he said, "I *saw* through my own windows you doing a very credible impersonation of a female spider having her abdomen tickled. Where did you learn to flirt your head like that? It was better than finger puppets."

"Mack always kisses me in the kitchen. It's a habit, it means nothing. You know for yourself how in love with Eleanor he is."

"So much he's divorcing her. His devotion verges on the quixotic."

"The divorce is her idea, you know that. He's a lost soul. I feel sorry for him."

"Yes, I saw that you do. You were like the Red Cross at Verdun."

"What I'd like to know is, why are you so pleased?"

"Pleased? I'm annihilated."

"You're delighted. Look at your smile in the mirror."

"You're so incredibly unapologetic, I guess I think you must be being ironical."

The telephone rang. Joan picked it up and said, "Hello," and Richard heard the click across the room. Joan replaced the receiver and said to him, "So. She thought I'd be playing tennis by now."

"Who's she?"

"You tell me. Your lover. Your loveress."

"It was clearly yours, and something in your voice warned him off."

"Go to her!" Joan suddenly cried, with a burst of the same defiant energy that made her, on other hungover mornings, rush through a mountain of housework. "Go to her like a man and stop trying to maneuver me into something I don't understand!

I have no lover! I let Mack kiss me because he's lonely and drunk! Stop trying to make me more interesting than I am! All I am is a beat-up housewife who wants to go play tennis with some other tired ladies!"

Mutely Richard fetched from their sports closet her tennis racket, which had recently been restrung with gut. Carrying it in his mouth like a dog retrieving a stick, he laid it at the toe of her sneaker. Richard Jr., their older son, a wiry nine-year-old presently obsessed by the accumulation of Batman cards, came into the living room, witnessed this pantomime, and laughed to hide his fright. "Dad, can I have my nickel for emptying the waste baskets?"

"Mommy's going to go out to play, Dickie," Richard said, licking from his lips the salty taste of the racket handle. "Let's all go to the five-and-ten and buy a Batmobile."

"Yippee," the small boy said limply, glancing wide-eyed from one of his parents to the other, as if the space between them had gone treacherous.

Richard took the children to the five-and-ten, to the playground, and to a hamburger stand for lunch. These blameless activities transmuted the residue of alcohol and phlegm into a woolly fatigue as pure as the sleep of infants. Obligingly he nodded while his son described a boundless plot: "... and then, see Dad, the Penguin had an umbrella smoke came out of, it was neat, and there were these two other guys with funny masks in the bank, filling it with water, I don't know why, to make it bust or something, and Robin was climbing up these slippery stacks of like half-dollars to get away from the water, and then, see Dad ..."

Back home, the children dispersed into the neighborhood on the same mysterious tide that on other days packed their back yard with unfamiliar urchins.

Joan returned from tennis glazed with sweat, her ankles coated with dust. Her body was swimming in the rose afterglow of exertion. He suggested they take a nap.

"Just a nap," she warned.

"Of course," he said. "I met my mistress at the playground and we satisfied each other on the jungle gym."

"Maureen and I beat Alice and Judy. It can't be any of those three, they were waiting for me half an hour."

In bed, the shades strangely drawn against the bright afternoon, a glass of stale water standing bubbled with secret light, he asked her, "You think I want to make you more interesting than you are?"

"Of course. You're bored. You left me and Mack alone deliberately. It was very uncharacteristic of you, to go out with a cold."

"It's sad, to think of you without a lover."

"I'm sorry."

"You're pretty interesting anyway. Here, and here, and here."

"I said really a nap."

In the upstairs hall, on the other side of the closed bedroom door, the telephone rang. After four peals— icy spears hurled from afar—the ringing stopped, unanswered. There was a puzzled pause. Then a tentative, questioning *pring*, as if someone in passing had bumped the table, followed by a determined series, strides of sound, imperative and plaintive, that did not stop until twelve had been counted; then the lover hung up.

Anton Chekhov

THE CHORUS GIRL

Translated by Constance Garnett

ONE DAY WHEN she was younger and better-looking, and when her voice was stronger, Nikolay Petrovitch Kolpakov, her adorer, was sitting in the outer room of her summer villa. It was intolerably hot and stifling. Kolpakov, who had just dined and drunk a whole bottle of inferior port, felt ill-humored and out of sorts. Both were bored and waiting for the heat of the day to be over in order to go for a walk.

All at once there was a sudden ring at the door. Kolpakov, who was sitting with his coat off, in his slippers, jumped up and looked inquiringly at Pasha.

"It must be the postman or one of the girls," said the singer.

Kolpakov did not mind being found by the postman or Pasha's lady friends, but by way of precaution gathered up his clothes and went into the next room, while Pasha ran to open the door. To her great surprise in the doorway stood, not the postman and not a girl friend, but an unknown woman, young and beautiful, who was dressed like a lady, and from all outward signs was one.

The stranger was pale and was breathing heavily

as though she had been running up a steep flight
of stairs.

"What is it?" asked Pasha.

The lady did not at once answer. She took a step
forward, slowly looked about the room, and sat down
in a way that suggested that from fatigue, or perhaps
illness, she could not stand; then for a long time her
pale lips quivered as she tried in vain to speak.

"Is my husband here?" she asked at last, raising
to Pasha her big eyes with their red tear-stained lids.

"Husband?" whispered Pasha, and was suddenly
so frightened that her hands and feet turned cold.

"What husband?" she repeated, beginning to
tremble.

"My husband, ... Nikolay Petrovitch Kolpakov."

"N ... no, madam ... I ... I don't know any
husband."

A minute passed in silence. The stranger several
times passed her handkerchief over her pale lips and
held her breath to stop her inward trembling, while
Pasha stood before her motionless, like a post, and
looked at her with astonishment and terror.

"So you say he is not here?" the lady asked, this
time speaking with a firm voice and smiling oddly.

"I ... I don't know who it is you are asking about."

"You are horrid, mean, vile ..." the stranger muttered, scanning Pasha with hatred and repulsion. "Yes,
yes ... you are horrid. I am very, very glad that at
last I can tell you so!"

Pasha felt that on this lady in black with the angry
eyes and white slender fingers she produced the
impression of something horrid and unseemly, and
she felt ashamed of her chubby red cheeks, the
pockmark on her nose, and the fringe on her forehead,
which never could be combed back. And it seemed
to her that if she had been thin, and had had no

powder on her face and no fringe on her forehead, then she could have disguised the fact that she was not "respectable," and she would not have felt so frightened and ashamed to stand facing this unknown, mysterious lady.

"Where is my husband?" the lady went on. "Though I don't care whether he is here or not, but I ought to tell you that the money has been missed, and they are looking for Nikolay Petrovitch.... They mean to arrest him. That's your doing!"

The lady got up and walked about the room in great excitement. Pasha looked at her and was so frightened that she could not understand.

"He'll be found and arrested today," said the lady, and she gave a sob, and in that sound could be heard her resentment and vexation. "I know who has brought him to this awful position! Low, horrid creature! Loathsome, mercenary hussy!" The lady's lips worked and her nose wrinkled up with disgust. "I am helpless, do you hear, you low woman? ... I am helpless; you are stronger than I am, but there is One to defend me and my children! God sees all! He is just! He will punish you for every tear I have shed, for all my sleepless nights! The time will come; you will think of me!...."

Silence followed again. The lady walked about the room and wrung her hands, while Pasha still gazed blankly at her in amazement, not understanding and expecting something terrible.

"I know nothing about it, madam," she said, and suddenly burst into tears.

"You are lying!" cried the lady, and her eyes flashed angrily at her. "I know all about it! I've known about you a long time. I know that for the last month he has been spending every day with you!"

"Yes. What then? What of it? I have a great many

visitors, but I don't force anyone to come. He is free to do as he likes."

"I tell you they have discovered that money is missing! He has embezzled money at the office! For the sake of such a ... creature as you, for your sake he has actually committed a crime. Listen," said the lady in a resolute voice, stopping short, facing Pasha. "You can have no principles: you live simply to do harm—that's your object; but one can't imagine you have fallen so low that you have no trace of human feeling left! He has a wife, children ... If he is condemned and sent into exile we shall starve, the children and I.... Understand that! And yet there is a chance of saving him and us from destitution and disgrace. If I take them nine hundred roubles today they will let him alone. Only nine hundred roubles!"

"What nine hundred roubles?" Pasha asked softly. "I ... I don't know ... I haven't taken it."

"I am not asking you for nine hundred roubles.... You have no money, and I don't want your money. I ask you for something else.... Men usually give expensive things to women like you. Only give me back the things my husband has given you!"

"Madam, he has never made me a present of anything!" Pasha wailed, beginning to understand.

"Where is the money? He has squandered his own and mine and other people's.... What has become of it all? Listen, I beg you! I was carried away by indignation and have said a lot of nasty things to you, but I apologize. You must hate me, I know, but if you are capable of sympathy, put yourself in my position! I implore you to give me back the things!"

"H'm!" said Pasha, and she shrugged her shoulders. "I would with pleasure, but, God is my witness, he never made me a present of anything. Believe me, on my conscience. However, you are right, though," said the singer in confusion, "he did bring me two little things. Certainly I will give them back, if you wish it."

Pasha pulled out one of the drawers in the toilet-table and took out of it a hollow gold bracelet and a thin ring with a ruby in it. "Here, madam!" she said, handing the visitor these articles.

The lady flushed and her face quivered. She was offended.

"What are you giving me?" she said. "I am not asking for charity, but for what does not belong to you ... what you have taken advantage of your position to squeeze out of my husband ... that weak, unhappy man.... On Thursday, when I saw you with my husband at the harbor you were wearing expensive brooches and bracelets. So it's no use your playing the innocent lamb to me! I ask you for the last time: will you give me the things, or not?"

"You are a queer one, upon my word," said Pasha, beginning to feel offended. "I assure you that, except the bracelet and this little ring, I've never seen a thing from your Nikolay Petrovitch. He brings me nothing but sweet cakes."

"Sweet cakes!" laughed the stranger. "At home the children have nothing to eat, and here you have sweet cakes. You absolutely refuse to restore the presents?"

Receiving no answer, the lady sat down and stared into space, pondering.

"What's to be done now?" she said. "If I don't get nine hundred roubles, he is ruined, and the children and I are ruined, too. Shall I kill this low woman or go down on my knees to her?"

The lady pressed her handkerchief to her face and broke into sobs.

"I beg you!" Pasha heard through the stranger's sobs. "You see you have plundered and ruined my husband. Save him.... You have no feeling for him, but the children ... the children.... What have the children done?"

Pasha imagined little children standing in the street, crying with hunger, and she, too, sobbed.

"What can I do, madam?" she said. "You say that I am a low woman and that I have ruined Nikolay Petrovitch, and I assure you ... before God Almighty, I have had nothing from him whatever.... There is only one girl in our chorus who has a rich admirer; all the rest of us live from hand to mouth on bread and kvass. Nikolay Petrovitch is a highly educated, refined gentleman, so I've made him welcome. We are bound to make gentlemen welcome."

"I ask you for the things! Give me the things! I am crying ... I am humiliating myself.... If you like I will go down on my knees! If you wish it!"

Pasha shrieked with horror and waved her hands. She felt that this pale, beautiful lady who expressed herself so grandly, as though she were on the stage, really might go down on her knees to her, simply from pride, from grandeur, to exalt herself and humiliate the chorus girl.

"Very well, I will give you things!" said Pasha, wiping her eyes and bustling about. "By all means. Only they are not from Nikolay Petrovitch.... I got these from other gentlemen. As you please...."

Pasha pulled out the upper drawer of the chest, took out a diamond brooch, a coral necklace, some rings and bracelets, and gave them all to the lady.

"Take them if you like, only I've never had anything from your husband. Take them and grow rich," Pasha went on, offended at the threat to go down on her knees. "And if you are a lady ... his lawful wife, you should keep him to yourself. I should think so! I did not ask him to come; he came of himself."

Through her tears the lady scrutinized the articles given her and said:

"This isn't everything.... There won't be five hundred roubles' worth here."

Pasha impulsively flung out of the chest a gold watch, a cigar-case and studs, and said, flinging up her hands:

"I've nothing else left.... You can search!"

The visitor gave a sigh, with trembling hands twisted the things up in her handkerchief, and went out without uttering a word, without even nodding her head.

The door from the next room opened and Kolpakov walked in. He was pale and kept shaking his head nervously, as though he had swallowed something very bitter; tears were glistening in his eyes.

"What presents did you make me?" Pasha asked, pouncing upon him. "When did you, allow me to ask you?"

"Presents ... that's no matter!" said Kolpakov, and he tossed his head. "My God! She cried before you, she humbled herself ..."

"I am asking you, what presents did you make me!" Pasha cried.

"My God! She, a lady, so proud, so pure.... She was ready to go down on her knees to ... to this wench! And I've brought her to this! I've allowed it!"

He clutched his head in his hands and moaned.

"No, I shall never forgive myself for this! I shall never forgive myself! Get away from me ... you low creature!" he cried with repulsion, backing away from Pasha, and thrusting her off with trembling hands. "She would have gone down on her knees, and ... and to you! Oh, my God!"

Pasha lay down, and began wailing aloud. She was already regretting her things which she had given away so impulsively, and her feelings were hurt. She remembered how three years ago a merchant had beaten her for no sort of reason, and she wailed more loudly than ever.

Sinclair Ross

A FIELD OF WHEAT

IT WAS THE BEST crop of wheat that John had ever grown; sturdy, higher than the knee, the heads long and filling well; a still, heat-hushed mile of it, undulating into a shimmer of summer-colts and crushed horizon blue. Martha finished pulling the little patch of mustard that John had told her about at noon, stood a minute with her shoulders strained back to ease the muscles that were sore from bending, then bunched up her apron filled with the yellow-blossomed weeds and started towards the road. She walked carefully, placing her feet edgeways between the rows of wheat to avoid trampling and crushing the stalks. The road was only a few rods distant, but several times she stopped before reaching it, holding her apron with one hand and with the other stroking the blades of grain that pressed close against her skirts, luxuriant and tall. Once she looked back, her eyes shaded, across the wheat to the dark fallow land beside it. John was there; she could see the long, slow-settling plume of dust thrown up by the horses and the harrow-cart. He was a fool for work, John. This year he was farming the whole section of land without help, managing with two outfits of horses, one for the morning and one for the afternoon; six, and sometimes even seven hours a shift.

It was John who gave such allure to the wheat. She thought of him hunched black and sweaty on the harrow-cart, twelve hours a day, smothering in dust, shoulders sagged wearily beneath the glare of sun. Her fingers touched the stalks of grain again and tightened on a supple blade until they made it squeak like a mouse. A crop like this was coming to him. He had had his share of failures and set-backs, if ever a man had, twenty times over.

Martha was thirty-seven. She had clinched with the body and substance of life; had loved, borne children—a boy had died—and yet the quickest aches of life, travail, heartbrokenness, they had never wrung as the wheat wrung. For the wheat allowed no respite. Wasting and unending it was struggle, struggle against wind and insects, drought and weeds. Not an heroic struggle to give a man courage and resolve, but a frantic, unavailing one. They were only poor, taunted, driven things; it was the wheat that was invincible. They only dreaded, built bright futures; waited for the first glint of green, watched timorous and eager while it thickened, merged, and at last leaned bravely to a ripple in the wind; then followed every slip of cloud into the horizon, turned to the wheat and away again. And it died tantalizingly sometimes, slowly: there would be a cool day, a pittance of rain.

Or perhaps it lived, perhaps the rain came, June, July, even into August, hope climbing, wish-patterns painted on the future. And then one day a clench and tremble to John's hand; his voice faltering, dull. Grasshoppers perhaps, sawflies or rust; no matter, they would grovel for a while, stand back helpless, then go on again. Go on in bitterness and cowardice, because there was nothing else but going-on.

She had loved John, for these sixteen years had stood close watching while he died—slowly, tantalizingly, as the parched wheat died. He had grown unkempt, ugly, morose. His voice was gruff, contentious, never broke into the deep, strong laughter that used to make her feel she was living at the heart of things. John was gone, love was gone; there was only wheat.

She plucked a blade; her eyes travelled hungrily up and down the field. Serene now, all its sting and torment sheathed. Beautiful, more beautiful than Annabelle's poppies, than her sunsets. Theirs—all of it. Three hundred acres ready to give perhaps a little of what it had taken from her—John, his love, his lips unclenched.

Three hundred acres. Bushels, thousands of bushels, she wouldn't even try to think how many. And prices up this year. It would make him young again, lift his head, give him spirit. Maybe he would shave twice a week as he used to when they were first married, buy new clothes, believe in himself again.

She walked down the road towards the house, her steps quickening to the pace of her thoughts until the sweat clung to her face like little beads of oil. It was the children now, Joe and Annabelle: this winter perhaps they could send them to school in town and let them take music lessons. Annabelle, anyway. At a pinch Joe could wait a while; he was only eight. It wouldn't take Annabelle long to pick up her notes; already she played hymn tunes by ear on the organ. She was bright, a real little lady for manners; among town people she would learn a lot. The farm was no place to bring her up. Running wild and barefoot, what would she be like in a few years? Who would ever want to marry her but some stupid country lout?

John had never been to school himself; he knew what it meant to go through life with nothing but his muscles to depend upon; and that was it, dread that Annabelle and Joe would be handicapped as he was, that was what had darkened him, made him harsh and dour. That was why he breasted the sun and dust a frantic, dogged fool, to spare them, to help them to a life that offered more than sweat and debts. Martha knew. He was a slow, inarticulate man, but she knew. Sometimes it even vexed her, brought a wrinkle of jealousy, his anxiety about the children, his sense of responsibility where they were concerned. He never seemed to feel that he owed her anything, never worried about her future. She could sweat, grow flat-footed and shapeless, but that never bothered him.

Her thoughts were on their old, trudging way, the way they always went; but then she halted suddenly, and with her eyes across the wheat again found freshening promise in its quiet expanse. The children must come first, but she and John—mightn't there be a little of life left for them too? A man was young at thirty-nine. And if she didn't have to work so hard, if she could get some new clothes, maybe some of the creams and things that other women had....

As she passed through the gate, Annabelle raced across the yard to meet her. "Do you know what Joe's done? He's taken off all his clothes and he's in the trough with Nipper!" She was a lanky girl, sunburned, barefoot, her face oval and regular, but spoiled by an expression that strained her mouth and brows into a reproachful primness. It was Martha who had taught her the expression, dinning manners and politeness into her, trying to make her better than the other little girls who went to the country school. She went on, her eyes wide and aghast, "And when I told him to come out he stood right up, all bare, and I had to come away."

"Well, you tell him he'd better be out before I get there."

"But how can I tell him? He's all bare."

Then Joe ran up, nothing on but little cotton knee-pants, strings of green scum from the water-trough still sticking to his face and arms. "She's been peekin'." He pointed at Annabelle. "Nipper and me just got into the trough to get cooled off, and she wouldn't mind her own business."

"Don't you tell lies about me." Annabelle pounced on him and slapped his bare back. "You're just a dirty little pig anyway, and the horses don't want to drink after you've been in the trough."

Joe squealed, and excited by the scuffle Nipper yelped and spattered Martha with a spray of water from his coat and tail. She reached out to cuff him, missed, and then to satisfy the itch in her fingers seized Joe and boxed his ears. "You put your shirt on and then go and pick peas for supper. Hurry now, both of you, and only the fat ones, mind. No, not you, Annabelle." There was something about Annabelle's face, burned and countrified, that changed Martha's mind. "You shell the peas when he gets them. You're in the sun too much as it is."

"But I've got a poppy out and if he goes to the garden by himself he'll pick it—just for spite." Annabelle spun round, and leaving the perplexity in her voice behind her, bolted for the garden. The next minute, before Martha had even reached the house, she was back again triumphant, a big fringed pink and purple poppy in her hand. Sitting down on the doorstep to admire the gaudy petals, she complained to herself, "They go so fast—the first little winds blow them all away." On her face, lengthening it, was bitten deeply the enigma of the flowers and the naked seed-pods. Why did the beauty flash and the bony stalks remain?

Martha had clothes to iron, and biscuits to bake for supper; Annabelle and Joe quarrelled about the peas until she shelled them herself. It was hot—heat so intense and breathless that it weighed like a solid. An ominous darkness came with it, gradual and unnoticed. All at once she turned away from the stove and stood strained, inert. The silence seemed to gather itself, hold its breath. She tried to speak to Nipper and the children, all three sprawled in a heap alongside the house, but the hush over everything was like a raised finger, forbidding her.

A long immobile minute; suddenly a bewildering awareness that the light was choked; and then, muffled, still distant, but charged with resolution, climaxing the stillness, a slow, long brooding heave of thunder.

Martha darted to the door, stumbled down the step and around the corner of the house. To the west there was no sky, only a gulf of blackness, so black that the landscape seemed slipping down the neck of a funnel. Above, almost overhead, a heavy, hard-lined bank of cloud swept its way across the sun-white blue in august, impassive fury.

"Annabelle!" She wanted to scream a warning, but it was a bare whisper. In front of her the blackness split—an abrupt, unforked gash of light as if angry hands had snatched to seal the rent.

"Annabelle! Quick—inside—!" Deep in the funnel shaggy thunder rolled, emerged and shook itself, then with hurtling strides leaped up to drum and burst itself on the advancing peak of cloud.

"Joe, come back here!" He was off in pursuit of Nipper, who had broken away from Annabelle when she tried to pull him into the house. "Before I warm you!"

Her voice broke. She stared into the blackness. There it was—the hail again—the same white twisting little cloud against the black one—just as she had seen it four years ago.

She craned her neck, looking to see whether John was coming. The wheat, the acres and acres of it, green and tall, if only he had put some insurance on it. Damned mule—just work and work. No head himself and too stubborn to listen to anyone else.

There was a swift gust of wind, thunder in a splintering avalanche, the ragged hail-cloud low and close. She wheeled, with a push sent Annabelle toppling into the house, and then ran to the stable to throw open the big doors. John would turn the horses loose—surely he would. She put a brace against one of the doors, and bashed the end into the ground with her foot. Surely—but he was a fool—such a fool at times. It would be just like him to risk a runaway for the sake of getting to the end of the field.

The first big drops of rain were spitting at her before she reached the house. Quietly, breathing hard, she closed the door, numb for a minute, afraid to think or move. At the other side of the kitchen Annabelle was tussling with Joe, trying to make him go down cellar with her. Frightened a little by her mother's excitement, but not really able to grasp the imminence of danger, she was set on exploiting the event; and to be compelled to seize her little brother and carry him down cellar struck her imagination as a superb way of crystallizing for all time the dreadfulness of the storm and her own dramatic part in it. But Martha shouted at her hoarsely, "Go and get pillows. Here, Joe, quick, up on the table." She snatched him off his feet and set him on the table beside the window.

"Be ready now when the hail starts, to hold the pillow tight against the glass. You, Annabelle, stay upstairs at the west window in my room."

The horses were coming, all six at a break-neck gallop, terrified by the thunder and the whip stripes John had given them when he turned them loose. They swept past the house, shaking the earth, their harness jangling tinny against the brattle of thunder, and collided headlong at the stable door.

John, too; through Joe's legs Martha caught sight of his long, scarecrow shape stooped low before the rain. Distractedly, without purpose, she ran upstairs two steps at a time to Annabelle. "Don't be scared, here comes your father!" Her own voice shook, craven. "Why don't you rest your arms? It hasn't started yet."

As she spoke there was a sharp, crunching blow on the roof, its sound abruptly dead, sickening, like a weapon that has sunk deep into flesh. Wildly she shook her hands, motioning Annabelle back to the window, and started for the stairs. Again the blow came; then swiftly a stuttered dozen of them.

She reached the kitchen just as John burst in. With their eyes screwed up against the pommelling roar of the hail they stared at each other. They were deafened, pinioned, crushed. His face was a livid blank, one cheek smeared with blood where a jagged stone had struck him. Taut with fear, her throat aching, she turned away and looked through Joe's legs again. It was like a furious fountain, the stones bouncing high and clashing with those behind them. They had buried the earth, blotted out the horizon; there was nothing but their crazy spew of whiteness. She cowered away, put her hands to her ears.

Then the window broke, and Joe and the pillow tumbled off the table before the howling inrush of the storm. The stones clattered on the floor and bounded up to the ceiling, lit on the stove and threw out sizzling steam. The wind whisked pots and kettles off their hooks, tugged at and whirled the sodden curtains, crashed down a shelf of lamps and crockery. John pushed Martha and Joe into the next room and shut the door. There they found Annabelle huddled at the foot of the stairs, round-eyed, biting her nails in terror. The window she had been holding was broken too; and she had run away without closing the bedroom door, leaving a wild tide of wind upstairs to rage unchecked. It was rocking the whole house, straining at the walls. Martha ran up to close the door, and came down whimpering.

There was hail heaped on the bed, the pictures were blown off the walls and broken, the floor was swimming; the water would soak through and spoil all the ceilings.

John's face quietened her. They all crowded together, silent, averting their eyes from one another. Martha wanted to cry again, but dared not. Joe, awed to calmness, kept looking furtively at the trickle of blood on his father's face. Annabelle's eyes went wide and glassy as suddenly she began to wonder about Nipper. In the excitement and terror of the storm they had all forgotten him.

When at last they could go outside they stumbled over his body on the step. He had run away from Joe before the storm started, crawled back to the house when he saw John go in, and crouching down against the door had been beaten lifeless. Martha held back the children, while John picked up the mangled heap and hurried away with it to the stable.

Neither Joe nor Annabelle cried. It was too annihilating, too much like a blow. They clung tightly to Martha's skirts, staring across the flayed yard and garden. The sun came out, sharp and brilliant on the drifts of hail. There was an icy wind that made them shiver in their thin cotton clothes. "No, it's too cold on your feet." Martha motioned them back to the step as she started towards the gate to join John. "I want to go with your father to look at the wheat. There's nothing anyway to see."

Nothing but the glitter of sun on hailstones. Nothing but their wheat crushed into little rags of muddy slime. Here and there an isolated straw standing bolt upright in headless defiance. Martha and John walked to the far end of the field. There was no sound but their shoes slipping and rattling on the pebbles of ice. Both of them wanted to speak, to break the atmosphere of calamity that hung over them, but the words they could find were too small for the sparkling serenity of wasted field. Even as waste it was indomitable. It tethered them to itself, so that they could not feel or comprehend. It had come and gone, that was all; before its tremendousness and havoc they were prostrate. They had not yet risen to cry out or protest.

It was when they were nearly back to the house that Martha started to whimper. "I can't go on any longer; I can't, John. There's no use, we've tried." With one hand she clutched him and with the other held her apron to her mouth. "It's driving me out of my mind. I'm so tired—heart-sick of it all. Can't you see?"

He laid his big hands on her shoulders. They looked at each other for a few seconds, then she dropped her head weakly against his greasy smock. Presently he roused her. "Here come Joe and Annabelle!" The pressure of his hands tightened. His bristly cheek touched her hair and forehead. "Straighten up, quick, before they see you!"

It was more of him than she had had for years. "Yes, John, I know—I'm all right now." There was a wistful little pull in her voice as if she would have had him hold her there, but hurriedly instead she began to dry her eyes with her apron. "And tell Joe you'll get him another dog."

Then he left her and she went back to the house. Mounting within her was a resolve, a bravery. It was the warming sunlight, the strength and nearness of John, a feeling of mattering, belonging. Swung far upwards by the rush and swell of recaptured life, she was suddenly as far above the desolation of the storm as a little while ago she had been abject before it. But in the house she was alone; there was no sunlight, only a cold wind through the broken window; and she crumpled again.

She tried to face the kitchen, to get the floor dried and the broken lamps swept up. But it was not the kitchen; it was tomorrow, next week, next year. The going on, the waste of life, the hopelessness.

Her hands fought the broom a moment, twisting the handle as if trying to unscrew the rusted cap of a jar; then abruptly she let it fall and strode outside. All very fine for John: he'd talk about education for Joe and Annabelle, and she could worry where the clothes were to come from so that they could go clean and decent even to the country school. It made no difference that she had wanted to take out hail insurance. He was the one that looked after things. She was just his wife; it wasn't for her to open her mouth. He'd pat her shoulder and let her come back to this. They'd be brave, go on again, forget about the crop. Go on, go on—next year and the next— go on till they were both ready for the scrapheap. But she'd had enough. This time he'd go on alone.

Not that she meant it. Not that she failed to understand what John was going through. It was just rebellion. Rebellion because their wheat was beaten to the ground, because there was this brutal, callous finish to everything she had planned, because she had will and needs and flesh, because she was alive. Rebellion, not John at all—but how rebel against a summer storm, how find the throat of a cloud?

So at a jerky little run she set off for the stable, for John. Just that she might release and spend herself, no matter against whom or what, unloose the fury that clawed within her, strike back a blow for the one that had flattened her.

The stable was quiet, only the push of hay as the horses nosed through the mangers, the lazy rub of their flanks and hips against the stall partitions; and before its quietness her anger subsided, took time for breath. She advanced slowly, almost on tiptoe, peering past the horses' rumps for a glimpse of John. To the last stall, back again. And then there was a sound different from the stable sounds. She paused.

She had not seen him the first time she passed because he was pressed against one of the horses, his head pushed into the big deep hollow of its neck and shoulder, one hand hooked by the fingers in the mane, his own shoulders drawn up and shaking. She stared, thrust out her head incredulously, moved her lips, but stood silent. John sobbing there, against the horse. It was the strangest, most frightening moment of her life. He had always been so strong and grim; had just kept on as if he couldn't feel, as if there were a bull's hide over him, and now he was beaten.

She crept away. It would be unbearable to watch his humiliation if he looked up and saw her. Joe was wandering about the yard, thinking about Nipper and disconsolately sucking hailstones, but she fled past him, head down, stricken with guilty shame as if it were she who had been caught broken and afraid.

He had always been so strong, a brute at times in his strength, and now—

Now—why now that it had come to this, he might never be able to get a grip on himself again. He might not want to keep on working, not if he were really beaten. If he lost heart, if he didn't care about Joe and Annabelle any more. Weeds and pests, drought and hail—it took so much fight for a man to hold his own against them all, just to hold his own, let alone make headway.

"Look at the sky!" It was Annabelle again, breathless and ecstatic. "The far one—look how it's opened like a fan!"

Withdrawn now in the eastern sky the storm clouds towered, gold-capped and flushed in the late sunlight, high still pyramids of snowiness and shadow. And one that Annabelle pointed to, apart, the farthest away of them all, this one in bronzed slow splendour spread up mountains high to a vast plateau-like summit.

Martha hurried inside. She started the fire again, then nailed a blanket over the broken window and lit the big brass parlour lamp—the only one the storm had spared. Her hands were quick and tense. John would need a good supper tonight. The biscuits were water-soaked, but she still had the peas. He liked peas. Lucky that they had picked them when they did. This winter they wouldn't have so much as an onion or potato.

SEEING IS BELIEVING

/a/

'WHY DON'T YOU JUST DO IT,' he said, 'and be done with it. Beginning, middle, end—the way stories have always been made. Go ahead, write.'

'It's so boring,' she muttered.

'It certainly isn't as boring as writing about writing.'

'I never said I wanted to write about writing.'

'Look,' he said, trying to be helpful, 'it's the way people live, in sequence, they meet and something doesn't happen and then they look at each other again or meet again and something does happen—somewhere in time, though maybe not connected, and that's a beginning and out of that happens a middle and maybe even an—'

'Dear god,' she groaned, 'it's so dull!'

'Damn it, why write at all then?'

'What else is there that's better?' she said.

/b/

Once upon a time in a land not too far away there lived a young maiden. She was intelligent and beautiful as maidens invariably are, and of course she was very unhappy. You see, her father who adored her had died while she was but a child and her stunningly beautiful though not particularly bright mother, not able to cope with the large estate her husband left her, quickly re-married. Her new husband, so considerate and courteous in courtship, turned out to be a clever brute on the make who blatantly favoured his twin sons from a previous marriage. Very soon the mother, worn out by cares in the usual patient suffering fashion, and with only slightly worse timing than intelligence, died.

It seems hardly necessary to elaborate on the fate of our heroine. Her twin step-brothers noticed her only to tease and, as they grew older, to chase her screaming around the great house. Her step-father was too occupied enlarging his enormous estate to notice anything; he simply kicked her aside when she got in his way. By the time she turned ten she was strong enough to be useful, and so she was sent to work in the barns. She carried hay and oats and water all day long to the one hundred horses stabled there, and after feeding she had to clean the aisles and gutters because of course the more those strong, beautiful animals ate, the more manure there was to shovel. Often she was so exhausted that she fell asleep on the straw in an empty stall, and one day her step-father noticed and said she might as well live there; it would save her time and probably be better for the horses. So she took her blanket and the picture of her father, which was all she owned, and cleared a small space for herself in the loft behind the hay bales. Soon she smelled so much like the stables that her step-brothers called her Barney.

As she grew older, she learned how to groom the horses as well, but of course she was never allowed to ride one. That was reserved for her step-father and step-brothers only. Every day at ten fifteen the brothers would walk into the stables in their beautiful riding costumes, smelling like Brut or Igor, and parade down the aisle poor Barney had laboured to clean, deciding which horses they would ride. Every day.

Until one spring morning. As Barney led out their mounts, the soft sunlight flickered a particular aura about her there between the shining horses against the dark opening of the barn. The twins broke off their usual banter, and stared. Silently Barney held out the reins to them, but they did not move. It seemed they were both seeing her for the very first time.

/c/

'De-constructionists are not smart-ass, you ninny,' she said. 'They are parodic, they are trying to break down our conventional understanding of language and rebuil—'

'All language is convention, what the hell else can it be? Look, it's the one, greatest cooperative venture known to humanity, without it—'

'Aren't there a few other «cooperative ventures»!'

'Silly, I mean on such a massive scale, see, we both agree this thing is called «bed», everybody who speaks English, maybe a billion people or so agree, this is «bed», otherwise—'

'They won't ever call it «bad», not «bed», «bad»?'

'Oh, some of them will have a poor accent, sure, a small handicap but we all know what they really mean, they're just not quite able to—'

'What if I know better, I can hear exactly what I'm saying and I say it that way because I mean it, this is not «bed», it's «bad».'

'That's de-constructionist all right,' he said, 'it probably started because they're all foreigners and can't talk properly anyway and that gave them the idea, probably Frenchmen or Marxists.'

/d/

In the high glass and concrete departure area of an airport echoing with arrivals and leavings, with persons repeatedly paged but apparently never appearing to lift receivers and to be heard by an ear waiting for a voice, somewhere, there was a small circle of people. If they had faced outward they would have resembled muskoxen of the Arctic islands backed around young to confront enemies, but these faced in upon themselves: they were bending gradually closer and closer together, intent only upon the slowly tightening sphere they made. It could have been a family, a mother, a son, several daughters, a father. Between the slabs of echoing glass a film of quiet gathered about them, it might have been that the father or a daughter was leaving. Certainly none of them had the worn, devastated skin of someone recently hurled for hours near the edges of space. Perhaps the son was leaving, or a daughter and they were vainly trying one last time to look into each other's eyes, to see as they never had all of themselves at the same instant while their hands and arms groped around and beyond the person pressed against them for the next, trying to feel every bone in every individual body they suddenly knew they loved with an overwhelming conviction into the very cell circle and absolute affirmation of their own fingers meeting to clutch themselves. It seemed they should really be hollow globes, inside and outside every one of each other, to be touching each other completely at every surface in the desperate singing of all the pullulating nerves they had discovered within themselves, everywhere. Perhaps the mother was leaving.

/e/

'Will you write me a letter every day?'

'Then I'd have time for nothing but to write you letters.'

'Really?'

'A good letter, yes.'

'That would be lovely. You're a superb writer, but you've never written me an all-day letter.'

'I will write you an all-day letter, the most perfect letter possible. Immediately, I will send it to you special delivery, Express as they say, and every day you'll read it all day and it will tell you everything you want to know of me and of you and about us, it will be a letter you can read forever and never grow tired of, absolutely satisfying whenever you so much as glance at it, you could wear out the paper reading it so you better put it under glass and never touch it again until your looking wears it out, wears the letters right off the paper through glass, I will type it perfectly on an electric typewriter on hard, white paper and you can read it forever and it will—'

'What will it say, tell me, this perfect letter?'

'Have you put it under glass?'

'Yes, of course, my eyes are wearing it out. What?'

'It will say, a b c d f g h i j k l m n o p q r s t u v w x y z. And I'll sign it, perfectly.'

'Every day I should read that?'

'Yes, perfectly complete, just arrange it, whatever you want it to say.'

'I guess that's all carpenters do too, arrange lumber, or potters mud or painters paint—'

'Every day I want to say exactly what you want me to say—isn't that good? The perfect letter.'

'I couldn't even make the word «love» in your letter.'

'Why couldn't you?'

'You left out the «e».'

'What?'

'You didn't say «e».'

She hesitated a moment, then she said, 'You noticed that?'

'Yes.'

'Actually,' she said, 'I did say it, I was talking fast and I said «a b c deef.» I just ran it together a little, that's all.'

'There isn't much of a letter you can make out of the lumber of the English alphabet if you don't have an «e».'

'You're not listening to me.'

'I am, and you didn't say it; if you had written out what you said, you'd have no argument. No «please», no «remember», or «beauty, sweetheart» ... «we» ... «love» ...'

'There's a lot of useable four letter words,' she said, 'without «e»s.'

'There is only *one* four letter word.'

'Yes,' she said, '«mama».'

'No. There is only *one* four letter word and I've never liked the smell of it. It stinks.'

'«Gold»?' she asked.

He would not answer. After a moment she spoke again, 'Could you write me a love letter without an «e»?'

He spoke then, very carefully, 'I-would-not-want-to-try.'

/f/

It was so dark they could not see each other's faces when the hunters finally heard the beaver coming. The sound of the creek running over stones played back to them from the cliffs in an endless lullaby and

they stood still as trees against the willows, their
shapes gone now from dark into darkness. They had
been waiting so long for that quiet splash, that
imperceptible breaking of surface in the pond before
them that at first they could not recognize the sound
for anything it might be: it seemed merely ... noise
... coming over the narrow water before them from
the sand bar overgrown with willows, a small racket
as if something was being dragged through willows
and alder brush, an ever louder bumping between
bushes. And nattering, like old workers trudging to
the job and already anticipating a weekend. And then
there fell into the indecipherable black sheet of water
before them such a clumsy ... plop! ... one seeming
bellyflop and then another, that the hunters nudged
each other in astonishment, the very turns of their
heads in the darkness betraying their utter incom-
prehension: these were the secret beaver they had
never seen, whose dams measured and tiered the
creek in steps between every bend and rapid where
each fall weekend revealed more poplars devastated
like wheatstraw, mown down and hurled against those
still, temporarily standing? The hunters strained to
see, still touching each other for fear one or the other
would make a sound, they tilted forward into the
darkness, and then they saw upon the invisible,
suddenly silent water a string of starlight slowly being
drawn.

'Okay, there,' one of them breathed.

A click, the black-green water surfaced in one spot
of brilliant light. A beaver head there, a small blotch
quickly turning and gone, the larger hump of back
and tail flipping, Smack!, into a roil of water and gone,
the hunters cursing each other almost aloud but
unable to finish an oath before the head again surfaced, the light centred on it, and there was a tre-

mendous CRASH. The cliffs hammered it back against
their heads like clubs and the water exploded, seemed
to smash in pieces out of the yellow light. And then
again, an instant too late, another crash, smashing
the pieces further into pieces.

'Shit!'

'Did you get the bugger?'

'Sure as hell you didn't!'

'Well I—'

'Sh-h-h . . .' the boy with the light hissed.

A head again; nose circling high out of the broken
water. Was it the other one stupidly searching in the
relentless light to smell its way into discovery, breath
invisibility there?

The tremendous crashes this time were simultane-
ous and so overwhelming that only a clanging hammered in the hunters' heads, on and on, while the
light wavered, searching over the pond. Gradually the
sound of the rapids returned through iron to its gentle
insistence. But there was nothing on the surface of
the water. Only a dark green glister, and then white
bits moving, it could have been autumn leaves; or
bone.

/g/

'What were you doing the day I turned sixteen?'

'I wasn't born yet.'

'So what were you doing, November sixteen?'

'I was with my mother. Looking at a van Gogh
exhibition.'

'In Canada? Where—Montreal?'

'No, Esterhazy, Saskatchewan—or maybe it was
Cereal, Alberta.'

'A van Gogh exhibition in Esterhazy or Cereal?'

'Why not? They'd never had one there before.'

'I suppose not.'

'It was the first and only van Gogh exhibition to ever travel to North America and the paintings were hung at three-foot intervals all around the school gym, just at eye level, all those thick blazing golden Arles vineyards and bridges and canals and purple wheeling nights and thick corn fields, they made the gymnasium stinking of basketball and wrestling mats burn with rainbows, I was swimming in rainbow fire, turning somersaults like a porpoise in the Gulf Stream.'

'Your mother really liked it.'

'Not really. It just gave her a gut ache.'

/h/

Barney, still holding the horses' bridles, looked from one brother to the other in similar amazement. Slowly she understood that, in their own peculiar way, the twins were as beautiful as any horses she had ever seen. Their very twinishness was like a mirror, doubling the seeing of them with tiny, charming particularities.

'Hey,' one of them laughed at last, it was Astor who had a small dusting of beard, 'why don't you ... come ride with us?'

'Yes,' Charles laughed also, 'please do.'

'I've never ridden,' Barney said, even more amazed. 'I wouldn't know how.'

'We'll teach you,' the twins said together, but they really did not have to. The bodies of horses were so familiar to Barney that when she at last mounted one, she felt with her legs what she had already always known with the rest of her body. So they rode all day, and if the estate had not been so enormous they certainly would have discovered every corner of it. They rode about in silent happiness: only occasionally would their glances meet and one or the other would suddenly laugh and break into a gallop or jump across a creek or a fence, and the other two would instantly follow. The sun was almost down before they noticed that their horses were exhausted and that they themselves were hungry.

'Come to the house for tea,' Charles said.

'Yes,' Astor laughed, 'please do.'

So after they had rubbed down the horses together, they went up into the house. In the rose arbour opening off the library, they were served tea. Through the glass doors Barney could see the room she remembered better than any other of the house she had once lived in: the foldy leather chairs, the globes and maps, books scattered and stacked, the dark bookshelves to the ceiling; it was almost as if she could smell her father's pipe, the faint sweetness of it. Then she realized that the twins had bent towards her; that each was holding one of her hands!

'Let's get married,' they both exclaimed together, laughing.

Barney was puzzled. 'Which one?' she said.

'It doesn't matter,' Astor said, and Charles finished his thought, 'Not even father can tell us apart—one day Astor has the beard and the next day I do.'

'We're both exactly the same,' Astor said, 'you want to see?'

And indeed, Charles and Astor were as alike as two roses. Then they all three put their arms around each other in the rose arbour and laughed and laughed.

'It would be perfect,' Charles said.

'Come, marry us,' Astor echoed.

/i/

'Would you love me even if we weren't married?'

'You believe I love you now?'

'You just said so.'

'That was at least fifteen minutes ago.'

'But your actions haven't changed in fifteen minutes, they—'

'Actions are reflex, habitual, one's body is too lazy to discover new ones.'

'I believe you love me.'

'Good.'

'Would you love me still even if—'

'I don't know.'

'I know.'

'What do you know?'

'That I want to love you, married or not.'

'Good. I want to too.'

'So show me you love me. I want to see it, right now.'

'We've done everything seeable, a thousand times over, on three continents, or four.'

'Come on, lover, you're the one with the famous imagination, now come on!'

'How about ... this?'

'Nice, but no good. You did that on June 23rd, 1981.'

'I did? This too?'

'Hmm ... I don't think so ... not then, that was on October 2nd, 1976.'

'You're sure, never since then?'

'Never.'

'Aw sweetheart, there is nothing on earth so reassuring as loving a computer.'

/j/

Under the quick knife, the body of the beaver slowly revealed itself. It was a knife-point unzippering, the gradual removal of a fur coat to expose a yellowish fat nakedness.

'You ever see a seal lying on a rock?' the skinner asked. 'Maybe in a zoo somewhere?'

The woman was looking at his knife with a certain abhorrent intensity; she said nothing, and since the man did not look up, he did not see the slight shake of her head, which might in any case have been no more than a suppressed shudder.

'They're a lot longer, but they have the same kind of bloated, boneless body,' the skinner continued. 'Maybe all water animals do, probably whales too, though I've never seen one. Skinned. Their skeletons are so deep inside layers of meat and fat, they don't seem to have any bones at all to look at. Look here, two and a half inches of fat, turning my big trees into fat, the bugger.'

The woman said nothing. His left hand was clenched in the roll of greasy fur and was tearing it back under the quick, short slashes of the knife; both his hands were thick with fat and blood, she could not imagine them touching her, anywhere.

'You cut a hole in it,' she said, pointing, 'there.'

'Shit!' his hands stopped and he looked up at her, grinning.

'You're watching me too close.'

'Don't you like me watching you?'

'You're the one doesn't like it,' and he bent to his work again.

'That's just a tiny cut, not like the bullet holes. I'll stretch it out carefully and you can sew it shut with two stitches. When it's dry, no one will ever notice.'

'What makes you think I'd touch that?'

'That's woman's work, sewing ... and when it's stretched and dry you have to chew it soft too, carefully day after day just chew it, till it's all soft and we can wrap it around our feet, keep warm at night.'

'All my six years of braces to chew a dry beaver-skin?'

He laughed, 'What are beautiful teeth good for?' and did not look up to see her baring them at him. 'You'll make this softer than layered silk, you'll see, the inner fur so soft you'll ... did you ever make love on beaver fur?'

She bent her slender legs up against her breast, wrapped her arms around them. Her chin found its notch between her knees.

'I don't know,' she said slowly, 'if I could make love to a beaver.'

'That's not what I meant,' he said. 'That is not what I meant, at all.'

What was left of the beaver lay on its back; when she looked at it with half-shut eyes it seemed to be a pale, bloated torpedo tipped with two enormous yellow teeth and black flares of nostrils. Its tiny front legs, its powerful hind legs with their webbed claws dangled down like helpless afterthoughts. When she opened her eyes wide, it looked like nothing but a plastic bag of bruised fat.

/k/

'No language is translatable.'

'You're exactly wrong, the genius of language is that it is eminently translatable.'

'No, it isn't. Every language has its own systems of meaning, of reflecting what you see. If you have no past tense in a language, you cannot think about pasts.'

'That's exactly where de-constructionists so-called

become so ridiculous. They take words with fine, perfectly ordinary meanings and break them up so you can't recognize the most usual—«desiring» becomes «de-siring», a beautiful word like «ineffable» becomes an obscenity contorted into a title like «Effing the Ineffable». It's dreadful.'

'That has nothing to do with what I was saying; and aren't your examples rather tendentious?'

'So what's tendentious? These so-called writers use the accidents of phonemology to get their tendentious meanings, usually obscene, into—'

'All words are play.'

'Don't jack around too. I'm talking about phonemes, sounds, not phenomes, facts.'

'I know,' she said. 'All words are play.'

'You're being ridiculous too! Words are the way human beings handle reality. You can make a game out of eating, but if you don't eat at all, you're dead.'

'I agree. Words are the deadliest game of all.'

'See, you're at it again, jacking around with words, once you start there's no stopping. It's like when you start to look for risque shapes, soon everything longer than it is wide is phallic, everything rounded is a breast—'

'Everything with a round opening, vaginal.'

'Exactly, so take it one step further, to translations.'

'I thought we agreed, languages are not translatable.'

'We didn't agree! If that thing can be «the slipper», it can certainly be «die Pantoffel» as well.'

'It's «der».'

'What?'

'It's «der Pantoffel».'

'Okay, okay, German expert, now, you're taking a boat cruise down the Rhine and you buy a card showing the Lorelei and you write me in Canada,

«Hey lover, here I am sailing down the River Clean and we've just passed the Laurel's Egg» ... isn't that ridiculous?'

'Hey, that's pretty good.'

'It's a joke, a silly meaningless joke based on phoneme accidents!'

'Actually, I find it ironically meaningful, really, the River Clean, I'll never—'

'Oh for pete's sake!'

'I'll never see that abused river the same way again, my sweet, and who is pete, eh?'

'The old pete, I'm sure, black with a glowing red pitchfork.'

'Oh ... I thought you had a pete—r.'

'Probably, and you no doubt have a hairy!'

'Isn't she nice?'

'Oh for—'

/n/

At first they could not believe it, but the fact was that the streets of the town were so narrow between overwhelming walls of whitewashed stone that they could not walk two abreast. Then they simply laughed; if anyone met them they would have to turn past each other sideways.

But fortunately they met no one as the cobblestones, rough as if gathered from a field, led them downwards towards the centre in the gradual evening and they were so excited by this ancientness, this definite, Before Christ antiquity still being lived in in a clustered town they had glimpsed like a white-tiled splotch against a cove of the blue Mediterranean; so ecstatic at their own nerve of turning away from their planned route and leaving their car locked in the shadow of a wall and just walking (they had seen immediately there was no question of driving down this topless tunnel), leaving the technological safety of their car and just walking with nothing but their handbags (*Never* leave your money or passport anywhere) firmly tucked under their arms; neither was even wearing stockings, just a loose cotton dress for the heat, and sandals.

They met no one. Perhaps it was time for the evening meal; they could hear voices and kettles, pots through open windows too high to look into but letting in, at last, the evening coolness though they were still perspiring from the tremendous sun all day, and then turning a corner they saw people passing far below them where it seemed another street perhaps as narrow as their own crossed; but when they got there, laughing to themselves a little in anticipation, they were still alone.

'Make your photos?'

It was a moment before either realized they had been spoken to; in English. In any case, the intersection would have forced them to decide in which of five directions to face here where the cobblestones emerged out of their straight narrowness and circled about themselves. Even the untrained soles of their feet could feel that; if they had been blind, if the whole town were blind, the circled stones would tell them exactly where they were; and then the tops of their feet felt suddenly cold as if along one of the streets a breath had come up from the sea. A man was standing in the fold of one wall. And then they realized that it was he who had spoken to them. A square camera, was it actually of wood?, stared at them, its black cloth draped over his arm.

'Oh!' the shorter woman said, frightened. 'Oh ... I ...'

'It's much too dark,' the other woman said with complete technological assurance.

'No,' the man said without moving and without inflection. And indeed the lens at the centre of the wooden face seemed to flicker, it clicked precisely even as they stood turned slightly away from it, their lower bodies poised as it seemed for flight and their faces caught exposed, perhaps quite open. His left hand moved, presenting a piece of paper.

'Oh no you don't,' the other woman said. 'We're driving on immediately, we're not staying anywhere to pick up a picture tomorrow, we're not going to be pressured by some unscrupulous—'

But the paper already in her hand was the picture. She recognized herself in bright sunlight: her back, she was getting out of a taxi in front of her own suburban house and there were her three tall children running, it seemed they were running down the curved walk to greet her! She could not believe what she saw in her hand, her three children, their faces . . .

'Where's mine?' the shorter woman demanded beside her.

The man had glanced once at the picture he had taken and now he quickly shook his head. 'No,' he said, crouching back as if he would have been happy to disappear into the wall, 'it is not good, no.'

'Where's John?' the other woman said, still staring at the picture.

'You're a fake!' the shorter woman spit out, 'You're all alike, fakes trying to get money out of us, well, what do I look like in front of my house, eh, show me! Come on!'

But the picture she received did not show her. There was no person on it at all. Only the straight walk between the two birches leading to the front door of her house. There was no one there at all.

'There's just the three kids,' the other woman said, still staring.

'I did not want to take it,' the man said to the shorter woman, his face hunched painfully together; his voice so deeply gentle, almost as if he were praying the miserare.

'Where's my John!' the other woman screamed.

They stood side by side feeling the circular stones under their unwilling feet. They had not even planned to visit this town, their car was waiting for them, with one slight twist of a key it would carry them instantly, permanently away. But here they felt the stones, revelations laid before their defenseless eyes.

/o/

'Please, don't do that.'

'Sweetheart, I want to talk to you about it.'

'Why?'

'Because I like it, I want to experience more of—'

'Then why not just read it again?'

'I will, I will.'

'Readers nowadays are such meaning hounds, sniffing, sniffing after nothing but meaning, yes, I get a whiff here, there's a spoor of meaning, sniff, sniff ... if that was all there was to meaning a writer could just make one big stink and be done with it: the husband is a son of a bitch! Period!'

'It means a lot more then—okay, I'm not looking for meanings, it just *is*, okay? But ... why did you arrange the parts in the order you did?'

'I don't know.'

'Look. I don't believe that, when you write you're so careful you—'

'That's why they're labelled «a», «b», «c» etc.—you can read them in any order you please.'

'But «b» comes after «a», and «h» always before «j», so—'

'Not when you write words they don't.'

'What? Are you trying to make a word out of—'

'Read them in any order you please, only please!'

'A story has to have a pattern!'

'Not necessarily. It could be—a necklace, with various beads in a relationship to each other, that's all.'

'Then ... I don't see the string.'

'Why do you have to see it? You sense perhaps it's there, somewhere at the centre of things, but in good necklaces you never see the string, only individual beads juxtaposed. Don't be so damned logical!'

'Okay, the true beauty of a necklace is brought out when it is hung around a neck, right? So whe—'

'Right! You're the neck.'

'Me?'

'Yes you. You've read my story, you're wearing the necklace.'

'Oh. Has it ...' he hesitated, then plunged on. 'Was it, has it made me beautiful?'

'You always are,' she said, suddenly moved by a profound love. 'I don't really know, about the necklace. Maybe you don't need it.'

'But I *want* it.'

'I know. But maybe the story isn't really a necklace. Maybe it's just a ... a random scatter of beads, as spilled on a bed.'

'Not a «bad»?'

'No, bed, b-e-d, bed.'

'Of course,' he laughed. 'If you want to, right away.'

William Faulkner

THAT EVENING SUN

MONDAY IS NO DIFFERENT from any other weekday in Jefferson now. The streets are paved now, and the telephone and electric companies are cutting down more and more of the shade trees—the water oaks, the maples and locusts and elms—to make room for iron poles bearing clusters of bloated and ghostly and bloodless grapes; and we have a city laundry which makes the rounds on Monday morning, gathering the bundles of clothes into bright colored, specially-made motorcars; the soiled wearing of a whole week now flees apparition-like behind alert and irritable electric horns, with a long diminishing noise of rubber and asphalt like tearing silk, and even the Negro women who still take in white people's washing after the old custom, fetch and deliver it in automobiles.

But fifteen years ago, on Monday morning the quiet, dusty, shady streets would be full of Negro women with, balanced on their steady, turbaned heads, bundles of clothes tied up in sheets, almost as large as cotton bales, carried so without touch of hand between the kitchen door of the white house and the blackened washpot beside a cabin door in Negro Hollow.

Nancy would set her bundle on the top of her head, then upon the bundle in turn she would set the black straw sailor hat which she wore winter and summer. She was tall, with a high, sad face sunken a little where her teeth were missing. Sometimes we would go a part of the way down the lane and across the pasture with her, to watch the balanced bundle and the hat that never bobbed nor wavered, even when she walked down into the ditch and up the other side and stooped through the fence. She would go down on her hands and knees and crawl through the gap, her head rigid, uptilted, the bundle steady as a rock or a balloon, and rise to her feet again and go on.

Sometimes the husbands of the washing women would fetch and deliver the clothes, but Jesus never did that for Nancy, even before Father told him to stay away from our house, even when Dilsey was sick and Nancy would come to cook for us.

And then about half the time we'd have to go down the lane to Nancy's cabin and tell her to come on and cook breakfast. We would stop at the ditch, because Father told us not to have anything to do with Jesus—he was a short black man, with a razor scar down his face—and we would throw rocks at Nancy's house until she came to the door, leaning her head around it without any clothes on.

"What yawl mean, chunking my house?" Nancy said. "What you little devils mean?"

"Father says for you to come on and get breakfast," Caddy said. "Father says it's over a half an hour now, and you've got to come this minute."

"I ain't studying no breakfast," Nancy said. "I going to get my sleep out."

"I bet you're drunk," Jason said. "Father says you're drunk. Are you drunk, Nancy?"

"Who says I is?" Nancy said. "I got to get my sleep out. I ain't studying no breakfast."

So after a while we quit chunking the cabin and went back home. When she finally came, it was too late for me to go to school. So we thought it was whiskey until that day they arrested her again and they were taking her to jail and they passed Mr. Stovall. He was the cashier in the bank and a deacon in the Baptist church, and Nancy began to say:

"When you going to pay me, white man? When you going to pay me, white man? It's been three times now since you paid me a cent—" Mr. Stovall knocked her down, but she kept on saying, "When you going to pay me, white man? It's been three times now since—" until Mr. Stovall kicked her in the mouth with his heel and the marshal caught Mr. Stovall back, and Nancy lying in the street, laughing. She turned her head and spat out some blood and teeth and said, "It's been three times now since he paid me a cent."

That was how she lost her teeth, and all that day they told about Nancy and Mr. Stovall, and all that night the ones that passed the jail could hear Nancy singing and yelling. They could see her hands holding to the window bars, and a lot of them stopped along the fence, listening to her and to the jailer trying to make her stop. She didn't shut up until almost daylight, when the jailer began to hear a bumping and scraping upstairs and he went up there and found Nancy hanging from the window bar. He said that it was cocaine and not whiskey, because no nigger would try to commit suicide unless he was full of cocaine, because a nigger full of cocaine wasn't a nigger any longer.

The jailer cut her down and revived her; then he beat her, whipped her. She had hung herself with her dress. She had fixed it all right, but when they arrested her she didn't have on anything except a dress and so she didn't have anything to tie her hands with and she couldn't make her hands let go of the window ledge. So the jailer heard the noise and ran up there and found Nancy hanging from the window, stark naked, her belly already swelling out a little, like a little balloon.

When Dilsey was sick in her cabin and Nancy was cooking for us, we could see her apron swelling out; that was before Father told Jesus to stay away from the house. Jesus was in the kitchen, sitting behind the stove, with his razor scar on his black face like a piece of dirty string. He said it was a watermelon that Nancy had under her dress.

"It never come off of your vine, though," Nancy said.

"Off of what vine?" Caddy said.

"I can cut down the vine it did come off of," Jesus said.

"What makes you want to talk like that before these chillen?" Nancy said. "Whyn't you go on to work? You done et. You want Mr. Jason to catch you hanging around his kitchen, talking that way before these chillen?"

"Talking what way?" Caddy said. "What vine?"

"I can't hang around white man's kitchen," Jesus said. "But white man can hang around mine. White man come in my house, but I can't stop him. When white man want to come in my house, I ain't got no house. I can't stop him, but he can't kick me outen it. He can't do that."

Dilsey was still sick in her cabin. Father told Jesus to stay off our place. Dilsey was still sick. It was a long time. We were in the library after supper.

"Isn't Nancy through in the kitchen yet?" Mother

said. "It seems to me that she has had plenty of time to have finished the dishes."

"Let Quentin go and see," Father said. "Go and see if Nancy is through, Quentin. Tell her she can go on home."

I went to the kitchen. Nancy was through. The dishes were put away and the fire was out. Nancy was sitting in a chair, close to the cold stove. She looked at me.

"Mother wants to know if you are through," I said.

"Yes," Nancy said. She looked at me. "I done finished." She looked at me.

"What is it?" I said. "What is it?"

"I ain't nothing but a nigger," Nancy said. "It ain't none of my fault."

She looked at me, sitting in the chair before the cold stove, the sailor hat on her head. I went back to the library. It was the cold stove and all, when you think of a kitchen being warm and busy and cheerful. And with a cold stove and the dishes all put away, and nobody wanting to eat at that hour.

"Is she through?" Mother said.

"Yessum," I said.

"What is she doing?" Mother said.

"She's not doing anything. She's through."

"I'll go and see," Father said.

"Maybe she's waiting for Jesus to come and take her home," Caddy said.

"Jesus is gone," I said. Nancy told us how one morning she woke up and Jesus was gone.

"He quit me," Nancy said. "Done gone to Memphis, I reckon. Dodging them city po-lice for a while, I reckon."

"And a good riddance," Father said. "I hope he stays there."

"Nancy's scaired of the dark," Jason said.

"So are you," Caddy said.

"I'm not," Jason said.

"Scairy cat," Caddy said.

"I'm not," Jason said.

"You, Candace!" Mother said. Father came back.

"I am going to walk down the lane with Nancy," he said. "She says that Jesus is back."

"Has she seen him?" Mother said.

"No. Some Negro sent her word that he was back in town. I won't be long."

"You'll leave me alone, to take Nancy home?" Mother said. "Is her safety more precious to you than mine?"

"I won't be long," Father said.

"You'll leave these children unprotected, with that Negro about?"

"I'm going too," Caddy said. "Let me go, Father."

"What would he do with them, if he were unfortunate enough to have them?" Father said.

"I want to go, too," Jason said.

"Jason!" Mother said. She was speaking to Father. You could tell that by the way she said the name. Like she believed that all day Father had been trying to think of doing the thing she wouldn't like the most, and that she knew all the time that after a while he would think of it. I stayed quiet, because Father and I both knew that Mother would want him to make me stay with her if she just thought of it in time. So Father didn't look at me. I was the oldest. I was nine and Caddy was seven and Jason was five.

"Nonsense," Father said. "We won't be long."

Nancy had her hat on. We came to the lane. "Jesus always been good to me," Nancy said. "Whenever he had two dollars, one of them was mine." We walked in the lane. "If I can just get through the lane," Nancy said, "I be all right then."

The lane was always dark. "This is where Jason got scaired on Hallowe'en," Caddy said.

"I didn't," Jason said.

"Can't Aunt Rachel do anything with him?" Father said. Aunt Rachel was old. She lived in a cabin beyond Nancy's, by herself. She had white hair and she smoked a pipe in the door, all day long; she didn't work any more. They said she was Jesus' mother. Sometimes she said she was and sometimes she said she wasn't any kin to Jesus.

"Yes you did," Caddy said. "You were scairder than Frony. You were scairder than T.P. even. Scairder than niggers."

"Can't nobody do nothing with him," Nancy said. "He say I done woke up the devil in him and ain't but one thing going to lay it down again."

"Well, he's gone now," Father said. "There's nothing for you to be afraid of now. And if you'd just let white men alone."

"Let what white men alone?" Caddy said. "How let them alone?"

"He ain't gone nowhere," Nancy said. "I can feel him. I can feel him now, in this lane. He hearing us talk, every word, hid somewhere, waiting. I ain't seen him, and I ain't going to see him again but once more, with that razor in his mouth. That razor on that string down his back, inside his shirt. And then I ain't going to be even surprised."

"I wasn't scaired," Jason said.

"If you'd behave yourself, you'd have kept out of this," Father said. "But it's all right now. He's probably in Saint Louis now. Probably got another wife by now and forgot all about you."

"If he has, I better not find out about it," Nancy said. "I'd stand there right over them, and every time he wropped her, I'd cut that arm off. I'd cut his head off and slit her belly and I'd shove—"

"Hush," Father said.

"Slit whose belly, Nancy?" Caddy said.

"I wasn't scaired," Jason said. "I'd walk right down this lane by myself."

"Yah," Caddy said. "You wouldn't dare to put your foot down in it if we were not here too."

II

DILSEY WAS STILL SICK, so we took Nancy home every night until Mother said, "How much longer is this going on? I to be left alone in this big house while you take home a frightened Negro?"

We fixed a pallet in the kitchen for Nancy. One night we waked up, hearing the sound. It was not singing and it was not crying, coming up the dark stairs. There was a light in Mother's room and we heard Father going down the hall, down the back stairs, and Caddy and I went into the hall. The floor was cold. Our toes curled away from it while we listened to the sound. It was like singing and it wasn't like singing, like the sound that Negroes make.

Then it stopped and we heard Father going down the back stairs, and we went to the head of the stairs. Then the sound began again, in the stairway, not loud, and we could see Nancy's eyes halfway up the stairs, against the wall. They looked like cat's eyes do, like a big cat against the wall, watching us. When we came down the steps to where she was, she quit making the sound again, and we stood there until Father came back up from the kitchen, with his pistol in his hand. He went back down with Nancy and they came back with Nancy's pallet.

We spread the pallet in our room. After the light in Mother's room went off, we could see Nancy's eyes again. "Nancy," Caddy whispered, "are you asleep, Nancy?"

Nancy whispered something. It was oh or no, I don't know which. Like nobody had made it, like it came from nowhere and went nowhere, until it was like Nancy was not there at all; that I had looked so hard at her eyes on the stairs that they had got printed on my eyeballs, like the sun does when you have closed your eyes and there is no sun. "Jesus," Nancy whispered. "Jesus."

"Was it Jesus?" Caddy said. "Did he try to come into the kitchen?"

"Jesus," Nancy said. Like this: Jeeeeeeeeeeeeeeeee-sus, until the sound went out, like a match or a candle does.

"It's the other Jesus she means," I said.

"Can you see us, Nancy?" Caddy whispered. "Can you see our eyes too?"

"I ain't nothing but a nigger," Nancy said. "God knows. God knows."

"What did you see down there in the kitchen?" Caddy whispered. "What tried to get in?"

"God knows," Nancy said. We could see her eyes. "God knows."

Dilsey got well. She cooked dinner. "You'd better stay in bed a day or two longer," Father said.

"What for?" Dilsey said. "If I had been a day later, this place would be to rack and ruin. Get on out of here now, and let me get my kitchen straight again."

Dilsey cooked supper too. And that night, just before dark, Nancy came into the kitchen.

"How do you know he's back?" Dilsey said. "You ain't seen him."

"Jesus is a nigger," Jason said.

"I can feel him," Nancy said. "I can feel him laying yonder in the ditch."

"Tonight?" Dilsey said. "Is he there tonight?"

"Dilsey's a nigger too," Jason said.

"You try to eat something," Dilsey said.

"I don't want nothing," Jason said.

"Drink some coffee," Dilsey said. She poured a cup of coffee for Nancy. "Do you know he's out there tonight? How come you know it's tonight?"

"I know," Nancy said. "He's there, waiting. I know. I done lived with him too long. I know what he is fixing to do fore he know it himself."

"Drink some coffee," Dilsey said. Nancy held the cup to her mouth and blew into the cup. Her mouth pursed out like a spreading adder's, like a rubber mouth, like she had blown all the color out of her lips with blowing the coffee.

"I ain't a nigger," Jason said. "Are you a nigger, Nancy?"

"I hellborn, child," Nancy said. "I won't be nothing soon. I going back where I come from soon."

III

SHE BEGAN TO DRINK the coffee. While she was drinking, holding the cup in both hands, she began to make the sound again. She made the sound into the cup and the coffee sploshed out onto her hands and her dress. Her eyes looked at us and she sat there, her elbows on her knees, holding the cup in both hands, looking at us across the wet cup, making the sound.

"Look at Nancy," Jason said. "Nancy can't cook for us now. Dilsey's got well now."

"You hush up," Dilsey said. Nancy held the cup in both hands, looking at us, making the sound, like there were two of them: one looking at us and the other making the sound. "Whyn't you let Mr. Jason telefoam the marshal?" Dilsey said. Nancy stopped then, holding the cup in her long brown hands. She tried to drink some coffee again, but it sploshed out of the cup, onto her hands and her dress, and she put the cup down. Jason watched her.

"I can't swallow it," Nancy said. "I swallows but it won't go down me."

"You go down to the cabin," Dilsey said. "Frony will fix you a pallet and I'll be there soon."

"Won't no nigger stop him," Nancy said.

"I ain't a nigger," Jason said. "Am I, Dilsey?"

"I reckon not," Dilsey said. She looked at Nancy. "I don't reckon so. What you going to do, then?"

Nancy looked at us. Her eyes went fast, like she was afraid there wasn't time to look, without hardly moving at all. She looked at us, at all three of us at one time. "You member that night I stayed in yawls' room?" she said. She told about how we waked up early the next morning, and played. We had to play quiet, on her pallet, until Father woke up and it was time to get breakfast. "Go and ask your maw to let me stay here tonight," Nancy said. "I won't need no pallet. We can play some more."

Caddy asked Mother. Jason went too. "I can't have Negroes sleeping in the bedrooms," Mother said. Jason cried. He cried until Mother said he couldn't have dessert for three days if he didn't stop. Then Jason said he would stop if Dilsey would make a chocolate cake. Father was there.

"Why don't you do something about it?" Mother said. "What do we have officers for?"

"Why is Nancy afraid of Jesus?" Caddy said. "Are you afraid of Father, Mother?"

"What could the officers do?" Father said. "If Nancy hasn't seen him, how could the officers find him?"

"Then why is she afraid?" Mother said.

"She says he is there. She says she knows he is there tonight."

"Yet we pay taxes," Mother said. "I must wait here alone in this big house while you take a Negro woman home."

"You know that I am not lying outside with a razor," Father said.

"I'll stop if Dilsey will make a chocolate cake," Jason said. Mother told us to go out and Father said he didn't know if Jason would get a chocolate cake or not, but he knew what Jason was going to get in about a minute. We went back to the kitchen and told Nancy.

"Father said for you to go home and lock the door, and you'll be all right," Caddy said. "All right from what, Nancy? Is Jesus mad at you?" Nancy was holding the coffee cup in her hands again, her elbows on her knees and her hands holding the cup between her knees. She was looking into the cup. "What have you done that made Jesus mad?" Caddy said. Nancy let the cup go. It didn't break on the floor, but the coffee spilled out, and Nancy sat there with her hands still making the shape of the cup. She began to make the sound again, not loud. Not singing and not unsinging. We watched her.

"Here," Dilsey said. "You quit that, now. You get aholt of yourself. You wait here. I going to get Versh to walk home with you." Dilsey went out.

We looked at Nancy. Her shoulders kept shaking, but she quit making the sound. We watched her.

"What's Jesus going to do to you?" Caddy said. "He went away."

Nancy looked at us. "We had fun that night I stayed in yawls' room, didn't we?"

"I didn't," Jason said. "I didn't have any fun."

"You were asleep in Mother's room," Caddy said. "You were not there."

"Let's go down to my house and have some more fun," Nancy said.

"Mother won't let us," I said. "It's too late now."

"Don't bother her," Nancy said. "We can tell her in the morning. She won't mind."

"She wouldn't let us," I said.

"Don't ask her now," Nancy said. "Don't bother her now."

"She didn't say we couldn't go," Caddy said.

"We didn't ask," I said.

"If you go, I'll tell," Jason said.

"We'll have fun," Nancy said. "They won't mind, just to my house. I been working for yawl a long time. They won't mind."

"I'm not afraid to go," Caddy said. "Jason is the one that's afraid. He'll tell."

"I'm not," Jason said.

"Yes, you are," Caddy said. "You'll tell."

"I won't tell," Jason said. "I'm not afraid."

"Jason ain't afraid to go with me," Nancy said. "Is you, Jason?"

"Jason is going to tell," Caddy said. The lane was dark. We passed the pasture gate. "I bet if something was to jump out from behind that gate, Jason would holler."

"I wouldn't," Jason said. We walked down the lane. Nancy was talking loud.

"What are you talking so loud for, Nancy?" Caddy said.

"Who, me?" Nancy said. "Listen at Quentin and Caddy and Jason saying I'm talking loud."

"You talk like there was five of us here," Caddy said. "You talk like Father was here too."

"Who; me talking loud, Mr. Jason?" Nancy said.

"Nancy called Jason 'Mister,'" Caddy said.

"Listen how Caddy and Quentin and Jason talk," Nancy said.

"We're not talking loud," Caddy said. "You're the one that's talking like Father—"

"Hush," Nancy said; "hush, Mr. Jason."

"Nancy called Jason 'Mister' aguh—"

"Hush," Nancy said. She was talking loud when we crossed the ditch and stooped through the fence where she used to stoop through with the clothes on her head. Then we came to her house. We were going fast then. She opened the door. The smell of the house was like the lamp and the smell of Nancy was like the wick, like they were waiting for one another to begin to smell. She lit the lamp and closed the door and put the bar up. Then she quit talking loud, looking at us.

"What're we going to do?" Caddy said.

"What do yawl want to do?" Nancy said.

"You said we would have some fun," Caddy said.

There was something about Nancy's house; something you could smell besides Nancy and the house. Jason smelled it, even. "I don't want to stay here," he said. "I want to go home."

"Go home, then," Caddy said.

"I don't want to go by myself," Jason said.

"We're going to have some fun," Nancy said.

"How?" Caddy said.

Nancy stood by the door. She was looking at us, only it was like she had emptied her eyes, like she had quit using them. "What do you want to do?" she said.

"Tell us a story," Caddy said. "Can you tell a story?"

"Yes," Nancy said.

"Tell it," Caddy said. We looked at Nancy. "You don't know any stories."

"Yes," Nancy said. "Yes I do."

She came and sat in a chair before the hearth. There was a little fire there. Nancy built it up, when it was already hot inside. She built a good blaze. She told a story. She talked like her eyes looked, like her eyes watching us and her voice talking to us did not belong to her. Like she was living somewhere else, waiting somewhere else. She was outside the cabin. Her voice was inside and the shape of her, the Nancy that could stoop under a barbed wire fence with a bundle of clothes balanced on her head as though without weight, like a balloon, was there. But that was all. "And so this here queen come walking up to the ditch, where that bad man was hiding. She was walking up to the ditch, and she say, 'If I can just get past this here ditch,' was what she say ..."

"What ditch?" Caddy said. "A ditch like that one out there? Why did a queen want to go into a ditch?"

"To get to her house," Nancy said. She looked at us. "She had to cross the ditch to get into her house quick and bar the door."

"Why did she want to go home and bar the door?" Caddy said.

IV

NANCY LOOKED AT US. She quit talking. She looked at us. Jason's legs stuck straight out of his pants where he sat on Nancy's lap. "I don't think that's a good story," he said. "I want to go home."

"Maybe we had better," Caddy said. She got up from the floor. "I bet they are looking for us right now." She went toward the door.

"No," Nancy said. "Don't open it." She got up quick and passed Caddy. She didn't touch the door, the wooden bar.

"Why not?" Caddy said.

"Come back to the lamp," Nancy said. "We'll have fun. You don't have to go."

"We ought to go," Caddy said. "Unless we have a lot of fun." She and Nancy came back to the fire, the lamp.

"I want to go home," Jason said. "I'm going to tell."

"I know another story," Nancy said. She stood close to the lamp. She looked at Caddy, like when your eyes look up at a stick balanced on your nose. She had to look down to see Caddy, but her eyes looked like that, like when you are balancing a stick.

"I won't listen to it," Jason said. "I'll bang on the floor."

"It's a good one," Nancy said. "It's better than the other one."

"What's it about?" Caddy said. Nancy was standing by the lamp. Her hand was on the lamp, against the light, long and brown.

"Your hand is on that hot globe," Caddy said. "Don't it feel hot to your hand?"

Nancy looked at her hand on the lamp chimney. She took her hand away, slow. She stood there, looking at Caddy, wringing her long hand as though it were tied to her wrist with a string.

"Let's do something else," Caddy said.

"I want to go home," Jason said.

"I got some popcorn," Nancy said. She looked at Caddy and then at Jason and then at me and then at Caddy again. "I got some popcorn."

"I don't like popcorn," Jason said. "I'd rather have candy."

Nancy looked at Jason. "You can hold the popper."

She was still wringing her hand; it was long and limp and brown.

"All right," Jason said. "I'll stay a while if I can do that. Caddy can't hold it. I'll want to go home again if Caddy holds the popper."

Nancy built up the fire. "Look at Nancy putting her hands in the fire," Caddy said. "What's the matter with you, Nancy?"

"I got popcorn," Nancy said. "I got some." She took the popper from under the bed. It was broken. Jason began to cry.

"Now we can't have any popcorn," he said.

"We ought to go home, anyway," Caddy said. "Come on, Quentin."

"Wait," Nancy said; "wait. I can fix it. Don't you want to help me fix it?"

"I don't think I want any," Caddy said. "It's too late now."

"You help me, Jason," Nancy said. "Don't you want to help me?"

"No," Jason said. "I want to go home."

"Hush," Nancy said; "hush. Watch. Watch me. I can fix it so Jason can hold it and pop the corn." She got a piece of wire and fixed the popper.

"It won't hold good," Caddy said.

"Yes it will," Nancy said. "Yawl watch. Yawl help me shell some corn."

The popcorn was under the bed too. We shelled it into the popper and Nancy helped Jason hold the popper over the fire.

"It's not popping," Jason said. "I want to go home."

"You wait," Nancy said. "It'll begin to pop. We'll have fun then."

She was sitting close to the fire. The lamp was turned up so high it was beginning to smoke. "Why don't you turn it down some?" I said.

"It's all right," Nancy said. "I'll clean it. Yawl wait. The popcorn will start in a minute."

"I don't believe it's going to start," Caddy said. "We ought to start home, anyway. They'll be worried."

"No," Nancy said. "It's going to pop. Dilsey will tell um yawl with me. I been working for yawl long time. They won't mind if yawl at my house. You wait, now. It'll start popping any minute now."

Then Jason got some smoke in his eyes and he began to cry. He dropped the popper into the fire. Nancy got a wet rag and wiped Jason's face, but he didn't stop crying.

"Hush," she said. "Hush." But he didn't hush. Caddy took the popper out of the fire.

"It's burned up," she said. "You'll have to get some more popcorn, Nancy."

"Did you put all of it in?" Nancy said.

"Yes," Caddy said. Nancy looked at Caddy. Then she took the popper and opened it and poured the cinders into her apron and began to sort the grains, her hands long and brown, and we watching her.

"Haven't you got any more?" Caddy said.

"Yes," Nancy said; "yes. Look. This here ain't burnt. All we need to do is—"

"I want to go home," Jason said. "I'm going to tell."

"Hush," Caddy said. We all listened. Nancy's head was already turned toward the barred door, her eyes filled with red lamplight. "Somebody is coming," Caddy said.

Then Nancy began to make that sound again, not loud, sitting there above the fire, her long hands dangling between her knees; all of a sudden water began to come out on her face in big drops, running down her face, carrying in each one a little turning ball of firelight like a spark until it dropped off her chin. "She's not crying," I said.

"I ain't crying," Nancy said. Her eyes were closed. "I ain't crying. Who is it?"

"I don't know," Caddy said. She went to the door and looked out. "We've got to go now," she said. "Here comes Father."

"I'm going to tell," Jason said. "Yawl made me come."

The water still ran down Nancy's face. She turned in her chair. "Listen. Tell him. Tell him we going to have fun. Tell him I take good care of yawl until in the morning. Tell him to let me come home with yawl and sleep on the floor. Tell him I won't need no pallet. We'll have fun. You member last time how we had so much fun?"

"I didn't have fun," Jason said. "You hurt me. You put smoke in my eyes. I'm going to tell."

V

FATHER CAME IN. He looked at us. Nancy did not get up.

"Tell him," she said.

"Caddy made us come down here," Jason said. "I didn't want to."

Father came to the fire. Nancy looked up at him. "Can't you go to Aunt Rachel's and stay?" he said. Nancy looked up at Father, her hands between her knees. "He's not here," Father said. "I would have seen him. There's not a soul in sight."

"He in the ditch," Nancy said. "He waiting in the ditch yonder."

"Nonsense," Father said. He looked at Nancy. "Do you know he's there?"

"I got the sign," Nancy said.

"What sign?"

"I got it. It was on the table when I come in. It

was a hogbone, with blood meat still on it, laying by the lamp. He's out there. When yawl walk out that door, I gone."

"Gone where, Nancy?" Caddy said.

"I'm not a tattletale," Jason said.

"Nonsense," Father said.

"He out there," Nancy said. "He looking through that window this minute, waiting for yawl to go. Then I gone."

"Nonsense," Father said. "Lock up your house and we'll take you to Aunt Rachel's."

"'Twont do no good," Nancy said. She didn't look at Father now, but he looked down at her, at her long, limp, moving hands. "Putting it off won't do no good."

"Then what do you want to do?" Father said.

"I don't know," Nancy said. "I can't do nothing. Just put it off. And that don't do no good. I reckon it belong to me. I reckon what I going to get ain't no more than mine."

"Get what?" Caddy said. "What's yours?"

"Nothing," Father said. "You all must get to bed."

"Caddy made me come," Jason said.

"Go on to Aunt Rachel's," Father said.

"It won't do no good," Nancy said. She sat before the fire, her elbows on her knees, her long hands between her knees. "When even your own kitchen wouldn't do no good. When even if I was sleeping on the floor in the room with your chillen, and the next morning there I am, and blood—"

"Hush," Father said. "Lock the door and put out the lamp and go to bed."

"I scaired of the dark," Nancy said. "I scaired for it to happen in the dark."

"You mean you're going to sit right here with the lamp lighted?" Father said. Then Nancy began to make the sound again, sitting before the fire, her long hands between her knees. "Ah, damnation," Father said. "Come along, chillen. It's past bedtime."

"When yawl go home, I gone," Nancy said. She talked quieter now, and her face looked quiet, like her hands. "Anyway, I got my coffin money saved up with Mr. Lovelady." Mr. Lovelady was a short, dirty man who collected the Negro insurance, coming around to the cabins or the kitchens every Saturday morning, to collect fifteen cents. He and his wife lived at the hotel. One morning his wife committed suicide. They had a child, a little girl. He and the child went away. After a week or two he came back alone. We would see him going along the lanes and the back streets on Saturday mornings.

"Nonsense," Father said. "You'll be the first thing I'll see in the kitchen tomorrow morning."

"You'll see what you'll see, I reckon," Nancy said. "But it will take the Lord to say what that will be."

VI

WE LEFT HER sitting before the fire.

"Come and put the bar up," Father said. But she didn't move. She didn't look at us again, sitting quietly there between the lamp and the fire. From some distance down the lane we could look back and see her through the open door.

"What, Father?" Caddy said. "What's going to happen?"

"Nothing," Father said. Jason was on Father's back, so Jason was the tallest of all of us. We went down into the ditch. I looked at it, quiet. I couldn't see much where the moonlight and the shadows tangled.

"If Jesus *is* hid here, he can see us, can't he?" Caddy said.

"He's not there," Father said. "He went away a long time ago."

"You made me come," Jason said, high; against the sky it looked like Father had two heads, a little one and a big one. "I didn't want to."

We went up out of the ditch. We could still see Nancy's house and the open door, but we couldn't see Nancy now, sitting before the fire with the door open, because she was tired. "I just done got tired," she said. "I just a nigger. It ain't no fault of mine."

But we could hear her, because she began just after we came up out of the ditch, the sound that was not singing and not unsinging. "Who will do our washing now, Father?" I said.

"I'm not a nigger," Jason said, high and close above Father's head.

"You're worse," Caddy said, "you are a tattletale. If something was to jump out, you'd be scairder than a nigger."

"I wouldn't," Jason said.

"You'd cry," Caddy said.

"Caddy," Father said.

"I wouldn't!" Jason said.

"Scairy cat," Caddy said.

"Candace!" Father said.

COUNTERPARTS

THE BELL RANG FURIOUSLY and, when Miss Parker went to the tube, a furious voice called out in a piercing North of Ireland accent:

—Send Farrington here!

Miss Parker returned to her machine, saying to a man who was writing at a desk:

—Mr Alleyne wants you upstairs.

The man muttered *Blast him!* under his breath and pushed back his chair to stand up. When he stood up he was tall and of great bulk. He had a hanging face, dark wine-coloured, with fair eyebrows and moustache: his eyes bulged forward slightly and the whites of them were dirty. He lifted up the counter and, passing by the clients, went out of the office with a heavy step.

He went heavily upstairs until he came to the second landing, where a door bore a brass plate with the inscription *Mr Alleyne*. Here he halted, puffing with labour and vexation, and knocked. The shrill voice cried:

—Come in!

The man entered Mr Alleyne's room. Simultaneously Mr Alleyne, a little man wearing gold-rimmed glasses on a clean-shaven face, shot his head up over a pile of documents. The head itself was so pink and hairless that it seemed like a large egg reposing on the papers. Mr Alleyne did not lose a moment:

—Farrington? What is the meaning of this? Why have I always to complain of you? May I ask you why you haven't made a copy of that contract between Bodley and Kirwan? I told you it must be ready by four o'clock.

—But Mr Shelley said, sir—

—*Mr Shelley said, sir*.... Kindly attend to what I say and not to what *Mr Shelley says, sir*. You have always some excuse or another for shirking work. Let me tell you that if the contract is not copied before this evening I'll lay the matter before Mr Crosbie.... Do you hear me now?

—Yes, sir.

—Do you hear me now? ... Ay and another little matter! I might as well be talking to the wall as talking to you. Understand once for all that you get a half an hour for your lunch and not an hour and a half. How many courses do you want, I'd like to know.... Do you mind me, now?

—Yes, sir.

Mr Alleyne bent his head again upon his pile of papers. The man stared fixedly at the polished skull which directed the affairs of Crosbie & Alleyne, gauging its fragility. A spasm of rage gripped his throat for a few moments and then passed, leaving after it a sharp sensation of thirst. The man recognised the sensation and felt that he must have a good night's drinking. The middle of the month was passed and, if he could get the copy done in time, Mr Alleyne might give him an order on the cashier. He stood still, gazing fixedly at the head upon the pile of papers. Suddenly Mr Alleyne began to upset all the papers, searching for something. Then, as if he had been unaware of the man's presence till that moment, he shot up his head again, saying:

—Eh? Are you going to stand there all day? Upon my word, Farrington, you take things easy!

—I was waiting to see ...

—Very good, you needn't wait to see. Go downstairs and do your work.

The man walked heavily towards the door and, as he went out of the room, he heard Mr Alleyne cry after him that if the contract was not copied by evening Mr Crosbie would hear of the matter.

He returned to his desk in the lower office and counted the sheets which remained to be copied. He took up his pen and dipped it in the ink but he continued to stare stupidly at the last words he had written: *In no case shall the said Bernard Bodley be ...* The evening was falling and in a few minutes they would be lighting the gas: then he could write. He felt that he must slake the thirst in his throat. He stood up from his desk and, lifting the counter as before, passed out of the office. As he was passing out the chief clerk looked at him inquiringly.

—It's all right, Mr Shelley, said the man, pointing with his finger to indicate the objective of his journey.

The chief clerk glanced at the hat-rack but, seeing the row complete, offered no remark. As soon as he was on the landing the man pulled a shepherd's plaid cap out of his pocket, put it on his head and ran quickly down the rickety stairs. From the street door he walked on furtively on the inner side of the path towards the corner and all at once dived into a doorway. He was now safe in the dark snug of O'Neill's shop, and, filling up the little window that looked into the bar with his inflamed face, the colour of dark wine or dark meat, he called out:

—Here, Pat, give us a g.p., like a good fellow.

The curate brought him a glass of plain porter. The man drank it at a gulp and asked for a caraway seed. He put his penny on the counter and, leaving the curate to grope for it in the gloom, retreated out of the snug as furtively as he had entered it.

Darkness, accompanied by a thick fog, was gaining upon the dusk of February and the lamps in Eustace Street had been lit. The man went up by the houses until he reached the door of the office, wondering whether he could finish his copy in time. On the stairs a moist pungent odour of perfumes saluted his nose: evidently Miss Delacour had come while he was out in O'Neill's. He crammed his cap back again into his pocket and re-entered the office, assuming an air of absent-mindedness.

—Mr Alleyne has been calling for you, said the chief clerk severely. Where were you?

The man glanced at the two clients who were standing at the counter as if to intimate that their presence prevented him from answering. As the clients were both male the chief clerk allowed himself a laugh.

—I know that game, he said. Five times in one day is a little bit.... Well, you better look sharp and get a copy of our correspondence in the Delacour case for Mr Alleyne.

This address in the presence of the public, his run upstairs and the porter he had gulped down so hastily confused the man and, as he sat down at his desk to get what was required, he realised how hopeless was the task of finishing his copy of the contract before half past five. The dark damp night was coming and he longed to spend it in the bars, drinking with his friends amid the glare of gas and the clatter of glasses. He got out the Delacour correspondence and passed out of the office. He hoped Mr Alleyne would not discover that the last two letters were missing.

The moist pungent perfume lay all the way up to Mr Alleyne's room. Miss Delacour was a middle-aged woman of Jewish appearance. Mr Alleyne was said to be sweet on her or on her money. She came to the office often and stayed a long time when she came. She was sitting beside his desk now in an aroma of perfumes, smoothing the handle of her umbrella and nodding the great black feather in her hat. Mr Alleyne had swivelled his chair round to face her and thrown his right foot jauntily upon his left knee. The man put the correspondence on the desk and bowed respectfully but neither Mr Alleyne nor Miss Delacour took any notice of his bow. Mr Alleyne tapped a finger on the correspondence and then flicked it towards him as if to say: *That's all right: you can go*.

The man returned to the lower office and sat down again at his desk. He stared intently at the incomplete phrase: *In no case shall the said Bernard Bodley be ...* and thought how strange it was that the last three words began with the same letter. The chief clerk began to hurry Miss Parker, saying she would never have the letters typed in time for post. The man listened to the clicking of the machine for a few minutes and then set to work to finish his copy. But his head was not clear and his mind wandered away to the glare and rattle of the public-house. It was a night for hot punches. He struggled on with his copy, but when the clock struck five he had still fourteen pages to write. Blast it! He couldn't finish it in time. He longed to execrate aloud, to bring his fist down on something violently. He was so enraged that he wrote *Bernard Bernard* instead of *Bernard Bodley* and had to begin again on a clean sheet.

He felt strong enough to clear out the whole office singlehanded. His body ached to do something, to rush out and revel in violence. All the indignities of his life enraged him.... Could he ask the cashier privately for an advance? No, the cashier was no good, no damn good: he wouldn't give an advance.... He knew where he would meet the boys: Leonard and O'Halloran and Nosey Flynn. The barometer of his emotional nature was set for a spell of riot.

His imagination had so abstracted him that his name was called twice before he answered. Mr Alleyne and Miss Delacour were standing outside the counter and all the clerks had turned round in anticipation of something. The man got up from his desk. Mr Alleyne began a tirade of abuse, saying that two letters were missing. The man answered that he knew nothing about them, that he had made a faithful copy. The tirade continued: it was so bitter and violent that the man could hardly restrain his fist from descending upon the head of the manikin before him.

—I know nothing about any other two letters, he said stupidly.

—*You-know-nothing*. Of course you know nothing, said Mr Alleyne. Tell me, he added, glancing first for approval to the lady beside him, do you take me for a fool? Do you think me an utter fool?

The man glanced from the lady's face to the little egg-shaped head and back again; and, almost before he was aware of it, his tongue had found a felicitous moment:

—I don't think, sir, he said, that that's a fair question to put to me.

There was a pause in the very breathing of the clerks. Everyone was astounded (the author of the witticism no less than his neighbours) and Miss Delacour, who was a stout amiable person, began to smile broadly. Mr Alleyne flushed to the hue of a wild rose and his mouth twitched with a dwarf's passion. He shook his fist in the man's face till it seemed to vibrate like the knob of some electric machine:

—You impertinent ruffian! You impertinent ruffian! I'll make short work of you! Wait till you see! You'll apologise to me for your impertinence or you'll quit the office instanter! You'll quit this, I'm telling you, or you'll apologise to me!

He stood in a doorway opposite the office watching to see if the cashier would come out alone. All the clerks passed out and finally the cashier came out with the chief clerk. It was no use trying to say a word to him when he was with the chief clerk. The man felt that his position was bad enough. He had been obliged to offer an abject apology to Mr Alleyne for his impertinence but he knew what a hornet's nest the office would be for him. He could remember the way in which Mr Alleyne had hounded little Peake out of the office in order to make room for his own nephew. He felt savage and thirsty and revengeful, annoyed with himself and with everyone else. Mr Alleyne would never give him an hour's rest; his life would be a hell to him. He had made a proper fool of himself this time. Could he not keep his tongue in his cheek? But they had never pulled together from the first, he and Mr Alleyne, ever since the day Mr Alleyne had overheard him mimicking his North of Ireland accent to amuse Higgins and Miss Parker: that had been the beginning of it. He might have tried Higgins for the money, but sure Higgins never had anything for himself. A man with two establishments to keep up, of course he couldn't. . . .

He felt his great body again aching for the comfort of the public-house. The fog had begun to chill him and he wondered could he touch Pat in O'Neill's. He could not touch him for more than a bob—and a bob was no use. Yet he must get money somewhere or other: he had spent his last penny for the g.p. and soon it would be too late for getting money anywhere. Suddenly, as he was fingering his watch-chain, he thought of Terry Kelly's pawn-office in Fleet Street. That was the dart! Why didn't he think of it sooner?

He went through the narrow alley of Temple Bar quickly, muttering to himself that they could all go to hell because he was going to have a good night of it. The clerk in Terry Kelly's said *A crown!* but the consignor held out for six shillings; and in the end the six shillings was allowed him literally. He came out of the pawn-office joyfully, making a little cylinder of the coins between his thumb and fingers. In Westmoreland Street the footpaths were crowded with young men and women returning from business and ragged urchins ran here and there yelling out the names of the evening editions. The man passed through the crowd, looking on the spectacle generally with proud satisfaction and staring masterfully at the office-girls. His head was full of the noises of tram-gongs and swishing trolleys and his nose already sniffed the curling fumes of punch. As he walked on he preconsidered the terms in which he would narrate the incident to the boys:

—So, I just looked at him—coolly, you know, and looked at her. Then I looked back at him again—taking my time, you know. *I don't think that that's a fair question to put to me*, says I.

Nosey Flynn was sitting up in his usual corner of Davy Byrne's and, when he heard the story, he stood Farrington a half-one, saying it was as smart a thing as ever he heard. Farrington stood a drink in his turn. After a while O'Halloran and Paddy Leonard came in and the story was repeated to them.

O'Halloran stood tailors of malt, hot, all round and told the story of the retort he had made to the chief clerk when he was in Callan's of Fownes's Street; but, as the retort was after the manner of the liberal shepherds in the eclogues, he had to admit that it was not so clever as Farrington's retort. At this Farrington told the boys to polish off that and have another.

Just as they were naming their poisons who should come in but Higgins! Of course he had to join in with the others. The men asked him to give his version of it, and he did so with great vivacity for the sight of five small hot whiskies was very exhilarating. Everyone roared laughing when he showed the way in which Mr Alleyne shook his fist in Farrington's face. Then he imitated Farrington, saying, *And here was my nabs, as cool as you please,* while Farrington looked at the company out of his heavy dirty eyes, smiling and at times drawing forth stray drops of liquor from his moustache with the aid of his lower lip.

When that round was over there was a pause. O'Halloran had money but neither of the other two seemed to have any; so the whole party left the shop somewhat regretfully. At the corner of Duke Street Higgins and Nosey Flynn bevelled off to the left while the other three turned back towards the city. Rain was drizzling down on the cold streets and, when they reached the Ballast Office, Farrington suggested the Scotch House. The bar was full of men and loud with the noise of tongues and glasses. The three men pushed past the whining match-sellers at the door and formed a little party at the corner of the counter. They began to exchange stories. Leonard introduced them to a young fellow named Weathers who was performing at the Tivoli as an acrobat and knockabout *artiste*. Farrington stood a drink all around. Weathers said he would take a small Irish and Apollinaris. Farrington, who had definite notions of what was what, asked the boys would they have an Apollinaris too; but the boys told Tim to make theirs hot. The talk became theatrical. O'Halloran stood a round and then Farrington stood another round, Weathers protesting that the hospitality was too Irish. He promised to get them in behind the scenes and introduce them to some nice girls. O'Halloran said that he and Leonard would go but that Farrington wouldn't because he was a married man; and Farrington's heavy dirty eyes leered at the company in token that he understood he was being chaffed. Weathers made them all have just one little tincture at his expense and promised to meet them later on at Mulligan's in Poolbeg Street.

When the Scotch House closed they went round to Mulligan's. They went into the parlour at the back and O'Halloran ordered small hot specials all round. They were all beginning to feel mellow. Farrington was just standing another round when Weathers came back. Much to Farrington's relief he drank a glass of bitter this time. Funds were running low but they had enough to keep them going. Presently two young women with big hats and a young man in a check suit came in and sat at a table close by. Weathers saluted them and told the company that they were out of the Tivoli. Farrington's eyes wandered at every moment in the direction of one of the young women. There was something striking in her appearance. An immense scarf of peacock-blue muslin was wound round her hat and knotted in a great bow under her chin; and she wore bright yellow gloves, reaching to the elbow. Farrington gazed admiringly at the plump arm which she moved very often and with much grace; and when, after a little time, she answered his gaze he admired still more her large dark brown eyes. The oblique staring expression in them fascinated him. She glanced at him once or twice and, when the party was leaving the room, she brushed against his chair and said *O, pardon!* in a London accent. He watched her leave the room in the hope that she would look back at him, but he was disappointed. He cursed his want of money and cursed all the rounds he had stood, particularly all the whiskies and Apollinaris which he had stood to Weathers. If there was one thing that he hated it was a sponge. He was so angry that he lost count of the conversation of his friends.

When Paddy Leonard called him he found that they were talking about feats of strength. Weathers was showing his biceps muscle to the company and boasting so much that the other two had called on Farrington to uphold the national honour. Farrington pulled up his sleeve accordingly and showed his biceps muscle to the company. The two arms were examined and compared and finally it was agreed to have a trial of strength. The table was cleared and the two men rested their elbows on it, clasping hands. When Paddy Leonard said *Go!* each was to try to bring down the other's hand on to the table. Farrington looked very serious and determined.

The trial began. After about thirty seconds Weathers brought his opponent's hand slowly down on to the table. Farrington's dark wine-coloured face flushed darker still with anger and humiliation at having been defeated by such a stripling.

—You're not to put the weight of your body behind it. Play fair, he said.

—Who's not playing fair? said the other.

—Come on again. The two best out of three.

The trial began again. The veins stood out on Farrington's forehead and the pallor of Weathers' complexion changed to peony. Their hands and arms trembled under the stress. After a long struggle Weathers again brought his opponent's hand slowly on to the table. There was a murmur of applause from the spectators. The curate, who was standing beside the table, nodded his red head towards the victor and said with loutish familiarity:

—Ah! that's the knack!

—What the hell do you know about it? said Farrington fiercely, turning on the man. What do you put in your gab for?

—Sh, sh! said O'Halloran, observing the violent expression of Farrington's face. Pony up, boys. We'll have just one little smahan more and then we'll be off.

A very sullen-faced man stood at the corner of O'Connell Bridge waiting for the little Sandymount tram to take him home. He was full of smouldering anger and revengefulness. He felt humiliated and discontented; he did not even feel drunk; and he had only twopence in his pocket. He cursed everything. He had done for himself in the office, pawned his watch, spent all his money; and he had not even got drunk. He began to feel thirsty again and he longed to be back again in the hot reeking public-house. He had lost his reputation as a strong man, having been defeated twice by a mere boy. His heart swelled with fury and, when he thought of the woman in the big hat who had brushed against him and said *Pardon!* his fury nearly choked him.

His tram let him down at Shelbourne Road and he steered his great body along in the shadow of the wall of the barracks. He loathed returning to his home. When he went in by the side-door he found

the kitchen empty and the kitchen fire nearly out.
He bawled upstairs:

—Ada! Ada!

His wife was a little sharp-faced woman who bullied
her husband when he was sober and was bullied by
him when he was drunk. They had five children. A
little boy came running down the stairs.

—Who is that? said the man, peering through the
darkness.

—Me, pa.

—Who are you? Charlie?

—No, pa. Tom.

—Where's your mother?

—She's out at the chapel.

—That's right.... Did she think of leaving any
dinner for me?

—Yes, pa. I—

—Light the lamp. What do you mean by having
the place in darkness? Are the other children in bed?

The man sat down heavily on one of the chairs
while the little boy lit the lamp. He began to mimic
his son's flat accent, saying half to himself: *At the chapel.
At the chapel, if you please!* When the lamp was lit he
banged his fist on the table and shouted:

—What's for my dinner?

—I'm going ... to cook it, pa, said the little boy.

The man jumped up furiously and pointed to the
fire.

—On that fire! You let the fire out! By God, I'll
teach you to do that again!

He took a step to the door and seized the walking-
stick which was standing behind it.

—I'll teach you to let the fire out! he said, rolling
up his sleeve in order to give his arm free play.

The little boy cried *O, pa!* and ran whimpering

round the table, but the man followed him and caught
him by the coat. The little boy looked about him wildly
but, seeing no way of escape, fell upon his knees.

—Now, you'll let the fire out the next time! said
the man, striking at him viciously with the stick. Take
that, you little whelp!

The boy uttered a squeal of pain as the stick cut
his thigh. He clasped his hands together in the air
and his voice shook with fright.

—O, pa! he cried. Don't beat me, pa! And I'll ...
I'll say a *Hail Mary* for you.... I'll say a *Hail Mary*
for you, pa, if you don't beat me.... I'll say a *Hail
Mary*....

Jack Hodgins

THE PLAGUE
CHILDREN

MAYBE THIS YOUTH is dangerous and maybe he isn't, nobody knows for sure. What's known is that he's running up the entire length of the Island, end to end. With his track shoes dipped in the Strait of Juan de Fuca he is pumping knees and elbows towards Port Hardy. If he isn't dangerous maybe he's just plain crazy. A sweat-band keeps that long pale hair from getting in his eyes; a beard that looks like rusty wire fans out across his chest; a wrinkled cotton shirt, embroidered like a table-cloth with daisies, flaps and flutters around the waist of his track-suit pants. Whether you see him flicker past behind a screen of trees or catch him stroking head-on up the highway, the effect is much the same. The rhythm of his footsteps never changes, his bone-jarred breaths maintain an even beat, no sweat breaks out across his forehead or soaks that flapping shirt. Maybe this youth is dangerous and maybe he isn't: there are some who even think he may not be human.

Here in Waterville they think they know this youth and what he means: a spy, a scout, an advance guard for a swarm of others. While those legs and elbows pump him north, those eyes are reconnoitering, the

brain behind the sweat-band taking notes. In Port
Hardy where the highway ends he'll catch his breath
and make a phone call south to launch this year's
attack. These people have seen it all before. When
he passes through this small community of farms they
brace themselves for war.

Yet only Frieda Macken acts. Even before the youth
is out of sight, she hurries out to the lean-to shed
behind her house and roots around in a clutter of
rusty machines and broken tools for a sack of lime.
In all that settlement of part-time farmers, only Frieda
Macken and her husband Eddie get out in their fields
to spread the harsh white powder with their hands,
squinting into the dust that burns their eyes. The
others, seeing that youth thump past with his cov-
etous eyes and his rusty prophetic beard, move inside
to wait for what they know is about to happen and
still refuse to believe. Not only scout, this youth is
harbinger as well. The invading horde is only a day
behind.

Read the papers. Find out where they're from.
Holland, California, Rome. The Philippines. Some from
as near as Vancouver, others from Katmandu. All of
them could be here from another planet. A few every
year get caught by police and fined. Copenhagen,
Tallahassee, Nome, nobody wants to believe the
addresses they print in the papers. Nobody believes
their names.

For the people who live in Waterville there is
something a little incredible in all of this. The place
has never wanted to be part of anyone's map. This
collection of thirty hobby farms along a four-mile
stretch of highway has never wanted to be anything
at all but what it is: a General Store and Post Office,
a community hall, and houses you pass on your way
to somewhere else. They don't even ask you to reduce

THE PLAGUE CHILDREN   231

your speed as you're driving through. Everyone here
has been here for fifty years at least, everyone here
is middle-aged or older. It's not easy for them to believe
that people in Holland, Colombia, Rome, when they
hear the name of this settlement, pack their bags and
immigrate in order to take part in this annual assault.
And yet in Saskatoon, in Florence, and in Oslo, they
wrench up whatever roots they have and join the
converging exodus around the world towards this
place. Word has gone out on some invisible global
network that the September rains have come to this
part of the world, the magic mushrooms are pushing
their way through the ground in record numbers, and
a fortune is waiting to be made by those who get
here first. Bring your family, bring your friends, bring
anyone with a pair of hands and a pair of legs for
running away from the law. Fresh air, fresh fruit, and
plenty of gardens to raid; a hefty profit and a month
of incredible highs.

Dennis Macken sees them first. They lean their bicy-
cles into the ditch outside his field, hide their motorbikes in the bush, and hop off hitch-hiked rides onto
the gravel shoulder of the highway. Then they climb
over, under, through his strands of barbed-wire fence.
They stretch it, twist it, leave bits of their own patched
sweaters snagged on it. One fat bearded man in leather
shorts grabs a cedar post and levers it back and forth
until it breaks off beneath the ground like a rotten
tooth. Now he and his long-skirted woman and their
four small children can walk unmolested onto Dennis
Macken's nearest pasture and start their bent-over
search in the damp September grass.
    Dennis Macken watches with a hand on the tele-
phone, his tongue exploring a cavity. Unlike his
brother and sister-in-law he's done nothing at all to

avoid this confrontation. Perhaps he even welcomes it. At any rate he doesn't stop himself from grinning. When it appears that no more of them will be coming this morning he calls the police, then moves out onto the step to watch. A woman with a baby strapped to her back pauses to wave, and smile. There is no one out there who is even half his age.

When the police arrive, he laughs out loud at the sight of that pack breaking up and scattering like panicked cattle—pails emptied, skirts hoisted, long hair flying, children screaming. Through his second fence, or over it, into the bush. By the time the Mounties have crossed the ditch and entered the field there's no one left in sight. The two of them stomp bravely towards the woods and disappear in alder. They come out again pulling a girl who kicks and screams and finally goes limp while they drag her back to their car. At the car she turns and shouts out something, a curse perhaps, at Dennis Macken, at those invisible pickers, at the world. Her words, of course, are in a language he cannot understand.

When the rest have come back to spread out over his field again, Macken moves inside his house and watches from a window. He knows that something is happening here but he doesn't know what it is. He only hopes they will have left for the day by the time he goes out for his evening chores. At sixty-three years old Dennis Macken still believes in the law. These people are trespassing on private property. They're tromping on the field he cleared himself with his home-made tractor. They're breaking down fences he worked hard weeks to build. He imagines himself with a rifle, picking them off from his window; he imagines his pasture a battlefield strewn with bodies; but he still believes in the law. He will phone the police every hour through the rest of this day. And tomorrow. And the day after that. Those young buggers may get their mushrooms in the end, but they'll get plenty of exercise, too.

His neighbour Angel Hopper doesn't believe in waiting for the law, he believes in fighting his battles himself. The sight of the second-day wave of pickers upsets his stomach, gives him migraines, sets his teeth on edge, but he doesn't phone the police. What Dennis Macken has is foolish faith, he says; what Angel Hopper has is a Hereford bull—a thick-necked, thick-shouldered, thick-legged miserable son-of-a-bitch that even Angel Hopper is scared of. A people-hater from birth. He rolls his bulging eyes and swings his head and paws at the ground at even a glimpse of something human, no matter how far away. In a small high-fenced corral behind the barn, he stands up to his knees in muck and swings his tail at flies while he munches hay and dreams of destroying the two-legged race. Sometimes just the sound of Angel Hopper moving around inside the barn is enough to make him circle his pen, work up some speed, and smash his head into the wall.

Hopper isn't half so mean as his bull but he can't help chuckling over what he knows will happen. A treat like this is worth a day off work—no logging company ever went belly-up just because one second-loader stayed home to protect his land. It is also worth the effort of doing it right—which means giving that ragged pack of youths some warning. He waits until all the young men in their crotch-patched overalls and pony-tails and the women in their ankle-length flowered skirts and the children with their pails and paper bags of lunch have crossed the ditch, have cut the strands of his fence and spread out over the field. Then he swaggers down into their midst with his twenty-two in his arms and approaches the only person who looks up, a girl in a purple velvet coat who reminds him of the runaway daughter of Frieda and Eddie Macken. "This is my property you're on," he says, as pleasantly as he knows how, "and I'd like to see you people off of here right away." He pauses and looks at the others, who don't even know he is there. "Please."

The girl frowns into his face as if she sees something at the back of his eyeballs that even he doesn't know is there. "Haven't you heard?" she says. "Nobody owns the earth. You got no business putting up fences and trying to keep us out."

"Thank you," Hopper says and heads for the barn. When the bull has been released to the field Hopper stands on the rusty seat of an abandoned hayfork to watch. Faced with so much humanity all at once, the bull hardly knows where to start. He bawls, drools, trots forward. He lowers his head and flings up dirt with his hoof and trots in a wide curve around the edge of the crowd. At last he charges. He seems to have chosen someone right in the middle. People scatter in all directions, screaming. Angel Hopper hoots and slaps his leg. No one would ever call him a sadist, but he is having a wonderful time. "Scare the hell out of them all, old Bull!" But Bull is intent on only the one original target, a youth with a rusty beard and a sweat-band who refuses to move. From this distance, Hopper thinks it may be the marathon youth. But marathon youth or whoever he is, this fellow has only to lift his arms and the bull nearly breaks his neck trying to put on the brakes. When he comes to a stiff-legged halt, his head lowered, he appears for a moment to be bowing to the youth. From their positions on top of fence posts and in the lower limbs of trees, the scattered pickers laugh. A few applaud.

The bull backs away from the youth and swings his head as if in apology. Then catching sight of Hopper on the seat of that rusty hayfork, he snorts and tosses his head and starts to run again. This time there's no indecision, the curve in his route is simply because his target is moving, is running towards the house. The bull cuts right through the fence like someone going through spiderweb, drags wire and broken post and several strands of honeysuckle vine behind him across the yard. Unhampered by so many accessories, Hopper is the first to get to the house. He even, for some reason or other, locks the door. While Hopper turns his basement upside down looking for strong enough rope to do something about that bull, the bull discovers a strong desire to travel. Out on the yellow centre line of the highway, he trots northward with his tail switching at flies. Perhaps he has an appointment he wants to keep in someone else's field. Perhaps he has simply developed an ambition to run the length of the Island.

Now all the world is draining into Waterville, it seems. There are people here from Taiwan, Turkey, and Tibet. There are people off the plane from New South Wales, from Ecuador, from Greece. Families of Alabamans. Couples from Japan. Four youths on motorbikes from California, migrant workers on the look-out for a crop more profitable and fun than grapes or beets or oranges. The fields are crowded. The woods are full. No one can escape them now. They hide behind the cattle in the pasture. They camp in the bush and sneak out after dark with miners' lamps beaming from their foreheads. Alan Powers finds a family sleeping in his hayloft. Ossie Greenfield discovers a naked couple making love in the attic of his house. All night long Grandma Barclay listens to the sounds of running footsteps, whispering voices, bodies brushing one another outside her bedroom walls. Strangers sleep in tractor sheds and pick-up cabs and cellars, children's voices cry from under trucks, the air at night is alive with whispers like the rustling sounds of rats.

Dennis Macken wakes at dawn and knows that someone else has slept beside him in his bed. The colour of his dreams has changed and the sheets are strangely warm and limp. Some of his forty-seven hats hanging around the wall are rearranged. He believes it is the marathon youth himself, who intends to push him off his place and use it as a headquarters for his operation. Being a long-time bachelor, Dennis Macken has the neatest house in the district, the most expensive furniture, the newest truck, the cleanest barn, and by far the biggest garden. Naturally, the rusty-bearded runner would choose it for his own. Macken is used to people wanting what he's got.

One of the things that people used to want was Dennis Macken himself. He had his turn as heart-throb for the entire district, years ago. Nearly every woman in Waterville once dreamed of catching him. Star pitcher for the valley baseball team, a heavy drinker, and a player of practical jokes. He also played the field since the field was so willing to be played, then in time chose Frieda Barclay out of all the rest. Amongst other things, he liked her turned-up nose. Frieda, however, liked the stronger, thicker nose of Eddie Macken and gave Dennis back his ring. Her choice was to be his sister-in-law instead of wife. His choice was to make no second choice at all from the well-played field but to travel twice around the world and hope to forget her. By the time he stopped his running she was pregnant and he settled into bachelorhood to watch her raise a family. Even after forty years of watching, her nose still drives him crazy.

He keeps his place so spick and span not only because it is where she grew up, the Barclay dairy farm he bought from her widowed mother, but also because he knows she despises dirt. He's the only man in the community who can match the floors and windows of her spotless home.

But it isn't Frieda Macken's home that he feels is most at stake. It's his. If he doesn't do something soon to stop that plague of mushroom-pickers from over-running the settlement they'll soon be crowding him off this earth.

Yet it appears that nothing can stop them now. Everyone knows that police arrests are a joke. These people are happy to forfeit their airline tickets to Norway or Egypt and hightail it back to the fields. Someone is making a fortune and it isn't the Waterville farmer. His cattle huddle in corners. His garden is picked nearly bare. His wife is afraid to step outside her own house. Coming from town with her station wagon full of groceries, Lenora Desmond finds her house overrun; people in every room. Something they ate has gone bad in their stomachs and they've converted her house to a hospital: people are in her beds, people are throwing up in her toilet, people are wrapped in blankets they've hauled from her closet. The whole house stinks of some foul concoction of weeds a girl is boiling on her stove. "Who is the doctor here?" she says. "Why are you in my house?" But they turn up their sad forgiving eyes and pity her for this bitter uncharity and refuse to move.

Aside from Eddie and Frieda Macken's silent farm, the General Store and Post Office is the only part of the community not alive with strangers. By the fourth day of the siege it is full of residents who've come in for the mail and won't go home. They buy groceries to justify a few more minutes of talk, they stand at the door until Em Madill brings out more chairs from her kitchen. Display shelves are shifted to one end of the room. Counters are cleared. Lenora Desmond moves every loaf of bread to the top of the meat counter so that Angel Hopper can perch to smoke his pipe and Em Madill has somewhere to set up her coffee pot and cups. Women's jaws are set. Men's eyes refuse to see the eyes of other men. They prefer to read the tiny print on the labels of the canned tomatoes.

"It's really very simple," Frieda Macken says. "Nobody picks on our property. Nobody tramples our fences. Nobody scares our cows. You spread lime and the mushrooms don't grow."

"Not that you're gloating," they say.

And she isn't gloating, she understands that no one has followed her lead simply because they can't believe this thing until it's already started to happen. She smiles at a time like this, and almost sings, as if what she's got to offer is astonishing news. "If you gave all of your fields a good dose of it now, would those people still want the mushrooms?"

"Probably yes."

"Those people are crazy, Frieda. They'll find some way of hallucinating on a mixture of mushrooms and lime. They're very young, they're capable of everything."

"The police are trying but they haven't got a hope. That helicopter of theirs nearly scared my pants off, they thought I was one of them and chased me right across my own field. I thought that noisy rig was going to land on my head."

Ernie Butcher tells everyone he fixed up a forty-five-gallon drum of liquid manure on his tractor and chased these long-legged freaks all over the field, spraying them. "I even sprayed their car, but damn if they didn't come back the next day and I had to do it again." He's getting his field fertilized, he says, but he isn't doing anything else at all.

Ella Korhonen says she heard that flooding your field with sea water would solve the problem, too bad this place was too far inland and all uphill.

Uphill or not, a couple of miles of pipe would be worth it if it didn't ruin the soil. Ernie Butcher says he's keeping his own hands off from now on, he saw a bunch of the pickers on Alan Powers' field yesterday and stopped to holler at them to get out of there. "They never paid me no attention so I starts out onto the field myself to give them a piece of my mind and then old Powers comes roaring out of his house with his shotgun in his hand and stops on the top of his well-head to fire. I yelled and waved my arms all over the place but he blasts off just the same and cripes, you shoulda seen me run! I heard some of that buckshot whining past my ear. Somebody's going to get killed if we don't do something quick."

"It's got so's a person can't even protect what he owns. Yesterday I heard that Grandma Barclay— Frieda's mother, eh, and Lenora's—how old is she now? I heard she . . ."

"Eighty-four," Lenora says. "And I know what you're going to say. Yesterday she came across one of them smoking in the doorway of our root cellar when she went past to get me some spuds and without even thinking she hauled off and hit him with the fork. This morning the guy comes around with the police and wants to charge her with assault! You can imagine how far they got with me in the door."

Hell, Alan Powers says, he don't have to worry about that anymore himself, this big fat fellow moved onto his property and thinks he owns the place, him and his gang, they chase everybody else away with sticks and even get into fights. "That bozo had the bloody cheek to tell me he made sixty thousand dollars off my place last year and he don't intend to share it with no one now! I told him, maybe him and that Back East Mafia is making a fortune off of this farm but they're tramping down my winter silage as well, which is the same as taking the money right out of my pocket. He laughed in my face. You think I'm going to tangle with him? Forget it."

"It isn't just that we own this land," says Ernie Butcher. "We put a lifetime of sweat into working it. Who do they think they are? If somebody shot just one ..."

"It wouldn't make any difference," Frieda says. "You'd go to jail and the rest would move into your house."

At the age of sixty, with her white hair and determined jaw, she has the air about her of a woman judge. People will balk at everything she says, but in the end they listen. Her smiling eyes and singsong voice give her an added advantage: she can deliver a judge's orders and pass a judge's sentence as if she's dispensing news that delights and surprises even herself. "We'll go in to town and buy every sack of lime we can find," she says. "Then we'll spend tomorrow spoiling their obscene fun!"

At six o'clock Dennis Macken wakens and feels the heat of a second body in his bed. He knows the heavy breathing isn't his own. He knows the odour of unwashed feet is not his own. Beside him the marathon youth is laid out on his back, asleep. His hands are behind his neck. The hair in his armpits is as bushy as the rusted wire of the beard which rests on his skinny chest. Macken opens his mouth to holler.

Then closes it. Who would he holler for? Instead he grunts, and moves to the edge of the bed, ready to leap. He wonders if he left his rifle loaded. He wonders, too, if he's left his senses altogether and taken a step into madness. Who is to say at this time of the morning whether the youth or himself is the intruder? How does he know for sure that this is his house?

Something he knows for sure is that the language he hears is not something he understands. Thick, European, full of sounds in the throat. The youth is awake, grinning. Without taking his hands from behind his neck he stretches his long skinny body, arches it right up off the sheet like a footbridge, then lets it collapse. "Jesus, I overslept," says the youth, in something a little closer to English. And sits up to swing his feet out onto the floor. While Macken still searches for words, the youth crosses the room, and bends to pick up his clothes from the rug.

"Just a minute," Macken says.

The youth drops his flowery shirt down over his upstretched arms and pushes his head through the neck. He pulls the track pants up his muscled legs. He crouches to lace his shoes. Then, running on the spot, he takes the sweat-band off his head and begins to comb his hair.

"What are you doing here? How the hell'd you get in?"

The youth, still combing, laughs, then takes one of Macken's forty-seven caps down off the wall and tries it on. It's a little small for all that hair but he keeps it anyway.

Macken leans back on his pillow and pulls the covers up to his neck. "Who are you?" he says. He is cold. No, he is frozen. His hands are blue. Ice-water runs through every vein, out to the ends of his toes, his fingers.

The youth dances like a boxer across the floor to Macken. "That doesn't matter," he says. "But who are you?"

For a moment Macken doesn't know. His name is a foreign sound that people used against him years ago. He can't recall it now. If this stranger should ask him his age, however, that is a different matter. Macken suddenly knows that this is old. "Get out," he says, too weak to put any force in the words. "Get out." He closes his eyes until he is sure there is no one in the room but himself. Even then he doesn't get out of bed.

Not even the sight of Frieda Macken in his bedroom is enough to raise him up. Not even the devastated look on her handsome face, or her plea for help. What are they going to do, she wants to know. She's learned, from people in town who claim to know these things, that lime kills every kind of mushroom you can think of except this psylo ... psylo ... whatever it is, this thing. What she and Eddie have done, she supposes, is wasted time and energy spreading lime on fields where none of those things would have had the inclination to grow anyway. And made fools of themselves with their smugness.

Dennis Macken is not surprised to discover that the mushrooms are indestructible. He sees them in his mind's eye multiplying undeterred until they carpet the entire valley, until they are the only crop that grows in this part of the world. All he wants to do is look at his hands. They're old. They're wrinkled and old and covered with splotches like some terrible disease. He's caught it, he thinks, from that youth who slept in his bed, but how can he tell that to Frieda without sounding insane? He can't. He'd rather be silent. He rests his hands on the top of his blankets and hopes she'll notice. She doesn't. His hands look no different to her than her own. It's his eyes she's worried about. His eyes look as if they've seen something they can't accept.

Dennis Macken knows that finding something that will kill the mushroom has nothing to do with anything, that even if every mushroom in the community turns to poison, the plague will not go away. It will increase the energy of its attack, like a horde of starving rats; it will overrun the district, destroying everything in sight. That's why he stays in bed until he's heard Frieda Macken's car pull out of his yard. That's why he listens until he is sure that the pickers are again at work, and gets up to watch from a kitchen window until everything he can see is alive with people. His own fields, Desmonds' fields, Powers' stumpy pasture. Down on their knees with their noses only inches from ground, they part the grass as if they've been told there are diamonds amongst the roots. He knows what they're after, he's seen it himself, a small pointed cap of flesh on a long wiry stem. The first few they find they will eat, to start the day off feeling good, the rest they will hoard in their tins or their plastic bags. He's heard three thousand dollars a pound is what they're worth. Having tasted one once, he can't understand why. All it did was give him a dizzy head.

A dizzy head is what time has given him too, with its incredible speed. Why has it gone so fast? One day you look out a window and dream of all you can do once you've grown into a man; the next, so it seems, you look out the window and find yourself wondering what you've done with it while it flew by. In his case, he wonders what Frieda has done with his life, the one he offered her years ago. Given it back. Having returned it, she seemed to have left everything else up to him. Some travel, a job, this little farm, helping his neighbours a bit—is this what they like to call life?

A pick-up truck slows down and parks in the shallow ditch. Close to a dozen people hop out of the back, and two more out of the cab. On the gravel shoulder they pause for a moment to look over his field, then climb through his fence and drop to their knees to start combing. One of them wears something that looks like pajamas. One is a child with a crutch. They haven't been there for even a minute when the people who got there before them stand up and converge to a knot in the centre of the field. Some carry sticks, a few swing their pails, all of them seem to be shouting. Macken sees, when they break apart and start walking towards the intruders, that the marathon youth takes the lead. Face to face, the groups engage in some conversation. An arm is raised. A short piece of lumber is swung. The bodies convulse in a brawl. Even inside he can hear the sounds of their yells. One of the newcomers breaks free and makes for the truck. Others follow his lead. Waving their fists from the back of the pick-up they make their escape, while the rest go back to their work.

Once he is dressed, Dennis Macken crosses the yard and climbs on board his tractor, a monster he's made from a hundred scrapyard wrecks. Big as a tank, it has back wheels that stand higher than he does and a bulldozer blade on the front. Its motor rattles windows. Its tracks cut patterns of three-inch holes in the ground. Its exhaust pipe stretches skyward like a flagpole, and flies his flag—a flowered rag that whips about in the blue exhaust as if it wants to tear free and have a life of its own. A life of his own is what Macken wants too, and up on his tractor he'll claim it.

He starts the engine and manoeuvres out onto the

grass. Selecting a cluster of adults down on their knees like pilgrims worshipping their god, he opens her up. Oh holy terror, the screams! Bodies leap up, fall away, scatter. Macken rattles on through. They yell at him, in thirteen different languages. Someone throws a jam tin that clatters against the hood. Someone throws a clod of grass that barely misses his face. He laughs, he laughs, he feels almost young again.

And now he is off to new encounters. This time they haven't the sense to scatter, they run in a pack, and he can't resist the need to give them chase. He stands, he hollers insults, he whoops like a cowboy. He follows them down the length of the field, as close as he dare on their heels. When they turn, he turns. Hair flies. Rags ripple and flap. The girl in a purple velvet coat who looks like Frieda Macken's runaway daughter trips and screams, crawls ahead of the blade, gets up in the nick of time. Macken swings to the left and heads for a new cluster of pickers, he won't be happy until he has them all stirred up, he won't be happy until he's given them all a scare, until he's made their lives so miserable they'll be glad to leave, get off his land, and spread the word that Dennis Macken's not a man to take advantage of. Off to one side he sees a car on the highway backing up for a better look, he sees Angel Hopper getting out of his truck, he sees Frieda Macken running in this direction across the Desmonds' fields.

One youth alone stands upright, steady, refuses to move. Macken decides to run over him. But the youth doesn't move, doesn't leap, except onto the top of Macken's blade where he rides with his rusty beard whipped up across his face, his powerful hands on the bar. He is wearing a Macken cap on his hairy head.

Macken stops for no one, not even this wild-eyed

youth on his nose. Not even the crowd of neighbours that's collected along his fence. Let them gawk, let them admire his pluck. He sets out on a new crusade. "Get off my field you pack of bastards, git!" But the marathon youth crawls up the engine hood towards Macken's face. "Get out of my way, you creep. I can't see where I'm going!" The eyes are so deep and frightening that Macken can't bear to look at them. The youth pushes his face up close to Macken's face, his breath in Macken's breath, his nose against Macken's nose. He says something that Macken can't understand, some foreign sounds, but he tastes their meaning with his teeth. He won't get out of this alive. Nobody will.

When the youth pulls out the key and rides the tractor to a stop it's already far too late. Behind them a child is lying in the grass and screaming. People are yelling again. People are running to see what Macken has done. Someone hauls him down off his tractor and shoves him towards the commotion. The girl who looks like Frieda Barclay's daughter stops in front of him and spits in his face. Terrified by what he sees, Macken is almost relieved when the marathon youth pushes the others away and hustles him forward towards the child. The crowd from outside his fence is running this way, all of Waterville seems to be here. Macken can hear someone calling his name.

Some faces in this crowd are familiar, some are not. That could be Frieda Macken trying to get to him, but it could be someone else. Macken can't tell his neighbours from these children of the plague. A confusion of bodies. He thinks he sees Angel Hopper pushing someone, he thinks he sees Alan Powers. How carefully does a plague select a territory it will attack? Macken thinks that maybe it doesn't strike blindly at everything in its way, as people believe, he thinks its victims probably select themselves. The magnetic force it can't resist is fear.

The magnetic force he can't resist is that fallen girl. People move back so that he can be pulled towards her. A youth in wire-rimmed glasses is down on his knees in the grass with his eyes squeezed shut and his hands clasped together beneath his chin. A young woman is down in the grass beside him, holding the child's head in her arms. An arm, crushed by one of his wheels, is bleeding. Her mouth is open and her scream is so high and loud that Macken's ears are unable to bear it. He thinks, instead, that he's hearing the sirens that announce the end of the world.

A few of their names are appearing in the papers even now, along with their exotic addresses. Mexico City, Marseilles. Most of the pickers, however, have gone. Like other crops, the magic mushroom has its time and disappears. The marathon youth buys an Oh Henry bar in the General Store and sets off running down the road with his even pace. And where will he go to now? Does he scout for other causes? Will he lead his herd into department stores and onto beaches, will he usher them into picket lines and protest marches and demonstrations? Few have the time to wonder. They pick up liquor bottles and plastic bags and peanut butter jars in the fields. They examine livestock for signs of abuse. They bury smouldering campfires with shovelled sand. Some start giant bonfires of their own to burn up everything those hands have touched. Everyone is fixing fence. Lenora and Albert Desmond scour their house and scrape dried vomit out of corners with a paring knife. Grandma Barclay announces she wants to move into an old folks' home in town. Eddie and Frieda Macken lock up and head for the ferry, in order to spend some time with Frieda's sister Bella in North Vancouver. No one wants to believe what has happened. This collection of thirty hobby farms has never wanted to be anything special at all, except what it's always been. Nearly everyone has lived here for fifty years or longer. Rumour has it that Angel Hopper has decided what he'll do next year when the pickers return, if he hasn't sold out first. He'll sit by the gate and hold out his hand. For a hundred dollars a day— adult or child—he'll let a person pick on his private land and promise not to cause trouble. So what if he's lost a war? Dirty money or not, it's better than breaking bones, it's better than crushing children under your tractor wheels, like somebody else he knows.

Dennis Macken still believes in law, but not the law of the courts. He believes in Macken's law, which will have something to do with magnetic force when he finally figures it out. Watching that youth pump past his fence-line heading south, he knows that some day someone will drag him out of his house and try to convince him with speeches and legal documents and perhaps with a gun that these forty acres don't belong to him any more, or to anyone else that he knows. They'll tell him that everything belongs to this entire race of children from another planet who follow that bearded runner in a swarm from place to place throughout the universe harvesting their crop of drugs. Maybe this youth is dangerous and maybe he isn't, nobody knows for sure. What Dennis Macken knows is that there's much he's never thought of in this world, and plenty more to be found. What Dennis Macken knows is that before that plague of mushroom pickers returns he has eleven months to find some way of stopping clocks or step outside of time.

Aritha van Herk

WAITING FOR THE RODEO

WARNING: DO NOT COME TO CALGARY. THERE
IS NO CRIME. NO MONEY. NO DISEASE. THE CITY
HAS BECOME COMPLETELY CONVENTIONAL
AND SHOULD BE AVOIDED. BY ORDER OF CAL-
GARY CITY COUNCIL. SIGNED, MAYOR RALPH
KLEIN

TIP DID NOT consciously decide to ignore the posters, the newspaper ads, the radio and television
bulletins. She was going to Calgary and she went,
without much consideration of the consequences.
That was the way she travelled; when the moment
came, she followed. If she had been one to listen to
horror stories, she would never have gone anywhere.
Every city had its drawbacks, its white-gloved com-
missionaires and fungus epidemics, its travelling
magic shows. Audiences watched magicians like
hawks; if they could detect a trick, the magician's
apprentice was allowed to saw the magician in half,
a ritual accompanied by goatish shouts and bellows.
Too, Tip had once contracted a bad case of the staggers
in Regina and had only been able to pull herself out
of it by flying to Amsterdam and walking the cob-

blestones for a week. That had given her a bad scare and she never wanted to see Saskatchewan again. But it didn't stop her following her life's lust—to live in every Canadian city substantially enough to flaunt its markings in public. Everyone else wore their armbands and tattoos with a tribal loyalty; they only travelled when they were looking for trouble or because there was a rash of work.

For the last five years Calgary had been swollen with outsider markings, so much so that it would have been hard to find a native, but now, Tip knew from the television, the streets were empty and the wind howled down the glass coulees without ruffling much more than cement dust. Everyone had played Monopoly, tossing their dice on the sidewalks in front of the buildings they were gambling for. But the game had tired and the players packed up their Chance and Opportunity Knocks cards and went west, leaving behind the hopscotch outline of their chalked dice squares.

Tip always ran with the climate; when a city boasted a high suicide, divorce, and amputation rate, she was one of the first to move there, knowing that it would be a hot spot, a pride place to live. But now the deterring ads yearned her toward Calgary. She had never stopped there, only passed through on the TransCanada. And her life was getting predictable; it might be more fun to play in an unfashionable city. Most of all, she wanted to evade plot.

Tip owned a rusty U-haul for her moves. She never actually unpacked it, just pulled it up on the sidewalk in front of her crash. She had shoved all the stuff to the back and lived in it a few times when she hit a city with a housing shortage. It held the masked and intermittent objects that she had collected, had narrowed her eyes and imagined a future use for. She towed it behind her Ford.

Tip arrived in Calgary two weeks before Rodeo. As an economic joust, she decided to turn her pennies in. She went to the bank and asked for penny rolls. The teller brought her a dozen.

"Oh, that won't be enough."

"How meny dew yew wand?"

"A hundred." Each roll held fifty pennies.

The teller squinted. "A hunderd?"

"Yes. I've been saving them." For four years, she might have added, chunking them into her ten piggy banks, clinking them into empty mayonnaise jars. Now they waited, fat and heavy, to be emptied; for the plugs, the slots, the lids to release their copper-brown stream. Tip anticipated the ritual, shaking each container onto a heap on the floor, kneeling to count by fistfuls, rolling them into the brown cylinders. It was an afternoon's occupation and by the end of it her hands would be greenish, she would roll the last fifty and fold the ends down with satisfaction. She saved it up for herself the same way she saved the pennies, catching them in her piggy banks once a week or when she sorted her purse. She was never one who said to the cashier, "Oh, I have two pennies." She took them home for deposit in her own poor box, surreptitious pleasure in their accumulation.

She waited for a rainy afternoon, then bundled in an old woolen sweater with frayed wrists, she began to heap the pennies, tipping them into a noisy pile on the floor. She stood to cascade the piggybanks empty, rattle them from a satisfying height. Then, on her knees, she began to count and roll. Occasionally, she would stop to add the accumulating cylinders— fourteen, thirty-seven, fifty-five, sixty (she stopped for a cup of tea and streaked black across her face), ninety-two, and finally one hundred. There was still a small heap left and she separated it into piles. Eighteen, she would have to get more rolls. One hundred and eighteen rolls, fifty-nine dollars. She rocked back on her heels and stroked the neat cylinders with her palm. She would turn them in, all that extra weight shed, and use the paper bills to entertain a day. She divided the pennies between three plastic grocery bags and scrubbed her face and hands, feeling that she had completed her move, that she was settled.

The bags were so heavy she had trouble lugging them into the bank and she set them down on the teller's counter with a terrific clunk. The teller scowled. "Yew cand hand doze in all ad onze."

"Why not?"

"We don wand dem. Dere's doo meny."

"What am I supposed to do, drag them off and bring them back two at a time?"

The teller shrugged.

"You're a bank, you're supposed to take them." Tip began hauling rolls out of the bags, slamming them down on the teller's desk pad. "Twofoursixeightten-twelvefourteensixteeneighteentwenty—"

"Hew meny are there?"

"Hundred and eighteen—twentytwotwentyfour-twentysixtwentyeightthirty—"

"All ride. Slew down." She counted, then re-counted them and put them back into the grocery bags before hauling them one at a time into the vault, wincing. When she returned to her computer stool she looked at Tip as if she were part of a hold-up. "Yeh?"

"You haven't given me the money. Fifty-nine dollars."

"Oh yeh." She opened her drawer and reluctantly extracted four tens, two fives and nine ones, crumpled and well-circulated. Several of the ones were criss-crossed with scotch tape.

"Don't you have any new money?"

"Newp."

Tip folded the bills once and tucked them into her hip pocket. She felt light as the dust that the wind was blowing across the parking lot in front of her feet.

To compound her re-location, she hung all her clothes up in her new mirrored closet and began to sort them, moving the hangers in a complicated chess of different seasons and occupations. Play clothes, work clothes, dress-up clothes, costume clothes, evening clothes, sexy clothes, maneuver clothes, impractical clothes, worn out but loved clothes. Then she re-sorted them according to their function. Pants, jeans, skirts, dresses, suits, blouses, ties, scarves, belts, sweaters, T-shirts, underwear. And then, began to tear them from their hangers, hold each considered item up for her critical eye; keep it or pitch it? It was hard for Tip to get rid of clothes—they had a past, they lacked the safe anonymity of pennies. Sorting clothes was unsettling; once the pile of hangers lay flung beside the pile of clothes to be discarded, she had doubts. Would she never wear that purple velvet again? Were those silk slacks really splitting at the seam, couldn't they be mended? The pile lay on the floor while she speculated, sometimes returning an item to a hanger and place in the closet, sometimes flinging even more onto the pile. Until she was utterly sick of the process, swept the bundle up in her arms and carried it down to the car wanting to be done with it once and for all. But then had to scan the yellow pages searching for where to abandon it: Goodwill, the Salvation Army? And thinking of that, had to consider consignment shops. Would someone else actually pay for her old clothes? She reviewed her discards again. She could take them to an amateur theatre; they must need costumes. The clothes wrinkled in the back window of the car while Tip tried to make up her mind. Finally, she stuffed them into the nearest clothing box in the nearest shopping center, not caring how wrinkled or stained they would get or who would parade them on the streets. And driving away, she saw in her rearview mirror the leg of a pair of red pants executing a limp kick out of the box's chute door.

She had worn those pants when she was the magician's apprentice, when she stood behind him on the stage after he seduced the audience by conjuring rabbits and scarves and flights of paper birds, after he sawed her in half. He had insisted that she wear red pants, that she wear red pants with a black scarf, that she conceal within her pant legs the accoutrements of his trade. They were filled with pockets, huge expanding pockets; driving away, Tip was worried that someone would try the pants on and discover herself the magician's apprentice without any real wish to follow that profession, without agreement or her own volition. But Tip had to get them out of her life; until she discarded them she would always be reminded of her role as his sidekick, the cantor to his liturgical exercises. The job had paid well, but night after night she grew increasingly tense as time for the concluding act drew near. His finale was to place her in a kind of pine coffin and saw the box in half, all very realistically, the saw rasping at the wood, the crumbs of sawdust flying so that the audience, certain of the act's authenticity, thrilled to be watching the terrible demise of what they took to be an endless stream of magician's girls (all tarts who had no life beyond magic), watching for a trickle of blood to appear on the floor under the coffin (which was always balanced, each end on a straight-backed chair); they held their breath as the magician finished his laborious work, would knock the two halves of the coffin apart and wave his hand, whereupon Tip was supposed to spring up, the two halves of enclosing wood falling away from her red pants, her sexy bosom. The truth was that the coffins (a new one delivered by the local coffin-maker every day) were slightly larger than they appeared, so that she could tuck up her legs and curl herself into a ball in one half of the coffin; but every night she watched and listened to the progress of the saw so close to her ear, her unseeing eye, that the job began to wear on her. One night, unforgivably, right before the magician's finale, she stole the gate receipts and ran away, changing her name, her hair color, her way of dressing so that he could not trace her. She even gained weight and consciously altered her walk. Magician's apprentices are not allowed to quit their jobs. They know too much. If he found her she was in trouble. So the red flag of her discarded apprentice pants signalled both relief and worry. If he happened to see them walking down the street on a body's legs, he would know she lived here in Calgary now; on the other hand, they cast a sinister light on the rest of her closet and she was glad to abandon them to thrift shops and second-hand dealers. She wanted no reminders of her failed vocation.

Next, she had to learn money machine etiquette. When she first came to Calgary, she barged up without waiting her turn, looked over people's shoulders and was surprised when they turned and snarled at her. The rules were unbendable. You came up while someone was using the machine. You stood exactly three feet behind them, directly behind them so that they could use their back as a shield, and if they glanced over their shoulder at you, you looked away into the distance. You were no machine thief, you had no intention of watching them punch in their number and then bashing them on the head in order to steal their card and commit computer crime, emptying their programmed and helpless accounts of their programmed limit.

While break-in artists left polite lists of what they had taken (for insurance purposes) and homeowners left a chicken in the fridge for hungry break-in artists, the elaborate ritual of money machines was played out 1900 times an hour all over Calgary, customers brandishing their punch-in cards, their key numbers cleverly memorized (one street in from the back door, the fourteen stations of the cross, subtract the last digit of my birthdate from the first), all following the indelible etiquette of the money machines, protocol as rigid and unyielding as the plastic and metal consoles it was performed for, an elaborate punctilio. Tip tried to ignore rules but the behavior proved infectious and she averted her eyes with as much disdainful courtesy as everyone else. "Who, me? I'm not trying to see your number. I'm just waiting my turn." Nobody knew where the money came from although everyone used the money machines and everyone had a different limit, seemed to have a different monetary designation. Trading numbers and cards had become a gambling racket—you threw yours in the pile to see if you could come off with a higher limit. Even better, the money that the machines doled out was always crisp and new, a pleasure to riffle between the fingers. Money machines were illegal down across the line.

Still, Tip needed a job. The most prevalent occupation in Calgary was that of doorman. Most places had at least one doorman; high class places two or three: a head doorman, an under-doorman, who stood a few steps in front of the head doorman, and a street doorman, who stood at sidewalk level. They were all dressed in top hats and tails, with gold-headed canes across the arms of the head doormen and whistles around the necks of the street doormen. The whistles were to summon rickshaws. The doormen, whose primary employment was staying on their feet, were always yawning, huge molar-displaying yawns that would crack a normal person's jaw, but the doormen were used to it. The problem was that the yawns were contagious, and if you passed a doorman you were sure to catch yourself in the middle of a yawn half a block farther. It got so that people would avert their faces when they passed, all the doormen saw were the backs of heads and determinedly walking bodies. Of course, when you came out of a cave at eleven o'clock at night, pitch black and raining hail-stones, there were no doormen around, they were all in the back gambling or trying on each other's uniforms. The biggest union issues were changes of color and cut for the tailcoats.

The big event came. Rodeo, when the city went naked, resulting in a carnivale levelling, everyone stripped of status and design. As compensation, the animals carried the people's clothes; there were cats with feather boas around their necks, horses wearing buffalo greatcoats, dogs in T-shirts. Because their hats and tailcoats were essential to their duties, the door-men kept those on, although they discarded shirts and pants and shoes, and were able to yawn just as effectively in semi-uniform. During Rodeo Tip got a job as a necromancer, using her magician's appren-ticeship as experience. Curled inside his wooden coffin she had indeed felt herself close to the dead, even wondered if she should try to get closer. She sometimes thought what would happen if she remained stretched flat in the coffin, if she lay with her hands folded across her breast and her eyes lightly closed, with her legs neatly stretched, knee to knee and ankle to ankle under the incipient scrape of the saw; if magic would really happen, if the toothed blade would caress its way through her body without noticeable harm. That recurring idea was what made her decide to run away from the job. Some night she might be tempted to try it and would end up as titillation for the diseased audience.

Necromancy was a good racket down six-gun alley; everyone needed to communicate with their dead, not so much because of the future but because of the present, which was as close as most of them could come to imagining the future. All Tip had to do was persuade them that the voice coming from the ceiling was the voice of their own particular loved one, and with some artificial smoke and red lighting, a heavy and pervasive incense, most people were quite willing to believe that their mother, who had had a soprano voice in real life, would have a raspy contralto in death. The answers to their questions were easy to devise. Falling in love had become unfashionable, and most people's questions had to do with careers and jobs. There was no predictable plot. Tip dressed in an old wedding gown minus veil and train and wrapped a tie-dyed scarf around her curly hair. She put on some half granny glasses for disguise and made sure that she was wearing tennis shoes and that the dress was easily torn off. If the magician stumbled onto her, she wanted to be able to run.

When she wanted to Rodeo dance she went to the Brass Ring. Like everything else in Calgary, you had to know how to get in. You could hear the music, you could see the bodies moving through intermittent windows, but you could not find the door; there was no door, you entered through a complicated series of interconnecting underground passages and back alleys which let out onto a box alley that was always carefully watched. This was no place for hunters or pickups but for real drinkers and dancers, people who wanted to move to the inspiration of alcohol in their bloodstreams and the music—all of it old and hardly heard or remembered by the young. The average age was forty and the bouncer made an attempt to keep everyone under thirty out. Tip slipped him a twenty and got in that way; found herself a table in a dark corner on the lower level and waited for the morning, watching the people thump the brilliantined floor, watching the bodies work their way closer as the night wore on; she danced too, with the lean bandannaed men in wrist and neckline tans, uneasy with the nakedness required by Rodeo. All the music that the headphoned jockey played was from the fifties, Tip's mother's tunes. For Tip, this was a better memory exercise than the machines in the arcades. This was human, noisy, sweaty, the determined bodies writhing or leaning over each other, the broken strobe, the massive bouncer flexing his arm across the door, the table girl's ferocious seating plan, pointing out tables with a six-gun; if you moved without her permission, she'd shoot, hit a hamstring or a funnybone with narrow-eyed deliberance. Everyone was terrified of her pointed bouncing breasts and her choppy walk, her levelled finger. All the bouncer did was watch the door, she didn't need muscle.

The Brass Ring filled you up, satisifed you. When you hit the cool air of the alley at four in the morning, you were high, strung at a pitch that could keep you vibrating for hours. When you went home to sleep the dancing went on and on in your ears. Tip went to the Brass Ring every night after her red-light necromancies, danced and danced until her breasts fell from bouncing, ran all the way home and high-kicked inside the door before she put her earrings in the fridge and fell fast asleep, not even hesitating to dream about the magician she knew was pursuing her.

Every night during Rodeo the hot-air balloons puffed their way south, south-east above the city; a house, an ice cream cone and a propane tank among the striped and shivering colored globes. They floated and duffed, rose and fell. Tip watched for them, the slight hiss that they gave to the air, their implacable float. All of Calgary's dogs hated them, perked their ears and twitched sleeping tails and growled, dived under chairs or ran to windows and barked, tore madly after the balloon's wake or burst through screen doors into their humans' houses. During Rodeo dogs scanned the sky before going outside, anxiety on their muzzles, their raised and pointed noses. The balloons began to fly longer, all day and all night, glowing teardrops hanging above the city in the darkness, the balloonists as a dare beginning to detonate fireworks from their baskets, lighting the sky in unpredictably celebratory purples and greens. The dog population of Calgary went crazy, neurosis and psychosis increasing until they refused to chase cars or cats, refused to water hydrants and instead spent all their time eyeing the transfixed sky. The balloon baskets carried groups of laughing people having champagne break-fasts and cognac lunches, tossing pennies into the sky for luck, renting a feather bed basket in order to become a member of the hot air club, piquancy to lovemaking in the air that did not exist in the hotels and alleys below. Tip fell in love with a balloonist, even though he never removed his leather goggles and aviator's helmet, mainly because she wanted him to teach her his trade. His eyes behind the brown circles were kind, were preoccupied, and when he was on the ground he was always looking up, wanting to hiss his way to the mare's tails of clouds that streamed above the city.

One night in the Brass Ring with her aviator, Tip saw the magician. He was in disguise but she knew it was him, she recognized his mustache. At first she froze, then comforted herself that he would not recognize her. But of course he did and came toward her table, even though the table girl pointed her pearl-handled six-gun at him. He held up his palms. "I know these people," and she spun her gun around her forefinger and walked away.

"I've missed you," he said to Tip.

"Haven't you found a replacement?"

"She's not as good as you were." He smiled.

Tip was starting to sweat. The balloonist looked at the ceiling, he didn't notice. "I've got a new job."

He twitched his mustache and smiled again. "I wouldn't mind," he said reasonably, "if I could get back the pants that I had specially made for you. They were expensive and I think they'd fit the new girl."

"I don't have them anymore."

The magician looked thoughtful and drew at the blue silk bandanna that was knotted around his neck. It came undone and at his gentle tugs grew larger and larger until he held up a new pair of apprentice pants, blue this time, the pockets even more capacious than those of the previous pair. "I'd like you back," he said. "I'd teach you my tricks and you could eventually take over."

Tip shook her head. "There's no future in it. I'd always be your apprentice." The balloonist stood up to go to the can and the magician dared to lay a soft white hand on her knee.

"It's more secure than Calgary. Come now, my dear. Hanging out with balloonists and doormen? Not your style is it?"

"I like it fine. Better than being sawn in half every night."

He ignored that. "I've added a couple of trunk escapes to my repertoire. You'd be perfect."

"What do you do? Stick swords through it?"

"See?" he said gently. "You know the trade. Clever girl." His hand vised itself over her knee. "Come on now, without making a scene. You know you were meant for me. Besides, the gate receipts . . ."

Tip had no weapon and the aviator must have encountered a lineup at the urinal. She stood up, the magician's hand squeezing her arm.

"No funny stuff now," he said happily.

Tip shook her head. They climbed the stairs, moved toward the edge of the dance floor which was right by the door. A greying cowboy lurched against them and turned to slur, "Hey sweetie, wanna dance?"

"Yes," said Tip. "Please." The magician had to let go. The cowboy steered her onto the floor of naked bodies and began to jive, spinning Tip around. She could see the magician by the door looking patient. There was only one exit.

"Please," she said to the cowboy, "I'm getting dizzy."

He swung her into a slow, belly-rubbing waltz and as they turned around the light-pinpointed floor, she worked him deeper and deeper into the crowd. At the end of the waltz she kissed his cheek and slithered to the floor, began to crawl toward the dark warren of tables. She knew without looking that the magician was starting to scan the crowd, check heads. She knew that in a few seconds he would act, would invade, if he had to, the whole of the Brass Ring, would either begin to perform or threaten: the tables would start flying through the air, the DJ's record would begin to spin backwards, the wind would begin to blow. Tip peered from under the edge of an askew tablecloth. One of his best tricks was making his apprentice disappear. Maybe, in the storm he was bound to create, in the energy he would have to unleash, she could make herself disappear. She chuckled suddenly. It was the old rule. If you guessed how he did it, the apprentice got to saw the magician in half; the apprentice became the magician. Tip knew the story had to come from somewhere, it had to be possible. She held her breath and concentrated.

When does a magician's apprentice know that she has absorbed her master's knowledge? If she knew, there might be more rebellions, more magicians sawn in half for inflamed crowds. When apprentice becomes magician history hesitates. It's a rare occasion; most apprentices never dare to try. Tip squeezed her eyes shut and willed herself to disappear. When she opened them, she was floating above the table she had been hiding under and the Brass Ring was in an uproar. The magician was flinging bolts of lightning from his palms. Half the crowd thought it was part of the floor show and the other half thought the situation was serious. The bouncer, who was closest to the magician, had grabbed him, only to find himself flat on his back in a corner with a lump on the side of his head and a chair leg bent around his wrist. There were screams, laughter, and Tip saw her preoccupied balloonist lose both his goggles and his flying helmet to an unseen hand. She almost giggled but caught herself in time. Putting on his knowledge with his power made her see the indifferent strength of his illusion.

She stayed where she was and watched the turn-table trail into silence, the confused jumble of the people on the dance floor, the lights going up to expose the stained walls and the empty glasses. The magician scanned the crowd for Tip, and then all his strength waned. He felt he had better sit down. She had escaped. He hadn't expected her to usurp his power, hadn't expected her to have the nerve to revolt so thoroughly. He was angry but he was also impressed. He knew enough to retreat gracefully.

He stood, bowed to the titsy table girl who strode up and levelled her six-gun at him. "You're supposed to stay at the table I give you," she said. "Those are the rules." She cocked the hammer of the gun.

"Would you like a job? I need an apprentice," he said.

She shook her head and pointed her gun toward the door. He looked at her and nodded and as he moved away, from his fingers drifted hundreds of tiny hot-air balloons that bobbed and swung in the draft of the room and its bodies, as though he were wishing Tip well.

The music began again.

The day after the Rodeo ended, Tip took her fifty-nine dollars and went downtown to look for an object to add to her U-haul collection. Her necromancing was over and now she planned to become a hot air pilot under the tutelage of her preoccupied balloonist. The dogs had returned to their occupations, the doormen to yawning and the people to clothes. An Indian slept on a bench on the Stephen Avenue Mall and a window washer performed his tenuous ballet high against the side of a golden-mirrored building.

Tip looked up at the chartreuse sky, down at the dusty sidewalk. She had found the blue silk pants with the capacious pockets folded into a neat square in her mailbox. What if the magician returned? She stopped in front of a gun store. Inside were racks of shotguns, velvet cases of pistols, knives in leather sheaths. She went in and fingered a double-bladed throwing knife, then shoved it back across the counter at the clerk. "I don't think I need it," she said. As she pulled the wooden door shut behind her, she saw the half-effaced sign stencilled in gothic script on its glass. ALL STORIES   ND. The rack of twenty-twos in the window winked at her.

She would stay here, live in Calgary and wait for next year's Rodeo.

Madeleine Ferron

BE FRUITFUL AND MULTIPLY

Translated by Sheila Watson

ABOUT EIGHT O'CLOCK they woke with a start. Amazed and confused, she shrank from the unexpectedness of her waking. She wasn't dreaming. It was true. She had been married the day before and was waking up with her husband in a bed in the neighbour's house. He was pushing back his hair and swearing as he painfully lifted his head. He had gone to bed dead drunk. "You cannot refuse," they said. "After all, you are the bridegroom."

Half way through the evening he was drunk already and a shock of brown hair had fallen forward over his face without his making any effort at all to throw it back with a shake of his head as he usually did. Shifting from leg to leg, her senses blunted with sleep, she watched, heavy-eyed, the progress of the festivity, diverted from time to time by the almost wild pleasure he was taking in his own wedding feast.

Since it was her wedding too, she resolutely stayed awake, all the while envying her cousin who slept peacefully, her head against the corner of the wall. They were the same age—thirteen-and-a-half. At that age sleep could be pardoned, she had heard them say again and again. Of course, but not on the night of one's wedding.

It was long after midnight when at last he signalled her to follow him. They went through the garden so that no one could see them or play mean tricks on them. She helped him to jump over the fence, to cross the ditch, and to climb the stairs. He fell across the bed and began to snore at once, his hands clenched like a child's. He was eighteen. She slept, curled round on an empty corner of the mattress.

They got up quickly as soon as they woke, ashamed to have stayed in bed so long. He ran to hitch up a buggy which he drove around in front of his in-laws' house. His wife's trunk was loaded on and he helped her up. He was formal, embarrassed; she, almost joyful. Then he turned the horse at a trot towards the property that had been prepared for them. He was to be the second neighbour down the road. She waved happily again and again and her mother, who was crying, kept watching, until they had rounded the corner, the blond braid that swung like a pendulum over the back of the buggy seat.

All day they worked eagerly getting settled. In the evening they went to bed early. He embraced her eagerly. Face to face with a heat that flamed and entangled her in its curious movement, she was frightened.

"What are you doing?" she asked.

He answered quietly, "You are the sheep and I am the ram."

"Oh," she said. It was simple when one had a reference point.

On the first mornings of their life together, after he had left for the fields, she ran quickly to her mother's.

"Are you managing?" her mother always asked.

"Yes," the child replied smiling.

"Your husband, is he good to you?"

"Oh yes," she said. "He says I am a pretty sheep."

Sheep ... sheep. The mother, fascinated, watched her daughter attentively but did not dare to question her further.

"Go back to your husband now," she said. "Busy yourself about the house and get his meal ready."

Since the girl hesitated uncertainly as if she did not understand, her mother sprinkled sugar on a slice of bread spread with cream, gave it to her and pushed her gently toward the door. The child went down the road eating her bread and the mother, reassured, leaned sadly against the wall of the house watching the thick swaying braid until the girl turned the corner of the road.

Little by little the young wife spaced her visits. In autumn when the cold rain began to fall, she came only on Sundays. She had found her own rhythm. Was she too eager, too ambitious? Perhaps she was simply inattentive. Her tempo was too swift. She always hurried now. She wove more bed covers than her chest could hold, cultivated more vegetables than they could eat, raised more calves than they knew how to sell.

And the children came quickly—almost faster than nature permits. She was never seen without a child in her arms, one in her belly, and another at her heels. She raised them well, mechanically, without counting them; accepted them as the seasons are accepted; watched them leave; not with fatalism or resignation but steadfast and untroubled, face to face with the ineluctable cycle that makes the apple fall when it is ripe.

The simple mechanism she had set in motion did not falter. She was the cog wheel that had no right to oversee the whole machine. Everything went well. Only the rhythm was too fast. She outstripped the seasons. The begetting of her children pressed unreasonably on that of her grandchildren and the order was broken. Her daughters and her sons already had many children when she was still bearing others— giving her grandsons uncles who were younger than they were and for whom they could have no respect.

She had twenty-two children. It was extravagant. Fortunately, as one child was carried in the front door, beribboned and wailing, one went out the rear door alone, its knapsack on its back. Nevertheless, it was extravagant. She never realized it.

When her husband was buried and her youngest son married, she caught her breath, decided finally on slippers and a rocking chair. The mechanism could not adjust to a new rhythm. It broke down. She found herself disoriented, incapable of directing the stranger she had become, whom she did not know, who turned round and round with outstretched arms, more and more agitated.

"And if I should visit my family?" she asked her neighbour one day. She had children settled in the four corners of the province, some even exiled to the United States. She would go to take the census or, rather, she would go like a bishop to make the rounds of the diocese.

She had been seen leaving one morning, walking slowly. She had climbed onto the bus, a small black cardboard suitcase in her hand. She had smiled at her neighbours but her eyes were still haggard.

She went first to the States. She was introduced to the wife of her grandson who spoke no French and to all the others whom she looked at searchingly.

"That one," she said, "is she my child or my child's child?"

The generations had become confused. She no longer knew.

She went back to Sept-Isles. One day, when she was rocking on the veranda with one of her sons, he pointed out a big dark-haired young man who was coming down the street.

"Look, mother," her son said, "He is my youngest." He was eighteen and a shock of hair fell forward over his face. She began to cry.

"It is he," she said, "it is my husband."

The next day she was taken to the home of one of her daughters, whom she called by her sister's name. Her daughter took care of her for several days and then took her to the house of the other daughter who, after much kindness, took her to the home of one of the oldest of the grandsons. She asked no questions. She cried.

Finally, one of her boys, chaplain in a home for the aged, came to get her. She followed him obediently. When he presented her to the assembled community, she turned to him and said quietly, "Tell me, are all these your brothers?"

Audrey G. Thomas

IF ONE GREEN BOTTLE ...

WHEN FLEEING, one should never look behind. Orpheus, Lot's wife ... penalties grotesque and terrible await us all. It does not pay to doubt ... to turn one's head ... to rely on the confusion ... the smoke ... the fleeing multitudes ... the satisfaction of the tumbling cities ... to distract the attention of the gods. Argus-eyed, they wait, he waits ... the golden chessmen spread upon the table ... the opponent's move already known, accounted for.... Your pawns, so vulnerable ... advancing with such care (if you step on a crack, then you'll break your mother's back). Already the monstrous hand trembles in anticipation ... the thick lips twitch with suppressed laughter ... then pawn, knight, castle, queen scooped up and tossed aside. "Check," and (click click) "check ... mmmate." The game is over, and you ... surprised (but why?) ... petulant ... your nose still raw from the cold ... your galoshes not yet dried ... really, it's indecent ... inhumane (why bother to come? answer: the bother of not coming) ... and not even the offer of a sandwich or a cup of tea ... discouraging ... disgusting. The great mouth opens ... like a whale really ... he strains you, one more bit of plankton, through his teeth. "Next week ...? At the same time ...? No, no, not at all. I do not find it boring in the least.... Each time a great improvement. Why, soon," the huge lips tremble violently, "ha, ha, *you'll* be beating *me*." Lies ... all lies. Yet, even as you go, echoes of Olympian laughter in your ears, you know you will return, will once more challenge ... and be defeated once again. Even plankton have to make a protest ... a stand ... what else can one do? "Besides, it passes the time ... keeps my hand in ... and you never know.... One time, perhaps ... a slip ... a flutter of the eyelids.... Even the gods grow old."

The tropical fan, three-bladed, omniscient, omnipotent, inexorable, churns up dust and mosquitoes, the damp smell of coming rain, the overripe smell of vegetation, of charcoal fires, of human excrement, of fear ... blown in through the open window, blown up from the walls and the floor. All is caught in the fan's embrace, the efficient arms of the unmoved mover. The deus in the machina, my old chum the chess-player, refuses to descend ... yet watches. Soon they will let down the nets and we will lie in the darkness, in our gauze houses, like so many lumps of cheese ... protected ... revealed. The night-fliers, dirty urchins, will press their noses at my windows and lick their hairy lips in hunger ... in frustration. Can they differentiate, I wonder, between the blood of my neighbor and mine? Are these aesthetes among the insects who will touch only the soft parts ... between the thighs ... under the armpits ... along the inner arm? Are there vintages and connoisseurs? I don't like the nights here: that is why I wanted it over before the night. One of the reasons. If am asleep I do not know who feeds on me, who has found the infinitesimal rip and invited his neighbors in. Besides, he promised it would be over before the night.

And one listens, doesn't one?... one always believes.... Absurd to rely on verbal consolation ...
clichés so worn they feel like old coins ... smooth
... slightly oily to the touch ... faceless.

Pain, the word, I mean, derived (not according to
Skeat) from "pay" and "Cain." How can there, then,
be an exit ... a way out? The darker the night, the
clearer the mark on the forehead ... the brighter the
blind man's cane at the crossing ... the louder the
sound of footsteps somewhere behind. Darkness
heightens the absurd sense of "situation" ... gives
the audience its kicks. But tonight ... really ... All
Souls' ... it's too ridiculous.... Somebody goofed. The
author has gone too far; the absurdity lies in one
banana skin, not two or three. After one, it becomes
too painful ... too involved ... too much like home.
Somebody will have to pay for this ... the reviews
... tomorrow ... will all be most severe. The actors
will sulk over their morning cup of coffee ... the angel
will beat his double breast above the empty pocket-
book ... the director will shout and stamp his feet....
The whole thing should have been revised ... re-
written ... we knew it from the first.

(This is the house that Jack built. This is the cat
that killed the rat that lived in the house that Jack
built. We are the maidens all shaven and shorn, that
milked the cow with the crumpled horn ... that loved
in the hearse that Joke built. Excuse me, please, was
this the Joke that killed the giant or the Jack who
tumbled down ... who broke his crown? Crown him
with many crowns, the lamb upon his throne. He
tumbled too ... it's inevitable.... It all, in the end,
comes back to the nursery.... Jill, Humpty Dumpty,
Rock-a-bye baby ... they-kiss-you, they-kiss-you ...
they all fall down. The nurses in the corner playing
Ludo ... centurions dicing. We are all betrayed by

Cock-a-Doodle-Doo.... We all fall down. Why, then, should I be exempt? ... presumptuous of me ... please forgive).

Edges of pain. Watch it, now, the tide is beginning to turn. Like a cautious bather, stick in one toe ... both feet ... "brr" ... the impact of the ocean ... the solidity of the thing, now that you've finally got under ... like swimming in an ice cube really. "Yes, I'm coming. Wait for me." The shock of the total immersion ... the pain breaking over the head. Don't cry out ... hold your breath ... so. "Not so bad, really, when one gets used to it." That's it ... just the right tone ... the brave swimmer.... Now wave a gay hand toward the shore. Don't let them know ... the indignities ... the chattering teeth ... the blue lips ... the sense of isolation.... Good.

And Mary, how did she take it, I wonder, the original, the appalling announcement ... the burden thrust upon her? "No, really, some other time ... the spring planting ... my aged mother ... quite impossible. Very good of you to think of me, of course, but I couldn't take it on. Perhaps you'd call in again this time next year." (Dismiss him firmly ... quickly, while there's still time. Don't let him get both feet in the door. Be firm and final. "No, I'm sorry, I never accept free gifts.") And then the growing awareness, the anger showing quick and hot under the warm brown of the cheeks. The voice ... like oil.... "I'm afraid I didn't make myself clear." (Like the detective novels.... "Allow me to present my card ... my credentials." The shock of recognition ... the horror. "Oh, I see.... Yes ... well, if it's like that.... Come this way." A gesture of resignation. She allows herself one sigh ... the ghost of a smile.) But no, it's all wrong. Mary ... peasant girl ... quite a different reaction implied. Dumbfounded ... remember Zachary. A shocked silence ... the rough fingers twisting together like snakes ... awe ... a certain rough pride ("Wait until I tell the other girls. The well ... tomorrow morning. ... I won't be proud about it, not really. But it is an honor. What will Mother say?") *Droit de seigneur* ... the servant summoned to the bedchamber ... honored ... afraid. Or perhaps like Leda. No preliminaries ... no thoughts at all. Too stupid ... too frightened ... the thing was, after all, over so quickly. That's it ... stupidity ... the necessary attribute. I can hear him now. "That girl ... whatzername? ... Mary. Mary will do. Must be a simple woman. ... That's where we made our first mistake. Eve too voluptuous ... too intelligent ... this time nothing must go wrong."

And the days were accomplished. Unfair to gloss that over ... to make so little of the waiting ... the months ... the hours. They make no mention of the hours; but of course, men wrote it down. How were they to know? After the immaculate conception, after the long and dreadful journey, after the refusal at the inn ... came the maculate delivery ... the manger. And all that noise ... cattle lowing (and doing other things besides) ... angels blaring away ... the eerie light. No peace ... no chance for sleep ... for rest between the pains ... for time to think ... to gather courage. Yet why should she be afraid ... downhearted ... ? Hadn't she had a sign ... the voice ... the presence of the star? (And notice well, they never told her about the other thing ... the third act.) It probably seemed worth it at the time ... the stench ... the noise ... the pain.

Robert the Bruce ... Constantine ... Noah. The spider ... the flaming cross ... the olive branch. ... With these signs ... I would be content with some-

thing far more simple. A breath of wind on the cheek
... the almost imperceptible movements of a curtain
... a single flash of lightning. Courage consists, perhaps, in the ability to recognize signs ... the symbolism of the spider. But for me ... tonight ... what
is there? The sound of far-off thunder ... the smell
of the coming rain which will wet, but not refresh
... that tropical fan. The curtain moves ... yes, I will
allow you that. But for me ... tonight ... there is only
a rat behind the arras. Jack's rat. This time there is
no exit ... no way out or up.

(You are not amused by my abstract speculations?
Listen ... I have more. Time. Time is an awareness,
either forward or backward, of Then, as opposed to
Now ... the stasis. Time is the moment between
thunder and lightning ... the interval at the street
corner when the light is amber, neither red nor green,
but shift gears, look both ways ... the oasis of pleasure
between pains ... the space between the darkness
and the dawn ... the conversations between courses
... the fear in the final stroke of twelve ... the nervous
fumbling with cloth and buttons, before the longed-
for contact of the flesh ... the ringing telephone ...
the solitary coffee cup ... the oasis of pleasure between
pains. Time ... and time again.)

That time when I was eleven and at Scout camp
... marching in a dusty serpentine to the fire tower
... the hearty counselors with sun-streaked hair and
muscular thighs ... enjoying themselves, enjoying
ourselves ... the long hike almost over. "Ten green
bottles standing on the wall. Ten green bottles standing on the wall. If one green bottle ... should accidentally fall, there'd be nine green bottles standing
on the wall." And that night ... after pigs in blankets
... cocoa ... campfire songs ... the older girls taught
us how to faint ... to hold our breath and count to

thirty ... then blow upon our thumbs. Gazing up at the stars ... the sudden sinking back into warmth and darkness ... the recovery ... the fresh attempt ... delicious. In the morning we climbed the fire tower (and I, afraid to look down or up, climbing blindly, relying on my sense of touch), reached the safety of the little room on top. We peered out the windows at the little world below ... and found six baby mice, all dead ... curled up, like dust kitties in the kitchen drawer. "How long d'you suppose they've been there?" "Too long. Ugh." "Throw them away." "Put them back where you found them." Disturbed ... distressed ... the pleasure marred. "Let's toss them down on Rachel. She was too scared to climb the tower. Baby." "Yes, let's toss them down. She ought to be paid back." (Everything all right now ... the day saved. Ararat ... Areopagus....) Giggling, invulnerable, we hurled the small bodies out the window at the Lilliputian form below. Were we punished? Curious ... I can't remember. And yet the rest ... so vivid ... as though it were yesterday ... this morning ... five minutes ago.... We must have been punished. Surely they wouldn't let us get away with that?

Waves of pain now ... positive whitecaps ... breakers.... Useless to try to remember ... to look behind ... to think. Swim for shore. Ignore the ringing in the ears ... the eyes half blind with water ... the waves breaking over the head. Just keep swimming ... keep moving forward ... rely on instinct ... your sense of direction ... don't look back or forward ... there isn't time for foolish speculation.... See? Flung up ... at last ... exhausted, but on the shore. Flotsam ... jetsam ... but there, you made it. Lie still.

The expected disaster is always the worst. One

waits for it ... is obsessed by it ... it nibbles at the
consciousness. Jack's rat. Far better the screech of
brakes ... the quick embrace of steel and shattered
glass ... or the sudden stumble from the wall. One
is prepared through being unprepared. A few thumps
of the old heart ... like a brief flourish of announcing
trumpets ... a roll of drums ... and then nothing.
This way ... tonight ... I wait for the crouching
darkness like a child waiting for that movement from
the shadows in the corner of the bedroom. It's all
wrong ... unfair ... there ought to be a law.... One
can keep up only a given number of chins ... one
keeps silent only a given number of hours. After that,
the final humiliation ... the loss of self-control ... the
oozing out upon the pavement.... Dumpty-like, one
refuses (or is unable?) to be reintegrated ... whimpers
for morphia and oblivion ... shouts and tears her
hair.... That must not happen.... Undignified ...
déclassé. I shall talk to my friend the fan ... gossip
with the night-fliers ... pit my small light against the
darkness, a miner descending the shaft. I have seen
the opening gambit ... am aware of the game's
inevitable conclusion. What does it matter? I shall
leap over the net ... extend my hand ... murmur,
"Well done," and walk away, stiff-backed and
shoulders high. I will drink the hemlock gaily ... I
will sing. Ten green bottles standing on the wall. Ten
green bottles standing on the wall. If one green bottle
should accidentally fall.... When it is over I will sit
up and call for tea ... ignore the covered basin ...
the bloody sheets (but what do they do with it
afterward ... where will they take it? I have no
experience in these matters). They will learn that the
death of a part is not the death of the whole. The
tables will be turned ... and overturned. The shield
of Achilles will compensate for his heel.

And yet, were we as innocent as all that ... as naive ... that we never wondered where the bottles came from? I never wondered.... I accepted them the way a small child draws the Christmas turkey ... brings the turkey home ... pins it on the playroom wall ... and then sits down to eat. One simply doesn't connect. Yet there they were ... lined up on the laboratory wall ... half-formed, some of them ... the tiny vestigial tails of the smallest ... like corpses of stillborn kittens ... or baby mice. Did we think that they had been like that always ... swimming forever in their little formaldehyde baths ... ships in bottles ... snowstorms in glass paperweights? The professor's voice ... droning like a complacent bee ... tapping his stick against each fragile glass shell ... cross-pollinating facts with facts ... our pencils racing over the paper. We accepted it all without question ... even went up afterward for a closer look ... boldly ... without hesitation. It was all so simple ... so uncomplex ... so scientific. Stupidity, the necessary attribute. And once we dissected a guinea pig, only to discover that she had been pregnant ... tiny little guinea pigs inside. We ... like children presented with one of those Russian dolls ... were delighted ... gratified. We had received a bonus .. a free gift.

Will they do that to part of me? How out of place it will look, bottled with the others ... standing on the laboratory wall. Will the black professor ... the brown-eyed students ... bend their delighted eyes upon this bonus, this free gift? (White. 24 weeks. Female ... or male.) But perhaps black babies are white ... or pink ... to begin. It is an interesting problem ... one which could be pursued ... speculated upon. I must ask someone. If black babies are not black before they are born, at what stage does the dark hand of heredity ... of race ... touch their small bodies? At the moment of birth perhaps? ... like silver exposed to the air. But remember their palms ... the soles of their feet. It's an interesting problem. And remember the beggar outside the central post office ... the terrible burned place on his arm ... the new skin ... translucent ... almost a shell pink. I turned away in disgust ... wincing at the shared memory of scalding liquid ... the pain. But really ... in retrospect ... it was beautiful. That pink skin ... that delicate ... Turneresque tint ... apple blossoms against dark branches.

That's it ... just the right tone.... Abstract speculation on birth ... on death ... on human suffering in general. Remember only the delicate tint ... sunset against a dark sky ... the pleasure of the Guernica. It's so simple, really ... all a question of organization ... of aesthetics. One can so easily escape the unpleasantness ... the shock of recognition. Cleopatra in her robes ... her crown.... "I have immortal longings in me." No fear ... the asp suckles peacefully and unreproved.... She wins ... and Caesar loses. Better than Falstaff "babbling of green fields." One needs the transcendentalism of the tragic hero. Forget the old man ... pathetic ... deserted ... broken. The gray iniquity. It's all a question of organization ... of aesthetics ... of tone. Brooke, for example. "In that rich earth a richer dust concealed...." Terrified out of his wits, of course, but still organizing ... still posturing.

(The pain is really quite bad now ... you will excuse me for a moment? I'll be back. I must not think for a moment ... must not struggle ... must let myself be carried over the crest of the wave ... face downward ... buoyant ... a badge of seaweed across the shoulder. It's easier this way ... not to think ... not to struggle.... It's quicker ... it's more humane.)

Still posturing. See the clown ... advancing slowly across the platform ... dragging the heavy rope ... Grunts ... strains ... the audience shivering with delight. Then the last ... the desperate ... tug. And what revealed? ... a carrot ... a bunch of grapes ... a small dog ... nothing. The audience in tears.... "Oh, God ... how funny.... One knows, of course ... all the time. And yet it never fails to amuse ... I never fail to be taken in." Smothered giggles in the darkened taxi ... the deserted streets.... "Oh, God, how amusing.... Did you see? The carrot ... the bunch of grapes ... the small dog ... nothing. All a masquerade ... a charade ... the rouge ... the powder ... the false hair of an old woman ... a clown." Babbling of green fields.

Once, when I was ten, I sat on a damp rock and watched my father fishing. Quiet ... on a damp rock ... I watched the flapping gills ... the frenzied tail ... the gasps for air ... the refusal to accept the hook's reality. Rainbow body swinging through the air ... the silver drops ... like tears. Watching quietly from the haven of my damp rock, I saw my father struggle with the fish ... the chased and beaten silver body. "Papa, let it go, Papa ... please!" My father ... annoyed ... astonished ... his communion disrupted ... his chalice overturned ... his paten trampled underfoot. He let it go ... unhooked it carelessly and tossed it lightly toward the center of the pool. After all, what did it matter ... to please the child ... and the damage already done. No recriminations ... only, perhaps (we never spoke of it), a certain loss of faith ... a fall, however imperceptible ... from grace?

The pain is harder now ... more frequent ... more intense. Don't think of it ... ignore it ... let it come. The symphony rises to its climax. No more andante ... no more moderato ... clashing cymbals ... blaring

horns.... Lean forward in your seat ... excited ...
intense ... a shiver of fear ... of anticipation. The
conductor ... a wild thing ... a clockwork toy gone
mad.... Arms flailing ... body arched ... head swinging loosely ... dum de dum de DUM DUM DUM.
The orchestra ... the audience ... all bewitched ...
heads nodding ... fingers moving, yes, oh, yes ... the
orgasm of sound ... the straining ... letting go. An
ecstasy ... a crescendo ... a coda ... it's over. "Whew."
"Terrific." (Wiping the sweat from their eyes.) Smiling
... self-conscious ... a bit embarrassed now.... "Funny
how you can get all worked up over a bit of music."
Get back to the formalities.... Get off the slippery
sand ... onto the warm, safe planks of conversation.
"Would you like a coffee ... a drink ... an ice?" The
oasis of pleasure between pains. For me, too, it will
soon be over ... and for you.

Noah on Ararat ... high and dry ... sends out the
dove to see if it is over. Waiting anxiously ... the dove
returning with the sign. Smug now ... self-satisfied
... know-it-all.... All those drowned neighbors ... all
those doubting Thomases ... gone ... washed away
... full fathoms five.... And he, safe ... the animals
pawing restlessly, scenting freedom after their long
confinement ... smelling the rich smell of spring ...
of tender shoots. Victory ... triumph ... the chosen
ones. Start again ... make the world safe for democracy
... cleansing ... purging ... Guernica ... Auschwitz
... God's fine Italian hand. Always the moral ... the
little tag ... the cautionary tale. Willie in one of his
bright new sashes/fell in the fire and was burnt to
ashes.... Suffering is good for the soul ... the effects
on the body are not to be considered. Fire and rain
... cleansing ... purging ... tempering the steel. Not
much longer now ... and soon they will let down
the nets. (He promised it would be over before the

dark. I do not like the dark here. Forgive me if I've mentioned this before.) We will sing to keep our courage up. Ten green bottles standing on the wall. Ten green bottles standing on the wall. If one green bottle....

The retreat from Russia ... feet bleeding on the white snow ... tired ... discouraged ... what was it all about anyway? ... we weren't prepared. Yet we go on ... feet bleeding on the white snow ... dreaming of warmth ... smooth arms and golden hair ... a glass of kvass. We'll get there yet. (But will we ever be the same?) A phoenix ... never refusing ... flying true and straight ... into the fire and out. Plunge downward now ... a few more minutes ... spread your wings ... the moment has come ... the fire blazes ... the priest is ready ... the worshippers are waiting. The battle over ... the death within expelled ... cast out ... the long hike done ... Ararat. Sleep now ... and rise again from the dying fire ... the ashes. It's over ... eyes heavy ... body broken but relaxed. All over. We made it, you and I.... It's all, is it not ... a question of organization ... of tone? Yet one would have been grateful at the last ... for a reason ... an explanation ... a sign. A spider ... a flaming cross ... a carrot ... a bunch of grapes ... a small dog. Not this nothing.

James Thurber

YOU COULD LOOK IT UP

IT ALL BEGUN when we dropped down to C'lumbus, Ohio, from Pittsburgh to play a exhibition game on our way out to St. Louis. It was gettin' on into September, and though we'd been leadin' the league by six, seven games most of the season, we was now in first place by a margin you could 'a' got into the eye of a thimble, bein' only a half a game ahead of St. Louis. Our slump had given the boys the leapin' jumps, and they was like a bunch a old ladies at a lawn fete with a thunderstorm comin' up, runnin' around snarlin' at each other, eatin' bad and sleepin' worse, and battin' for a team average of maybe .186. Half the time nobody'd speak to nobody else, without it was to bawl 'em out.

Squawks Magrew was managin' the boys at the time, and he was darn near crazy. They called him "Squawks" 'cause when things was goin' bad he lost his voice, or pretty near lost it, and squealed at you like a little girl you stepped on her doll or somethin'. He yelled at everybody and wouldn't listen to nobody, without maybe it was me. I'd been trainin' the boys for ten year, and he'd take more lip from me than from anybody else. He knowed I was smarter'n him, anyways, like you're goin' to hear.

This was thirty, thirty-one year ago; you could look it up, 'cause it was the same year C'lumbus decided to call itself the Arch City, on account of a lot of iron arches with electric-light bulbs into 'em which stretched acrost High Street. Thomas Albert Edison sent 'em a telegram, and they was speeches and maybe even President Taft opened the celebration by pushin' a button. It was a great week for the Buckeye capital, which was why they got us out there for this exhibition game.

Well, we just lose a double-header to Pittsburgh 11 to 5 and 7 to 3, so we snarled all the way to C'lumbus, where we put up at the Chittaden Hotel, still snarlin'. Everybody was tetchy, and when Billy Klinger took a sock at Whitey Cott at breakfast, Whitey throwed marmalade all over his face.

"Blind each other, whatta I care?" says Magrew. "You can't see nothin' anyways."

C'lumbus win the exhibition game, 3 to 2, whilst Magrew set in the dugout, mutterin' and cursin' like a fourteen-year-old Scotty. He bad-mouthed everybody on the ball club and he bad-mouthed everybody offa the ball club, includin' the Wright brothers, who, he claimed, had yet to build a airship big enough for any of our boys to hit with a ball bat.

"I wisht I was dead," he says to me. "I wisht I was in heaven with the angels."

I told him to pull hisself together, 'cause he was drivin' the boys crazy, the way he was goin' on, sulkin' and bad-mouthin' and whinin'. I was older'n he was and smarter'n he was, and he knowed it. I was ten times smarter'n he was about this Pearl du Monville, first time I ever laid eyes on the little guy, which was one of the saddest days of my life.

Now, most people name of Pearl is girls, but this

Pearl du Monville was a man, if you could call a fella a man who was only thirty-four, thirty-five inches high. Pearl du Monville was a midget. He was part French and part Hungarian, and maybe even part Bulgarian or somethin'. I can see him now, a sneer on his little pushed-in pan, swingin' a bamboo cane and smokin' a big cigar. He had a gray suit with a big black check into it, and he had a gray felt hat with one of them rainbow-colored hatbands onto it, like the young fellas wore in them days. He talked like he was talkin' into a tin can, but he didn't have no foreign accent. He might a been fifteen or he might a been a hundred, you couldn't tell. Pearl du Monville.

After the game with C'lumbus, Magrew headed straight for the Chittaden bar—the train for St. Louis wasn't goin' for three, four hours—and there he set, drinkin' rye and talkin' to this bartender.

"How I pity me, brother," Magrew was tellin' this bartender. "How I pity me." That was alwuz his favorite tune.

So he was settin' there, tellin' this bartender how heartbreakin' it was to be manager of a bunch of blindfolded circus clowns, when up pops this Pearl du Monville outa nowheres.

It give Magrew the leapin' jumps. He thought at first maybe the D.T.'s had come back on him; he claimed he'd had 'em once, and little guys had popped up all around him, wearin' red, white and blue hats.

"Go on, now!" Magrew yells, "Get away from me!"

But the midget clumb up on a chair acrost the table from Magrew and says, "I seen that game today, Junior, and you ain't got no ball club. What you got there, Junior," he says, "is a side show."

"Whatta ya mean, 'Junior'?" says Magrew, touchin' the little guy to satisfy hisself he was real.

"Don't pay him no attention, mister," says the

bartender. "Pearl calls everybody 'Junior,' 'cause it alwuz turns out he's a year older'n anybody else."

"Yeh?" says Magrew. "How old is he?"

"How old are you, Junior?" says the midget.

"Who, me? I'm fifty-three," says Magrew.

"Well, I'm fifty-four," says the midget.

Magrew grins and asts him what he'll have, and that was the beginnin' of their beautiful friendship, if you don't care what you say.

Pearl du Monville stood up on his chair and waved his cane around and pretended like he was ballyhooin' for a circus. "Right this way, folks!" he yells. "Come on in and see the greatest collection of freaks in the world! See the armless pitchers, see the eyeless batters, see the infielders with five thumbs!" and on and on like that, feedin' Magrew gall and handin' him a laugh at the same time, you might say.

You could hear him and Pearl du Monville hootin' and hollerin' and singin' way up to the fourth floor of the Chittaden, where the boys was packin' up. When it come time to go to the station, you can imagine how disgusted we was when we crowded into the doorway of that bar and seen them two singin' and goin' on.

"Well, well, well," says Magrew, lookin' up and spottin' us. "Look who's here. . . . Clowns, this is Pearl du Monville, a monseer of the old, old school. . . . Don't shake hands with 'em, Pearl, 'cause their fingers is made of chalk and would bust right off in your paws," he says, and he starts guffawin' and Pearl starts titterin' and we stand there givin' 'em the iron eye, it bein' the lowest ebb a ball-club manager'd got hisself down to since the national pastime we started.

Then the midget begun givin' us the ballyhoo. "Come on in!" he says, wavin' his cane. "See the legless base runners, see the outfielders with the butter fingers, see the southpaw with the arm of a little chee-ild!"

Then him and Magrew begun to hoop and holler and nudge each other till you'd of thought this little guy was the funniest guy than even Charlie Chaplin. The fellas filed outa the bar without a word and went on up to the Union Depot, leavin' me to handle Magrew and his new-found crony.

Well, I got 'em outa there finely. I had to take the little guy along, 'cause Magrew had a holt onto him like a vise and I couldn't pry him loose.

"He's comin' along as masket," says Magrew, holdin' the midget in the crouch of his arm like a football. And come along he did, hollerin' and protestin' and beatin' at Magrew with his little fists.

"Cut it out, will ya, Junior?" the little guy kept whinin'. "Come on, leave a man loose, will ya, Junior?"

But Junior kept a holt onto him and begun yellin', "See the guys with the glass arm, see the guys with the cast-iron brains; see the fielders with the feet on their wrists!"

So it goes, right through the whole Union Depot, with people starin' and catcallin', and he don't put the midget down till he gets him through the gates.

"How'm I goin' to go along without no tooth-brush?" the midget asts. "What'm I goin' to do without no other suit?" he says.

"Doc here," says Magrew, meanin' me—"doc here will look after you like you was his own son, won't you, doc?"

I give him the iron eye, and he finely got on the train and prob'ly went to sleep with his clothes on.

This left me alone with the midget. "Lookit," I says to him. "Why don't you go on home now? Come mornin', Magrew'll forget all about you. He'll prob'ly think you was somethin' he seen in a nightmare maybe. And he ain't goin' to laugh so easy in the mornin', neither," I says. "So why don't you go on home?"

"Nix," he says to me. "Skiddoo," he says, "twenty-three for you," and he tosses his cane up into the vestibule of the coach and clam'ers on up after it like a cat. So that's the way Pearl du Monville come to go to St. Louis with the ball club.

I seen 'em first at breakfast the next day, settin' opposite each other; the midget playin' "Turkey in the Straw" on a harmonium and Magrew starin' at his eggs and bacon like they was a uncooked bird with its feathers still on.

"Remember where you found this?" I says, jerkin' my thumb at the midget. "Or maybe you think they come with breakfast on these trains," I says, bein' a good hand at turnin' a sharp remark in them days.

The midget puts down the harmonium and turns on me. "Sneeze," he says; "your brains is dusty." Then he snaps a couple drops of water at me from a tumbler. "Drown," he says, tryin' to make his voice deep.

Now, both them cracks is Civil War cracks, but you'd of thought they was brand new and the funniest than any crack Magrew'd ever heard in his whole life. He started hoopin' and hollerin', and the midget started hoopin' and hollerin', so I walked on away and set down with Bugs Courtney and Hank Metters, payin' no attention to this weak-minded Damon and Phidias acrost the aisle.

Well, sir, the first game with St. Louis was rained out, and there we was facin' a double-header next day. Like maybe I told you, we lose the last three double-headers we play, makin' maybe twenty-five errors in the six games, which is all right for the intimates of a school for the blind, but is disgraceful for the world's champions. It was too wet to go to the zoo, and Magrew wouldn't let us go to the movies, 'cause they flickered so bad in them days. So we just set around, stew-in' and frettin'.

One of the newspaper boys come over to take a pitture of Billy Klinger and Whitey Cott shakin' hands—this reporter'd heard about the fight—and whilst they was standin' there, toe to toe, shakin' hands, Billy gave a back lunge and a jerk, and throwed Whitey over his shoulder into a corner of the room, like a sack a salt. Whitey come back at him with a chair, and Bethlehem broke loose in that there room. The camera was tromped to pieces like a berry basket. When we finely got 'em pulled apart, I heard a laugh, and there was Magrew and the midget standin' in the door and givin' us the iron eye.

"Wrasslers," says Magrew, cold-like, "that's what I got for a ball club, Mr. Du Monville, wrasslers— and not very good wrasslers at that, you ast me."

"A man can't be good at everythin'," says Pearl, "but he oughta be good at somethin'."

This sets Magrew guffawin' again, and away they go, the midget taggin' along by his side like a hound dog and handin' him a fast line of so-called comic cracks.

When we went out to face that battlin' St. Louis club in a double-header the next afternoon, the boys was jumpy as tin toys with keys in their back. We lose the first game, 7 to 2, and are trailin', 4 to 0, when the second game ain't but ten minutes old. Magrew set there like a stone statue, speakin' to nobody. Then, in their half a the fourth, somebody singled to center and knocked in two more runs for St. Louis.

That made Magrew squawk. "I wisht one thing," he says. "I wisht I was manager of a old ladies' sewin' circus 'stead of a ball club."

"You are, Junior, you are," says a familyer and disagreeable voice.

It was that Pearl du Monville again, poppin' up outa nowheres, swingin' his bamboo cane and smokin' a cigar that's three sizes too big for his face. By this time we'd finely got the other side out, and Hank Metters slithered a bat acrost the ground, and the midget had to jump to keep both his ankles from bein' broke.

I thought Magrew'd bust a blood vessel. "You hurt Pearl and I'll break your neck!" he yelled.

Hank muttered somethin' and went on up to the plate and struck out.

We managed to get a couple runs acrost in our half a the sixth, but they come back with three more in their half a the seventh, and this was too much for Magrew.

"Come on, Pearl," he says. "We're gettin' outa here."

"Where you think you're goin'?" I ast him.

"To the lawyer's again," he says cryptly.

"I didn't know you'd been to the lawyer's once, yet," I says.

"Which that goes to show how much you don't know," he says.

With that, they was gone, and I didn't see 'em the rest of the day, nor know what they was up to, which was a God's blessin'. We lose the nightcap, 9 to 3, and that puts us into second place plenty, and as low in our mind as a ball club can get.

The next day was a horrible day, like anybody that lived through it can tell you. Practice was just over and the St. Louis club was takin' the field, when I hears this strange sound from the stands. It sounds like the nervous whickerin' a horse gives when he smells somethin' funny on the wind. It was the fans ketchin' sight of Pearl du Monville, like you have

prob'ly guessed. The midget had popped up onto
the field all dressed up in a minacher club uniform,
sox, cap, little letters sewed onto his chest, and all.
He was swingin' a kid's bat and the only thing kept
him from lookin' like a real ball-player seen through
the wrong end of a microscope was this cigar he was
smokin'.

Bugs Courtney reached over and jerked it outa his
mouth and throwed it away. "You're wearin' that suit
on the playin' field," he says to him, severe as a judge.
"You go insultin' it and I'll take you out to the zoo
and feed you to the bears."

Pearl just blowed some smoke at him which he
still had in his mouth.

Whilst Whitey was foulin' off four or five prior to
strikin' out, I went on over to Magrew. "If I was as
comic as you," I says, "I'd laugh myself to death,"
I says. "Is that any way to treat the uniform, makin'
a mockery out of it?"

"I might surprise you to know I ain't makin' no
mockery outa the uniform," says Magrew. "Pearl du
Monville here has been made a bone-of-fida member
of this so-called ball club. I fixed it up with the front
office by long-distance phone."

"Yeh?" I says. "I can just hear Mr. Dillworth or
Bart Jenkins agreein' to hire a midget for the ball club.
I can just hear 'em." Mr. Dillworth was the owner
of the club and Bart Jenkins was the secretary, and
they never stood for no monkey business. 'May I be
so bold as to inquire," I says, "just what you told
'em?"

"I told 'em," he says, "I wanted to sign up a guy
they ain't no pitcher in the league can strike him
out."

"Uh-huh," I says, "and did you tell 'em what size
of a man he is?"

"Never mind about that," he says. "I got papers on me, made out legal and proper, constitutin' one Pearl du Monville a bone-of-fida member of this former ball club. Maybe that'll shame them big babies into gettin' in there and swingin', knowin' I can replace any one of 'em with a midget, if I have a mind to. A St. Louis lawyer I seen twice tells me it's all legal and proper."

"A St. Louis lawyer would," I says, "seein' nothin' could make him happier than havin' you makin' a mockery outa this one-time baseball outfit," I says.

Well, sir, it'll all be there in the papers of thirty, thirty-one year ago, and you could look it up. The game went along without no scorin' for seven innings, and since they ain't nothin' much to watch but guys poppin' up or strikin' out, the fans pay most of their attention to the goin's-on of Pearl du Monville. He's out there in front a the dugout, turnin' handsprings, balancin' his bat on his chin, walkin' a imaginary line, and so on. The fans clapped and laughed at him, and he ate it up.

So it went up to the last a the eighth, nothin' to nothin', not more'n seven, eight hits all told, and no errors on neither side. Our pitcher gets the first two men out easy in the eighth. Then up come a fella name of Porter or Billings, or some such name, and he lammed one up against the tobacco sign for three bases. The next guy up slapped the first ball out into left for a base hit, and in come the fella from third for the only run of the ball game so far. The crowd yelled, the look a death come onto Magrew's face again, and even the midget quit his tom-foolin'. Their next man fouled out back a third, and we come up for our last bats like a bunch a schoolgirls steppin' into a pool of cold water. I was lower in my mind than I'd been since the day in Nineteen-four when

Chesbro throwed the wild pitch in the ninth inning with a man on third and lost the pennant for the Highlanders. I knowed something just as bad was goin' to happen, which shows I'm a clairvoyun, or was then.

When Gordy Mills hit out to second, I just closed my eyes. I opened 'em up again to see Dutch Muller standin' on second, dustin' off his pants, him havin' got his first hit in maybe twenty times to the plate. Next up was Harry Loesing, battin' for our pitcher, and he got a base on balls, walkin' on a fourth one you could a combed your hair with.

Then up come Whitey Cott, our lead-off man. He crotches down in what was prob'ly the most fearsome stanch in organized ball, but all he can do is pop out to short. That brung up Billy Klinger, with two down and a man on first and second. Billy took a cut at one you could a knocked a plug hat offa this here Carnera with it, but then he gets sense enough to wait 'em out, and finely he walks, too, fillin' the bases.

Yes, sir, there you are; the tyin' run on third and the winnin' run on second, first a the ninth, two men down, and Hank Metters comin' to the bat. Hank was built like a Pope-Hartford and he couldn't run no faster'n President Taft, but he had five home runs to his credit for the season, and that wasn't bad in them days. Hank was still hittin' better'n anybody else on the ball club, and it was mighty heartenin', seein' him stridin' up towards the plate. But he never got there.

"Wait a minute!" yells Magrew, jumpin' to his feet. "I'm sendin' in a pinch hitter!" he yells.

You could a heard a bomb drop. When a ball-club manager says he's sendin' in a pinch hitter for the best batter on the club, you know and I know and everybody knows he's lost his hold.

"They're goin' to be sendin' the funny wagon for you, if you don't watch out," I says, grabbin' a holt of his arm.

But he pulled away and run out towards the plate, yellin', "Du Monville battin' for Metters!"

All the fellas begun squawlin' at once, except Hank, and he just stood there starin' at Magrew like he'd gone crazy and was claimin' to be Ty Cobb's grandma or somethin'. Their pitcher stood out there with his hands on his hips and a disagreeable look on his face, and the plate umpire told Magrew to go on and get a batter up. Magrew told him again Du Monville was battin' for Metters, and the St. Louis manager finely got the idea. It brung him outa his dugout, howlin' and bawlin' like he'd lost a female dog and her seven pups.

Magrew pushed the midget towards the plate and he says to him, he says, "Just stand up there and hold the bat on your shoulder. They ain't a man in the world can throw three strikes in there 'fore he throws four balls!" he says.

"I get it, Junior!" says the midget. "He'll walk me and force in the tyin' run!" And he starts on up to the plate as cocky as if he was Willie Keeler.

I don't need to tell you Bethlehem broke loose on that there ball field. The fans got onto their hind legs, yellin' and whistlin', and everybody on the field begun wavin' their arms and hollerin' and shovin'. The plate umpire stalked over to Magrew like a traffic cop, waggin' his jaw and pointin' his finger, and the St. Louis manager kept yellin' like his house was on fire. When Pearl got up to the plate and stood there, the pitcher slammed his glove down onto the ground and started stompin' on it, and they ain't nobody can blame him. He's just walked two normal-sized human bein's, and now here's a guy up to the plate they ain't more'n twenty inches between his knees and his shoulders.

The plate umpire called in the field umpire, and they talked a while, like a couple doctors seein' the bucolic plague or somethin' for the first time. Then the plate umpire come over to Magrew with his arms folded acrost his chest, and he told him to go on and get a batter up, or he'd forfeit the game to St. Louis. He pulled out his watch, but somebody batted it outa his hand in the scuffin', and I thought there'd be a free-for-all, with everybody yellin' and shovin' except Pearl du Monville, who stood up at the plate with his little bat on his shoulder, not movin' a muscle.

Then Magrew played his ace. I seen him pull some papers outa his pocket and show 'em to the plate umpire. The umpire begun lookin' at 'em like they was bills for somethin' he not only never bought it, he never even heard of it. The other umpire studied 'em like they was a death warren, and all this time the St. Louis manager and the fans and the players is yellin' and hollerin'.

Well, sir, they fought about him bein' a midget, and they fought about him usin' a kid's bat, and they fought about where'd he been all season. They was eight or nine rule books brung out and everybody was thumbin' through 'em, tryin' to find out what it says about midgets, but it don't say nothin' about midgets, cause this was somethin' never'd come up in the history of the game before, and nobody'd ever dreamed about it, even when they has nightmares. Maybe you can't send no midgets in to bat nowadays, 'cause the old game's changed a lot, mostly for the worst, but you could then, it turned out.

The plate umpire finely decided the contract papers was all legal and proper, like Magrew said, so he waved the St. Louis players back to their places and he pointed his finger at their manager and told him to quit hollerin' and get on back in the dugout. The manager says the game is percedin' under protest, and the umpire bawls, "Play ball!" over 'n' above the yellin' and booin', him havin' a voice like a hog-caller.

The St. Louis pitcher picked up his glove and beat at it with his fist six or eight times, and then got set on the mound and studied the situation. The fans realized he was really goin' to pitch to the midget, and they went crazy, hoopin' and hollerin' louder'n ever, and throwin' pop bottles and hats and cushions down onto the field. It took five, ten minutes to get the fans quieted down again, whilst our fellas that was on base set down on the bags and waited. And Pearl du Monville kept standin' up there with the bat on his shoulder, like he'd been told to.

So the pitcher starts studyin' the setup again, and you got to admit it was the strangest setup in a ball game since the players cut off their beards and begun wearin' gloves. I wisht I could call the pitcher's name— it wasn't old Barney Pelty nor Nig Jack Powell nor Harry Howell. He was a big right-hander, but I can't call his name. You could look it up. Even in a crotchin' position, the ketcher towers over the midget like the Washington Monument.

The plate umpire tries standin' on his tiptoes, then he tries crotchin' down, and he finely get hisself into a stanch nobody'd ever seen on a ball field before, kinda squattin' down on his hanches.

Well, the pitcher is sore as a old buggy horse in fly time. He slams in the first pitch, hard and wild, and maybe two foot higher'n the midget's head.

"Ball one!" hollers the umpire over 'n' above the

racket, 'cause everybody is yellin' worsten ever.

The ketcher goes on out towards the mound and talks to the pitcher and hands him the ball. This time the big right-hander tried a undershoot, and it comes in a little closer, maybe no higher'n a foot, foot and a half above Pearl's head. It would a been a strike with a human bein' in there, but the umpire's got to call it, and he does.

"Ball two!" he bellers.

The ketcher walks on out to the mound again, and the whole infield comes over and gives advice to the pitcher about what they'd do in a case like this, with two balls and no strikes on a batter that oughta be in a bottle of alcohol 'stead of up there at the plate in a big-league game between the teams that is fightin' for first place.

For the third pitch, the pitcher stands there flat-footed and tosses up the ball like he's playin' ketch with a little girl.

Pearl stands there motionless as a hitchin' post, and the ball comes in big and slow and high—high for Pearl, that is, it bein' about on a level with his eyes, or a little higher'n a grown man's knees.

They ain't nothin' else for the umpire to do, so he calls, "Ball three!"

Everybody is onto their feet, hoopin' and hollerin', as the pitcher sets to throw ball four. The St. Louis manager is makin' signs and faces like he was a contorturer, and the infield is givin' the pitcher some more advice about what to do this time. Our boys who was on base stick right onto the bag, runnin' no risk of bein' nipped for the last out.

Well, the pitcher decides to give him a toss again, seein' he come closer with that than with a fast ball. They ain't nobody ever seen a slower ball throwed. It come in big as a balloon and slower'n any ball ever throwed before in the major leagues. It come right in over the plate in front of Pearl's chest, lookin' prob'ly big as a full moon to Pearl. They ain't never been a minute like the minute that followed since the United States was founded by the Pilgrim grandfathers.

Pearl du Monville took a cut at that ball, and he hit it! Magrew give a groan like a poleaxed steer as the ball rolls out in front a the plate into fair territory.

"Fair ball!" yells the umpire, and the midget starts runnin' for first, still carryin' that little bat, and makin' maybe ninety foot an hour. Bethlehem breaks loose on that ball field in them stands. They ain't never been nothin' like it since creation was begun.

The ball's rollin' slow, on down towards third, goin' maybe eight, ten foot. The infield comes in fast and our boys break from their bases like hares in a brush fire. Everybody is standin' up, yellin' and hollerin', and Magrew is tearin' his hair outa his head, and the midget is scamperin' for first with all the speed of one of them little dashbounds carryin' a satchel in his mouth.

The ketcher gets to the ball first, but he boots it on out past the pitcher's box, the pitcher fallin' on his face tryin' to stop it, the shortstop sprawlin' after it full length and zaggin' it on over towards the second baseman, whilst Muller is scorin' with the tyin' run and Loesing is roundin' third with the winnin' run. Ty Cobb could a made a three-bagger outa that bunt, with everybody fallin' over theirself tryin' to pick the ball up. But Pearl is still maybe fifteen, twenty feet from the bag, toddlin' like a baby and yeepin' like a trapped raibbit, when the second baseman finely gets a holt of that ball and slams it over to first. The first baseman ketches it and stomps on the bag, the base umpire waves Pearl out, and there goes your old ball game, the craziest ball game every played in the history of the organized world.

Their players start runnin' in, and then I see Magrew. He starts after Pearl, runnin' faster'n any man ever run before. Pearl sees him comin' and runs behind the base umpire's legs and gets a holt onto 'em. Magrew comes up, pantin' and roarin', and him and the midget plays ring-around-a-rosy with the umpire, who keeps shovin' at Magrew with one hand and tryin' to slap the midget loose from his legs with the other.

Finely Magrew ketches the midget, who is still yeepin' like a stuck sheep. He gets holt of that little guy by both his ankles and starts whirlin' him round and round his head like Magrew was a hammer thrower and Pearl was the hammer. Nobody can stop him without gettin' their head knocked off, so everybody just stands there and yells. Then Magrew lets the midget fly. He flies on out towards second, high and fast, like a human home run, headed for the soap sign in center field.

Their shortstop tries to get to him, but he can't make it, and I knowed the little fella was goin' to bust to pieces like a dollar wach on a asphalt street when he hit the ground. But it so happens their center fielder is just crossin' second, and he starts runnin' back, tryin' to get under the midget, who had took to spiralin' like a football 'stead of turnin' head over foot, which give him more speed and more distance.

I know you never seen a midget ketched, and you prob'ly never seen one throwed. To ketch a midget that's been throwed by a heavy-muscled man and is flyin' through the air, you got to run under him and with him and pull your hands and arms back and down when you ketch him, to break the compact of his body, or you'll bust him in two like a matchstick.

I seen Bill Lange and Willie Keeler and Tris Speaker made some wonderful ketches in my day, but I never seen nothin' like that center fielder. He goes back and back and still further back and he pulls that midget down outa the air like he was liftin' a sleepin' baby from a cradle. They wasn't a bruise onto him, only his face was the color of cat's meat and he ain't got no air in his chest. In his excitement, the base umpire, who was runnin' back with the center fielder when he ketched Pearl, yells, "Out!" and that give hysteries to the Bethlehem which was ragin' like Niagry on that ball field.

Everybody was hoopin' and hollerin' and yellin' and runnin', with the fans swarmin' onto the field, and the cops tryin' to keep order, and some guys laughin' and some of the women fans cryin', and six or eight of us holdin' onto Magrew to keep him from gettin' at that midget and finishin' him off. Some of the fans picks up the St. Louis pitcher and the center fielder, and starts carryin' 'em around on their shoulders, and they was the craziest goin's-on knowed to the history of organized ball on this side of the 'Lantic Ocean.

I seen Pearl du Monville strugglin' in the arms of a lady fan with a ample bosom, who was laughin' and cryin' at the same time, and him beatin' at her with his little fists and bawlin' and yellin'. He clawed his way loose finely and disappeared in the forest of legs which made that ball field look like it was Coney Island on a hot summer's day.

That was the last I ever seen of Pearl du Monville. I never seen hide nor hair of him from that day to this, and neither did nobody else. He just vanished into the thin of the air, as the fella says. He was ketched for the final out of the ball game and that was the end of him, just like it was the end of the ball game, you might say, and also the end of our losin' streak, like I'm goin' to tell you.

That night we piled onto a train for Chicago, but we wasn't snarlin' and snappin' any more. No, sir, the ice was finely broke and a new spirit come into that ball club. The old zip come back with the disappearance of Pearl du Monville out back a second base. We got to laughin' and talkin' and kiddin' together, and 'fore long Magrew was laughin' with us. He got a human look onto his pan again, and he quit whinin' and complainin' and wishtin' he was in heaven with the angels.

Well, sir, we wiped up that Chicago series winnin' all four games, and makin' seventeen hits in one of 'em. Funny thing was, St. Louis was so shook up by that last game with us, they never did hit their stride again. Their center fielder took to misjudgin' everything that come his way, and the rest a the fellas followed suit, the way a club'll do when one guy blows up.

'Fore we left Chicago, I and some of the fellas went out and bought a pair of them little baby shoes, which we had 'em golded over and give 'em to Magrew for a souvenir, and he took it all in good spirit. Whitey Cott and Billy Klinger made up and was fast friends again, and we hit our home lot like a ton of dynamite and they was nothin' could stop us from then on.

I don't recollect things as clear as I did thirty, forty year ago. I can't read no fine print no more, and the only person I got to check with on the golden days of the national pastime, as the fella says, is my friend, old Milt Kline, over in Springfield, and his mind ain't as strong as it once was.

He gets Rube Waddell mixed up with Rube Marquard, for one thing, and anybody does that oughta be put away where he won't bother nobody. So I can't tell you the exact margin we win the pennant by. Maybe it was two and a half games, or maybe it was three and a half. But it'll all be there in the newspapers and record books of thirty, thirty-one year ago and, like I was sayin', you could look it up.

Ernest Hemingway

AFTER THE STORM

IT WASN'T ABOUT ANYTHING, something about making punch, and then we started fighting and I slipped and he had me down kneeling on my chest and choking me with both hands like he was trying to kill me and all the time I was trying to get the knife out of my pocket to cut him loose. Everybody was too drunk to pull him off me. He was choking me and hammering my head on the floor and I got the knife out and opened it up; and I cut the muscle right across his arm and he let go of me. He couldn't have held on if he wanted to. Then he rolled and hung onto that arm and started to cry and I said:

"What the hell you want to choke me for?"

I'd have killed him. I couldn't swallow for a week. He hurt my throat bad.

Well, I went out of there and there were plenty of them with him and some came out after me and I made a turn and was down by the docks and I met a fellow and he said somebody killed a man up the street. I said "Who killed him?" and he said "I don't know who killed him but he's dead all right," and it was dark and there was water standing in the street and no lights and windows broke and boats all up in the town and trees blown down and everything all blown and I got a skiff and went out and found my boat where I had her inside of Mango Key and she was all right only she was full of water. So I bailed her out and pumped her out and there was a moon but plenty of clouds and still plenty rough and I took it down along; and when it was daylight I was off Eastern Harbor.

Brother, that was some storm. I was the first boat out and you never saw water like that was. It was just as white as a lye barrel and coming from Eastern Harbor to Sou'west Key you couldn't recognize the shore. There was a big channel blown right out through the middle of the beach. Trees and all blown out and a channel cut through and all the water white as chalk and everything on it; branches and whole trees and dead birds, and all floating. Inside the keys were all the pelicans in the world and all kinds of birds flying. They must have gone inside there when they knew it was coming.

I lay at Sou'west Key a day and nobody came after me. I was the first boat out and I seen a spar floating and I knew there must be a wreck and I started out to look for her. I found her. She was a three-masted schooner and I could just see the stumps of her spars out of water. She was in too deep water and I didn't get anything off of her. So I went on looking for something else. I had the start on all of them and I knew I ought to get whatever there was. I went on down over the sand-bars from where I left that three-masted schooner and I didn't find anything and I went on a long way. I was way out toward the quicksands and I didn't find anything so I went on. Then when I was in sight of the Rebecca Light I saw all kinds of birds making over something and I headed over for them to see what it was and there was a cloud of birds all right.

I could see something looked like a spar up out of the water and when I got over close the birds all went up in the air and stayed all around me. The water was clear out there and there was a spar of some kind sticking out just above the water and when I come up close to it I saw it was all dark under water like a long shadow and I came right over it and there under water was a liner; just lying there all under water as big as the whole world. I drifted over her in the boat. She lay on her side and the stern was deep down. The port holes were all shut tight and I could see the glass shine in the water and the whole of her; the biggest boat I ever saw in my life laying there and I went along the whole length of her and then I went over and anchored and I had the skiff on the deck forward and I shoved it down into the water and sculled over with the birds all around me.

I had a water glass like we use sponging and my hand shook so I could hardly hold it. All the port holes were shut that you could see going along over her but way down below near the bottom something must have been open because there were pieces of things floating out all the time. You couldn't tell what they were. Just pieces. That's what the birds were after. You never saw so many birds. They were all around me; crazy yelling.

I could see everything sharp and clear. I could see her rounded over and she looked a mile long under the water. She was lying on a clear white bank of sand and the spar was a sort of foremast or some sort of tackle that slanted out of water the way she was laying on her side. Her bow wasn't very far under. I could stand on the letters of her name on her bow and my head was just out of water. But the nearest port hole was twelve feet down. I could just reach it with the grains pole and I tried to break it with that but I couldn't. The glass was too stout. So I sculled back to the boat and got a wrench and lashed it to the end of the grains pole and I couldn't break it. There I was looking down through the glass at that liner with everything in her and I was the first one to her and I couldn't get into her. She must have had five million dollars worth in her.

It made me shaky to think how much she must have in her. Inside the port hole that was closest I could see something but I couldn't make it out through the water glass. I couldn't do any good with the grains pole and I took off my clothes and stood and took a couple of deep breaths and dove over off the stern with the wrench in my hand and swam down. I could hold on for a second to the edge of the port hole and I could see in and there was a woman inside with her hair floating all out. I could see her floating plain and I hit the glass twice with the wrench hard and I heard the noise clink in my ears but it wouldn't break and I had to come up.

I hung onto the dinghy and got my breath and then I climbed in and took a couple of breaths and dove again. I swam down and took hold of the edge of the port hole with my fingers and held it and hit the glass as hard as I could with the wrench. I could see the woman floated in the water through the glass. Her hair was tied once close to her head and it floated all out in the water. I could see the rings on one of her hands. She was right up close to the port hole and I hit the glass twice and I didn't even crack it. When I came up I thought I wouldn't make it to the top before I'd have to breathe.

I went down once more and I cracked the glass, only cracked it, and when I came up my nose was bleeding and I stood on the bow of the liner with my bare feet on the letters of her name and my head

just out and rested there and then I swam over to
the skiff and pulled up into it and sat there waiting
for my head to stop aching and looking down into
the water glass, but I bled so I had to wash out the
water glass. Then I lay back in the skiff and held my
hand under my nose to stop it and I lay there with
my head back looking up and there was a million
birds above and all around.

When I quit bleeding I took another look through
the glass and then I sculled over to the boat to try
and find something heavier than the wrench but I
couldn't find a thing; not even a sponge hook. I went
back and the water was clearer all the time and you
could see everything that floated out over that white
bank of sand. I looked for sharks but there weren't
any. You could have seen a shark a long way away.
The water was so clear and the sand white. There
was a grapple for an anchor on the skiff and I cut
it off and went overboard and down with it. It carried
me right down and past the port hole and I grabbed
and couldn't hold anything and went on down and
down, sliding along the curved side of her. I had to
let go of the grapple. I heard it bump once and it
seemed like a year before I came up through to the
top of the water. The skiff was floated away with the
tide and I swam over to her with my nose bleeding
in the water while I swam and I was plenty glad
there weren't sharks; but I was tired.

My head felt cracked open and I lay in the skiff
and rested and then I sculled back. It was getting
along in the afternoon. I went down once more with
the wrench and it didn't do any good. That wrench
was too light. It wasn't any good diving unless you
had a big hammer or something heavy enough to
do good. Then I lashed the wrench to the grains pole
again and I watched through the water glass and

pounded on the glass and hammered until the wrench came off and I saw it in the glass, clear and sharp, go sliding down along her and then off and down to the quicksand and go in. Then I couldn't do a thing. The wrench was gone and I'd lost the grapple so I sculled back to the boat. I was too tired to get the skiff aboard and the sun was pretty low. The birds were all pulling out and leaving her and I headed for Sou'west Key towing the skiff and the birds going on ahead of me and behind me. I was plenty tired.

That night it came on to blow and it blew for a week. You couldn't get out to her. They come out from town and told me the fellow I'd had to cut was all right except for his arm and I went back to town and they put me under five hundred dollars bond. It came out all right because some of them, friends of mine, swore he was after me with an ax, but by the time we got back out to her the Greeks had blown her open and cleaned her out. They got the safe out with dynamite. Nobody ever knows how much they got. She carried gold and they got it all. They stripped her clean. I found her and I never got a nickel out of her.

It was a hell of a thing all right. They say she was just outside of Havana harbor when the hurricane hit and she couldn't get in or the owners wouldn't let the captain chance coming in; they say he wanted to try; so she had to go with it and in the dark they were running with it trying to go through the gulf between Rebecca and Tortugas when she struck on the quicksands. Maybe her rudder was carried away. Maybe they weren't even steering. But anyway they couldn't have known they were quicksands and when she struck the captain must have ordered them to open up the ballast tanks so she'd lay solid. But it was quicksand she'd hit and when they opened the tank she went in stern first and then over on her beam ends. There were four hundred and fifty passengers and the crew on board of her and they must all have been aboard of her when I found her. They must have opened the tanks as soon as she struck and the minute she settled on it the quicksands took her down. Then her boilers must have burst and that must have been what made those pieces that came out. It was funny there weren't any sharks though. There wasn't a fish. I could have seen them on that clear white sand.

Plenty of fish now though; jewfish, the biggest kind. The biggest part of her's under the sand now but they live inside of her; the biggest kind of jewfish. Some weigh three to four hundred pounds. Sometime we'll go out and get some. You can see the Rebecca light from where she is. They've got a buoy on her now. She's right at the end of the quicksand right at the edge of the gulf. She only missed going through by about a hundred yards. In the dark in the storm they just missed it; raining the way it was they couldn't have seen the Rebecca. Then they're not used to that sort of thing. The captain of a liner isn't used to scudding that way. They have a course and they tell me they set some sort of a compass and it steers itself. They probably didn't know where they were when they ran with that blow but they come close to making it. Maybe they'd lost the rudder though. Anyway there wasn't another thing for them to hit till they'd get to Mexico once they were in that gulf. Must have been something though when they struck in that rain and wind and he told them to open her tanks. Nobody could have been on deck in that blow and rain. Everybody must have been below. They couldn't have lived on deck. There must have been some scenes inside all right because you know she settled fast. I saw that wrench go into the sand. The captain couldn't have known it was quicksand when she struck unless he knew these waters. He just knew it wasn't rock. He must have seen it all up in the bridge. He must have known what it was about when she settled. I wonder how fast she made it. I wonder if the mate was there with him. Do you think they stayed inside the bridge or do you think they took it outside? They never found any bodies. Not a one. Nobody floating. They float a long way with life belts too. They must have took it inside. Well, the Greeks got it all. Everything. They must have come fast all right. They picked her clean. First there was the birds, then me, then the Greeks, and even the birds got more out of her than I did.

Albert Camus

THE GUEST

Translated by Justin O'Brien

THE SCHOOLMASTER WAS WATCHING the two
men climb toward him. One was on horseback, the
other on foot. They had not yet tackled the abrupt
rise leading to the schoolhouse built on the hillside.
They were toiling onward, making slow progress in
the snow, among the stones, on the vast expanse of
the high, deserted plateau. From time to time the horse
stumbled. Without hearing anything yet, he could see
the breath issuing from the horse's nostrils. One of
the men, at least, knew the region. They were following
the trail although it had disappeared days ago under
a layer of dirty white snow. The schoolmaster cal-
culated that it would take them half an hour to get
onto the hill. It was cold; he went back into the school
to get a sweater.

He crossed the empty, frigid classroom. On the
blackboard the four rivers of France, drawn with four
different colored chalks, had been flowing toward
their estuaries for the past three days. Snow had
suddenly fallen in mid-October after eight months
of drought without the transition of rain, and the
twenty pupils, more or less, who lived in the villages
scattered over the plateau had stopped coming. With

fair weather they would return. Daru now heated only the single room that was his lodging, adjoining the classroom and giving also onto the plateau to the east. Like the class windows, his window looked to the south too. On that side the school was a few kilometers from the point where the plateau began to slope toward the south. In clear weather could be seen the purple mass of the mountain range where the gap opened onto the desert.

Somewhat warmed, Daru returned to the window from which he had first seen the two men. They were no longer visible. Hence they must have tackled the rise. The sky was not so dark, for the snow had stopped falling during the night. The morning had opened with a dirty light which had scarcely become brighter as the ceiling of clouds lifted. At two in the afternoon it seemed as if the day were merely beginning. But still this was better than those three days when the thick snow was falling amidst unbroken darkness with little gusts of wind that rattled the double door of the classroom. Then Daru had spent long hours in his room, leaving it only to go to the shed and feed the chickens or get some coal. Fortunately the delivery truck from Tadjid, the nearest village to the north, had brought his supplies two days before the blizzard. It would return in forty-eight hours.

Besides, he had enough to resist a siege, for the little room was cluttered with bags of wheat that the administration left as a stock to distribute to those of his pupils whose families had suffered from the drought. Actually they had all been victims because they were all poor. Every day Daru would distribute a ration to the children. They had missed it, he knew, during these bad days. Possibly one of the fathers or big brothers would come this afternoon and he could supply them with grain. It was just a matter of carrying them over to the next harvest. Now shiploads of wheat were arriving from France and the worst was over. But it would be hard to forget that poverty, that army of ragged ghosts wandering in the sunlight, the plateaus burned to a cinder month after month, the earth shriveled up little by little, literally scorched, every stone bursting into dust under one's foot. The sheep had died then by thousands and even a few men, here and there, sometimes without anyone's knowing.

In contrast with such poverty, he who lived almost like a monk in his remote schoolhouse, nonetheless satisfied with the little he had and with the rough life, had felt like a lord with his whitewashed walls, his narrow couch, his unpainted shelves, his well, and his weekly provision of water and food. And suddenly this snow, without warning, without the foretaste of rain. This is the way the region was, cruel to live in, even without men—who didn't help matters either. But Daru had been born here. Everywhere else, he felt exiled.

He stepped out onto the terrace in front of the schoolhouse. The two men were now halfway up the slope. He recognized the horseman as Balducci, the old gendarme he had known for a long time. Balducci was holding on the end of a rope an Arab who was walking behind him with hands bound and head lowered. The gendarme waved a greeting to which Daru did not reply, lost as he was in contemplation of the Arab dressed in a faded blue jellaba, his feet in sandals but covered with socks of heavy raw wool, his head surmounted by a narrow, short *chèche*. They were approaching. Balducci was holding back his horse in order not to hurt the Arab, and the group was advancing slowly.

Within earshot, Balducci shouted: "One hour to do

the three kilometers from El Ameur!" Daru did not answer. Short and square in his thick sweater, he watched them climb. Not once had the Arab raised his head. "Hello," said Daru when they got up onto the terrace. "Come in and warm up." Balducci painfully got down from his horse without letting go of the rope. From under his bristling mustache he smiled at the schoolmaster. His little dark eyes, deep-set under a tanned forehead, and his mouth surrounded with wrinkles made him look attentive and studious. Daru took the bridle, led the horse to the shed, and came back to the two men, who were now waiting for him in the school. He led them into his room. "I am going to heat up the classroom," he said. "We'll be more comfortable there." When he entered the room again, Balducci was on the couch. He had undone the rope tying him to the Arab, who had squatted near the stove. His hands still bound, the *chèche* pushed back on his head, he was looking toward the window. At first Daru noticed only his huge lips, fat, smooth, almost Negroid; yet his nose was straight, his eyes were dark and full of fever. The *chèche* revealed an obstinate forehead and, under the weathered skin now rather discolored by the cold, the whole face had a restless and rebellious look that struck Daru when the Arab, turning his face toward him, looked him straight in the eyes. "Go into the other room," said the schoolmaster, "and I'll make you some mint tea." "Thanks," Balducci said. "What a chore! How I long for retirement." And addressing his prisoner in Arabic: "Come on, you." The Arab got up and, slowly, holding his bound wrists in front of him, went into the classroom.

With the tea, Daru brought a chair. But Balducci was already enthroned on the nearest pupil's desk and the Arab had squatted against the teacher's

platform facing the stove, which stood between the
desk and the window. When he held out the glass
of tea to the prisoner, Daru hesitated at the sight
of his bound hands. "He might perhaps be untied."
"Sure," said Balducci. "That was for the trip." He
started to get to his feet. But Daru, setting the glass
on the floor, had knelt beside the Arab. Without saying
anything, the Arab watched him with his feverish
eyes. Once his hands were free, he rubbed his swollen
wrists against each other, took the glass of tea, and
sucked up the burning liquid in swift little sips.

"Good," said Daru. "And where are you headed?"

Balducci withdrew his mustache from the tea.
"Here, son."

"Odd pupils! And you're spending the night?"

"No. I'm going back to El Ameur. And you will
deliver this fellow to Tinguit. He is expected at police
headquarters."

Balducci was looking at Daru with a friendly little
smile.

"What's this story?" asked the schoolmaster. "Are
you pulling my leg?"

"No, son. Those are the orders."

"The orders? I'm not ..." Daru hesitated, not wanting to hurt the old Corsican. "I mean, that's not my
job."

"What! What's the meaning of that? In wartime
people do all kinds of jobs."

"Then I'll wait for the declaration of war!"

Balducci nodded.

"O.K. But the orders exist and they concern you
too. Things are brewing, it appears. There is talk of
a forthcoming revolt. We are mobilized, in a way."

Daru still had his obstinate look.

"Listen, son," Balducci said. "I like you and you
must understand. There's only a dozen of us at El

Ameur to patrol throughout the whole territory of a small department and I must get back in a hurry. I was told to hand this guy over to you and return without delay. He couldn't be kept there. His village was beginning to stir; they wanted to take him back. You must take him to Tinguit tomorrow before the day is over. Twenty kilometers shouldn't faze a husky fellow like you. After that, all will be over. You'll come back to your pupils and your comfortable life."

Behind the wall the horse could be heard snorting and pawing the earth. Daru was looking out the window. Decidedly, the weather was clearing and the light was increasing over the snowy plateau. When all the snow was melted, the sun would take over again and once more would burn the fields of stone. For days, still, the unchanging sky would shed its dry light on the solitary expanse where nothing had any connection with man.

"After all," he said, turning around toward Balducci, "what did he do?" And, before the gendarme had opened his mouth, he asked: "Does he speak French?"

"No, not a word. We had been looking for him for a month, but they were hiding him. He killed his cousin."

"Is he against us?"

"I don't think so. But you can never be sure."

"Why did he kill?"

"A family squabble, I think. One owed the other grain, it seems. It's not at all clear. In short, he killed his cousin with a billhook. You know, like a sheep, *kreezk!*"

Balducci made the gesture of drawing a blade across his throat and the Arab, his attention attracted, watched him with a sort of anxiety. Daru felt a sudden wrath against the man, against all men with their rotten spite, their tireless hates, their blood lust.

But the kettle was singing on the stove. He served Balducci more tea, hesitated, then served the Arab again, who, a second time, drank avidly. His raised arms made the jellaba fall open and the schoolmaster saw his thin, muscular chest.

"Thanks, kid," Balducci said. "And now, I'm off."

He got up and went toward the Arab, taking a small rope from his pocket.

"What are you doing?" Daru asked dryly.

Balducci, disconcerted, showed him the rope.

"Don't bother."

The old gendarme hesitated. "It's up to you. Of course, you are armed?"

"I have my shotgun."

"Where?"

"In the trunk."

"You ought to have it near your bed."

"Why? I have nothing to fear."

"You're crazy, son. If there's an uprising, no one is safe, we're all in the same boat."

"I'll defend myself. I'll have time to see them coming."

Balducci began to laugh, then suddenly the mustache covered the white teeth. "You'll have time? O.K. That's just what I was saying. You have always been a little cracked. That's why I like you, my son was like that."

At the same time he took out his revolver and put it on the desk.

"Keep it; I don't need two weapons from here to El Ameur."

The revolver shone against the black paint of the table. When the gendarme turned toward him, the schoolmaster caught the smell of leather and horseflesh.

"Listen, Balducci," Daru said suddenly, "every bit

of this disgusts me, and first of all your fellow here. But I won't hand him over. Fight, yes, if I have to. But not that."

The old gendarme stood in front of him and looked at him severely.

"You're being a fool," he said slowly. "I don't like it either. You don't get used to putting a rope on a man even after years of it, and you're even ashamed—yes, ashamed. But you can't let them have their way."

"I won't hand him over," Daru said again.

"It's an order, son, and I repeat it."

"That's right. Repeat to them what I've said to you: I won't hand him over."

Balducci made a visible effort to reflect. He looked at the Arab and at Daru. At last he decided.

"No, I won't tell them anything. If you want to drop us, go ahead; I'll not denounce you. I have an order to deliver the prisoner and I'm doing so. And now you'll just sign this paper for me."

"There's no need. I'll not deny that you left him with me."

"Don't be mean with me. I know you'll tell the truth. You're from hereabouts and you are a man. But you must sign, that's the rule."

Daru opened his drawer, took out a little square bottle of purple ink, the red wooden penholder with the "sergeant-major" pen he used for making models of penmanship, and signed. The gendarme carefully folded the paper and put it into his wallet. Then he moved toward the door.

"I'll see you off," Daru said.

"No," said Balducci. "There's no use being polite. You insulted me."

He looked at the Arab, motionless in the same spot, sniffed peevishly, and turned away toward the door.

"Good-by, son," he said. The door shut behind him. Balducci appeared outside the window and then disappeared. His footsteps were muffled by the snow. The horse stirred on the other side of the wall and several chickens fluttered in fright. A moment later Balducci reappeared outside the window leading the horse by the bridle. He walked toward the little rise without turning around and disappeared from sight with the horse following him. A big stone could be heard bouncing down. Daru walked back toward the prisoner, who, without stirring, never took his eyes off him. "Wait," the schoolmaster said in Arabic and went toward the bedroom. As he was going through the door, he had a second thought, went to the desk, took the revolver, and stuck it in his pocket. Then, without looking back, he went into his room.

For some time he lay on his couch watching the sky gradually close over, listening to the silence. It was this silence that had seemed painful to him during the first days here, after the war. He had requested a post in the little town at the base of the foothills separating the upper plateaus from the desert. There, rocky walls, green and black to the north, pink and lavender to the south, marked the frontier of eternal summer. He had been named to a post farther north, on the plateau itself. In the beginning, the solitude and the silence had been hard for him on these wastelands peopled only by stones. Occasionally, furrows suggested cultivation, but they had been dug to uncover a certain kind of stone good for building. The only plowing here was to harvest rocks. Elsewhere a thin layer of soil accumulated in the hollows would be scraped out to enrich paltry village gardens. This is the way it was: bare rock covered three quarters of the region. Towns sprang up, flourished, then disappeared; men came by, loved one another or fought bitterly, then died. No one in this desert, neither he nor his guest, mattered. And yet, outside this desert neither of them, Daru knew, could have really lived.

When he got up, no noise came from the classroom. He was amazed at the unmixed joy he derived from the mere thought that the Arab might have fled and that he would be alone with no decision to make. But the prisoner was there. He had merely stretched out between the stove and the desk. With eyes open, he was staring at the ceiling. In that position, his thick lips were particularly noticeable, giving him a pouting look. "Come," said Daru. The Arab got up and followed him. In the bedroom, the schoolmaster pointed to a chair near the table under the window. The Arab sat down without taking his eyes off Daru.

"Are you hungry?"

"Yes," the prisoner said.

Daru set the table for two. He took flour and oil, shaped a cake in a frying-pan, and lighted the little stove that functioned on bottled gas. While the cake was cooking, he went out to the shed to get cheese, eggs, dates, and condensed milk. When the cake was done he set it on the window sill to cool, heated some condensed milk diluted with water, and beat up the eggs into an omelette. In one of his motions he knocked against the revolver stuck in his right pocket. He set the bowl down, went into the classroom, and put the revolver in his desk drawer. When he came back to the room, night was falling. He put on the light and served the Arab. "Eat," he said. The Arab took a piece of the cake, lifted it eagerly to his mouth, and stopped short.

"And you?" he asked.

"After you. I'll eat too."

The thick lips opened slightly. The Arab hesitated,

then bit into the cake determinedly.

The meal over, the Arab looked at the schoolmaster. "Are you the judge?"

"No, I'm simply keeping you until tomorrow."

"Why do you eat with me?"

"I'm hungry."

The Arab fell silent. Daru got up and went out. He brought back a folding bed from the shed, set it up between the table and the stove, perpendicular to his own bed. From a large suitcase which, upright in a corner, served as a shelf for papers, he took two blankets and arranged them on the camp bed. Then he stopped, felt useless, and sat down on his bed. There was nothing more to do or to get ready. He had to look at this man. He looked at him, therefore, trying to imagine his face bursting with rage. He couldn't do so. He could see nothing but the dark yet shining eyes and the animal mouth.

"Why did you kill him?" he asked in a voice whose hostile tone surprised him.

The Arab looked away. "He ran away. I ran after him."

He raised his eyes to Daru again and they were full of a sort of woeful interrogation. "Now what will they do to me?"

"Are you afraid?"

He stiffened, turning his eyes away.

"Are you sorry?"

The Arab stared at him openmouthed. Obviously he did not understand. Daru's annoyance was growing. At the same time he felt awkward and self-conscious with his big body wedged between the two beds.

"Lie down there," he said impatiently. "That's your bed."

The Arab didn't move. He called to Daru:

"Tell me!"

The schoolmaster looked at him.

"Is the gendarme coming back tomorrow?"

"I don't know."

"Are you coming with us?"

"I don't know. Why?"

The prisoner got up and stretched out on top of the blankets, his feet toward the window. The light from the electric bulb shone straight into his eyes and he closed them at once.

"Why?" Daru repeated, standing beside the bed.

The Arab opened his eyes under the blinding light and looked at him, trying not to blink.

"Come with us," he said.

In the middle of the night, Daru was still not asleep. He had gone to bed after undressing completely; he generally slept naked. But when he suddenly realized that he had nothing on, he hesitated. He felt vulnerable and the temptation came to him to put his clothes back on. Then he shrugged his shoulders; after all, he wasn't a child and, if need be, he could break his adversary in two. From his bed he could observe him, lying on his back, still motionless with his eyes closed under the harsh light. When Daru turned out the light, the darkness seemed to coagulate all of a sudden. Little by little, the night came back to life in the window where the starless sky was stirring gently. The schoolmaster soon made out the body lying at his feet. The Arab still did not move, but his eyes seemed open. A faint wind was prowling around the schoolhouse. Perhaps it would drive away the clouds and the sun would reappear.

During the night the wind increased. The hens fluttered a little and then were silent. The Arab turned over on his side with his back to Daru, who thought he heard him moan. Then he listened for his guest's breathing, become heavier and more regular. He listened to that breath so close to him and mused without being able to go to sleep. In this room where he had been sleeping alone for a year, this presence bothered him. But it bothered him also by imposing on him a sort of brotherhood he knew well but refused to accept in the present circumstances. Men who share the same rooms, soldiers or prisoners, develop a strange alliance as if, having cast off their armor with their clothing, they fraternized every evening, over and above their differences, in the ancient community of dream and fatigue. But Daru shook himself; he didn't like such musings, and it was essential to sleep.

A little later, however, when the Arab stirred slightly, the schoolmaster was still not asleep. When the prisoner made a second move, he stiffened, on the alert. The Arab was lifting himself slowly on his arms with almost the motion of a sleepwalker. Seated upright in bed, he waited motionless without turning his head toward Daru, as if he were listening attentively. Daru did not stir; it had just occurred to him that the revolver was still in the drawer of his desk. It was better to act at once. Yet he continued to observe the prisoner, who, with the same slithery motion, put his feet on the ground, waited again, then began to stand up slowly. Daru was about to call out to him when the Arab began to walk, in a quite natural but extraordinarily silent way. He was heading toward the door at the end of the room that opened into the shed. He lifted the latch with precaution and went out, pushing the door behind him but without shutting it. Daru had not stirred. "He is running away," he merely thought. "Good riddance!" Yet he listened attentively. The hens were not fluttering; the guest must be on the plateau. A faint sound of water reached

him, and he didn't know what it was until the Arab
again stood framed in the doorway, closed the door
carefully, and came back to bed without a sound. Then
Daru turned his back on him and fell asleep. Still
later he seemed, from the depths of his sleep, to hear
furtive steps around the schoolhouse. "I'm dreaming!
I'm dreaming!" he repeated to himself. And he went
on sleeping.

When he awoke, the sky was clear; the loose window
let in a cold, pure air. The Arab was asleep, hunched
up under the blankets now, his mouth open, utterly
relaxed. But when Daru shook him, he started dreadfully, staring at Daru with wild eyes as if he had
never seen him and such a frightened expression that
the schoolmaster stepped back. "Don't be afraid. It's
me. You must eat." The Arab nodded his head and
said yes. Calm had returned to his face, but his
expression was vacant and listless.

The coffee was ready. They drank it seated together
on the folding bed as they munched their pieces of
the cake. Then Daru led the Arab under the shed
and showed him the faucet where he washed. He went
back into the room, folded the blankets and the bed,
made his own bed and put the room in order. Then
he went through the classroom and out onto the
terrace. The sun was already rising in the blue sky;
a soft, bright light was bathing the deserted plateau.
On the ridge the snow was melting in spots. The
stones were about to reappear. Crouched on the edge
of the plateau, the schoolmaster looked at the deserted
expanse. He thought of Balducci. He had hurt him,
for he had sent him off in a way as if he didn't want
to be associated with him. He could still hear the
gendarme's farewell and, without knowing why, he
felt strangely empty and vulnerable. At that moment,
from the other side of the schoolhouse, the prisoner

coughed. Daru listened to him almost despite himself and then, furious, threw a pebble that whistled through the air before sinking into the snow. That man's stupid crime revolted him, but to hand him over was contrary to honor. Merely thinking of it made him smart with humiliation. And he cursed at one and the same time his own people who had sent him this Arab and the Arab too who had dared to kill and not managed to get away. Daru got up, walked in a circle on the terrace, waited motionless, and then went back into the schoolhouse.

The Arab, leaning over the cement floor of the shed, was washing his teeth with two fingers. Daru looked at him and said: "Come." He went back into the room ahead of the prisoner. He slipped a hunting-jacket on over his sweater and put on walking-shoes. Standing, he waited until the Arab had put on his *chèche* and sandals. They went into the classroom and the schoolmaster pointed to the exit, saying: "Go ahead." The fellow didn't budge. "I'm coming," said Daru. The Arab went out. Daru went back into the room and made a package of pieces of rusk, dates, and sugar. In the classroom, before going out, he hesitated a second in front of his desk, then crossed the threshold and locked the door. "That's the way," he said. He started toward the east, followed by the prisoner. But, a short distance from the schoolhouse, he thought he heard a slight sound behind them. He retraced his steps and examined the surroundings of the house; there was no one there. The Arab watched him without seeming to understand. "Come on," said Daru.

They walked for an hour and rested beside a sharp peak of limestone. The snow was melting faster and faster and the sun was drinking up the puddles at once, rapidly cleaning the plateau, which gradually dried and vibrated like the air itself. When they resumed walking, the ground rang under their feet. From time to time a bird rent the space in front of them with a joyful cry. Daru breathed in deeply the fresh morning light. He felt a sort of rapture before the vast familiar expanse, now almost entirely yellow under its dome of blue sky. They walked an hour more, descending toward the south. They reached a level height made up of crumbly rocks. From there on, the plateau sloped down, eastward toward a low plain where there were a few spindly trees and, to the south, toward outcroppings of rock that gave the landscape a chaotic look.

Daru surveyed the two directions. There was nothing but the sky on the horizon. Not a man could be seen. He turned toward the Arab, who was looking at him blankly. Daru held out the package to him. "Take it," he said. "There are dates, bread, and sugar. You can hold out for two days. Here are a thousand francs too." The Arab took the package and the money but kept his full hands at chest level as if he didn't know what to do with what was being given him. "Now look," the schoolmaster said as he pointed in the direction of the east, "there's the way to Tinguit. You have a two-hour walk. At Tinguit you'll find the administration and the police. They are expecting you." The Arab looked toward the east, still holding the package and the money against his chest. Daru took his elbow and turned him rather roughly toward the south. At the foot of the height on which they stood could be seen a faint path. "That's the trail across the plateau. In a day's walk from here you'll find pasturelands and the first nomads. They'll take you in and shelter you according to their law." The Arab had now turned toward Daru and a sort of panic was visible in his expression. "Listen," he said. Daru shook his head. "No, be quiet. Now I'm leaving you."

He turned his back on him, took two long steps in the direction of the school, looked hesitantly at the motionless Arab, and started off again. For a few minutes he heard nothing but his own step resounding on the cold ground and did not turn his head. A moment later, however, he turned around. The Arab was still there on the edge of the hill, his arms hanging now, and he was looking at the schoolmaster. Daru felt something rise in his throat. But he swore with impatience, waved vaguely, and started off again. He had already gone some distance when he again stopped and looked. There was no longer anyone on the hill.

Daru hesitated. The sun was now rather high in the sky and was beginning to beat down on his head. The schoolmaster retraced his steps, at first somewhat uncertainly, then with decision. When he reached the little hill, he was bathed in sweat. He climbed it as fast as he could and stopped, out of breath, at the top. The rock-fields to the south stood out sharply against the blue sky, but on the plain to the east a steamy heat was already rising. And in that slight haze, Daru, with heavy heart, made out the Arab walking slowly on the road to prison.

A little later, standing before the window of the classroom, the schoolmaster was watching the clear light bathing the whole surface of the plateau, but he hardly saw it. Behind him on the blackboard, among the winding French rivers, sprawled the clumsily chalked-up words he had just read: "You handed over our brother. You will pay for this." Daru looked at the sky, the plateau, and, beyond, the invisible lands stretching all the way to the sea. In this vast landscape he had loved so much, he was alone.

Heinrich Böll

THE POST CARD

Translated by Leila Vennewitz

NONE OF MY FRIENDS can understand the care
with which I preserve a scrap of paper that has no
value whatever: it merely keeps alive the memory of
a certain day in my life, and to it I owe a reputation
for sentimentality which is considered unworthy of
my social position: I am the assistant manager of a
textile firm. But I protest the accusation of sentimentality and am continually trying to invest this scrap
of paper with some documentary value. It is a tiny,
rectangular piece of ordinary paper, the size, but not
the shape, of a stamp—it is narrower and longer than
a stamp—and although it originated in the post office
it has not the slightest collector's value. It has a bright
red border and is divided by another red line into
two rectangles of different sizes; in the smaller of these
rectangles there is a big black R, in the larger one,
in black print, "Düsseldorf" and a number—the
number 634. That is all, and the bit of paper is yellow
and thin with age, and now that I have described
it minutely I have decided to throw it away: an
ordinary registration sticker, such as every post office
slaps on every day by the dozen.
     And yet this scrap of paper reminds me of a day

in my life which is truly unforgettable, although many attempts have been made to erase it from my memory. But my memory functions too well.

First of all, when I think of that day, I smell vanilla custard, a warm sweet cloud creeping under my bedroom door and reminding me of my mother's goodness: I had asked her to make some vanilla ice cream for my first day of vacation, and when I woke up I could smell it.

It was half past ten. I lit a cigarette, pushed up my pillow, and considered how I would spend the afternoon. I decided to go swimming; after lunch I would take the streetcar to the beach, have a bit of a swim, read, smoke, and wait for one of the girls at the office who had promised to come down to the beach after five.

In the kitchen my mother was pounding meat, and when she stopped for a moment I could hear her humming a tune. It was a hymn. I felt very happy. The previous day I had passed my test, I had a good job in a textile factory, a job with opportunities for advancement—but now I was on vacation, two weeks' vacation, and it was summertime. It was hot outside, but in those days I still loved hot weather: through the slits in the shutters I could see the heat haze, I could see the green of the trees in front of our house, I could hear the streetcar. And I was looking forward to breakfast. Then I heard my mother coming to listen at my door; she crossed the hall, stopped by my door, it was silent for a moment in our apartment, and I was just about to call "Mother" when the bell rang downstairs. My mother went to our front door, and I heard the funny high-pitched purring of the buzzer down below, it buzzed four, five, six times, my mother was talking on the landing to Frau Kurz, who lived in the next apartment. Then I heard a man's voice, and I knew at once it was the mailman, although I had only seen him a few times. The mailman came into our entrance hall, Mother said: "What?" and he said: "Here—sign here, please." It was very quiet for a moment, the mailman said "Thanks," my mother closed the door after him, and I heard her go back into the kitchen.

Shortly after that I got up and went into the bathroom. I shaved, had a leisurely wash, and when I turned off the faucet I could hear my mother grinding the coffee. It was like Sunday, except that I had not been to church.

Nobody will believe it, but my heart suddenly felt heavy. I don't know why, but it was heavy. I could no longer hear the coffee mill. I dried myself off, put on my shirt and trousers, socks and shoes, combed my hair and went into the living room. There were flowers on the table, pale pink carnations, it all looked fresh and neat, and on my plate lay a red pack of cigarettes.

Then Mother came in from the kitchen carrying the coffeepot and I saw at once she had been crying. In one hand she was holding the coffeepot, in the other a little pile of mail, and her eyes were red. I went over to her, took the pot from her, kissed her cheek and said: "Good morning." She looked at me, said: "Good morning, did you sleep well?" and tried to smile, but did not succeed.

We sat down, my mother poured the coffee, and I opened the red pack lying on my plate and lit a cigarette. I had suddenly lost my appetite. I stirred milk and sugar into my coffee, tried to look at Mother, but each time I quickly lowered my eyes. "Was there any mail?" I asked, a senseless question, since Mother's small red hand was resting on the little pile on top of which lay the newspaper.

"Yes," she said, pushing the pile toward me. I opened the newspaper while my mother began to butter some bread for me. The front page bore the headline: "Outrages continue against Germans in the Polish Corridor!" There had been headlines like that for weeks on the front pages of the papers. Reports "of rifle fire along the Polish border and refugees escaping from the sphere of Polish harassment and fleeing to the Reich." I put the paper aside. Next I read the brochure of a wine merchant who used to supply us sometimes when Father was still alive. Various types of Riesling were being offered at exceptionally low prices. I put the brochure aside too.

Meanwhile my mother had finished buttering the slice of bread for me. She put it on my plate saying: "Please eat something!" She burst into violent sobs. I could not bring myself to look at her. I can't look at anyone who is really suffering—but now for the first time I realized it must have something to do with the mail. It must be the mail. I stubbed out my cigarette, took a bite of the bread-and-butter and picked up the next letter, and as I did so I saw there was a post card lying underneath. But I had not noticed the registration sticker, that tiny scrap of paper I still possess and to which I owe a reputation for sentimentality. So I read the letter first. The letter was from Uncle Eddy. Uncle Eddy wrote that at last, after many years as an assistant instructor, he was now a full-fledged teacher, but it had meant being transferred to a little one-horse town; financially speaking, he was hardly any better off than before, since he was now being paid at the local scale. And his kids had had whooping cough, and the way things were going made him feel sick to his stomach, he didn't have to tell us why. No, he didn't, and it made us feel sick too. It made a lot of people feel sick.

THE POST CARD 333

When I reached for the post card I saw it had gone.
My mother had picked it up, she was holding it up
and looking at it, and I kept my eyes on my half-
eaten slice of bread, stirred my coffee and waited.

I shall never forget it. Only once had my mother
ever cried so terribly: when my father died; and then
I had not dared to look at her either. A nameless
diffidence had prevented me from comforting her.

I tried to bite into the bread, but my throat closed
up, for I suddenly realized that what was upsetting
Mother so much could only be something to do with
me. Mother said something I didn't catch and handed
me the post card, and it was then I saw the registration
sticker: that red-bordered rectangle, divided by a red
line into two other rectangles, of which the smaller
one contained a big black R and the bigger one the
word "Düsseldorf" and the number 634. Otherwise
the post card was quite normal, it was addressed to
me and on the back were the words: "Mr. Bruno
Schneider: You are required to report on August 5,
1939, to the Schlieffen Barracks in Adenbrück for an
eight-week period of military training." The words
Bruno Schneider, the date and Adenbrück were typed,
everything else was printed, and at the bottom was
a vague scrawl and the printed word "Major."

Today I know that the scrawl was superfluous. A
machine for printing majors' signatures would do the
job just as well. The only thing that mattered was
the little sticker on the front for which my mother
had had to sign a receipt.

I put my hand on her arm and said: "Now look,
Mother, it's only eight weeks." And my mother said:
"I know."

"Only eight weeks," I said, and I knew I was lying,
and my mother dried her tears, said: "Yes, of course,"
we were both lying, without knowing why we were

lying, but we were and we knew we were.

I was just picking up my bread-and-butter again when it struck me that today was the fourth and that on the following day at ten o'clock I had to be over two hundred miles away to the east. I felt myself going pale, put down the bread and got up, ignoring my mother. I went to my room. I stood at my desk, opened the drawer, closed it again. I looked round, felt something had happened and didn't know what. The room was no longer mine. That was all. Today I know, but that day I did meaningless things to reassure myself that the room still belonged to me. It was useless to rummage around in the box containing my letters, or to straighten my books. Before I knew what I was doing I had begun to pack my briefcase: shirt, pants, towel and socks, and I went into the bathroom to get my shaving things. My mother was still sitting at the breakfast table. She had stopped crying. My half-eaten slice of bread was still on my plate, there was still some coffee in my cup, and I said to my mother: "I'm going over to the Giesselbachs to phone about my train."

When I came back from the Giesselbachs it was just striking twelve noon. Our entrance hall smelled of roast pork and cauliflower, and my mother had begun to break up ice in a bag to put into our little ice-cream machine.

My train was leaving at eight that evening, and I would be in Adenbrück next morning about six. It was only fifteen minutes' walk to the station, but I left the house at three o'clock. I lied to my mother, who did not know how long it took to get to Adenbrück.

Those last three hours I spent in the house seem, on looking back, worse and longer than the whole time I spent away, and that was a long time. I don't

know what we did. We had no appetite for dinner.
My mother soon took back the roast, the cauliflower,
the potatoes, and the vanilla ice cream to the kitchen.
Then we drank the breakfast coffee which had been
kept warm under a yellow cosy, and I smoked
cigarettes, and now and again we exchanged a few
words. "Eight weeks," I said, and my mother said:
"Yes—yes, of course," and she didn't cry any more.
For three hours we lied to each other, till I couldn't
stand it any longer. My mother blessed me, kissed
me on both cheeks, and as I closed the front door
behind me I knew she was crying.

I walked to the station. The station was bustling
with activity. It was vacation time: happy sun-tanned
people were milling around. I had a beer in the waiting
room and about half past three decided to call up
the girl from the office whom I had arranged to meet
at the beach.

While I was dialing the number, and the perforated
nickel dial kept clicking back into place—five times—
I almost regretted it, but I dialed the sixth figure,
and when her voice asked: "Who is it?" I was silent
for a moment, then said slowly: "Bruno" and: "Can
you come? I have to go off—I've been drafted."

"Right now?" she asked.

"Yes."

She thought it over for a moment, and through the
phone I could hear the voices of the others, who were
apparently collecting money to buy some ice cream.

"All right," she said, "I'll come. Are you at the
station?"

"Yes," I said.

She arrived at the station very quickly, and to this
day I don't know, although she has been my wife
now for ten years, to this day I don't know whether
I ought to regret that phone call. After all, she kept

my job open for me with the firm, she revived my defunct ambition when I came home, and she is actually the one I have to thank for the fact that those opportunities for advancement have now become reality.

But I didn't stay as long as I could have with her either. We went to the movies, and in the cinema, which was empty, dark and very hot, I kissed her, though I didn't feel much like it.

I kept on kissing her, and I went to the station at six o'clock, although I need not have gone till eight. On the platform I kissed her again and boarded the first eastbound train. Ever since then I have not been able to look at a beach without a pang: the sun, the water, the cheerfulness of the people seem all wrong, and I prefer to stroll alone through the town on a rainy day and go to a movie where I don't have to kiss anybody. My opportunities for advancement with the firm are not yet exhausted. I might become a director, and I probably will, according to the law of paradoxical inertia. For people are convinced I am loyal to the firm and will do a great deal for it. But I am not loyal to it and I haven't the slightest intention of doing anything for it. . . .

Lost in thought I have often contemplated that registration sticker which gave such a sudden twist to my life. And when the tests are held in summer and our young employees come to me afterward with beaming faces to be congratulated, it is my job to make a little speech in which the words "opportunities for advancement" play a traditional role.

Pär Lagerkvist

THE CHILDREN'S CAMPAIGN

Translated by Alain Blair

EVEN THE CHILDREN at that time received military training, were assembled in army units and exercised just as though on active service, had their own headquarters and annual maneuvers when everything was conducted as in a real state of war. The grownups had nothing directly to do with this training; the children actually exercised themselves and all command was entrusted to them. The only use made of adult experience was to arrange officers' training courses for especially suitable boys, who were chosen with the greatest care and who were then put in charge of the military education of their comrades in the ranks.

These schools were of high standing and there was hardly a boy throughout the land who did not dream of going to them. But the entrance tests were particularly hard; not only a perfect physique was required but also a highly developed intelligence and character. The age of admission was six to seven years and the small cadets then received an excellent training, both purely military and in all other respects, chiefly the further molding of character. It was also greatly to one's credit in after life to have passed through one of these schools. It was really on the splendid foundation laid here that the quality, organization and efficiency of the child army rested.

Thereafter, as already mentioned, the grownups in no way interfered but everything was entrusted to the children themselves. No adult might meddle in the command, in organizational details or matters of promotion. Everything was managed and supervised by the children; all decisions, even the most vital, being reached by their own little general staff. No one over fourteen was allowed. The boys then passed automatically into the first age group of the regular troops with no mean military training already behind them.

The large child army, which was the object of the whole nation's love and admiration, amounted to three army corps of four divisions: infantry, light field artillery, medical and service corps. All physically fit boys were enrolled in it and a large number of girls belonged to it as nurses, all volunteers.

Now it so happened that a smaller, quite insigificant nation behaved in a high-handed and unseemly way toward its powerful neighbor, and the insult was all the greater since this nation was by no means an equal. Indignation was great and general and, since people's feelings were running high, it was necessary to rebuke the malapert and and at the same time take the chance to subjugate the country in question. In this situation the child army came forward and through its high command asked to be charged with the crushing and subduing of the foe. The news of this caused a sensation and a wave of fervor throughout the country. The proposal was given serious consideration in supreme quarters and as a result the commission was given, with some hesitation, to the children. It was in fact a task well suited to this army, and the people's obvious wishes in the matter had also to be met, if possible.

The Foreign Office therefore sent the defiant country an unacceptable ultimatum and, pending the reply, the child army was mobilized within twenty-four hours. The reply was found to be unsatisfactory and war was declared immediately.

Unparalleled enthusiasm marked the departure for the front. The intrepid little youngsters had green sprigs in the barrels of their rifles and were pelted with flowers. As is so often the case, the campaign was begun in the spring, and this time the general opinion was that there was something symbolic in it. In the capital the little commander in chief and chief of general staff, in the presence of huge crowds, made a passionate speech to the troops in which he expressed the gravity of the hour and his conviction of their unswerving valor and willingness to offer their lives for their country.

The speech, made in a strong voice, aroused the greatest ecstasy. The boy—who had a brilliant career behind him and had reached his exalted position at the age of only twelve and a half—was acclaimed with wild rejoicing and from this moment was the avowed hero of the entire nation. There was not a dry eye and those of the many mothers especially shone with pride and happiness. For them it was the greatest day in their lives. The troops marched past below fluttering banners, each regiment with its music corps at the head. It was an unforgettable spectacle.

There were also many touching incidents, evincing a proud patriotism, as when a little four-year-old, who had been lifted up on his mother's arm so that he could see, howled with despair and shouted, "I want

to go, too. I want to go, too!" while his mother tried
to hush him, explaining that he was too small. "Small
am I, eh?" he exclaimed, punching her face so that
her nose bled. The evening papers were full of such
episodes showing the mood of the people and of the
troops who were so sure of victory. The big march
past was broadcast and the c in c's speech, which
had been recorded, was broadcast every evening
during the days that followed at 7:15 p.m.

Military operations had already begun, however,
and reports of victory began to come in at once from
the front. The children had quickly taken the offensive
and on one sector of the front had inflicted a heavy
defeat on the enemy, seven hundred dead and
wounded and over twelve hundred prisoners, while
their own losses amounted to only a hundred or so
fallen. The victory was celebrated at home with indescribable rejoicing and with thanksgiving services
in the churches. The newspapers were filled with
accounts of individual instances of valor and pictures
several columns wide of the high command, of which
the leading personalities, later so well-known, began
to appear now for the first time. In their joy, mothers
and aunts sent so much chocolate and other sweets
to the army that headquarters had to issue a strict
order that all such parcels were, for the time being
at any rate, forbidden, since they made whole reg-
iments unfit for battle and these in their turn had
nearly been surrounded by the enemy.

For the child army was already far inside enemy
territory and still managed to keep the initiative. The
advance sector did retreat slightly in order to establish
contact with its wings but only improved its positions
by so doing. A stalemate ensued in the theater of
war for some time after this.

During July, however, troops were concentrated for

a big attack along the whole line and huge reserves—
the child army's, in comparison with those of its
opponent, were almost inexhaustible—were mustered
to the front. The new offensive, which lasted for several
weeks, resulted, too, in an almost decisive victory for
the whole army, even though casualties were high.
The children defeated the enemy all along the line
but did not manage to pursue him and thereby exploit
their success to the full, because he was greatly
favored by the fact that his legs were so much longer,
an advantage of which he made good use. By dint
of forced marches, however, the children finally succeeded in cutting the enemy's right flank to pieces.
They were now in the very heart of the country and
their outposts were only a few days' march from the
capital.

It was a pitched battle on a big scale and the
newspapers had enormous headlines every day which
depicted the dramatic course of events. At set hours
the radio broadcast the gunfire and a résumé of the
position. The war correspondents described in rapturous words and vivid colors the state of affairs at
the front—the children's incredible feats, their indomitable courage and self-sacrifice, the whole morale of
the army. It was no exaggeration. The youngsters
showed the greatest bravery; they really behaved like
heroes. One only had to see their discipline and
contempt of death during an attack, as though they
had been grown-up men at least.

It was an unforgettable sight to see them storm
ahead under murderous machine gun fire and the
small medical orderlies dart nimbly forward and pick
them up as they fell. Or the wounded and dying who
were moved behind the front, those who had had
a leg shot away or their bellies ripped open by a
bayonet so that their entrails hung out—but without

one sound of complaint crossing their small lips. The hand-to-hand fighting had been very fierce and a great number of children fell in this, while they were superior in the actual firing. Losses were estimated at 4,000 on the enemy side and 7,000 among the children, according to the secret reports. The victory had been hard won but all the more complete.

This battle became very famous and was also of far greater importance than any previously. It was now clear beyond all doubt that the children were incomparably superior in tactics, discipline and individual courage. At the same time, however, it was admitted by experts that the enemy's headlong retreat was very skillfully carried out, that his strength was evidently in defense and that he should not be underrated too much. Toward the end, also, he had unexpectedly made a stubborn resistance which had prevented any further penetration.

This observation was not without truth. In actual fact the enemy was anything but a warlike nation, and indeed his forces found it very difficult to hold their own. Nevertheless, they improved with practice during the fighting and became more efficient as time went on. This meant that they caused the children a good deal of trouble in each succeeding battle. They also had certain advantages on their side. As their opponents were so small, for instance, it was possible after a little practice to spit several of them on the bayonet at once, and often a kick was enough to fell them to the ground.

But against this, the children were so much more numerous and also braver. They were everywhere. They swarmed over one and in between one's legs and the unwarlike people were nearly demented by all these small monsters who fought like fiends. Little fiends was also what they were generally called—

not without reason—and this name was even adopted in the children's homeland, but there it was a mark of honor and a pet name. The enemy troops had all their work cut out merely defending themselves. At last, however, they were able to check the others' advance and even venture on one or two counter-attacks. Everything then came to a standstill for a while and there was a breathing space.

The children were now in possession of a large part of the country. But this was not always so easy. The population did not particularly like them and proved not to be very fond of children. It was alleged that snipers fired on the boys from houses and that they were ambushed when they moved in small detachments. Children had even been found impaled on stakes or with their eyes gouged out, so it was said. And in many cases these stories were no doubt true. The population had quite lost their heads, were obviously goaded into a frenzy, and as they were of little use as a warlike nation and their cruelty could therefore find no natural outlet, they tried to revenge themselves by atrocities. They felt overrun by all the foreign children as by troublesome vermin and, being at their wits' end, they simply killed whenever they had the chance. In order to put an end to these outrages the children burned one village after the other and shot hundreds of people daily, but this did not improve matters. The despicable deeds of these craven guerrillas caused them endless trouble.

At home, the accounts of all this naturally aroused the most bitter resentment. People's blood boiled to think that their small soldiers were treated in this way by those who had nothing to do with the war, by barbarous civilians who had no notion of estab-lished and judicial forms. Even greater indignation was caused, however, by an incident that occurred inside the occupied area some time after the big summer battle just mentioned.

A lieutenant who was out walking in the countryside came to a stream where a large, fat woman knelt washing clothes. He asked her the way to a village close by. The woman, who probably suspected him of evil intent, retorted, "What are you doing here? You ought to be at home with your mother." Whereupon the lieutenant drew his saber to kill her, but the woman grabbed hold of him and, putting him over her knee, thwacked him black and blue with her washboard so that he was unable to sit down for several days afterward. He was so taken aback that he did nothing, armed though he was to the teeth. Luckily no one saw the incident, but there were orders that all outrages on the part of the population were to be reported to headquarters. The lieutenant therefore duly reported what had happened to him. True, it gave him little satisfaction, but as he had to obey orders he had no choice. And so it all came out.

The incident aroused a storm of rage, particularly among those at home. The infamous deed was a humiliation for the country, an insult which nothing could wipe out. It implied a deliberate violation by this militarily ignorant people of the simplest rules of warfare. Everywhere, in the press, in propaganda speeches, in ordinary conversation, the deepest contempt and disgust for the deed was expressed. The lieutenant who had so flagrantly shamed the army had his officer's epaulettes ripped off in front of the assembled troops and was declared unworthy to serve any longer in the field. He was instantly sent home to his parents, who belonged to one of the most noted families but who now had to retire into obscurity in a remote part of the country.

The woman, on the other hand, became a heroic figure among her people and the object of their rapturous admiration. During the whole of the war she and her deed were a rallying national symbol which people looked up to and which spurred them on to further effort. She subsequently became a favorite motif in the profuse literature about their desperate struggle for freedom; a vastly popular figure, brought to life again and again as time passed, now in a rugged, everyday way which appealed to the man in the street, now in heroic female form on a grandiose scale, to become gradually more and more legendary, wreathed in saga and myth. In some versions she was shot by the enemy; in others she lived to a ripe old age, loved and revered by her people.

This incident, more than anything else, helped to increase the bad feelings between the two countries and to make them wage the war with ever greater ruthlessness. In the late summer, before the autumn rains began, both armies, ignorant of each other's plans, simultaneously launched a violent offensive, which devastated both sides. On large sectors of the front the troops completely annihilated each other so that there was not a single survivor left. Any peaceful inhabitants thereabouts who were still alive and ventured out of their cellars thought that the war was over, because all were slain.

But soon new detachments came up and began fighting again. Great confusion arose in other quarters from the fact that in the heat of attack men ran past each other and had to turn around in order to go on fighting; and that some parts of the line rushed ahead while others came behind, so that the troops were both in front of and behind where they should have been and time and again attacked each other in the rear. The battle raged in this way with extreme violence and shots were fired from all directions at once.

When at last the fighting ceased and stock was taken of the situation, it appeared that no one had won. On both sides there was an equal number of fallen, 12,924, and after all attacks and retreats the position of the armies was exactly the same as at the start of the battle. It was agreed that both should claim the victory. Thereafter the rain set in and the armies went to earth in trenches and put up barbed wire entanglements.

The children were the first to finish their trenches, since they had had more to do with that kind of thing, and settled down in them as best they could. They soon felt at home. Filthy and lousy, they lived there in the darkness as though they had never done anything else. With the adaptability of children they quickly got into the way of it. The enemy found this more difficult; he felt miserable and homesick for the life above ground to which he was accustomed. Not so the children. When one saw them in their small gray uniforms, which were caked thick with mud, and their small gas masks, one could easily think they had been born to this existence. They crept in and out of the holes down into the earth and scampered about the passages like mice. When their burrows were attacked they were instantly up on the parapet and snapped back in blind fury. As the months passed, this hopeless, harrowing life put endurance to an increasingly severe test. But they never lost courage or the will to fight.

For the enemy the strain was often too much; the glaring pointlessness of it all made many completely apathetic. But the little ones did not react like this. Children are really more fitted for war and take more pleasure in it, while grownups tire of it after a while and think it is boring. The boys continued to find the whole thing exciting and they wanted to go on living as they were now. They also had a more natural herd instinct; their unity and camaraderie helped them a great deal, made it easier to hold out.

But, of course, even they suffered great hardship. Especially when winter set in with its incessant rain, a cold sleet which made everything sodden and filled the trenches with mud. It was enough to unman anyone. But it would never have entered their heads to complain. However bad things were, nothing could have made them admit it. At home everyone was very proud of them. All the cinemas showed parades behind the front and the little c in c and his generals pinning medals for bravery on their soldiers' breasts. People thought of them a great deal out there, of their little fiends, realizing that they must be having a hard time.

At Christmas, in particular, thoughts went out to them, to the lighted Christmas trees and all the sparkling childish eyes out in the trenches; in every home people sat wondering how they were faring. But the children did not think of home. They were soldiers out and out, absorbed by their duty and their new life. They attacked in several places on the morning of Christmas Eve, inflicting fairly big losses on the enemy in killed and wounded, and did not stop until it was time to open their parcels. They had the real fighting spirit which might have been a lesson even to adults.

There was nothing sentimental about them. The war had hardened and developed them, made them men. It did happen that one poor little chap burst into tears when the Christmas tree was lighted, but he was made the laughing-stock of them all. "Are you homesick for your mummy, you bastard?" they said, and kept on jeering at him all evening. He was the object of their scorn all through Christmas; he behaved suspiciously and tried to keep to himself. Once he walked a hundred yards away from the post and, because he might well have been thinking of flight, he was seized and courtmartialed. He could give no reason for having absented himself and since he had obviously intended to desert he was shot.

If those at home had been fully aware of the morale out there, they need not have worried. As it was, they wondered if the children could really hold their ground and half-regretted having entrusted them with the campaign, now that it was dragging on so long because of this nerve-racking stationary warfare. After the New Year help was even offered in secret, but it was rejected with proud indignation.

The morale of the enemy, on the other hand, was not so high. They did intend to fight to the last man, but the certainty of a complete victory was not so general as it should have been. They could not help thinking, either, how hopeless their fight really was; that in the long run they could not hold their own against these people who were armed to the very milk teeth, and this often dampened their courage.

Hardly had nature begun to come to life and seethe with the newly awakened forces of spring before the children started with incredible intensity to prepare for the decisive battle. Heavy mechanized artillery was brought up and placed in strong positions; huge troop movements went on night and day; all available fighting forces were concentrated in the very front lines. After murderous gunfire which lasted for six days, an attack was launched with great force and extreme skill. Individual bravery was, if possible, more dazzling than ever. The whole army was also a year older, and that means much at that age. But their opponents, too, were determined to do their utmost. They had assembled all their reserves, and their spirits, now that the rain had stopped and the weather was fine, were full of hope.

It was a terrible battle. The hospital trains immediately started going back from both sides packed with wounded and dying. Machine guns, tanks and gas played fearful havoc. For several days the outcome was impossible to foresee, since both armies appeared equally strong and the tide of battle constantly changed. The position gradually cleared, however. The enemy had expected the main attack in the center, but the child army turned out to be weakest there. Use was made of this, especially because they themselves were best prepared at this very point, and this part of the children's front was soon made to waver and was forced farther and farther back by repeated attack. Advantage was also taken of an ideal evening breeze from just the right quarter to gas the children in thousands. Encouraged by their victory, the troops pursued the offensive with all their might and with equal success.

The child army's retreat, however, turned out to be a stratagem, brilliantly conceived and carried out. Its center gave way more and more and the enemy, giving all his attention to this, forgot that at the same time he himself was wavering on both wings. In this way he ran his head into a noose. When the children considered that they had retreated far enough they halted, while the troops on the outermost wings, already far ahead, advanced swiftly until they met behind the enemy's back. The latter's entire army was thereby surrounded and in the grip of an iron hand. All the children's army had to do now was to draw the noose tighter. At last the gallant defenders had to surrender and let themselves be taken prisoner, which in fact they already were. It was the most disastrous defeat in history; not a single one escaped other than by death.

This victory became much more famous than any of the others and was eagerly studied at all military academies on account of its brilliantly executed, doubly effective encircling movement. The great general Sludelsnorp borrowed its tactics outright seventy years later at his victory over the Slivokvarks in the year 2048.

The war could not go on any longer now, because there was nothing left to fight, and the children marched to the capital with the imprisoned army between them to dictate the peace terms. These were handed over by the little commander in chief in the hall of mirrors in the stately old palace at a historic scene which was to be immortalized time and again in art and even now was reproduced everywhere in the weekly press. The film cameras whirred, the flashlights hissed and the radio broadcast the great moment to the world. The commander in chief, with austere and haughty mien and one foot slightly in front of the other, delivered the historic document with his right hand. The first and most important condition was the complete cession of the country, besides which the expenses of its capture were to be borne by the enemy, who thus had to pay the cost of the war on both sides, the last clause on account of the fact that he had been the challenging party and, according to his own admission, the cause of the war. The document was signed in dead silence, the only sound was the scratching of the fountain pen, which, according to the commentator's whisper, was solid gold and undoubtedly a future museum piece.

With this, everything was settled and the children's

army returned to its own country, where it was received with indescribable rapture. Everywhere along the roads the troops were greeted with wild rejoicing; their homecoming was one long victory parade. The march into the capital and the dismissal there of the troops, which took place before vast crowds, were especially impressive. People waved and shouted in the streets as they passed, were beside themselves with enthusiasm, bands played, eyes were filled with tears of joy. Some of the loudest cheering was for the small invalids at the rear of the procession, blind and with limbs amputated, who had sacrificed themselves for their country. Many of them had already got small artificial arms and legs so that they looked just the same as before. The victory salute thundered, bayonets flashed in the sun. It was an unforgettable spectacle.

A strange, new leaf was written in the great book of history which would be read with admiration in time to come. The nation had seen many illustrious deeds performed, but never anything as proud as this. What these children had done in their devotion and fervent patriotism could never be forgotten.

Nor was it. Each spring, on the day of victory, school children marched out with flags in their hands to the cemeteries with all the small graves where the heroes rested under their small white crosses. The mounds were strewn with flowers and passionate speeches were made, reminding everyone of the glorious past, their imperishable honor and youthful, heroic spirit of self-sacrifice. The flags floated in the sun and the voices rang out clear as they sang their rousing songs, radiant childish eyes looking ahead to new deeds of glory.

Alain Robbe-Grillet

THE SECRET ROOM

To Gustave Moreau
Translated by Barbara Wright

THE FIRST THING TO BE SEEN is a red stain, of a deep, dark, shiny red, with almost black shadows. It is in the form of an irregular rosette, sharply outlined, extending in several directions in wide outflows of unequal length, dividing and dwindling afterward into single sinuous streaks. The whole stands out against a smooth, pale surface, round in shape, at once dull and pearly, a hemisphere joined by gentle curves to an expanse of the same pale color—white darkened by the shadowy quality of the place: a dungeon, a sunken room, or a cathedral—glowing with a diffused brilliance in the semi-darkness.

Further back, the space is filled with the cylindrical trunks of columns, repeated with progressive vagueness in their retreat toward the beginning of a vast stone stairway, turning slightly as it rises, growing narrower and narrower as it approaches the high vaults where it disappears.

The whole setting is empty, stairway and colonnades. Alone, in the foreground, the stretched-out body gleams feebly, marked with the red stain—a white body whose full, supple flesh can be sensed, fragile, no doubt, and vulnerable. Alongside the bloody hemisphere another identical round form, this one intact, is seen at almost the same angle of view; but the haloed point at its summit, of darker tint, is in this case quite recognizable, whereas the other one is entirely destroyed, or at least covered by the wound.

In the background, near the top of the stairway, a black silhouette is seen fleeing, a man wrapped in a long floating cape, ascending the last steps without turning around, his deed accomplished. A thin smoke rises in twisting scrolls from a sort of incense burner placed on a high stand of ironwork with a silvery glint. Nearby lies the milkwhite body, with wide streaks of blood running from the left breast, along the flank and on the hip.

It is a fully rounded woman's body, but not heavy, completely nude, lying on the back, the bust raised up somewhat by thick cushions thrown down on the floor, which is covered with oriental rugs. The waist is very narrow, the neck long and thin, curved to one side, the head thrown back into a darker area where, even so, may be discerned the facial features, the partly opened mouth, the wide-staring eyes, shining with a fixed brilliance, and the mass of long, black hair spread out in a complicated wavy disorder over a heavily folded cloth, of velvet perhaps, on which also rest the arm and shoulder.

It is a uniformly colored velvet of dark purple, or which seems so in this lighting. But purple, brown, blue also seem to dominate in the colors of the cushions—only a small portion of which is hidden beneath the velvet cloth, and which protrude notice-ably, lower down, beneath the bust and waist—as well as in the oriental patterns of the rugs on the floor. Further on, these same colors are picked up again in the stone of the paving and the columns, the vaulted archways, the stairs, and the less discernible surfaces that disappear into the farthest reaches of the room.

The dimensions of this room are difficult to determine exactly; the body of the young sacrificial victim seems at first glance to occupy a substantial portion of it, but the vast size of the stairway leading down to it would imply rather that this is not the whole room, whose considerable space must in reality extend all around, right and left, as it does toward the far-away browns and blues among the columns standing in line, in every direction, perhaps toward other sofas, thick carpets, piles of cushions and fabrics, other tortured bodies, other incense burners.

It is also difficult to say where the light comes from. No clue, on the columns or on the floor, suggests the direction of the rays. Nor is any window or torch visible. The milk-white body itself seems to light the scene, with its full breasts, the curve of its thighs, the rounded belly, the full buttocks, the stretched-out legs, widely spread, and the black tuft of the exposed sex, provocative, proffered, useless now.

The man has already moved several steps back. He is now on the first steps of the stairs, ready to go up. The bottom steps are wide and deep, like the steps leading up to some great building, a temple or theatre; they grow smaller as they ascend, and at the same time describe a wide helical curve, so gradually that the stairway has not yet made a halfturn by the time that it disappears near the top of the vaults, reduced then to a steep, narrow flight of steps without handrail, vaguely outlined, moreover, in the thickening darkness beyond.

But the man does not look in this direction, where

his movement nonetheless carries him; his left foot on the second step and his right foot already touching the third, with his knee bent, he has turned around to look at the spectacle for one last time. The long, floating cape thrown hastily over his shoulders, clasped in one hand at his waist, has been whirled around by the rapid circular motion that has just caused his head and chest to turn in the opposite direction, and a corner of the cloth remains suspended in the air as if blown by a gust of wind; this corner, twisting around upon itself in the form of a loose S, reveals the red silk lining with its gold embroidery.

The man's features are impassive, but tense, as if in expectation—or perhaps fear—of some sudden event, or surveying with one last glance the total immobility of the scene. Though he is looking backward, his whole body is turned slightly forward, as if he were continuing up the stairs. His right arm—not the one holding the edge of the cape—is bent sharply toward the left, toward a point in space where the balustrade should be, if this stairway had one, an interrupted gesture, almost incomprehensible, unless it arose from an instinctive movement to grasp the absent support.

As to the direction of his glance, it is certainly aimed at the body of the victim lying on the cushions, its extended members stretched out in the form of a cross, its bust raised up, its head thrown back. But the face is perhaps hidden from the man's eyes by one of the columns, standing at the foot of the stairs. The young woman's right hand touches the floor just at the foot of this column. The fragile wrist is encircled by an iron bracelet. The arm is almost in darkness, only the hand receiving enough light to make the thin, outspread fingers clearly visible against the circular protrusion at the base of the stone column. A black metal chain running around the column passes through a ring affixed to the bracelet, binding the wrist tightly to the column.

At the top of the arm a rounded shoulder, raised up by the cushions, also stands out well lighted, as well as the neck, the throat, and the other shoulder, the armpit with its soft hair, the left arm likewise pulled back with its wrist bound in the same manner to the base of another column, in the extreme foreground; here the iron bracelet and the chain are fully displayed, represented with perfect clarity down to the slightest details.

The same is true, still in the foreground but at the other side, for a similar chain, but not quite as thick, wound directly around the ankle, running twice around the column and terminating in a heavy iron ring embedded in the floor. About a yard further back, or perhaps slightly further, the right foot is identically chained. But it is the left foot, and its chain, that are the most minutely depicted.

The foot is small, delicate, finely molded. In several places the chain has broken the skin, causing noticeable if not extensive depressions in the flesh. The chain links are oval, thick, the size of an eye. The ring in the floor resembles those used to attach horses; it lies almost touching the stone pavement to which it is riveted by a massive iron peg. A few inches away is the edge of a rug; it is grossly wrinkled at this point, doubtless as a result of the convulsive, but necessarily very restricted, movements of the victim attempting to struggle.

The man is still standing about a yard away, half leaning over her. He looks at her face, seen upside down, her dark eyes made larger by their surrounding eye-shadow, her mouth wide open as if screaming. The man's posture allows his face to be seen only in a vague profile, but one senses in it a violent exaltation, despite the rigid attitude, the silence, the immobility. His back is slightly arched. His left hand, the only one visible, holds up at some distance from the body a piece of cloth, some dark colored piece of clothing, which drags on the carpet, and which must be the long cape with its gold embroidered lining.

This immense silhouette hides most of the bare flesh over which the red stain, spreading from the globe of the breast, runs in long rivulets that branch out, growing narrower, upon the pale background of the bust and the flank. One thread has reached the armpit and runs in an almost straight, thin line along the arm; others have run down toward the waist and traced out, along one side of the belly, the hip, the top of the thigh, a more random network already starting to congeal. Three or four tiny veins have reached the hollow between the legs, meeting in a sinuous line, touching the point of the V formed by the outspread legs, and disappearing into the black tuft.

Look, now the flesh is still intact: the black tuft and the white belly, the soft curve of the hips, the narrow waist, and, higher up, the pearly breasts rising and falling in time with the rapid breathing, whose rhythm grows more accelerated. The man, close to her, one knee on the floor, leans further over. The head, with its long, curly hair, and which is alone free to move somewhat, turns from side to side, struggling; finally the woman's mouth twists open, while the flesh is torn open, the blood spurts out over the tender skin, stretched tight, the carefully shadowed eyes grow abnormally larger, the mouth opens wider, the head twists violently, one last time, from right to left, then more gently, to fall back finally and become still, amid the mass of black hair spread out on the velvet.

At the very top of the stone stairway, the little door has opened, allowing a yellowish but sustained shaft of light to enter, against which stands out the dark silhouette of the man wrapped in his long cloak. He has but to climb a few more steps to reach the threshold.

Afterward, the whole setting is empty, the enormous room with its purple shadows and its stone columns proliferating in all directions, the monumental staircase with no handrail that twists upward, growing narrower and vaguer as it rises into the darkness, toward the top of the vaults where it disappears.

Near the body, whose wound has stiffened, whose brilliance is already growing dim, the thin smoke from the incense burner traces complicated scrolls in the still air: first a coil turned horizontally to the left, which then straightens out and rises slightly, then returns to the axis of its point of origin, which it crosses as it moves to the right, then turns back in the first direction, only to wind back again, thus forming an irregular sinusoidal curve, more and more flattened out, and rising, vertically, toward the top of the canvas.

Graham Greene

THE SECOND DEATH

SHE FOUND ME IN THE EVENING under trees that
grew outside the village. I had never cared for her
and would have hidden myself if I'd seen her coming.
She was to blame, I'm certain, for her son's vices. If
they were vices, but I'm very far from admitting that
they were. At any rate he was generous, never mean,
like others in the village I could mention if I chose.

I was staring hard at a leaf or she would never
have found me. It was dangling from its twig, its stalk
torn across by the wind or else by a stone one of
the village children had flung. Only the green tough
skin of the stalk held it there suspended. I was
watching closely, because a caterpillar was crawling
across the surface, making the leaf sway to and fro.
The caterpillar was aiming at the twig, and I wondered
whether it would reach it in safety or whether the
leaf would fall with it into the water. There was a
pool underneath the trees, and the water always
appeared red, because of the heavy clay in the soil.

I never knew whether the caterpillar reached the
twig, for, as I've said, the wretched woman found me.
The first I knew of her coming was her voice just
behind my ear.

"I've been looking in all the pubs for you," she

said in her old shrill voice. It was typical of her to say "all the pubs" when there were only two in the place. She always wanted credit for trouble she hadn't really taken.

I was annoyed and I couldn't help speaking a little harshly. "You might have saved yourself the trouble," I said, "you should have known I wouldn't be in a pub on a fine night like this."

The old vixen became quite humble. She was always smooth enough when she wanted anything. "It's for my poor son," she said. That meant that he was ill. When he was well I never heard her say anything better than "that dratted boy." She'd make him be in the house by midnight every day of the week, as if there were any serious mischief a man could get up to in a little village like ours. Of course we soon found a way to cheat her, but it was the principle of the thing I objected to—a grown man of over thirty ordered about by his mother, just because she hadn't a husband to control. But when he was ill, though it might be with only a small chill, it was "my poor son."

"He's dying," she said, "and God knows what I shall do without him."

"Well, I don't see how I can help you," I said. I was angry, because he'd been dying once before and she'd done everything but actually bury him. I imagined it was the same sort of dying this time, the sort a man gets over. I'd seen him about the week before on his way up the hill to see the big-breasted girl at the farm. I'd watched him till he was like a little black dot, which stayed suddenly by a square grey box in a field. That was the barn where they used to meet. I've very good eyes and it amuses me to try how far and how clearly they can see. I met him again some time after midnight and helped him get into the house without his mother knowing, and he was well enough then—only a little sleepy and tired.

The old vixen was at it again. "He's been asking for you," she shrilled at me.

"If he's as ill as you make out," I said, "it would be better for him to ask for a doctor."

"Doctor's there, but he can't do anything." That startled me for a moment, I'll admit it, until I thought, "the old devil's malingering. He's got some plan or other." He was quite clever enough to cheat a doctor. I had seen him throw a fit that would have deceived Moses.

"For God's sake come," she said, "he seems frightened." Her voice broke quite genuinely, for I suppose in her way she was fond of him. I couldn't help pitying her a little, for I knew that he had never cared a mite for her and had never troubled to disguise the fact.

I left the trees and the red pool and the struggling caterpillar, for I knew that she would never leave me alone, now that her "poor boy" was asking for me. Yet a week ago there was nothing she wouldn't have done to keep us apart. She thought me responsible for his ways, as though any mortal man could have kept him off a likely woman when his appetite was up.

I think it must have been the first time I had entered their cottage by the front door, since I came to the village ten years ago. I threw an amused glance at his window. I thought I could see the marks on the wall of the ladder we'd used the week before. We'd had a little difficulty in putting it straight, but his mother slept sound. He had brought the ladder down from the barn, and when he'd got safely in, I carried it up there again. But you could never trust his word. He'd lie to his best friend, and when I reached the barn I found the girl had gone. If he couldn't bribe you with his mother's money, he'd bribe you with other people's promises.

I began to feel uneasy directly I got inside the door. It was natural that the house should be quiet, for the pair of them never had any friends to stay, although the old woman had a sister-in-law living only a few miles away. But I didn't like the sound of the doctor's feet, as he came downstairs to meet us. He'd twisted his face into a pious solemnity for our benefit, as though there was something holy about death, even about the death of my friend.

"He's conscious," he said, "but he's going. There's nothing I can do. If you want him to die in peace, better let his friend go along up. He's frightened about something."

The doctor was right. I could tell that as soon as I bent under the lintel and entered my friend's room. He was propped up on a pillow, and his eyes were on the door, waiting for me to come. They were very bright and frightened, and his hair lay across his forehead in sticky stripes. I'd never realised before what an ugly fellow he was. He had got sly eyes that looked at you too much out of the corners, but when he was in ordinary health, they held a twinkle that made you forget the slyness. There was something pleasant and brazen in the twinkle, as much as to say "I know I'm sly and ugly. But what does that matter? I've got guts." It was that twinkle, I think, some women found attractive and stimulating. Now when the twinkle was gone, he looked a rogue and nothing else.

I thought it my duty to cheer him up, so I made a small joke out of the fact that he was alone in bed. He didn't seem to relish it, and I was beginning to fear that he, too, was taking a religious view of his death, when he told me to sit down, speaking quite sharply.

"I'm dying," he said, talking very fast, "and I want to ask you something. That doctor's no good—he'd think me delirious. I'm frightened, old man. I want to be reassured," and then after a long pause, "someone with common sense." He slipped a little farther down in his bed.

"I've only once been badly ill before," he said. "That was before you settled here. I wasn't much more than a boy. People tell me that I was even supposed to be dead. They were carrying me out to burial, when a doctor stopped them just in time."

I'd heard plenty of cases like that, and I saw no reason why he should want to tell me about it. And then I thought I saw his point. His mother had not been too anxious once before to see if he were properly dead, though I had little doubt that she made a great show of grief—"My poor boy. I don't know what I shall do without him." And I'm certain that she believed herself then, as she believed herself now. She wasn't a murderess. She was only inclined to be premature.

"Look here, old man," I said, and I propped him a little higher on his pillow, "you needn't be frightened. You aren't going to die, and anyway I'd see that the doctor cut a vein or something before they moved you. But that's all morbid stuff. Why, I'd stake my shirt that you've got plenty more years in front of you. And plenty more girls too," I added to make him smile.

"Can't you cut out all that?" he said, and I knew then that he had turned religious. "Why," he said, "if I lived, I wouldn't touch another girl. I wouldn't, not one."

I tried not to smile at that, but it wasn't easy to

keep a straight face. There's always something a bit funny about a sick man's morals. "Anyway," I said, "you needn't be frightened."

"It's not that," he said. "Old man, when I came round that other time, I thought that I'd been dead. It wasn't like sleep at all. Or rest in peace. There was someone there, all round me, who knew everything. Every girl I'd ever had. Even that young one who hadn't understood. It was before your time. She lived a mile down the road, where Rachel lives now, but she and her family went away afterwards. Even the money I'd taken from mother. I don't call that stealing. It's in the family. I never had a chance to explain. Even the thoughts I'd had. A man can't help his thoughts."

"A nightmare," I said.

"Yes, it must have been a dream, mustn't it? The sort of dream people do get when they are ill. And I saw what was coming to me too. I can't bear being hurt. It wasn't fair. And I wanted to faint and I couldn't, because I was dead."

"In the dream," I said. His fear made me nervous. "In the dream," I said again.

"Yes, it must have been a dream—mustn't it?— because I woke up. The curious thing was I felt quite well and strong. I got up and stood in the road, and a little farther down, kicking up the dust, was a small crowd, going off with a man—the doctor who had stopped them burying me."

"Well," I said.

"Old man," he said, "suppose it was true. Suppose I had been dead. I believed it then, you know, and so did my mother. But you can't trust her. I went straight for a couple of years. I thought it might be a sort of second chance. Then things got fogged and somehow.... It didn't seem really possible. It's not possible. Of course it's not possible. You know it isn't, don't you?"

"Why no," I said. "Miracles of that sort don't happen nowadays. And anyway, they aren't likely to happen to you are they? And there of all places under the sun."

"It would be so dreadful," he said, "if it had been true, and I'd got to go through all that again. You don't know what things were going to happen to me in that dream. And they'd be worse now." He stopped and then, after a moment, he added as though he were stating a fact: "When one's dead there's no unconsciousness any more for ever."

"Of course it was a dream," I said and squeezed his hand. He was frightening me with his fancies. I wished that he'd die quickly, so that I could get away from his sly, bloodshot and terrified eyes and see something cheerful and amusing, like the Rachel he had mentioned, who lived a mile down the road.

"Why," I said, "if there had been a man about working miracles like that, we should have heard of others, you may be sure. Even poked away in this God-forsaken spot," I said.

"There were some others," he said. "But the stories only went round among the poor, and they'll believe anything, won't they? There were lots of diseased and crippled they said he'd cured. And there was a man, who'd been born blind, and he came and just touched his eyelids and sight came to him. Those were all old wives' tales, weren't they?" he asked me, stammering with fear, and then lying suddenly still and bunched up at the side of the bed.

I began to say, "Of course, they were all lies," but I stopped, because there was no need. All I could do was to go downstairs and tell his mother to come up and close his eyes. I wouldn't have touched them for all the money in the world. It was a long time since I'd thought of that day, ages and ages ago, when I felt a cold touch like spittle on my lids and opening my eyes had seen a man like a tree surrounded by other trees walking away.

Margaret Atwood

WHEN IT HAPPENS

MRS. BURRIDGE is putting up green tomato pickles. There are twelve quarts in each lot with a bit left over, and that is the end of the jars. At the store they tell her there's a strike on at the factory where they get made. She doesn't know anything about that but you can't buy them anywhere, and even before this they were double what they were last year; she considers herself lucky she had those in the cellar. She has a lot of green tomatoes because she heard on the weather last night there was going to be a killer frost, so she put on her parka and her work gloves and took the lantern out to the garden in the pitch dark and picked off all the ones she could see, over three bushels. She can lift the full baskets herself but she asked Frank to carry them in for her; he grumbles, but he likes it when she asks. In the morning the news said the growers had been hit and that would shoot the price up, not that the growers would get any of it themselves, everyone knows it's the stores that make the money.

She feels richer than she did yesterday, but on the other hand there isn't that much you can do with green tomatoes. The pickles hardly made a dint in them, and Frank has said, as he does every year, that they will never eat twenty-four quarts of green tomato pickle with just the two of them and the children gone. Except when they come to visit and eat me out of house and home, Mrs. Burridge adds silently. The truth is she has always made two batches and the children never liked it anyway, it was Frank ate them all and she knows perfectly well he'll do it again, without even noticing. He likes it on bread and cheese when he's watching the hockey games, during every commercial he goes out to the kitchen and makes himself another slice, even if he's just had a big meal, leaving a trail of crumbs and bits of pickle from the counter across the floor and over the front room rug to his big chair. It used to annoy Mrs. Burridge, especially the crumbs, but now she watches him with a kind of sadness; she once thought their life together would go on forever but she has come to realize this is not the case.

She doesn't even feel like teasing him about his spare tire any more, though she does it all the same because he would miss it if she stopped. "There you go," she says, in the angular, prodding, metallic voice she cannot change because everyone expects it from her, if she spoke any other way they would think she was ill, "you keep on munching away like that and it'll be easy for me to get you out of bed in the mornings, I'll just give you a push and you'll roll all the way down the stairs like a barrel." And he answers in his methodical voice, pretending to be lazy even though he isn't, "You need a little fun in life," as though his pickles and cheese are slightly disreputable, almost like an orgy. Every year he tells her she's made too much but there would be a fuss all right if he went down to the cellar one day and there wasn't any left.

Mrs. Burridge has made her own pickles since 1952, which was the first year she had the garden. She remembers it especially because her daughter Sarah was on the way and she had trouble bending down to do the weeding. When she herself was growing up everyone did their own pickles, and their own canning and preserving too. But after the war most women gave it up, there was more money then and it was easier to buy things at the store. Mrs. Burridge never gave it up, though most of her friends thought she was wasting her time, and now she is glad she didn't, it kept her in practice while the others were having to learn all over again. Though with the sugar going up the way it is, she can't understand how long anyone is going to be able to afford even the home-made things.

On paper Frank is making more money than he ever has; yet they seem to have less to spend. They could always sell the farm, she supposes, to people from the city who would use it as a weekend place; they could get what seems like a very high price, several of the farms south of them have gone that way. But Mrs. Burridge does not have much faith in money; also it is a waste of the land, and this is her home, she has it arranged the way she wants it.

When the second batch is on and simmering she goes to the back door, opens it, and stands with her arms folded across her stomach, looking out. She catches herself doing this four or five times a day now and she doesn't quite know why. There isn't much to see, just the barn and the back field with the row of dead elms Frank keeps saying he's going to cut down, and the top of Clarke's place sticking over the hill. She isn't sure what she is looking for but she has the odd idea she may see something burning, smoke coming up from the horizon, a column of it or perhaps more than one column, off to the south. This is such a peculiar thought for her to have that she hasn't told it to any one else. Yesterday Frank saw her standing at the back door and asked her about it at dinner; anything he wants to talk to her about he saves up till dinner, even if he thinks about it in the morning. He wondered why she was at the back door, doing nothing at all for over ten minutes, and Mrs. Burridge told him a lie, which made her very uneasy. She said she heard a strange dog barking, which wasn't a good story because their own dogs were right there and they didn't notice a thing. But Frank let it pass; perhaps he thinks she is getting funny in her old age and doesn't want to call attention to it, which would be like him. He'll track mud all over her nice shiny kitchen floor but he'd hate to hurt anyone's feelings. Mrs. Burridge decides, a little wistfully, that despite his pig-headedness he is a kind and likable man, and for her this is like renouncing a cherished and unquestionable belief, such as the flatness of the earth. He has made her angry so many times.

When the pickles are cool she labels them as she always does with the name and the date and carries them down the cellar stairs. The cellar is the old kind, with stone walls and a dirt floor. Mrs. Burridge likes to have everything neat—she still irons her sheets— so she had Frank build her some shelves right after they were married. The pickles go on one side, jams and jellies on the other, and the quarts of preserves along the bottom. It used to make her feel safe to have all that food in the cellar; she would think to herself, well, if there's a snowstorm or anything and we're cut off, it won't be so bad. It doesn't make her feel safe any more. Instead she thinks that if she has to leave suddenly she won't be able to take any of the jars with her, they'd be too heavy to carry.

She comes back up the stairs after the last trip.

It's not as easy as it used to be, her knee still bothers her as it has ever since she fell six years ago, she tripped on the second-last step. She's asked Frank a million times to fix the stairs but he hasn't done it, that's what she means by pig-headed. If she asks him more than twice to do something he calls it nagging, and maybe it is, but who's going to do it if he won't? The cold vacant hole at the back of this question is too much for her.

She has to stop herself from going to the back door again. Instead she goes to the back window and looks out, she can see almost the same things anyway. Frank is going towards the barn, carrying something, it looks like a wrench. The way he walks, slower than he used to, bent forward a little—from the back he's like an old man, how many years has he been walking that way?—makes her think, *He can't protect me*. She doesn't think this on purpose, it simply occurs to her, and it isn't only him, it's all of them, they've lost the power, you can tell by the way they walk. They are all waiting, just as Mrs. Burridge is, for whatever it is to happen. Whether they realize it or not. Lately when she's gone to the Dominion Store in town she has seen a look on the faces of the women there—she knows most of them, she wouldn't be mistaken—an anxious, closed look, as if they are frightened of something but won't talk about it. They're wondering what they will do, perhaps they think there's nothing they can do. This air of helplessness exasperates Mrs. Burridge, who has always been practical.

For weeks she has wanted to go to Frank and ask him to teach her how to use the gun. In fact he has two guns, a shotgun and a twenty-two rifle; he used to like going after a few ducks in the fall, and of course there are the groundhogs, they have to be shot because of the holes they make in the fields Frank drives over on the tractor five or six times a year. A lot of men get injured by overturning tractors. But she can't ask him because she can't explain to him why she needs to know, and if she doesn't explain he will only tease. "Anyone can shoot a gun," he'll say, "all you have to do is pull the trigger ... oh, you mean you want to hit something, well now, that's different, who you planning to kill?" Perhaps he won't say that; perhaps this is only the way he talked twenty years ago, before she stopped taking an interest in things outside the house. But Mrs. Burridge will never know because she will never ask. She doesn't have the heart to say to him, *Maybe you'll be dead. Maybe you'll go off somewhere when it happens, maybe there will be a war.* She can remember the last war.

Nothing has changed outside the window, so she turns away and sits down at the kitchen table to make out her shopping list. Tomorrow is their day for going into town. She tries to plan the day so she can sit down at intervals; otherwise her feet start swelling up. That began with Sarah and got worse with the other two children and it's never really gone away. All her life, ever since she got married, she has made lists of things that have to be bought, sewed, planted, cooked, stored; she already has her list made for next Christmas, all the names and the gift she will buy for each, and the list of what she needs for Christmas dinner. But she can't seem to get interested in it, it's too far away. She can't believe in a distant future that is orderly like the past, she no longer seems to have the energy; it's as if she is saving it up for when she will have to use it.

She is even having trouble with the shopping list. Instead of concentrating on the paper—she writes on the backs of the used-up days off the page-a-day calendar Frank gives her every New Year's—she is gazing around the kitchen, looking at all the things she will have to leave behind when she goes. That will be the hardest part. Her mother's china, her silver, even though it is an old-fashioned pattern and the silver is wearing off, the egg timer in the shape of a chicken Sarah gave her when she was twelve, the ceramic salt-and-pepper shakers, green horses with perforated heads, that one of the other children brought back from the Ex. She thinks of walking up the stairs, the sheets folded in the chest, the towels stacked neatly on the shelves, the beds made, the quilt that was her grandmother's, it makes her want to cry. On her bureau, the wedding picture, herself in a shiny satin gown (the satin was a mistake, it emphasized her hips), Frank in the suit he has not worn since except to funerals, his hair cut too short on the sides and a surprising tuft at the top, like a woodpecker's. The children when they were babies. She thinks of her girls now and hopes they will not have babies; it is no longer the right time for it.

Mrs. Burridge wishes someone would be more precise, so she could make better plans. Everyone knows something is going to happen, you can tell by reading the newspapers and watching the television, but nobody is sure what it will be, nobody can be exact. She has her own ideas about it though. At first it will simply become quieter. She will have an odd feeling that something is wrong but it will be a few days before she is able to pin it down. Then she will notice that the planes are no longer flying over on their way to the Malton Airport, and that the noise from the highway two miles away, which is quite distinct when the leaves are off the trees, has almost disappeared. The television will be non-committal about it; in fact, the television, which right now is filled with bad news, of strikes, shortages,

famines, layoffs and price increases, will become
sweet-tempered and placating, and long intervals of
classical music will appear on the radio. About this
time Mrs. Burridge will realize that the news is being
censored as it was during the war.

Mrs. Burridge is not positive about what will
happen next; that is, she knows what will happen
but she is not positive about the order. She expects
it will be the gas and oil: the oil delivery man will
simply not turn up at his usual time, and one morning
the corner filling station will be closed. Just that, no
explanations, because of course they—she does not
know who "they" are, but she has always believed
in their existence—they do not want people to panic.
They are trying to keep things looking normal, possibly they have already started on this program and
that is in fact why things still do look normal. Luckily
she and Frank have the diesel fuel tank in the shed,
it is three-quarters full, and they don't use the filling
station anyway, they have their own gas pump. She
has Frank bring in the old wood stove, the one they
stored under the barn when they had the furnace
and the electricity put in, and for once she blesses
Frank's habit of putting things off. She was after him
for years to take that stove to the dump. He cuts
down the dead elms, finally, and they burn them in
the stove.

The telephone wires are blown down in a storm
and no one comes to fix them; or this is what Mrs.
Burridge deduces. At any rate, the phone goes dead.
Mrs. Burridge doesn't particularly mind, she never
liked using the phone much anyway, but it does make
her feel cut off.

About now men begin to appear on the back road,
the gravel road that goes past the gate, walking usually
by themselves, sometimes in pairs. They seem to be

heading north. Most of them are young, in their twenties, Mrs. Burridge would guess. They are not dressed like the men around here. It's been so long since she has seen anyone *walking* along this road that she becomes alarmed. She begins leaving the dogs off their chains, she has kept them chained at night ever since one of them bit a Jehovah's Witness early one Sunday morning. Mrs. Burridge doesn't hold with the Witnesses—she is United—but she respects their perseverance, at least they have the courage of their convictions which is more than you can say for some members of her own church, and she always buys a *Watchtower*. Maybe they have been right all along.

It is about this time too that she takes one of the guns, she thinks it will be the shotgun as she will have a better chance of hitting something, and hides it, along with the shells, under a piece of roofing behind the barn. She does not tell Frank; he will have the twenty-two. She has already picked out the spot.

They do not want to waste the little gasoline they still have left in the pump so they do not make unnecessary trips. They begin to eat the chickens, which Mrs. Burridge does not look forward to. She hates cleaning and plucking them, and the angriest she ever got at Frank was the time he and Henry Clarke decided to go into turkey farming. They did it too, despite all she had to say against it, and she had to cope with the turkeys escaping and scratching in the garden and impossible to catch, in her opinion they were the stupidest birds in God's creation, and she had to clean and pluck a turkey a week until luckily the blackhead wiped out a third of the flock, which was enough to discourage them, they sold off the rest at a loss. It was the only time she was actually glad to see Frank lose money on one of his ventures.

Mrs. Burridge will feel things are getting serious

on the day the electricity goes off and does not come back on. She knows, with a kind of fatalism, that this will happen in November, when the freezer is full of the vegetables but before it is cold enough to keep the packages frozen outside. She stands and looks at the pliofilm bags of beans and corn and spinach and carrots, melting and sodden, and thinks, *Why couldn't they have waited till spring*. It is the waste, of food and also of her hard work, that aggravates her the most. She salvages what she can. During the Depression, she remembers, they used to say those on farms were better off than those in the city, because at least they had food; if you could keep the farm, that is; but she is no longer sure this is true. She feels beleaguered, isolated, like someone shut up inside a fortress, though no one has bothered them, in fact no one has passed their way for days, not even any of the solitary walking men.

With the electricity off they can no longer get the television. The radio stations, when they broadcast at all, give out nothing but soothing music, which Mrs. Burridge does not find soothing in the least.

One morning she goes to the back door and looks out and there are the columns of smoke, right where she's been expecting to see them, off to the south. She calls Frank and they stand watching. The smoke is thick and black, oily, as though something has exploded. She does not know what Frank is thinking; she herself is wondering about the children. She has had no news of them in weeks, but how could she? They stopped delivering mail some time ago.

Fifteen minutes later, Henry Clarke drives into the yard in his half-ton truck. This is very unusual as no one has been driving anywhere lately. There is another man with him, and Mrs. Burridge identifies him as the man three farms up who moved in four or five years ago. Frank goes out and talks with them, and they drive over to the gas pump and start pumping the rest of the precious gas into the truck. Frank comes back to the house. He tells her there's a little trouble down the road, they are going along to see about it and she isn't to worry. He goes into the back room, comes out with the twenty-two, asks her where the shotgun is. She says she doesn't know. He searches for it, fruitlessly—she can hear him swearing, he does not swear in her presence—until he gives up. He comes out, kisses her goodbye, which is unusual too, and says he'll be back in a couple of hours. She watches the three of them drive off in Henry Clarke's truck, towards the smoke; she knows he will not come back. She supposes she ought to feel more emotional about it, but she is well prepared, she has been saying goodbye to him silently for years.

She re-enters the house and closes the door. She is fifty-one, her feet hurt, and she does not know where she can go, but she realizes she cannot stay here. There will now be a lot of hungry people, those that can make it this far out of the cities will be young and tough, her house is a beacon, signalling warmth and food. It will be fought over, but not by her.

She goes upstairs, searches in the cupboard, and puts on her heavy slacks and her two thickest sweaters. Downstairs she gathers up all the food that will be light enough for her to carry: raisins, cooking chocolate, dried prunes and apricots, half a loaf of bread, some milk powder which she puts into a quart freezer bag, a piece of cheese. Then she unearths the shotgun from behind the barn. She thinks briefly of killing the livestock, the chickens, the heifers and the pig, so no one will do it who does not know the right way; but she herself does not know the right way, she has never killed anything in her life, Frank always did it, so she contents herself with opening the hen-house door and the gate into the back field. She hopes the animals will run away but she knows they prob-ably will not.

She takes one last look around the house. As an afterthought, she adds her toothbrush to the bundle: she does not like the feel of unbrushed teeth. She does not go down into the cellar but she has an image of her carefully sealed bottles and jars, red and yellow and purple, shattered on the floor, in a sticky puddle that looks like blood. Those who come will be wasteful, what they cannot eat themselves they will destroy. She thinks about setting fire to the house herself, before anyone else can do it.

Mrs. Burridge sits at her kitchen table. On the back of her calendar page, it's for a Monday, she has written *Oatmeal*, in her evenly spaced public school hand-writing that always got a star and has not changed very much since then. The dogs are a problem. After some thought she unchains them, but she does not let them past the gate: at a crucial moment they might give her away. She walks north in her heavy boots, carrying her parka because it is not yet cold enough to put it on, and her package of food and the shotgun which she has taken care to load. She passes the cemetery where her father and mother and her grand-mother and grandfather are buried; the church used to be there but it burned down sixteen years ago and was rebuilt closer to the highway. Frank's people are in the other cemetery, his go back to the great-grandfather but they are Anglican, not that he kept it up. There is no one else on the road; she feels a little foolish. What if she is wrong and Frank comes back after all, what if nothing, really, is the matter? *Shortening*, she writes. She intends to make a lemon meringue pie for Sunday, when two of the children are coming up from the city for dinner.

It is almost evening and Mrs. Burridge is tired. She is in a part of the country she cannot remember, though she has stayed on the same road and it is a road she knows well; she has driven along it many times with Frank. But walking is not the same as driving. On one side there is a field, no buildings, on the other a woodlot; a stream flows through a culvert under the road. Mrs. Burridge kneels down to drink: the water is ice-cold and tastes of iron. Later there will be a frost, she can feel it. She puts on her parka and her gloves, and turns into the forest where she will not be seen. There she will eat some raisins and cheese and try to rest, waiting for the moon to rise so she can continue walking. It is now quite dark. She smells earth, wood, rotting leaves.

Suddenly her eye is caught by a flicker of red, and before she can turn back—how can this happen so quickly?—it takes shape, it is a small fire, off to the right, and two men are crouching near it. They have seen her, too: one of them rises and comes towards her. His teeth bare, he is smiling; he thinks she will be easy, an old woman. He says something but she cannot imagine what it is, she does not know how people dressed like that would talk.

They have spotted her gun, their eyes have fastened on it, they want it. Mrs. Burridge knows what she must do. She must wait until they are close enough and then she must raise the gun and shoot them, using one barrel for each, aiming at the faces. Otherwise they will kill her, she has no doubt about that. She will have to be fast, which is too bad because her hands feel thick and wooden; she is afraid, she does not want the loud noise or the burst of red that will follow, she has never killed anything in her life. She has no pictures beyond this point. You never know how you will act in a thing like that until it actually happens.

Mrs. Burridge looks at the kitchen clock. On her list she writes *Cheese*, they are eating more cheese now than they used to because of the price of meat. She gets up and goes to the kitchen door.

Franz Kafka

A Country Doctor

Translated by Willa and Edwin Muir

I WAS IN GREAT PERPLEXITY; I had to start on
an urgent journey; a seriously ill patient was waiting
for me in a village ten miles off; a thick blizzard of
snow filled all the wide spaces between him and me;
I had a gig, a light gig with big wheels, exactly right
for our country roads; muffled in furs, my bag of
instruments in my hand, I was in the courtyard all
ready for the journey; but there was no horse to be
had, no horse. My own horse had died in the night,
worn out by the fatigues of this icy winter; my servant
girl was now running around the village trying to
borrow a horse; but it was hopeless, I knew it, and
I stood there forlornly, with the snow gathering more
and more thickly upon me, more and more unable
to move. In the gateway the girl appeared, alone, and
waved the lantern; of course, who would lend a horse
at this time for such a journey? I strode through the
courtyard once more; I could see no way out; in my
confused distress I kicked at the dilapidated door of
the yearlong uninhabited pigsty. It flew open and
flapped to and fro on its hinges. A steam and smell
as of horses came out from it. A dim stable lantern
was swinging inside from a rope. A man, crouching

on his hams in that low space, showed an open blue-
eyed face. "Shall I yoke up?" he asked, crawling out
on all fours. I did not know what to say and merely
stooped down to see what else was in the sty. The
servant girl was standing beside me. "You never know
what you're going to find in your own house," she
said, and we both laughed. "Hey there, Brother, hey
there, Sister!" called the groom, and two horses,
enormous creatures with powerful flanks, one after
the other, their legs tucked close to their bodies, each
well-shaped head lowered like a camel's, by sheer
strength of buttocking squeezed out through the door
hole which they filled entirely. But at once they were
standing up, their legs long and their bodies steaming
thickly. "Give him a hand," I said, and the willing
girl hurried to help the groom with the harnessing.
Yet hardly was she beside him when the groom
clipped hold of her and pushed his face against hers.
She screamed and fled back to me; on her cheek stood
out in red the marks of two rows of teeth. "You brute,"
I yelled in fury, "do you want a whipping?" but in
the same moment reflected that the man was a
stranger; that I did not know where he came from,
and that of his own free will he was helping me out
when everyone else had failed me. As if he knew my
thoughts he took no offense at my threat but, still
busied with the horses, only turned around once
toward me. "Get in," he said then, and indeed:
everything was ready. A magnificent pair of horses,
I observed, such as I had never sat behind, and I
climbed in happily. "But I'll drive, you don't know
the way," I said. "Of course," said he, "I'm not coming
with you anyway, I'm staying with Rose." "No,"
shrieked Rose, fleeing into the house with a justified
presentiment that her fate was inescapable; I heard
the door chain rattle as she put it up; I heard the

key turn in the lock; I could see, moreover, how she put out the lights in the entrance hall and in further flight all through the rooms to keep herself from being discovered. "You're coming with me," I said to the groom, "or I won't go, urgent as my journey is. I'm not thinking of paying for it by handing the girl over to you." "Gee up!" he said; clapped his hands; the gig whirled off like a log in a freshet; I could just hear the door of my house splitting and bursting as the groom charged at it and then I was deafened and blinded by a storming rush that steadily buffeted all my senses. But this only for a moment, since, as if my patient's farmyard had opened out just before my courtyard gate, I was already there; the horses had come quietly to a standstill; the blizzard had stopped; moonlight all around; my patient's parents hurried out of the house, his sister behind them; I was almost lifted out of the gig; from their confused ejaculations I gathered not a word; in the sickroom the air was almost unbreathable; the neglected stove was smoking; I wanted to push open a window; but first I had to look at my patient. Gaunt, without any fever, not cold, not warm, with vacant eyes, without a shirt, the youngster heaved himself up from under the feather bedding, threw his arms around my neck, and whispered in my ear: "Doctor, let me die." I glanced around the room; no one had heard it; the parents were leaning forward in silence waiting for my verdict; the sister had set a chair for my handbag; I opened the bag and hunted among my instruments; the boy kept clutching at me from his bed to remind me of his entreaty; I picked up a pair of tweezers, examined them in the candlelight, and laid them down again. "Yes," I thought blasphemously, "in cases like this the gods are helpful, send the missing horse, add to it a second because of the urgency, and to crown everything bestow even a groom————" And only now did I remember Rose again; what was I to do, how could I rescue her, how could I pull her away from under that groom at ten miles' distance, with a team of horses I couldn't control. These horses, now, they had somehow slipped the reins loose, pushed the windows open from outside; I did not know how; each of them had stuck a head in at a window and, quite unmoved by the startled cries of the family, stood eyeing the patient. "Better go back at once," I thought, as if the horses were summoning me to the return journey, yet I permitted the patient's sister, who fancied that I was dazed by the heat, to take my fur coat from me. A glass of rum was poured out for me, the old man clapped me on the shoulder, a familiarity justified by this offer of his treasure. I shook my head; in the narrow confines of the old man's thoughts I felt ill; that was my only reason for refusing the drink. The mother stood by the bedside and cajoled me toward it; I yielded, and while one of the horses whinnied loudly to the ceiling, laid my head to the boy's breast, which shivered under my wet beard. I confirmed what I already knew; the boy was quite sound, something a little wrong with his circulation, saturated with coffee by his solicitous mother, but sound and best turned out of bed with one shove. I am no world reformer and so I let him lie. I was the district doctor and did my duty to the uttermost, to the point where it became almost too much. I was badly paid and yet generous and helpful to the poor. I had still to see that Rose was all right, and then the boy might have his way and I wanted to die too. What was I doing there in that endless winter! My horse was dead, and not a single person in the village would lend me another. I had to get my team out of the pigsty; if they hadn't chanced

to be horses I should have had to travel with swine.
That was how it was. And I nodded to the family.
They knew nothing about it, and, had they known,
would not have believed it. To write prescriptions is
easy, but to come to an understanding with people
is hard. Well, this should be the end of my visit, I
had once more been called out needlessly, I was used
to that, the whole district made my life a torment
with my night bell, but that I should have to sacrifice
Rose this time as well, the pretty girl who had lived
in my house for years almost without my noticing
her—that sacrifice was too much to ask, and I had
somehow to get it reasoned out in my head with the
help of what craft I could muster, in order not to
let fly at this family, which with the best will in the
world could not restore Rose to me. But as I shut
my bag and put an arm out for my fur coat, the family
meanwhile standing together, the father sniffing at
the glass of rum in his hand, the mother, apparently
disappointed in me—why, what do people expect?—
biting her lips with tears in her eyes, the sister
fluttering a blood-soaked towel, I was somehow ready
to admit conditionally that the boy might be ill after
all. I went toward him, he welcomed me smiling as
if I were bringing him the most nourishing invalid
broth—ah, now both horses were whinnying together;
the noise, I suppose, was ordained by heaven to assist
my examination of the patient—and this time I discovered that the boy was indeed ill. In his right side,
near the hip, was an open wound as big as the palm
of my hand. Rose-red, in many variations of shade,
dark in the hollows, lighter at the edges, softly
granulated, with irregular clots of blood, open as a
surface mine to the daylight. That was how it looked
from a distance. But on a closer inspection there was
another complication. I could not help a low whistle

of surprise. Worms, as thick and as long as my little finger, themselves rose-red and blood-spotted as well, were wriggling from their fastness in the interior of the wound toward the light, with small white heads and many little legs. Poor boy, you were past helping. I had discovered your great wound; this blossom in your side was destroying you. The family was pleased; they saw me busying myself; the sister told the mother, the mother the father, the father told several guests who were coming in, through the moonlight at the open door, walking on tiptoe, keeping their balance with outstretched arms. "Will you save me?" whispered the boy with a sob, quite blinded by the life within his wound. That is what people are like in my district. Always expecting the impossible from the doctor. They have lost their ancient beliefs; the parson sits at home and unravels his vestments, one after another; but the doctor is supposed to be omnipotent with his merciful surgeon's hand. Well, as it pleases them; I have not thrust my services on them; if they misuse me for sacred ends, I let that happen to me too; what better do I want, old country doctor that I am, bereft of my servant girl? And so they came, the family and the village elders, and stripped my clothes off me; a school choir with the teacher at the head of it stood before the house and sang these words to an utterly simple tune:

> Strip his clothes off, then he'll heal us,
> If he doesn't, kill him dead!
> Only a doctor, only a doctor.

Then my clothes were off and I looked at the people quietly, my fingers in my beard and my head cocked to one side. I was altogether composed and equal to the situation and remained so, although it was no help to me, since they now took me by the head and feet and carried me to the bed. They laid me down in it next to the wall, on the side of the wound. Then they all left the room; the door was shut; the singing stopped; clouds covered the moon; the bedding was warm around me; the horses' heads in the open windows wavered like shadows. "Do you know," said a voice in my ear, "I have very little confidence in you. Why, you were only blown in here, you didn't come on your own feet. Instead of helping me, you're cramping me on my deathbed. What I'd like best is to scratch your eyes out." "Right," I said, "it is a shame. And yet I am a doctor. What am I to do? Believe me, it is not too easy for me either." "Am I supposed to be content with this apology? Oh, I must be, I can't help it. I always have to put up with things. A fine wound is all I brought into the world; that was my sole endowment." "My young friend," said I, "your mistake is: you have not a wide enough view. I have been in all the sickrooms, far and wide, and I tell you: your wound is not so bad. Done in a tight corner with two strokes of the ax. Many a one proffers his side and can hardly hear the ax in the forest, far less that it is coming nearer to him." "Is that really so, or are you deluding me in my fever?" "It is really so, take the word of honor of an official doctor." And he took it and lay still. But now it was time for me to think of escaping. The horses were still standing faithfully in their places. My clothes, my fur coat, my bag were quickly collected; I didn't want to waste time dressing; if the horses raced home as they had come, I should only be springing, as it were, out of this bed into my own. Obediently a horse backed away from the window; I threw my bundle into the gig; the fur coat missed its mark and was caught on a hook only by the sleeve. Good enough. I swung myself onto the horse. With the reins loosely trailing, one horse barely fastened to the other, the gig swaying behind, my fur coat last of all in the snow. "Gee up!" I said, but there was no galloping; slowly, like old men, we crawled through the snowy wastes; a long time echoed behind us the new but faulty song of the children:

> O be joyful, all you patients,
> The doctor's laid in bed beside you!

Never shall I reach home at this rate; my flourishing practice is done for; my successor is robbing me, but in vain, for he cannot take my place; in my house the disgusting groom is raging; Rose is his victim; I do not want to think about it anymore. Naked, exposed to the frost of this most unhappy of ages, with an earthly vehicle, unearthly horses, old man that I am, I wander astray. My fur coat is hanging from the back of the gig, but I cannot reach it, and none of my limber pack of patients lifts a finger. Betrayed! Betrayed! A false alarm on the night bell once answered—it cannot be made good, not ever.

Isaac Bashevis Singer

GIMPEL THE FOOL

Translated by Saul Bellow

I AM GIMPEL THE FOOL. I don't think myself a fool. On the contrary. But that's what folks call me. They gave me the name while I was still in school. I had seven names in all: imbecile, donkey, flax-head, dope, glump, ninny, and fool. The last name stuck. What did my foolishness consist of? I was easy to take in. They said, "Gimpel, you know the rabbi's wife has been brought to childbed?" So I skipped school. Well, it turned out to be a lie. How was I supposed to know? She hadn't had a big belly. But I never looked at her belly. Was that really so foolish? The gang laughed and hee-hawed, stomped and danced and chanted a good-night prayer. And instead of the raisins they give when a woman's lying in, they stuffed my hand full of goat turds. I was no weakling. If I slapped someone he'd see all the way to Cracow. But I'm really not a slugger by nature. I think to myself: Let it pass. So they take advantage of me.

I was coming home from school and heard a dog barking. I'm not afraid of dogs, but of course I never want to start up with them. One of them may be mad, and if he bites there's not a Tartar in the world who can help you. So I made tracks. Then I looked around and saw the whole market place wild with laughter. It was no dog at all but Wolf-Leib the Thief. How was I supposed to know it was he? It sounded like a howling bitch.

When the pranksters and leg-pullers found that I was easy to fool, every one of them tried his luck with me. "Gimpel, the Czar is coming to Frampol; Gimpel, the moon fell down in Turbeen; Gimpel, little Hodel Furpiece found a treasure behind the bathhouse." And I like a golem believed everyone. In the first place, everything is possible, as it is written in the Wisdom of the Fathers, I've forgotten just how. Second, I had to believe when the whole town came down on me! If I ever dared to say, "Ah, you're kidding!" there was trouble. People got angry. "What do you mean! You want to call everyone a liar?" What was I to do? I believed them, and I hope at least that did them some good.

I was an orphan. My grandfather who brought me up was already bent toward the grave. So they turned me over to a baker, and what a time they gave me there! Every woman or girl who came to bake a batch of noodles had to fool me at least once. "Gimpel, there's a fair in heaven; Gimpel, the rabbi gave birth to a calf in the seventh month; Gimpel, a cow flew over the roof and laid brass eggs." A student from the yeshiva came once to buy a roll, and he said, "You, Gimpel, while you stand here scraping with your baker's shovel the Messiah has come. The dead have arisen." "What do you mean?" I said. "I heard no one blowing the ram's horn!" He said, "Are you deaf?" And all began to cry, "We heard it, we heard!" Then in came Rietze the Candle-dipper and called out in her hoarse voice, "Gimpel, your father and mother have stood up from the grave. They're looking for you."

To tell the truth, I knew very well that nothing of the sort had happened, but all the same, as folks were talking, I threw on my wool vest and went out. Maybe something had happened. What did I stand to lose by looking? Well, what a cat music went up! And then I took a vow to believe nothing more. But that was no go either. They confused me so that I didn't know the big end from the small.

I went to the rabbi to get some advice. He said, "It is written, better to be a fool all your days than for one hour to be evil. You are not a fool. They are the fools. For he who causes his neighbor to feel shame loses Paradise himself." Nevertheless the rabbi's daughter took me in. As I left the rabbinical court she said, "Have you kissed the wall yet?" I said, "No; what for?" She answered, "It's the law; you've got to do it after every visit." Well, there didn't seem to be any harm in it. And she burst out laughing. It was a fine trick. She put one over on me, all right.

I wanted to go off to another town, but then everyone got busy matchmaking, and they were after me so they nearly tore my coat tails off. They talked at me and talked until I got water on the ear. She was no chaste maiden, but they told me she was virgin pure. She had a limp, and they said it was deliberate, from coyness. She had a bastard, and they told me the child was her little brother. I cried, "You're wasting your time, I'll never marry that whore." But they said indignantly, "What a way to talk! Aren't you ashamed of yourself? We can take you to the rabbi and have you fined for giving her a bad name." I saw then that I wouldn't escape them so easily and I thought: They're set on making me their butt. But when you're married the husband's the master, and if that's all right with her it's agreeable to me too. Besides, you can't pass through life unscathed, nor expect to.

I went to her clay house, which was built on the sand, and the whole gang, hollering and chorusing, came after me. They acted like bear-baiters. When we came to the well they stopped all the same. They were afraid to start anything with Elka. Her mouth would open as if it were on a hinge, and she had a fierce tongue. I entered the house. Lines were strung from wall to wall and clothes were drying. Barefoot she stood by the tub, doing the wash. She was dressed in a worn hand-me-down gown of plush. She had her hair put up in braids and pinned across her head. It took my breath away, almost, the reek of it all.

Evidently she knew who I was. She took a look at me and said, "Look who's here! He's come, the drip. Grab a seat."

I told her all; I denied nothing. "Tell me the truth," I said, "are you really a virgin, and is that mischievous Yechiel actually your little brother? Don't be deceitful with me, for I'm an orphan."

"I'm an orphan myself," she answered, "and whoever tries to twist you up, may the end of his nose take a twist. But don't let them think they can take advantage of me. I want a dowry of fifty guilders, and let them take up a collection besides. Otherwise they can kiss my you-know-what." She was very plainspoken. I said, "It's the bride and not the groom who gives the dowry." Then she said, "Don't bargain with me. Either a flat 'yes' or a flat 'no'—Go back where you came from."

I thought: No bread will ever be baked from *this* dough. But ours is not a poor town. They consented to everything and proceeded with the wedding. It so happened that there was a dysentery epidemic at the time. The ceremony was held at the cemetery gates, near the little corpse-washing hut. The fellows got drunk. While the marriage contract was being drawn up I heard the most pious high rabbi ask, "Is the bride a widow or a divorced woman?" And the sexton's wife answered for her, "Both a widow and divorced." It was a black moment for me. But what was I to do, run away from under the marriage canopy?

There was singing and dancing. An old granny danced opposite me, hugging a braided white *chalah*. The master of revels made a "God 'a mercy" in memory of the bride's parents. The schoolboys threw burrs, as on Tishe b'Av fast day. There were a lot of gifts after the sermon: a noodle board, a kneading trough, a bucket, brooms, ladles, household articles galore. Then I took a look and saw two strapping young men carrying a crib. "What do we need this for?" I asked. So they said, "Don't rack your brains about it. It's all right, it'll come in handy." I realized I was going to be rooked. Take it another way though, what did I stand to lose? I reflected; I'll see what comes of it. A whole town can't go altogether crazy.

II

AT NIGHT I came where my wife lay, but she wouldn't let me in. "Say, look here, is this what they married us for?" I said. And she said, "My monthly has come." "But yesterday they took you to the ritual bath, and that's afterward, isn't it supposed to be?" "Today isn't yesterday," said she, "and yesterday's not today. You can beat it if you don't like it." In short, I waited.

Not four months later she was in childbed. The townsfolk hid their laughter with their knuckles. But what could I do? She suffered intolerable pains and clawed at the walls. "Gimpel," she cried, "I'm going. Forgive me!" The house filled with women. They were boiling pans of water. The screams rose to the welkin.

The thing to do was to go to the House of Prayer to repeat Psalms, and that was what I did.

The townsfolk liked that, all right. I stood in a corner saying Psalms and prayers, and they shook their heads at me. "Pray, pray!" they told me. "Prayer never made any woman pregnant." One of the congregation put a straw to my mouth and said, "Hay for the cows." There was something to that too, by God!

She gave birth to a boy. Friday at the synagogue the sexton stood up before the Ark, pounded on the reading table, and announced, "The wealthy Reb Gimpel invites the congregation to a feast in honor of the birth of a son." The whole House of Prayer rang with laughter. My face was flaming. But there was nothing I could do. After all, I *was* the one responsible for the circumcision honors and rituals.

Half the town came running. You couldn't wedge another soul in. Women brought peppered chick-peas, and there was a keg of beer from the tavern. I ate and drank as much as anyone, and they all congratulated me. Then there was a circumcision, and I named the boy after my father, may he rest in peace. When all were gone and I was left with my wife alone, she thrust her head through the bed-curtain and called me to her.

"Gimpel," said she, "why are you silent? Has your ship gone and sunk?"

"What shall I say?" I answered. "A fine thing you've done to me! If my mother had known of it she'd have died a second time."

She said, "Are you crazy, or what?"

"How can you make such a fool," I said, "of one who should be the lord and master?"

"What's the matter with you?" she said. "What have you taken it into your head to imagine?"

I saw that I must speak bluntly and openly. "Do you think this is the way to use an orphan?" I said. "You have borne a bastard."

She answered, "Drive this foolishness out of your head. The child is yours."

"How can he be mine?" I argued. "He was born seventeen weeks after the wedding."

She told me then that he was premature. I said, "Isn't he a little too premature?" She said, she had had a grandmother who carried just as short a time and she resembled this grandmother of hers as one drop of water does another. She swore to it with such oaths that you would have believed a peasant at the fair if he had used them. To tell the plain truth, I didn't believe her; but when I talked it over next day with the schoolmaster he told me that the very same thing had happened to Adam and Eve. Two they went to bed, and four they descended.

"There isn't a woman in the world who is not the grandaughter of Eve," he said.

That was how it was; they argued me dumb. But then, who really knows how such things are?

I began to forget my sorrow. I loved the child madly, and he loved me too. As soon as he saw me he'd wave his little hands and want me to pick him up, and when he was colicky I was the only one who could pacify him. I bought him a little bone teething ring and a little gilded cap. He was forever catching the evil eye from someone, and then I had to run to get one of those abracadabras for him that would get him out of it. I worked like an ox. You know how expenses go up when there's an infant in the house. I don't want to lie about it; I didn't dislike Elka either, for that matter. She swore at me and cursed, and I couldn't get enough of her. What strength she had! One of her looks could rob you of the power of speech.

And her orations! Pitch and sulphur, that's what they were full of, and yet somehow also full of charm. I adored her every word. She gave me bloody wounds though.

In the evening I brought her a white loaf as well as a dark one, and also poppyseed rolls I baked myself. I thieved because of her and swiped everything I could lay hands on: macaroons, raisins, almonds, cakes. I hope I may be forgiven for stealing from the Saturday pots the women left to warm in the baker's oven. I would take out scraps of meat, a chunk of pudding, a chicken leg or head, a piece of tripe, whatever I could nip quickly. She ate and became fat and handsome.

I had to sleep away from home all during the week, at the bakery. On Friday nights when I got home she always made an excuse of some sort. Either she had heartburn, or a stitch in the side, or hiccups, or headaches. You know what women's excuses are. I had a bitter time of it. It was rough. To add to it, this little brother of hers, the bastard, was growing bigger. He'd put lumps on me, and when I wanted to hit back she'd open her mouth and curse so powerfully I saw a green haze floating before my eyes. Ten times a day she threatened to divorce me. Another man in my place would have taken French leave and disappeared. But I'm the type that bears it and says nothing. What's one to do? Shoulders are from God, and burdens too.

One night there was a calamity in the bakery; the oven burst, and we almost had a fire. There was nothing to do but go home, so I went home. Let me, I thought, also taste the joy of sleeping in bed in mid-week. I didn't want to wake the sleeping mite and tiptoed into the house. Coming in, it seemed to me that I heard not the snoring of one but, as it were, a double snore, one a thin enough snore and the other like the snoring of a slaughtered ox. Oh, I didn't like that! I didn't like it at all. I went up to the bed, and things suddenly turned black. Next to Elka lay a man's form. Another in my place would have made an uproar, and enough noise to rouse the whole town, but the thought occurred to me that I might wake the child. A little thing like that—why frighten a little swallow, I thought. All right then, I went back to the bakery and stretched out on a sack of flour and till morning I never shut an eye. I shivered as if I had had malaria. "Enough of being a donkey," I said to myself. "Gimpel isn't going to be a sucker all his life. There's a limit even to the foolishness of a fool like Gimpel."

In the morning I went to the rabbi to get advice, and it made a great commotion in the town. They sent the beadle for Elka right away. She came, carrying the child. And what do you think she did? She denied it, denied everything, bone and stone! "He's out of his head," she said. "I know nothing of dreams or divinations." They yelled at her, warned her, hammered on the table, but she stuck to her guns: it was a false accusation, she said.

The butchers and the horse-traders took her part. One of the lads from the slaughterhouse came by and said to me, "We've got our eye on you, you're a marked man." Meanwhile the child started to bear down and soiled itself. In the rabbinical court there was an Ark of the Covenant, and they couldn't allow that, so they sent Elka away.

I said to the rabbi, "What shall I do?"

"You must divorce her at once," said he.

"And what if she refuses?" I asked.

He said, "You must serve the divorce. That's all you'll have to do."

I said, "Well, all right, Rabbi. Let me think about it."

"There's nothing to think about," said he. "You mustn't remain under the same roof with her."

"And if I want to see the child?" I asked.

"Let her go, the harlot," said he, "and her brood of bastards with her."

The verdict he gave was that I mustn't even cross her threshold—never again, as long as I should live.

During the day it didn't bother me so much. I thought: It was bound to happen, the abscess had to burst. But at night when I stretched out upon the sacks I felt it all very bitterly. A longing took me, for her and for the child. I wanted to be angry, but that's my misfortune exactly, I don't have it in me to be really angry. In the first place—this was how my thoughts went—there's bound to be a slip sometimes. You can't live without errors. Probably that lad who was with her led her on and gave her presents and what not, and women are often long on hair and short on sense, and so he got around her. And then since she denies it so, maybe I was only seeing things? Hallucinations do happen. You see a figure or a mannikin or something, but when you come up closer it's nothing, there's not a thing there. And if that's so, I'm doing her an injustice. And when I got so far in my thoughts I started to weep. I sobbed so that I wet the flour where I lay. In the morning I went to the rabbi and told him that I had made a mistake. The rabbi wrote on with his quill, and he said that if that were so he would have to reconsider the whole case. Until he had finished I wasn't to go near my wife, but I might send her bread and money by messenger.

III

NINE MONTHS PASSED before all the rabbis could
come to an agreement. Letters went back and forth.
I hadn't realized that there could be so much erudition
about a matter like this.

Meanwhile Elka gave birth to still another child,
a girl this time. On the Sabbath I went to the
synagogue and invoked a blessing on her. They called
me up to the Torah, and I named the child for my
mother-in-law—may she rest in peace. The louts and
loudmouths of the town who came into the bakery
gave me a going over. All Frampol refreshed its spirits
because of my trouble and grief. However, I resolved
that I would always believe what I was told. What's
the good of *not* believing? Today it's your wife you
don't believe; tomorrow it's God himself you won't
take stock in.

By an apprentice who was her neighbor I sent her
daily a corn or a wheat loaf, or a piece of pastry,
rolls or bagels, or, when I got the chance, a slab of
pudding, a slice of honeycake, or wedding strudel—
whatever came my way. The apprentice was a good-
hearted lad, and more than once he added something
on his own. He had formerly annoyed me a lot,
plucking my nose and digging me in the ribs, but
when he started to be a visitor to my house he became
kind and friendly. "Hey, you, Gimpel," he said to me,
"you have a very decent little wife and two fine kids.
You don't deserve them."

"But the things people say about her," I said.

"Well, they have long tongues," he said, "and
nothing to do with them but babble. Ignore it as you
ignore the cold of last winter."

One day the rabbi sent for me and said, "Are you
certain, Gimpel, that you were wrong about your
wife?"

I said, "I'm certain."

"Why, but look here! You yourself saw it."

"It must have been a shadow," I said.

"The shadow of what?"

"Just of one of the beams, I think."

"You can go home then. You owe thanks to the Yanover rabbi. He found an obscure reference in Maimonides that favored you."

I seized the rabbi's hand and kissed it.

I wanted to run home immediately. It's no small thing to be separated for so long a time from wife and child. Then I reflected: I'd better go back to work now, and go home in the evening. I said nothing to anyone, although as far as my heart was concerned it was like one of the Holy Days. The women teased and twitted me as they did every day, but my thought was: Go on, with your loose talk. The truth is out, like the oil upon the water. Maimonides says it's right, and therefore it is right!

At night, when I had covered the dough to let it rise, I took my share of bread and a little sack of flour and started homeward. The moon was full and the stars were glistening, something to terrify the soul. I hurried onward, and before me darted a long shadow. It was winter, and a fresh snow had fallen. I had a mind to sing, but it was growing late and I didn't want to wake the householders. Then I felt like whistling, but I remembered that you don't whistle at night because it brings the demons out. So I was silent and walked as fast as I could.

Dogs in the Christian yards barked at me when I passed, but I thought: Bark your teeth out! What are you but mere dogs? Whereas I am a man, the husband of a fine wife, the father of promising children.

As I approached the house my heart started to

pound as though it were the heart of a criminal. I felt no fear, but my heart went thump! thump! Well, no drawing back. I quietly lifted the latch and went in. Elka was asleep. I looked at the infant's cradle. The shutter was closed, but the moon forced its way through the cracks. I saw the newborn child's face and loved it as soon as I saw it—immediately—each tiny bone.

Then I came nearer to the bed. And what did I see but the apprentice lying there beside Elka. The moon went out all at once. It was utterly black, and I trembled. My teeth chattered. The bread fell from my hands, and my wife waked and said, "Who is that, ah?"

I muttered, "It's me."

"Gimpel?" she asked. "How come you're here? I thought it was forbidden."

"The rabbi said," I answered and shook as with a fever.

"Listen to me, Gimpel," she said, "go out to the shed and see if the goat's all right. It seems she's been sick." I have forgotten to say that we had a goat. When I heard she was unwell I went into the yard. The nannygoat was a good little creature. I had a nearly human feeling for her.

With hesitant steps I went up to the shed and opened the door. The goat stood there on her four feet. I felt her everywhere, drew her by the horns, examined her udders, and found nothing wrong. She had probably eaten too much bark. "Good night, little goat," I said. "Keep well." And the little beast answered with a "Maa" as though to thank me for the good will.

I went back. The apprentice had vanished.

"Where," I asked, "is the lad?"

"What lad?" my wife answered.

"What do you mean?" I said. "The apprentice. You were sleeping with him."

"The things I have dreamed this night and the night before," she said, "may they come true and lay you low, body and soul! An evil spirit has taken root in you and dazzles your sight." She screamed out, "You hateful creature! You moon calf! You spook! You uncouth man! Get out, or I'll scream all Frampol out of bed!"

Before I could move, her brother sprang out from behind the oven and struck me a blow on the back of the head. I thought he had broken my neck. I felt that something about me was deeply wrong, and I said, "Don't make a scandal. All that's needed now is that people should accuse me of raising spooks and *dybbuks*." For that was what she had meant. "No one will touch bread of my baking."

In short, I somehow calmed her.

"Well," she said, "that enough. Lie down, and be shattered by wheels."

Next morning I called the apprentice aside. "Listen here, brother?" I said. And so on and so forth. "What do you say?" He stared at me as though I had dropped from the roof or something.

"I swear," he said, "you'd better go to an herb doctor or some healer. I'm afraid you have a screw loose, but I'll hush it up for you." And that's how the thing stood.

To make a long story short, I lived twenty years with my wife. She bore me six children, four daughters and two sons. All kinds of things happened, but I neither saw nor heard. I believed, and that's all. The rabbi recently said to me, "Belief in itself is beneficial. It is written that a good man lives by his faith."

Suddenly my wife took sick. It began with a trifle, a little growth upon the breast. But she evidently was not destined to live long; she had no years. I spent a fortune on her. I have forgotten to say that by this time I had a bakery of my own and in Frampol was considered to be something of a rich man. Daily the healer came, and every witch doctor in the neighborhood was brought. They decided to use leeches, and after that to try cupping. They even called a doctor from Lublin, but it was too late. Before she died she called me to her bed and said, "Forgive me, Gimpel."

I said, "What is there to forgive? You have been a good and faithful wife."

"Woe, Gimpel!" she said. "It was ugly how I deceived you all these years. I want to go clean to my Maker, and so I have to tell you that the children are not yours."

If I had been clouted on the head with a piece of wood it couldn't have bewildered me more.

"Whose are they?" I asked.

"I don't know," she said. "There were a lot ... but they're not yours." And as she spoke she tossed her head to the side, her eyes turned glassy, and it was all up with Elka. On her whitened lips there remained a smile.

I imagined that, dead as she was, she was saying, "I deceived Gimpel. That was the meaning of my brief life."

IV

ONE NIGHT, when the period of mourning was done, as I lay dreaming on the flour sacks, there came the Spirit of Evil himself and said to me, "Gimpel, why do you sleep?"

I said, "What should I be doing? Eating *kreplach*?"

"The whole world deceives you," he said, "and you ought to deceive the world in your turn."

"How can I deceive all the world?" I asked him.

He answered, "You might accumulate a bucket of urine every day and at night pour it into the dough. Let the sages of Frampol eat filth."

"What about the judgment in the world to come?" I said.

"There is no world to come," he said. "They've sold you a bill of goods and talked you into believing you carried a cat in your belly. What nonsense!"

"Well then," I said, "and is there a God?"

He answered, "There is no God either."

"What," I said, "*is* there, then?"

"A thick mire."

He stood before my eyes with a goatish beard and horn, long-toothed, and with a tail. Hearing such words, I wanted to snatch him by the tail, but I tumbled from the flour sacks and nearly broke a rib. Then it happened that I had to answer the call of nature, and, passing, I saw the risen dough, which seemed to say to me, "Do it!" In brief, I let myself be persuaded.

At dawn the apprentice came. We kneaded the bread, scattered caraway seeds on it, and set it to bake. Then the apprentice went away, and I was left sitting in the little trench, by the oven, on a pile of rags. Well, Gimpel, I thought, you've revenged yourself on them for all the shame they've put on you. Outside the frost glittered, but it was warm beside the oven. The flames heated my face. I bent my head and fell into a doze.

I saw in a dream, at once, Elka in her shroud. She called to me, "What have you done, Gimpel?"

I said to her, "It's all your fault," and started to cry.

"You fool!" she said. "You fool! Because I was false is everything false too? I never deceived anyone but myself. I'm paying for it all, Gimpel. They spare you nothing here."

I looked at her face. It was black; I was startled and waked, and remained sitting dumb. I sensed that everything hung in the balance. A false step now and I'd lose Eternal Life. But God gave me His help. I seized the long shovel and took out the loaves, carried them into the yard, and started to dig a hole in the frozen earth.

My apprentice came back as I was doing it. "What are you doing boss?" he said, and grew pale as a corpse.

"I know what I'm doing," I said, and I buried it all before his very eyes.

Then I went home, took my hoard from its hiding place, and divided it among the children. "I saw your mother tonight," I said. "She's turning black, poor thing."

They were so astounded they couldn't speak a word.

"Be well," I said, "and forget that such a one as Gimpel ever existed." I put on my short coat, a pair of boots, took the bag that held my prayer shawl in one hand, my stock in the other, and kissed the *mezzuzah*. When people saw me in the street they were greatly surprised.

"Where are you going?" they said.

I answered, "Into the world." And so I departed from Frampol.

I wandered over the land, and good people did not neglect me. After many years I became old and white; I heard a great deal, many lies and falsehoods, but the longer I lived the more I understood that there were really no lies. Whatever doesn't really happen is dreamed at night. It happens to one if it doesn't happen to another, tomorrow if not today, or a century hence if not next year. What difference can it make? Often I heard tales of which I said, "Now this is a thing that cannot happen." But before a year had elapsed I heard that it actually had come to pass somewhere.

Going from place to place, eating at strange tables, it often happens that I spin yarns—improbable things that could never have happened—about devils, magicians, windmills, and the like. The children run after me, calling, "Grandfather, tell us a story." Sometimes they ask for particular stories, and I try to please them. A fat young boy once said to me, "Grandfather, it's the same story you told us before." The little rogue, he was right.

So it is with dreams too. It is many years since I left Frampol, but as soon as I shut my eyes I am there again. And whom do you think I see? Elka. She is standing by the washtub, as at our first encounter, but her face is shining and her eyes are as radiant as the eyes of a saint, and she speaks outlandish words to me, strange things. When I wake I have forgotten it all. But while the dream lasts I am comforted. She answers all my queries, and what comes out is that all is right. I weep and implore, "Let me be with you." And she consoles me and tells me to be patient. The time is nearer than it is far. Sometimes she strokes and kisses me and weeps upon my face. When I awaken I feel her lips and taste the salt of her tears.

No doubt the world is entirely an imaginary world, but it is only once removed from the true world. At the door of the hovel where I lie, there stands the plank on which the dead are taken away. The gravedigger Jew has his spade ready. The grave waits and the worms are hungry; the shrouds are prepared— I carry them in my beggar's sack. Another *shnorrer* is waiting to inherit my bed of straw. When the time comes I will go joyfully. Whatever may be there, it will be real, without complication, without ridicule, without deception. God be praised: there even Gimpel cannot be deceived.

Flannery O'Connor

REVELATION

THE DOCTOR'S WAITING ROOM, which was very small, was almost full when the Turpins entered and Mrs. Turpin, who was very large, made it look even smaller by her presence. She stood looming at the head of the magazine table set in the center of it, a living demonstration that the room was inadequate and ridiculous. Her little bright black eyes took in all the patients as she sized up the seating situation. There was one vacant chair and a place on the sofa occupied by a blond child in a dirty blue romper who should have been told to move over and make room for the lady. He was five or six, but Mrs. Turpin saw at once that no one was going to tell him to move over. He was slumped down in the seat, his arms idle at his sides and his eyes idle in his head; his nose ran unchecked.

Mrs. Turpin put a firm hand on Claud's shoulder and said in a voice that included anyone who wanted to listen, "Claud, you sit in that chair there," and gave him a push down into the vacant one. Claud was florid and bald and sturdy, somewhat shorter than Mrs. Turpin, but he sat down as if he were accustomed to doing what she told him to.

Mrs. Turpin remained standing. The only man in

the room besides Claud was a lean stringy old fellow with a rusty hand spread out on each knee, whose eyes were closed as if he were asleep or dead or pretending to be so as not to get up and offer her his seat. Her gaze settled agreeably on a well-dressed grey-haired lady whose eyes met hers and whose expression said: if that child belonged to me, he would have some manners and move over—there's plenty of room there for you and him too.

Claud looked up with a sigh and made as if to rise.

"Sit down," Mrs. Turpin said. "You know you're not supposed to stand on that leg. He has an ulcer on his leg," she explained.

Claud lifted his foot onto the magazine table and rolled his trouser leg up to reveal a purple swelling on a plump marble-white calf.

"My!" the pleasant lady said. "How did you do that?"

"A cow kicked him," Mrs. Turpin said.

"Goodness!" said the lady.

Claud rolled his trouser leg down.

"Maybe the little boy would move over," the lady suggested, but the child did not stir.

"Somebody will be leaving in a minute," Mrs. Turpin said. She could not understand why a doctor— with as much money as they made charging five dollars a day to just stick their heads in the hospital door and look at you—couldn't afford a decent-sized waiting room. This one was hardly bigger than a garage. The table was cluttered with limp-looking magazines and at one end of it there was a big green glass ash tray full of cigaret butts and cotton wads with little blood spots on them. If she had anything to do with the running of the place, that would have been emptied every so often. There were no chairs against the wall at the head of the room. It had a rectangular-shaped panel in it that permitted a view of the office where the nurse came and went and the secretary listened to the radio. A plastic fern in a gold pot sat in the opening and trailed its fronds down almost to the floor. The radio was softly playing gospel music.

Just then the inner door opened and a nurse with the highest stack of yellow hair Mrs. Turpin had ever seen put her face in the crack and called for the next patient. The woman sitting beside Claud grasped the two arms of her chair and hoisted herself up; she pulled her dress free from her legs and lumbered through the door where the nurse had disappeared.

Mrs. Turpin eased into the vacant chair, which held her tight as a corset. "I wish I could reduce," she said, and rolled her eyes and gave a comic sigh.

"Oh, *you* aren't fat," the stylish lady said.

"Ooooo I am too," Mrs. Turpin said. "Claud he eats all he wants to and never weighs over one hundred and seventy-five pounds, but me I just look at something good to eat and I gain some weight," and her stomach and shoulders shook with laughter. "You can eat all you want to, can't you, Claud?" she asked, turning to him.

Claud only grinned.

"Well, as long as you have such a good disposition," the stylish lady said, "I don't think it makes a bit of difference what size you are. You just can't beat a good disposition."

Next to her was a fat girl of eighteen or nineteen, scowling into a thick blue book which Mrs. Turpin saw was entitled *Human Development.* The girl raised her head and directed her scowl at Mrs. Turpin as if she did not like her looks. She appeared annoyed that anyone should speak while she tried to read.

The poor girl's face was blue with acne and Mrs. Turpin thought how pitiful it was to have a face like that at that age. She gave the girl a friendly smile but the girl only scowled the harder. Mrs. Turpin herself was fat but she had always had good skin, and, though she was forty-seven years old, there was not a wrinkle in her face except around her eyes from laughing too much.

Next to the ugly girl was the child, still in exactly the same position, and next to him was a thin leathery old woman in a cotton print dress. She and Claud had three sacks of chicken feed in their pump house that was in the same print. She had seen from the first that the child belonged with the old woman. She could tell by the way they sat—kind of vacant and white-trashy, as if they would sit there until Dooms-day if nobody called and told them to get up. And at right angles but next to the well-dressed pleasant lady was a lank-faced woman who was certainly the child's mother. She had on a yellow sweat shirt and wine-colored slacks, both gritty-looking, and the rims of her lips were stained with snuff. Her dirty yellow hair was tied behind with a little piece of red paper ribbon. Worse than niggers any day, Mrs. Turpin thought.

The gospel hymn playing was, "When I looked up and He looked down," and Mrs. Turpin, who knew it, supplied the last line mentally, "And wona these days I know I'll we-eara crown."

Without appearing to, Mrs. Turpin always noticed people's feet. The well-dressed lady had on red and grey suede shoes to match her dress. Mrs. Turpin had on her good black patent leather pumps. The ugly girl had on Girl Scout shoes and heavy socks. The old woman had on tennis shoes and the white-trashy mother had on what appeared to be bedroom slippers, black straw with gold braid threaded through them—exactly what you would have expected her to have on.

Sometimes at night when she couldn't go to sleep, Mrs. Turpin would occupy herself with the question of who she would have chosen to be if she couldn't have been herself. If Jesus had said to her before he made her, "There's only two places available for you. You can either be a nigger or white-trash," what would she have said? "Please, Jesus, please," she would have said, "just let me wait until there's another place available," and he would have said, "No, you have to go right now and I have only those two places so make up your mind." She would have wiggled and squirmed and begged and pleaded but it would have been no use and finally she would have said, "All right, make me a nigger then—but that don't mean a trashy one." And he would have made her a neat clean respectable Negro woman, herself but black.

Next to the child's mother was a red-headed youngish woman, reading one of the magazines and working a piece of chewing gum, hell for leather, as Claud would say. Mrs. Turpin could not see the woman's feet. She was not white-trash, just common. Sometimes Mrs. Turpin occupied herself at night naming the classes of people. On the bottom of the heap were most colored people, not the kind she would have been if she had been one, but most of them; then next to them—not above, just away from—were the white-trash; then above them were the home-owners, and above them the home-and-land owners, to which she and Claud belonged. Above she and Claud were people with a lot of money and much bigger houses and much more land. But here the complexity of it would begin to bear in on her, for some of the people with a lot of money were common and ought to be

below she and Claud and some of the people who
had good blood had lost their money and had to rent
and then there were colored people who owned their
homes and land as well. There was a colored dentist
in town who had two red Lincolns and a swimming
pool and a farm with registered white-face cattle on
it. Usually by the time she had fallen asleep all the
classes of people were moiling and roiling around in
her head, and she would dream they were all crammed
in together in a box car, being ridden off to be put
in a gas oven.

"That's a beautiful clock," she said and nodded to
her right. It was a big wall clock, the face encased
in a brass sunburst.

"Yes, it's very pretty," the stylish lady said agreeably. "And right on the dot too," she added, glancing
at her watch.

The ugly girl beside her cast an eye upward at
the clock, smirked, then looked directly at Mrs. Turpin
and smirked again. Then she returned her eyes to
her book. She was obviously the lady's daughter
because, although they didn't look anything alike as
to disposition, they both had the same shape of face
and the same blue eyes. On the lady they sparkled
pleasantly but in the girl's seared face they appeared
alternately to smolder and to blaze.

What if Jesus had said, "All right, you can be white-
trash or a nigger or ugly"!

Mrs. Turpin felt an awful pity for the girl, though
she thought it was one thing to be ugly and another
to act ugly.

The woman with the snuff-stained lips turned
around in her chair and looked up at the clock. Then
she turned back and appeared to look a little to the
side of Mrs. Turpin. There was a cast in one of her
eyes. "You want to know wher you can get you one

of themther clocks?" she asked in a loud voice.

"No, I already have a nice clock," Mrs. Turpin said. Once somebody like her got a leg in the conversation, she would be all over it.

"You can get you one with green stamps," the woman said. "That's most likely wher he got hisn. Save you up enough you can get you most anythang. I got me some joo'ry."

Ought to have got you a wash rag and some soap, Mrs. Turpin thought.

"I get contour sheets with mine," the pleasant lady said.

The daughter slammed her book shut. She looked straight in front of her, directly through Mrs. Turpin and on through the yellow curtain and the plate glass window which made the wall behind her. The girl's eyes seemed lit all of a sudden with a peculiar light, an unnatural light like night road signs give. Mrs. Turpin turned her head to see if there was anything going on outside that she should see, but she could not see anything. Figures passing cast only a pale shadow through the curtain. There was no reason the girl should single her out for her ugly looks.

"Miss Finley," the nurse said, cracking the door. The gum-chewing woman got up and passed in front of her and Claud and went into the office. She had on red high-heeled shoes.

Directly across the table, the ugly girl's eyes were fixed on Mrs. Turpin as if she had some very special reason for disliking her.

"This is wonderful weather, isn't it?" the girl's mother said.

"It's good weather for cotton if you can get the niggers to pick it," Mrs. Turpin said, "but niggers don't want to pick cotton any more. You can't get the white folks to pick it and now you can't get the niggers—

because they got to be right up there with the white folks."

"They gonna *try* anyways," the white-trash woman said, leaning forward.

"Do you have one of those cotton-picking machines?" the pleasant lady asked.

"No," Mrs. Turpin said, "they leave half the cotton in the field. We don't have much cotton anyway. If you want to make it farming now, you have to have a little of everything. We got a couple of acres of cotton and a few hogs and chickens and just enough white-face that Claud can look after them himself."

"One thang I don't want," the white-trash woman said, wiping her mouth with the back of her hand. "Hogs. Nasty stinking things, a-gruntin and a-rootin all over the place."

Mrs. Turpin gave her the merest edge of her attention. "Our hogs are not dirty and they don't stink," she said. "They're cleaner than some children I've seen. Their feet never touch the ground. We have a pig-parlor—that's where you raise them on concrete," she explained to the pleasant lady, "and Claud scoots them down with the hose every afternoon and washes off the floor." Cleaner by far than that child right there, she thought. Poor nasty little thing. He had not moved except to put the thumb of his dirty hand into his mouth.

The woman turned her face away from Mrs. Turpin. "I know I wouldn't scoot down no hog with no hose," she said to the wall.

You wouldn't have no hog to scoot down, Mrs. Turpin said to herself.

"A-gruntin and a-rootin and a-groanin," the woman muttered.

"We got a little of everything," Mrs. Turpin said to the pleasant lady. "It's no use in having more than you can handle yourself with help like it is. We found enough niggers to pick our cotton this year but Claud he has to go after them and take them home again in the evening. They can't walk that half a mile. No they can't. I tell you," she said and laughed merrily, "I sure am tired of buttering up niggers, but you got to love em if you want em to work for you. When they come in the morning, I run out and I say, 'Hi yawl this morning?' and when Claud drives them off to the field I just wave to beat the band and they just wave back." And she waved her hand rapidly to illustrate.

"Like you read out of the same book," the lady said, showing she understood perfectly.

"Child, yes," Mrs. Turpin said. "And when they come in from the field, I run out with a bucket of icewater. That's the way it's going to be from now on," she said. "You may as well face it."

"One thang I know," the white-trash woman said. "Two thangs I ain't going to do: love no niggers or scoot down no hog with no hose." And she let out a bark of contempt.

The look that Mrs. Turpin and the pleasant lady exchanged indicated they both understood that you had to *have* certain things before you could *know* certain things. But every time Mrs. Turpin exchanged a look with the lady, she was aware that the ugly girl's peculiar eyes were still on her, and she had trouble bringing her attention back to the conversation.

"When you got something," she said, "you got to look after it." And when you ain't got a thing but breath and britches, she added to herself, you can afford to come to town every morning and just sit on the Court House coping and spit.

A grotesque revolving shadow passed across the

curtain behind her and was thrown palely on the opposite wall. Then a bicycle clattered down against the outside of the building. The door opened and a colored boy glided in with a tray from the drug store. It had two large red and white paper cups on it with tops on them. He was a tall, very black boy in discolored white pants and a green nylon shirt. He was chewing gum slowly, as if to music. He set the tray down in the office opening next to the fern and stuck his head through to look for the secretary. She was not in there. He rested his arms on the ledge and waited, his narrow bottom stuck out, swaying slowly to the left and right. He raised a hand over his head and scratched the base of his skull.

"You see that button there, boy?" Mrs. Turpin said. "You can punch that and she'll come. She's probably in the back somewhere."

"Is that right?" the boy said agreeably, as if he had never seen the button before. He leaned to the right and put his finger on it. "She sometime out," he said and twisted around to face his audience, his elbows behind him on the counter. The nurse appeared and he twisted back again. She handed him a dollar and he rooted in his pocket and made the change and counted it out to her. She gave him fifteen cents for a tip and he went out with the empty tray. The heavy door swung to slowly and closed at length with the sound of suction. For a moment no one spoke.

"They ought to send all them niggers back to Africa," the white-trash woman said. "That's wher they come from in the first place."

"Oh, I couldn't do without my good colored friends," the pleasant lady said.

"There's a heap of things worse than a nigger," Mrs. Turpin agreed. "It's all kinds of them just like it's all kinds of us."

"Yes, and it takes all kinds to make the world go round," the lady said in her musical voice.

As she said it, the raw-complexioned girl snapped her teeth together. Her lower lip turned downwards and inside out, revealing the pale pink inside of her mouth. After a second it rolled back up. It was the ugliest face Mrs. Turpin had ever seen anyone make and for a moment she was certain that the girl had made it at her. She was looking at her as if she had known and disliked her all her life—all of Mrs. Turpin's life, it seemed too, not just all the girl's life. Why, girl, I don't even know you, Mrs. Turpin said silently.

She forced her attention back to the discussion. "It wouldn't be practical to send them back to Africa," she said. "They wouldn't want to go. They got it too good here."

"Wouldn't be what they wanted—if I had anything to do with it," the woman said.

"It wouldn't be a way in the world you could get all the niggers back over there," Mrs. Turpin said. "They'd be hiding out and lying down and turning sick on you and wailing and hollering and raring and pitching. It wouldn't be a way in the world to get them over there."

"They got over here," the trashy woman said. "Get back like they got over."

"It wasn't so many of them then," Mrs. Turpin explained.

The woman looked at Mrs. Turpin as if here was an idiot indeed but Mrs. Turpin was not bothered by the look, considering where it came from.

"Nooo," she said, "they're going to stay here where they can go to New York and marry white folks and improve their color. That's what they all want to do, every one of them, improve their color."

"You know what comes of that, don't you?" Claud asked.

"No, Claud, what?" Mrs. Turpin said.

Claud's eyes twinkled. "White-faced niggers." he said with never a smile.

Everybody in the office laughed except the white-trash and the ugly girl. The girl gripped the book in her lap with white fingers. The trashy woman looked around her from face to face as if she thought they were all idiots. The old woman in the feed sack dress continued to gaze expressionless across the floor at the high-top shoes of the man opposite her, the one who had been pretending to be asleep when the Turpins came in. He was laughing heartily, his hands still spread out on his knees. The child had fallen to the side and was lying now almost face down in the old woman's lap.

While they recovered from their laughter, the nasal chorus on the radio kept the room from silence.

> *"You go to blank blank*
> *And I'll go to mine*
> *But we'll all blank along*
> *To-geth-ther,*
> *And all along the blank*
> *We'll hep eachother out*
> *Smile-ling in any kind of*
> *Weath-ther!"*

Mrs. Turpin didn't catch every word but she caught enough to agree with the spirit of the song and it turned her thoughts sober. To help anybody out that needed it was her philosophy of life. She never spared herself when she found somebody in need, whether they were white or black, trash or decent. And of all she had to be thankful for, she was most thankful that this was so. If Jesus had said, "You can be high society and have all the money you want and be thin and svelte-like, but you can't be a good woman with it," she would have had to say, "Well don't make me that then. Make me a good woman and it don't matter what else, how fat or how ugly or how poor!" Her heart rose. He had not made her a nigger or white-trash or ugly! He had made her herself and given her a little of everything. Jesus, thank you! she said. Thank you thank you thank you! Whenever she counted her blessings she felt as buoyant as if she weighed one hundred and twenty-five pounds instead of one hundred and eighty.

"What's wrong with your little boy?" the pleasant lady asked the white-trashy woman.

"He has a ulcer," the woman said proudly. "He ain't give me a minute's peace since he was born. Him and her are just alike," she said, nodding at the old woman, who was running her leathery fingers through the child's pale hair. "Look like I can't get nothing down them two but Co' Cola and candy."

That's all you try to get down em, Mrs. Turpin said to herself. Too lazy to light the fire. There was nothing you could tell her about people like them that she didn't know already. And it was not just that they didn't have anything. Because if you gave them everything, in two weeks it would all be broken or filthy or they would have chopped it up for lightwood. She knew all this from her own experience. Help them you must, but help them you couldn't.

All at once the ugly girl turned her lips inside out again. Her eyes were fixed like two drills on Mrs. Turpin. This time there was no mistaking that there was something urgent behind them.

Girl, Mrs. Turpin exclaimed silently, I haven't done a thing to you! The girl might be confusing her with somebody else. There was no need to sit by and let herself by intimidated. "You must be in college," she said boldly, looking directly at the girl. "I see you reading a book there."

The girl continued to stare and pointedly did not answer.

Her mother blushed at this rudeness. "The lady asked you a question, Mary Grace," she said under her breath.

"I have ears," Mary Grace said.

The poor mother blushed again. "Mary Grace goes to Wellesley College," she explained. She twisted one of the buttons on her dress. "In Massachusetts," she added with a grimace. "And in the summer she just keeps right on studying. Just reads all the time, a real book worm. She's done real well at Wellesley; she's taking English and Math and History and Psychology and Social Studies," she rattled on, "and I think it's too much. I think she ought to get out and have fun."

The girl looked as if she would like to hurl them all through the plate glass window.

"Way up north," Mrs. Turpin murmured and thought, well, it hasn't done much for her manners.

"I'd almost rather to have him sick," the white-trash woman said, wrenching the attention back to herself. "He's so mean when he ain't. Look like some children just take natural to meanness. It's some gets bad when they get sick but he was the opposite. Took sick and turned good. He don't give me no trouble now. It's me waitin to see the doctor," she said.

If I was going to send anybody back to Africa, Mrs. Turpin thought, it would be your kind, woman. "Yes, indeed," she said aloud, but looking up at the ceiling, "it's a heap of things worse than a nigger." And dirtier than a hog, she added to herself.

"I think people with bad dispositions are more to be pitied than anyone on earth," the pleasant lady said in a voice that was decidedly thin.

"I thank the Lord he has blessed me with a good one," Mrs. Turpin said. "The day has never dawned that I couldn't find something to laugh at."

"Not since she married me anyways," Claud said with a comical straight face.

Everybody laughed except the girl and the white-trash.

Mrs. Turpin's stomach shook. "He's such a caution," she said, "that I can't help but laugh at him."

The girl made a loud ugly noise through her teeth.

Her mother's mouth grew thin and tight. "I think the worst thing in the world," she said, "is an ungrateful person. To have everything and not appreciate it. I know a girl," she said, "who has parents who would give her anything, a little brother who loves her dearly, who is getting a good education, who wears the best clothes, but who can never say a kind word to anyone, who never smiles, who just criticizes and complains all day long."

"Is she too old to paddle?" Claud asked.

The girl's face was almost purple.

"Yes," the lady said, "I'm afraid there's nothing to do but leave her to her folly. Some day she'll wake up and it'll be too late."

"It never hurt anyone to smile," Mrs. Turpin said. "It just makes you feel better all over."

"Of course," the lady said sadly, "but there are just some people you can't tell anything to. They can't take criticism."

"If it's one thing I am," Mrs. Turpin said with feeling, "it's grateful. When I think who all I could have been besides myself and what all I got, a little of everything, and a good disposition besides, I just feel like shouting,

'Thank you, Jesus, for making everything the way it is!' It could have been different!" For one thing, somebody else could have got Claud. At the thought of this, she was flooded with gratitude and a terrible pang of joy ran through her. "Oh thank you, Jesus, Jesus, thank you!" she cried aloud.

The book struck her directly over her left eye. It struck almost at the same instant that she realized the girl was about to hurl it. Before she could utter a sound, the raw face came crashing across the table toward her, howling. The girl's fingers sank like clamps into the soft flesh of her neck. She heard the mother cry out and Claud shout, "Whoa!" There was an instant when she was certain that she was about to be in an earthquake.

All at once her vision narrowed and she saw everything as if it were happening in a small room far away, or as if she were looking at it through the wrong end of a telescope. Claud's face crumpled and fell out of sight. The nurse ran in, then out, then in again. Then the gangling figure of the doctor rushed out of the inner door. Magazines flew this way and that as the table turned over. The girl fell with a thud and Mrs. Turpin's vision suddenly reversed itself and she saw everything large instead of small. The eyes of the white-trashy woman were staring hugely at the floor. There the girl, held down on one side by the nurse and on the other by her mother, was wrenching and turning in their grasp. The doctor was kneeling astride her, trying to hold her arm down. He managed after a second to sink a long needle into it.

Mrs. Turpin felt entirely hollow except for her heart which swung from side to side as if it were agitated in a great empty drum of flesh.

"Somebody that's not busy call for the ambulance,"

the doctor said in the off-hand voice young doctors adopt for terrible occasions.

Mrs. Turpin could not have moved a finger. The old man who had been sitting next to her skipped nimbly into the office and made the call, for the secretary still seemed to be gone.

"Claud!" Mrs. Turpin called.

He was not in his chair. She knew she must jump up and find him but she felt like some one trying to catch a train in a dream, when everything moves in slow motion and the faster you try to run the slower you go.

"Here I am," a suffocated voice, very unlike Claud's, said.

He was doubled up in the corner on the floor, pale as paper, holding his leg. She wanted to get up and go to him but she could not move. Instead, her gaze was drawn slowly downward to the churning face on the floor, which she could see over the doctor's shoulder.

The girl's eyes stopped rolling and focused on her. They seemed a much lighter blue than before, as if a door that had been tightly closed behind them was now open to admit light and air.

Mrs. Turpin's head cleared and her power of motion returned. She leaned forward until she was looking directly into the fierce brilliant eyes. There was no doubt in her mind that the girl did know her, knew her in some intense and personal way, beyond time and place and condition. "What you got to say to me?" she asked hoarsely and held her breath, waiting, as for a revelation.

The girl raised her head. Her gaze locked with Mrs. Turpin's. "Go back to hell where you came from, you old wart hog," she whispered. Her voice was low but clear. Her eyes burned for a moment as if she saw with pleasure that her message had struck its target.

Mrs. Turpin sank back in her chair.

After a moment the girl's eyes closed and she turned her head wearily to the side.

The doctor rose and handed the nurse the empty syringe. He leaned over and put both hands for a moment on the mother's shoulders, which were shaking. She was sitting on the floor, her lips pressed together, holding Mary Grace's hand in her lap. The girl's fingers were gripped like a baby's around her thumb. "Go on to the hospital," he said. "I'll call and make the arrangements."

"Now let's see that neck," he said in a jovial voice to Mrs. Turpin. He began to inspect her neck with his first two fingers. Two little moon-shaped lines like pink fish bones were indented over her windpipe. There was the beginning of an angry red swelling above her eye. His fingers passed over this also.

"Lea' me be," she said thickly and shook him off. "See about Claud. She kicked him."

"I'll see about him in a minute," he said and felt her pulse. He was a thin grey-haired man, given to pleasantries. "Go home and have yourself a vacation the rest of the day," he said and patted her on the shoulder.

Quit your pattin me, Mrs. Turpin growled to herself.

"And put an ice pack over that eye," he said. Then he went and squatted down beside Claud and looked at his leg. After a moment he pulled him up and Claud limped after him into the office.

Until the ambulance came, the only sounds in the room were the tremulous moans of the girl's mother, who continued to sit on the floor. The white-trash woman did not take her eyes off the girl. Mrs. Turpin looked straight ahead at nothing. Presently the ambulance drew up, a long dark shadow, behind the curtain.

The attendants came in and set the stretcher down beside the girl and lifted her expertly onto it and carried her out. The nurse helped the mother gather up her things. The shadow of the ambulance moved silently away and the nurse came back in the office.

"That ther girl is going to be a lunatic, ain't she?" the white-trash woman asked the nurse, but the nurse kept on to the back and never answered her.

"Yes, she's going to be a lunatic," the white-trash woman said to the rest of them.

"Po' critter," the old woman murmured. The child's face was still in her lap. His eyes looked idly out over her knees. He had not moved during the disturbance except to draw one leg up under him.

"I thank Gawd," the white-trash woman said fervently, "I ain't a lunatic."

Claud came limping out and the Turpins went home.

As their pick-up truck turned into their own dirt road and made the crest of the hill, Mrs. Turpin gripped the window ledge and looked out suspiciously. The land sloped gracefully down through a field dotted with lavender weeds and at the start of the rise their small yellow frame house, with its little flower beds spread out around it like a fancy apron, sat primly in its accustomed place between two giant hickory trees. She would not have been startled to see a burnt wound between two blackened chimneys.

Neither of them felt like eating so they put on their house clothes and lowered the shade in the bedroom and lay down, Claud with his leg on a pillow and herself with a damp washcloth over her eye. The instant she was flat on her back, the image of a razor-backed hog with warts on its face and horns coming out behind its ears snorted into her head. She moaned, a low quiet moan.

"I am not," she said tearfully, "a wart hog. From hell." But the denial had no force. The girl's eyes and her words, even the tone of her voice, low but clear, directed only to her, brooked no repudiation. She had been singled out for the message, though there was trash in the room to whom it might just have been applied. The full force of this fact struck her only now. There was a woman there who was neglecting her own child but she had been overlooked. The message had been given to Ruby Turpin, a respectable, hard-working, church-going woman. The tears dried. Her eyes began to burn instead with wrath.

She rose on her elbow and the washcloth fell into her hand. Claud was lying on his back, snoring. She wanted to tell him what the girl had said. At the same time, she did not wish to put the image of herself as a wart hog from hell into his mind.

"Hey, Claud," she muttered and pushed his shoulder.

Claud opened one pale baby blue eye.

She looked into it warily. He did not think about anything. He just went his way.

"Wha, whasit?" he said and closed the eye again.

"Nothing," she said. "Does your leg pain you?"

"Hurts like hell," Claud said.

"It'll quit terreckly," she said and lay back down. In a moment Claud was snoring again. For the rest of the afternoon they lay there. Claud slept. She scowled at the ceiling. Occasionally she raised her fist and made a small stabbing motion over her chest as if she was defending her innocence to invisible guests who were like the comforters of Job, reasonable-seeming but wrong.

About five-thirty Claud stirred. "Got to go after those niggers," he sighed, not moving.

She was looking straight up as if there were unintelligible handwriting on the ceiling. The protuberance over her eye had turned a greenish-blue. "Listen here," she said.

"What?"

"Kiss me."

Claud leaned over and kissed her loudly on the mouth. He pinched her side and their hands interlocked. Her expression of ferocious concentration did not change. Claud got up, groaning and growling, and limped off. She continued to study the ceiling.

She did not get up until she heard the pick-up truck coming back with the Negroes. Then she rose and thrust her feet in her brown oxfords, which she did not bother to lace, and stumped out onto the back porch and got her red plastic bucket. She emptied a tray of ice cubes into it and filled it half full of water and went out into the back yard. Every afternoon after Claud brought the hands in, one of the boys helped him put out hay and the rest waited in the back of the truck until he was ready to take them home. The truck was parked in the shade under one of the hickory trees.

"Hi yawl this evening?" Mrs. Turpin asked grimly, appearing with the bucket and the dipper. There were three women and a boy in the truck.

"Us doin nicely," the oldest woman said. "Hi you doin?" and her gaze stuck immediately on the dark lump on Mrs. Turpin's forehead. "You done fell down, ain't you?" she asked in a solicitous voice. The old woman was dark and almost toothless. She had on an old felt hat of Claud's set back on her head. The other two women were younger and lighter and they both had new bright green sun hats. One of them had hers on her head; the other had taken hers off and the boy was grinning beneath it.

Mrs. Turpin set the bucket down on the floor of the truck. "Yawl help yourselves," she said. She looked around to make sure Claud had gone. "No. I didn't fall down," she said, folding her arms. "It was something worse than that."

"Ain't nothing bad happen to you!" the old woman said. She said it as if they all knew that Mrs. Turpin was protected in some special way by Divine Providence. "You just had you a little fall."

"We were in town at the doctor's office for where the cow kicked Mr. Turpin," Mrs. Turpin said in a flat tone that indicated they could leave off their foolishness. "And there was this girl there. A big fat girl with her face all broke out. I could look at that girl and tell she was peculiar but I couldn't tell how. And me and her mama were just talking and going along and all of a sudden WHAM! She throws this big book she was reading at me and ..."

"Naw!" the old woman cried out.

"And then she jumps over the table and commences to choke me."

"Naw!" they all exclaimed, "naw!"

"Hi come she do that?" the old woman asked. "What ail her?"

Mrs. Turpin only glared in front of her.

"Somethin ail her," the old woman said.

"They carried her off in an ambulance," Mrs. Turpin continued, "but before she went she was rolling on the floor and they were trying to hold her down to give her a shot and she said something to me." She paused. "You know what she said to me?"

"What she say?" they asked.

"She said," Mrs. Turpin began, and stopped, her face very dark and heavy. The sun was getting whiter and whiter, blanching the sky overhead so that the leaves of the hickory tree were black in the face of it. She could not bring forth the words. "Something real ugly," she muttered.

"She sho shouldn't said nothin ugly to you," the old woman said. "You so sweet. You the sweetest lady I know."

"She pretty too," the one with the hat on said.

"And stout," the other one said. "I never knowed no sweeter white lady."

"That's the truth befo' Jesus," the old woman said. "Amen! You des as sweet and pretty as you can be."

Mrs. Turpin knew just exactly how much Negro flattery was worth and it added to her rage. "She said," she began again and finished this time with a fierce rush of breath, "that I was an old wart hog from hell."

There was an astounded silence.

"Where she at?" the youngest woman cried in a piercing voice.

"Lemme see her. I'll kill her!"

"I'll kill her with you!" the other one cried.

"She b'long in the sylum," the old woman said emphatically. "You the sweetest white lady I know."

"She pretty too," the other two said. "Stout as she can be and sweet. Jesus satisfied with her!"

"Deed he is," the old woman declared.

Idiots! Mrs. Turpin growled to herself. You could never say anything intelligent to a nigger. You could talk at them but not with them. "Yawl ain't drunk your water," she said shortly. "Leave the bucket in the truck when you're finished with it. I got more to do than just stand around and pass the time of day," and she moved off and into the house.

She stood for a moment in the middle of the kitchen. The dark protuberance over her eye looked like a miniature tornado cloud which might any moment sweep across the horizon of her brow. Her lower lip protruded dangerously. She squared her massive shoulders. Then she marched into the front of the house and out the side door and started down the road to the pig parlor. She had the look of a woman going single-handed, weaponless, into battle.

The sun was a deep yellow now like a harvest moon and was riding westward very fast over the far tree line as if it meant to reach the hogs before she did. The road was rutted and she kicked several good-sized stones out of her path as she strode along. The pig parlor was on a little knoll at the end of a lane that ran off from the side of the barn. It was a square of concrete as large as a small room, with a board fence about four feet high round it. The concrete floor sloped slightly so that the hog wash could drain off into a trench where it was carried to the field for fertilizer. Claud was standing on the outside, on the edge of the concrete, hanging onto the top board, hosing down the floor inside. The hose was connected to the faucet of a water trough nearby.

Mrs. Turpin climbed up beside him and glowered down at the hogs inside. There were seven long-snouted bristly shoats in it—tan with liver-colored spots—and an old sow a few weeks off from farrowing. She was lying on her side grunting. The shoats were running about shaking themselves like idiot children, their little slit pig eyes searching the floor for anything left. She had read that pigs were the most intelligent animal. She doubted it. They were supposed to be smarter than dogs. There had even been a pig astronaut. He had performed his assignment perfectly but died of a heart attack afterwards because they left him in his electric suit, sitting upright throughout his examination when naturally a hog should be on all fours.

A-gruntin and a-rootin and a-groanin.

"Gimme that hose," she said, yanking it away from Claud. "Go on and carry them niggers home and then get off that leg."

"You look like you might have swallowed a mad dog," Claud observed, but he got down and limped off. He paid no attention to her humors.

Until he was out of earshot, Mrs. Turpin stood on the side of the pen, holding the hose and pointing the stream of water at the hind quarters of any shoat that looked as if it might try to lie down. When he had had time to get over the hill, she turned her head slightly and her wrathful eyes scanned the path. He was nowhere in sight. She turned back again and seemed to gather herself up. Her shoulders rose and she drew in her breath.

"What do you send me a message like that for?" she said in a low fierce voice, barely above a whisper but with the force of a shout in its concentrated fury. "How am I a hog and me both? How am I saved and from hell too?" Her free fist was knotted and with the other she gripped the hose, blindly pointing the stream of water in and out of the eye of the old sow whose outraged squeal she did not hear.

The pig parlor commanded a view of the back pasture where their twenty beef cows were gathered around the haybales Claud and the boy had put out. The freshly cut pasture sloped down to the highway. Across it was their cotton field and beyond that a dark green dusty wood which they owned as well. The sun was behind the wood, very red, looking over the paling of trees like a farmer inspecting his own hogs.

"Why me?" she rumbled. "It's no trash around here, black or white, that I haven't given to. And break my back to the bone every day working. And do for the church."

She appeared to be the right size woman to command the arena before her. "How am I a hog?" she demanded. "Exactly how am I like them?" and she jabbed the stream of water at the shoats. "There was plenty of trash there. It didn't have to be me.

"If you like trash better, go get yourself some trash then," she railed. "You could have made me trash. Or a nigger. If trash is what you wanted why didn't you make me trash?" She shook her fist with the hose in it and a watery snake appeared momentarily in the air. "I could quit working and take it easy and be filthy," she growled. "Lounge about the sidewalks all day drinking root beer. Dip snuff and spit in every puddle and have it all over my face. I could be nasty.

"Or you could have made me a nigger. It's too late for me to be a nigger," she said with deep sarcasm, "but I could act like one. Lay down in the middle of the road and stop traffic. Roll on the ground."

In the deepening light everything was taking on a mysterious hue. The pasture was growing a peculiar glassy green and the streak of highway had turned lavender. She braced herself for a final assault and this time her voice rolled out over the pasture. "Go on," she yelled, "call me a hog! Call me a hog again. From hell. Call me a wart hog from hell. Put that bottom rail on top. There'll still be a top and a bottom!"

A garbled echo returned to her.

A final surge of fury shook her and she roared, "Who do you think you are?"

The color of everything, field and crimson sky, burned for a moment with a transparent intensity. The question carried over the pasture and across the highway and the cotton field and returned to her clearly like an answer from beyond the wood.

She opened her mouth but no sound came out of it.

A tiny truck, Claud's, appeared on the highway, heading rapidly out of sight. Its gears scraped thinly. It looked like a child's toy. At any moment a bigger truck might smash into it and scatter Claud's and the niggers' brains all over the road.

Mrs. Turpin stood there, her gaze fixed on the highway, all her muscles rigid, until in five or six minutes the truck reappeared, returning. She waited until it had had time to turn into their own road. Then like a monumental statue coming to life, she bent her head slowly and gazed, as if through the very heart of mystery, down into the pig parlor at the hogs. They had settled all in one corner around the old sow who was grunting softly. A red glow suffused them. They appeared to pant with a secret life.

Until the sun slipped finally behind the tree line, Mrs. Turpin remained there with her gaze bent to them as if she were absorbing some abysmal life-giving knowledge. At last she lifted her head. There was only a purple streak in the sky, cutting through a field of crimson and leading, like an extension of the highway, into the descending dusk. She raised her hands from the side of the pen in a gesture hieratic and profound. A visionary light settled in her eyes. She saw the streak as a vast swinging bridge extending upward from the earth through a field of living fire. Upon it a vast horde of souls were rumbling toward heaven. There were whole companies of white-trash, clean for the first time in their lives, and bands of black niggers in white robes, and battalions of freaks and lunatics shouting and clapping and leaping like frogs. And bringing up the end of the procession was a tribe of people whom she recognized at once as those who, like herself and Claud, had always had a little of everything and the God-given wit to use it right. She leaned forward to observe them closer. They were marching behind the others with great dignity, accountable as they had always been for good order and common sense and respectable behavior. They alone were on key. Yet she could see by their shocked and altered faces that even their virtues were being burned away. She lowered her hands and gripped the rail of the hog pen, her eyes small but fixed unblinkingly on what lay ahead. In a moment the vision faded but she remained where she was, immobile.

At length she got down and turned off the faucet and made her slow way on the darkening path to the house. In the woods around her the invisible cricket choruses had struck up, but what she heard were the voices of the souls climbing upward into the starry field and shouting hallelujah.

BIOGRAPHICAL NOTES

Prepared by Alfred Klassen and Sara Harasym.

Margaret Atwood (1939–   ) was born in Ottawa, Ontario. Poet, novelist, editor and cartoonist, Atwood is an active writer and spokesperson on current social and political issues. Her most recent novel, *The Handmaid's Tale*, is a feminist dystopia. Her works include ten volumes of poetry, six novels, three books of short fiction (including, *Dancing Girls and Other Stories*, 1977 in which "When It Happens" appears), two books of criticism and her edition of the *New Oxford Book of Canadian Verse in English*.

Isaac Babel (1894–1941). Born in Odessa, he served in the Soviet political police force and in Budyonny's Red Cavalry before blossoming as a writer. His hard, compact style relates him to Maupassant and Hemingway, but his portrayal of peasant life is in the great Russian story tradition. "The Sin of Jesus" is from *Lyubka the Cossack and Other Stories*, 1963. Other collections of short stories: *Collected Stories*, *You Must Know Everything*.

Sandra Birdsell (1943–   ) was born and grew up in Morris, Manitoba; she now lives in Winnipeg. Her stories subtly expose the socio-sexual networks and the games of power people create and play. "Falling in Love" appears in the collection *Ladies of the House*, 1984. *Night Travellers* was her first short story collection, about the Lafrenier family.

Clark Blaise (1940–   ) novelist, short story writer, and editor, was born in North Dakota and has lived in the American south, the urban north and various regions in Canada. Much of his work explores the crossing of cultural borders in a semi-autobiographical, satiric manner. "A North American Education" is from a collection by the same name (1973). His other works include *Days and Nights in Calcutta*, *Tribal Justice* and *Resident Alien*.

Heinrich Böll (1917–1985) was born in Cologne, Germany. War, defeat and anxiety as it is felt in a complex postwar world are the major themes of his novels. "The Post Card" is from *Eighteen Stories*, 1966. His novels include *The Train Was on Time*, *Billiards at Half Past Nine*, and *The Clown*.

Albert Camus (1913–1960). Born in Algeria and writing in French, he nevertheless continues to exercise a world-wide influence through his many translations. Playwright and novelist, he speaks to the modern existential dilemma. "The Guest" is from *Exile and the Kingdom*, 1957. His novels include *The Stranger*, *The Plague* and *The Fall*.

Anton Chekhov (1860–1904) was born in South Russia. Educated to be a physician, he became instead a master of the short story and a brilliant playwright. He believed that all the artist could do was "draw life as it is"; this example determined to a large extent the development of the short story in the twentieth century. "The Chorus Girl" was first published in 1893. His works include *Collected Stories*, *The Duel*, *The Seagull* and *The Cherry Orchard*.

William Faulkner (1897–1962) was born in Mississippi. Although he had little formal education, with stylistic and technical fictional genius he fashioned a world of legendary proportions out of the raw materials of the Southern United States. "That Evening Sun" is from *Collected Stories of William Faulkner*, 1931. His novels include *The Sound and the Fury*, *As I Lay Dying* and *The Snopes Trilogy*.

Madeleine Ferron (1922–   ) was born and educated in Louiseville, Quebec, and studied ethnography at the University of Montreal. Her novels, stories and plays draw upon the local folk fables of Quebec. "Be Fruitful and Multiply" first appeared in the collection of contes, *Coeur de Sucre*, 1966. Sheila Watson translated this ironic feminist fable in 1974. Ferron's texts include *La Fin des Loups-Garous*, *Le Baron Ecarlate*, *Quand le Peuple fait la loi* and *Sur le chemin Craig*.

Graham Greene (1904–   ) was born in England. His versatility as a writer embraces drama, fiction, travel literature, and motion picture script. Intrigue and suspense dominate his lighter work, while his more serious novels develop the themes of guilt and redemption. "The Second Death" is from *Twentyone Stories*, 1935. His novels include *Brighton Rock*, *The Power and the Glory*, *Monsignor Quixote* and *Dr. Fischer of Geneva*.

Ernest Hemingway (1899–1961) was born in Illinois. His experience of World War I, the Spanish Civil War, and the Second World War supplied the matrix of his major work. Hemingway's unornamented narrative style has exerted a strong influence on contemporary writers. "After the Storm" is from *Winner Take Nothing*, 1933. Volumes of short stories include *In Our Time*, *Men Without Women* and *The Short Stories*; novels, *A Farewell to Arms*, *For Whom the Bell Tolls* and *The Sun Also Rises*.

Jack Hodgins (1938–   ) was born and educated on Vancouver Island, British Columbia. Much of Hodgins' work combines anecdotal traditions and vernacular exaggeration with fantasy. "The Plague Children" is from the *Barclay Family Theatre*, 1981. His books include *Split Delaney's Island*, *The Invention of the World* and *The Resurrection of Joseph Bourne*.

James Joyce (1882–1941), Irish novelist born in Dublin, chose to live a life of voluntary exile on continental Europe, largely France. "Counterparts" is from his only collection of short stories, *Dubliners*, accepted for publication in 1906 but delayed until 1914. His often stylistically and technically innovative work eventually gained worldwide recognition. His novels include *A Portrait of the Artist as a Young Man*, *Ulysses* and *Finnegan's Wake*.

Franz Kafka (1883-1924) was born in Prague. Having studied law, he accepted various positions in the Austrian civil service while writing. In a realistic style he created the symbols that have ever since invited allegorical interpretations of his work. "A Country Doctor" was first published in 1920 and in English translation in 1933. Other works include: *The Metamorphosis*, *The Trial* and *In the Penal Colony*.

Pär Lagerkvist (1891-1974) was born in Sweden. When he received the Nobel Prize in 1951, he had already caught and transcribed in literature the sinister forces loosed upon Europe in the previous decade. "The Children's Campaign" is from *The Eternal Smile and Other Stories*, 1954. Short stories include *Iron and Men*, *Evil Tales*, *In That Time* and *Struggling Spirit*. Novels include *The Hangman*, *The Dwarf* and *The Sybil*.

D.H. Lawrence (1885-1930) was born the son of a coal miner in Eastwood Notts, England. A prolific writer, he wrote twelve novels, sixty stories, and over nine hundred poems dealing particularly with the personal and sexual conflicts of the English class-dominated society. "The Horse-Dealer's Daughter" (first published in 1922) is from *The Complete Short Stories of D.H. Lawrence*, Vol. II. His work includes *Sons and Lovers*, *Women in Love*, *Lady Chatterly's Lover* and *The Rainbow*.

Katherine Mansfield (1888-1923) was born in New Zealand and educated in London. She travelled widely for her health while writing four volumes of short stories. An admirer of Chekhov, she was part of the literary circle surrounding D.H. Lawrence. "The Wind Blows" is from *The Short Stories of Katherine Mansfield*, 1920. Books of short stories are *Bliss, The Garden Party, The Dove's Nest* and *Something Childish*.

Gabriel García Márquez (1928–   ), a Colombian storyteller, is best known for his book *One Hundred Years of Solitude* (1967), a novel in which realistic and fantastic elements interact to create a microcosm of the social, political and personal world of Latin America. Winner of the Nobel Prize for Literature in 1982, Márquez's works include *Leaf Storm and Other Stories, No One Writes to the Colonel and Other Stories, The Autumn of the Patriarch* and *Chronicle of a Death Foretold*.

Alice Munro (1931–   ) was born in Wingham, Ontario and now lives nearby in Clinton. Many of her stories reflect this landscape as they focus upon the social and personal restrictions her characters are caught within and attempt to break free from. "Thanks for the Ride" first appeared in the *Tamarack Review* and was later collected in *Dance of the Happy Shades*, 1968. Other works include *Lives of Girls and Women, Something I've Been Meaning to Tell You, Who Do You Think You Are?* and *The Moons of Jupiter*.

Joyce Carol Oates (1938–   ) grew up in New York. She is a university lecturer, critic, poet, novelist, and short story writer whose novel, *Expensive People*, was a leading contender for the 1969 National Book Award. "The Molesters" was first published in the *Quarterly Review of Literature*, and was Chapter 14 of *Expensive People*. Other works include *By The North Gate, A Garden of Earthly Delights* and *They*. She has published over forty books in two decades.

Flannery O'Connor (1924–1964) was born in Georgia. Due to a rare congenital disease, she spent

most of her life on her parents' farm. She attended
college and university, however, and despite her
illness produced a small but highly original body of
work. "Revelation" is from *Everything That Rises Must
Converge*, 1965. Her short stories include *A Good Man
Is Hard To Find*; her novels, *The Violent Bear It Away*
and *Wise Blood*.

Alain Robbe-Grillet (1922–   ) was born in
France. His aim as a writer is to give his creation
an independent, non-didactic entity; to blend sub-
jective with objective existence. "The Secret Room"
is from *Snapshots*, 1968. Novels available in translation
are *The Erasers*, *The Voyeur*, *Jealousy* and *In the Labyrinth*.
His best known movie script is *Last Year at Marienbad*.

Sinclair Ross (1908–   ) was born in Saskatchewan. A long-time bank employee, he chronicled the
time of dust and depression in the Canadian West.
Though written in the thirties and forties, his stories
were not collected until 1968. "A Field of Wheat" is
from *The Lamp at Noon and Other Stories*, 1968. His novels
include *As For Me and My House, Sawbones Memorial*.

Philip Roth (1933–   ) was born in New Jersey.
His first book, *Goodbye Columbus*, won him the National
Book Award for fiction. He registers social, religious,
and moral change against the background of the
Jewish community in America. "The Conversion of
the Jews" is from *Goodbye Columbus*, 1959. Novels
include *Letting Go, When She Was Good, Portnoy's Complaint* and *Zuckerman Unbound*.

Isaac Bashevis Singer (1894–   ) was born in
Poland. When he moved to the United States in 1935
he had already produced a large body of work as
an essayist and story writer. He still writes mostly
in Yiddish about the Europe he knew as a boy.
"Gimpel the Fool" first appeared in English translated
by Saul Bellow in *A Treasury of Yiddish Stories*, 1953.

Also available are *The Magician of Lublin, Short Friday and Other Stories* and numerous novels. He won the Nobel Prize for Literature in 1978.

Audrey G. Thomas (1935–   ), short story writer and novelist, was born in Binghampton, New York, but has lived all of her writing life in Canada. Thomas' varied repertoire of characters draw attention to the sexual, social and political problems in the various countries where she has lived and travelled. "If One Green Bottle . . ." is from the collection *Ten Green Bottles*, 1967. Her other collections include *Real Mothers* and *Good-bye Harold, Good-Luck*. Novels include *Blown Figures, Latakia* and *Intertidal Life*.

James Thurber (1894–1961) was born in Ohio. A brilliant satirist of American life, James Thurber contributed stories, cartoons, and articles to *The New Yorker* for many years. "You Could Look It Up" was first printed in *The Saturday Evening Post*, 1941. Published works include *My Life and Hard Times, Fables for Our Times* and *The Thurber Carnival*.

John Updike (1932–   ) was born in Pennsylvania. He worked for several years as a reporter for *The New Yorker*, which has subsequently published most of his stories. A prolific writer and an accomplished stylist, Updike writes poetry, novels, and short stories. "Your Lover Just Called" is from *Museums and Women and Other Stories*, 1972. His numerous novels include *Rabbit, Run, Couples, The Centaur* and *The Witches of Eastwick*.

Aritha van Herk (1954–   ) grew up on a farm near Edberg, Alberta, and studied at the University of Alberta. "Waiting for the Rodeo" first appeared in *Glass Canyons: A Collection of Calgary Fiction and Poetry*, 1985. Her stories and essays have appeared in a variety of international journals and anthologies. Winner of the Seal Books First Canadian Novel Award in 1978 for *Judith*, she has published two other novels—*The Tent Peg* and *No Fixed Address*.

Rudy Wiebe (1934–   ) was born in Saskatchewan. After study and travel in Europe, South America and the United States he teaches writing and literature at the University of Alberta. "Seeing is Believing" is from *Kunapipi*, Vol. 6, #2, 1984. His novels include *The Temptations of Big Bear*, *The Blue Mountains of China* and *My Lovely Enemy*.